Befo

By the same author:

Fiction, published by Eagle:
  Laura
  Katharine
  To Live Again

Non-fiction:
  Eye of the Storm
  My Unknown Child
  Only the Best
  When Suffering Comes

BEFORE THE DAWN

Noreen Riols

eagle
Guildford, Surrey

British Library Cataloguing in Publication Data. A catalogue
record for this book is available from the British Library.

Published by Eagle, an imprint of Inter Publishing Service
(IPS) Ltd, St Nicholas House, 14 The Mount, Guildford,
Surrey GU2 5HN.

Typeset by Palimpsest Book Production Limited,
Polmont, Stirlingshire
Printed and bound in Great Britain by
Caledonian International Book Manufacturing Ltd, Glasgow

ISBN No: 0 86347 182 X

ACKNOWLEDGEMENTS

My grateful thanks to Monsieur Jean-Louis Leimbacher, Managing-Director of the Hôtel du Palais in Biarritz, for his gracious help, Dr Claude Lemonnier, who kindly advised me on medical matters, and Commandant de Police Henri Prévost-Brouillet, who shared his personal experience of the Algerian crisis.

Chapter
1

'What on earth is Armand doing on the platform at this hour of the morning?' Maxime exclaimed, pulling down the window and waving frantically as the night express from Paris steamed into Narbonne station and panted to a halt.

Katharine, adjusting her hat in the small mirror above the washbasin, crossed to her husband's side. But her great-uncle's frail figure had already shot past.

Seeing his eyes searching the trundling compartments her mind flashed to their three young sons. Something terrible must have happened to them.

Jumping down onto the platform Maxime held out his hand to her. He smiled reassuringly. But she could see that he was far from reassured. There was concern in his eyes too.

Armand, who had been anxiously scanning the alighting passengers turned and, catching sight of them, raised his stick in a half salute as he hurried towards them.

'What's happened?' Katharine choked as he bent to kiss her. 'The boys? . . .'

Armand smiled. But it was a sad smile which did nothing to allay her fears.

'Tell me uncle,' she pleaded. 'What is it?'

He took her arm and began to walk towards the exit.

'It's Léonie . . .'

And for a few seconds he was unable to continue.

Katharine felt a sudden overwhelming relief immediately followed by a wave a guilt. Her great-grandmother was very dear to her.

'What's happened to Bonne Maman?' Maxime enquired. They had reached the station yard where Emile was busy piling the luggage into the boot of the car.

'She had a stroke early yesterday evening,' Armand said slowly, as if he were having difficulty enunciating the words. 'She is paralysed down her right side, but fully conscious. Mercifully, she can still speak.'

'But why didn't you let us know?' Katharine exclaimed, climbing into the car.

'We didn't immediately realise the seriousness of the situation. It wasn't until after midnight that the doctor said he thought I should contact the family, and by then you had already left. I thought that by meeting you at the station it would save time.'

'It's as bad as that?' Maxime enquired.

'I'm afraid so.'

Armand shrugged resignedly as the car drew up in front of the imposing house in Narbonne.

'After all these years it will be strange to be without her,' he murmured, as if for him Léonie was already in the past.

Katharine jumped out of the car and ran up the steps to the house scarcely pausing to greet Jeanne, standing at the door, her homely old face puffy from weeping. It would be strange for Jeanne too after all these years Katharine thought, her feet barely touching the stairs as she raced up them two at a time. The old woman had been in Léonie's service all her working life.

Outside the heavy double doors leading to her great-grandmother's bedroom, her hand raised to knock, Katharine paused. And she was suddenly afraid. Death and heartache seemed to have stalked her for so much of her adult life that she was not sure she wanted to enter. To witness Léonie's last moments. See the great-grandmother whom she had come to think of as indestructible reduced to a lifeless shell.

Her husband came silently to her side.

'Shall we go in together?' he said softly, putting an arm round her waist and drawing her close. He guessed the thoughts which were revolving round her mind.

'Oh Maxime,' she cried, and wearily closing her eyes leant her head against his shoulder.

'We can wait a little,' he murmured. 'Or I can go in on my own.'

'No,' she whispered, and raising her fist knocked gently on the door.

There was a slight shuffle from inside and then Germaine, who had been Léonie's faithful companion for as long as anyone could remember, quietly opened it.

Seeing them she smiled, but only with her lips. Like Jeanne, the light had gone from her eyes too.

'Madame is expecting you,' she murmured softly, standing aside to let them in.

Holding her breath, Katharine tiptoed into the room, already shaded against the early morning rays of bright June sunlight.

Léonie turned her head slightly.

'Bonne Maman,' Katharine cried, throwing herself on her knees beside her great-grandmother's bed, grasping her dry paper thin hand in both her own and gently rubbing it, willing it back to life. She looked up into the nut brown eyes she knew so well. They were still bright, still inquisitive. And Katharine took heart.

'Katharine,' Léonie murmured, her voice barely audible. With an effort she stretched her left arm across the vast bed and lovingly stroked her great-granddaughter's hair. 'My dear, dear Katharine.'

But the effort seemed to exhaust her. As Maxime came to stand behind his wife Léonie closed her eyes and her hand fell from Katharine's shining chestnut curls.

Katharine looked up at Maxime a flicker of hope in her eyes.

'Perhaps . . .?' she pleaded.

'Perhaps,' he smiled, lifting her to her feet. 'One never knows.'

She saw the look which passed between her husband and Germaine. And her mind raced back to that day in a London hospital almost thirteen years earlier when she had knelt beside her mother's bed desperately willing her to live. The Sister had been evasive then. But the same look had passed between her and Katharine's great-aunt Lavinia. And once again Katharine knew there was no hope.

'Let's join Armand for breakfast,' Maxime suggested.

'I want to stay . . .'

'Germaine and the nurse are both here', her husband said firmly. 'They will call us if necessary.'

'I think Armand needs support,' he added guiding her towards the door. 'There's only Toinette here at the moment and you know how hopeless she is. We should stay with him until some other members of the family arrive. At eighty-five it's a great burden for him to carry alone.'

* * *

After toying with breakfast Katharine hurried back to Léonie's room. But her great-grandmother was asleep and the nurse insisted that there was no change, even implying that Katharine's presence might disturb her.

So she wandered into the library where Maxime and

4

Armand were leafing through the morning papers. Curling up in one of the deep leather armchairs, she wondered what to do. Everything seemed unreal. Léonie's house which had always run on oiled wheels now appeared to be in complete disarray. The family, gradually beginning to gather, wandered aimlessly around in silent bewilderment. The aged servants stunned, performing their duties like zombies. The reins had at last fallen from Léonie's firm hands and, for the time being, no one seemed capable of picking them up.

'Is my father on his way?' Katharine enquired, realising that so far no one had mentioned Xavier.

Armand looked up from the newspaper he was pretending to read, relieved at the diversion.

'I don't know my dear. I have been trying to get in touch with him, but no one seems to know where he is.'

Katharine frowned, then fumbled in her handbag.

'He left a telephone number where he could be contacted,' she volunteered. 'I have it here. He *was* in Algiers, but he does move about.'

'That's just it,' Armand replied. 'He left Algiers to go into the desert a week or two ago. They are trying to contact him, but whether he'll arrive in time . . .'

Katharine's eyes widened in fright.

'Don't *say* that,' she protested, her heart refusing to believe what her mind knew was inevitable.

Armand looked at her sadly. And he wondered how she was going to accept the fact that Léonie was not eternal.

The gong sounded in the hall.

'Ah, lunch,' he said rising shakily to his feet. 'I wonder how many we will be? Honoré has just arrived. And your great-aunts are due back from Vichy this afternoon.'

He shook his head bewilderedly.

'I'm losing count I'm afraid.'

*   *   *

But Xavier did not arrive in time. And no news came from him.

Two days later as the golden shadows of early evening lengthened and twilight turned the cloudless sky above Narbonne a delicate green, Léonie de Montval's reluctant eyelids yielded open. Her eyes wandered round the shaded room in which she had slept for eighty-six years. The room where she had borne her children and known both passion and pain. The room to which Hugues had brought her as his bride. As her gaze gradually focused she saw them all gathered round her bed, her children, her grandchildren and her great grandchildren. The fruits of that passion and pain. And she knew that the long wait was over. She was at last going to be with Hugues.

Léonie smiled.

Her eyes, roving slowly round the group, held no fear. Hugues was there beside her. The room was full of his presence. A lingering sigh escaped from her colourless lips and she feebly held out her arms, longing to feel him close once again.

In the distance she heard the cathedral bells ringing out the Angelus, their peals carried by the warm scented air across the town where she had been born and lived her life. Listening to those tumbling chimes the misty veils of time parted and Léonie was seventeen again, a radiant bride walking down the aisle of St Just Cathedral to the peal of those same bells, her hand resting lightly on her husband's arm.

Making one last effort she raised a hand in farewell to her family, that dynasty born of their love. Then her tired lids drooped. The faint movement beneath the beautifully embroidered sheet ceased. And Léonie de Montval slipped quietly away from them and out of this world.

Before the Dawn

Katharine buried her face in the cool linen sheet, her great-grandmother's lifeless hand grasped tightly in her own. As the rest of the family crossed themselves and dropped to their knees, her shoulders shook with noiseless sobs.

'*Requiem eternam dona ea Domine*' intoned the bent old priest, who had been born in a cottage on the Montval estate and grown old with Léonie.

Raising her tear-streaked face Katharine realised that for him today was the end of an era.

It was 30th of June.

Tomorrow would have been Léonie's 103rd birthday.

Chapter
2

On the morning of the funeral there was still no news from Xavier.

'I'm worried, Maxime,' Katharine frowned as she fitted the hat with the trailing matching veil into place. She tutted in annoyance. Her whole appearance, dressed in black from head to foot, spelled gloom. It was *so* unlike Léonie, who had loved life yet been ready to die. But she knew that if she refused to wear deep mourning it would only upset her dear great-uncle Armand. He would imagine that she was being disrespectful to the memory of the mother for whom he had sacrificed his own life.

Katharine vaguely wondered in what horrendous disguise his sister Toinette would appear. Toinette thrived on melodrama and nothing excited her more than a funeral. She had drooped around the house for the past three days looking like a Victorian undertaker, positively revelling when it was her turn to keep watch, with another member of the family, beside her mother's open coffin in the shaded room lit only by tall flickering white candles placed at the four corners of the bier.

Whatever garment she wears, Katharine reflected, is bound to be outrageous with trailing black veils, bordering on the lunatic, fluttering everywhere.

Maxime stretched his neck as he knotted his black tie.

'What's worrying you?' he enquired, smiling at her across the room.

'It's Zag,' Katharine went on, her anxious frown hidden by the veil. 'It's not like him to leave us without news . . . especially now. Bonne Maman was very special to him. I can't understand why he hasn't arrived.'

'You've lived in Morocco,' Maxime said placidly. 'You know the desert. It can't be easy trying to track your father down. He could be *anywhere* on that vast expanse of sand. I'm sure there's some reasonable explanation.'

They entered the drawing-room and once again Katharine was astonished by the number of relatives she possessed. Through the black veil which covered her face, she looked up at Maxime wondering how he was feeling. The last time they had attended such a gathering in this room had been for his mother's funeral almost six years ago. But his face was impassive. If the scene brought back painful memories, he kept them to himself.

Before the long elaborate service in the cathedral drew to a close Katharine began to feel slightly sick. The incense was overpowering. And she was dreading that one of the bevy of priests officiating at the altar would once again sprinkle it over the bier and those surrounding it. She glanced sideways at the ornate coffin covered by a cross of white lilies, Armand's farewell tribute. The family had insisted that it was to be his wreath which covered the casket containing his mother's earthly remains. Katharine still could not believe that her great-grandmother's frail body lay inside that heavy coffin. Looking at the mountain of wreaths and sprays which surrounded it, spilling over to form a carpet of flowers almost to the altar she wished that Léonie had been there to see them.

The organ boomed out and the choir once again rose to sing. One by one the family bowed before Léonie's mortal remains. Each in turn taking the sprinkler filled with holy water, which an altar boy handed them, and making the sign of the cross with it over the coffin. Then at last it was over. The bearers came forward and the family stepped in procession behind them walking slowly back down the aisle as the organ played a requiem.

Forming in line at the back of the cathedral in generational age to receive condolences, Armand signalled to Germaine and Jeanne, Antonin and Huguette, Baptiste and his wife and the few remaining retainers at Castérat who had faithfully served Léonie for most of their lives, to join them.

Katharine looked up. The great cathedral was full. Her eyes scanned the crowd leaving their seats and forming a long solemn line to express sympathy and shake hands with each family member. But her father was not among them, squeezing his way to her side.

And once again that horrible fear entangled her in its web. Something *must* have happened to him.

Maxime, sensing her distress, surreptitiously sought her hand and held it firmly until the the first of the crowd, walking with bowed heads down the line, arrived in front of him.

As the family climbed into cars behind the flower-laden hearse on the last lap of Léonie's earthly pilgrimage, the solitary bell, booming from the spire announced to Narbonne that the great lady was finally to be laid to rest.

This was the part which Katharine dreaded, knowing how it had affected her when Elisabeth's coffin had been slotted into the Montredon family vault beside her husband's and those of so many other long dead members of Maxime's family. She steeled herself as they entered the vast echoing vault and Léonie was placed in the compartment reserved for her beside Hugues. The silence was oppressive, the heavy scent of incense still seeming to cling to them, wavering in the cold air as the priest intoned the final prayer. Katharine gritted her teeth and closed her eyes.

Suddenly a firm hand grasped her elbow and an arm went around her shoulders holding her tightly. And with a quick intake of breath Katharine knew. Her father had arrived. As he had promised her on her wedding day, he was there at the moment when she needed him.

Looking up through eyes blurred with tears, she leant against him gratefully.

'I'd hoped to make it for the mass,' he whispered bending close to her ear. 'But I arrived just as the cars left the cathedral.'

'Never mind,' she whispered back. 'You're here. That's all that matters.'

Katharine looked from her father to her husband, standing at her other side. And suddenly the gloom lifted. Grasping Maxime's hand in hers as they turned to leave the eerie vault and walk back into the warm July sunshine her fears vanished. And she felt at peace again.

* * *

'But you surely can't be rushing off so soon,' Katharine protested.

It was a week later and Xavier had come to Le Moulin to say goodbye to his grandsons.

'Yes darling,' he smiled. 'I think Armand is all right now. I was worried about him when I arrived but he's very resilient and has many interests. *Now* at last he'll be able to live his own life.'

He grimaced.

'I only hope it isn't too late.'

'But we see so little of you,' Katharine grumbled. 'You could at least stay for the summer.'

11

Xavier put down three-year-old Jehan who had climbed on his knee and crossing over sat down beside her.

'You have your own life now,' he said quietly. 'And I have mine. Don't you remember the pact I made with you at the end of the war? I promised we'd be together until you found happiness.'

His eyes strayed over the lawn across which Jehan had scampered to play ball with his two older brothers.

'You've found that happiness Katharine. Now let me continue the task God has given me to do. There is such a harvest of lost souls waiting to be gathered in. And as I told you once before, we only have today. Tomorrow may be too late.'

Katharine looked up, the sullen expression gone.

'You're right Zag,' she smiled. 'I'm sorry. It's just that . . . I'll miss you.'

'Have another baby', he joked. 'And I'll be there.'

His words were almost prophetic.

That night the reality of Léonie's death finally hit Katharine. Until then, everything had been disrupted and life had seemed unreal. But, tossing and turning in their vast canopied bed, she realised that nothing would ever be the same again. Léonie had ruled at Castérat for almost seventy years and with her passing a great gulf yawned beneath them all.

Would this be the end of the family as she had known it? she wondered. How could the annual September reunion at Castérat ever be the same?

Armand, as eldest son, would take over. But he had never married. What would happen when his turn to join his ancestors finally arrived?

Katharine, lying sleepless, looked out at the dark night sky, its blackness accentuated by the brightness of the glittering stars. And she asked herself where was Léonie?

Her great-grandmother had been very devout. But Katharine wondered whether she had ever really met her Lord. Or had Bonne Maman's devotion been to the elaborate ritual of the church? Léonie had seemed confident and ready to die. But had she the certainty, which Katharine had, that when her eyes closed for the last time on this world, she would open them looking into the eyes of Jesus?

Agonising over her great-grandmother's fate Katharine cried out to the Jesus she had accepted as her Saviour. But even as she did so, she knew it was too late. The decision as to our eternal destination has to be made this side of the grave. And yet she took heart from her father's words in that small Arab restaurant in the Souk at Er Rachidia.

'We mortals can never condemn anyone to eternal separation from God,' Zag had remarked. 'God is a just God. I'm convinced that even in the last second of life Jesus comes to offer one last chance.'

Katharine settled back on her pillows. Léonie had done her best. God was also a merciful God. He would have given her that chance.

Maxime turned and stretched out his hand to her.

'What is it darling?' he murmured sleepily.

'I was wondering where Léonie was.'

Turning he gathered her slight body to him and held her close.

And that electric current which had shattered her body on that faraway day when Maxime had first taken her in his arms shot through her once again. It was just as vivid, just as breathtaking as it had been then. Feeling an overpowering love for him shuddering through her, Maxime instantly responded. He kissed her eager lips. Then, his body now aflame, his kisses became more urgent in the passion of their embrace.

13

The spray of stars which had sparkled in through their bedroom window faded. The dark sky lightened giving place to the lemon tints of early morning as Katharine lay back on her pillows, satiated and at peace.

'Darling,' she breathed, opening her eyes and gazing at her husband, tenderly tucking the lace-edged sheet round her bare shoulders. 'Oh *darling* . . .'

He smiled, raising his eyebrows quizzically.

'I think Zag's prophecy before he left has just come true,' she whispered huskily. 'We're going to have our little Elisabeth after all.'

And without further explanation to her bewildered husband she turned and fell into a dreamless sleep.

* * *

True to his word Xavier was there when on the 29th March the cathedral bells, which had so recently tolled for Léonie, rang their joyful Easter morning peals across the awakening town, Katharine gave birth to her fourth son.

When she heard the doctor announce the baby's arrival, she gasped.

For nine months she had cherished this child, hugging it to her, talking to it, singing to it, caressingly calling it by the name she had chosen. Convincing herself that God had given her a daughter: the little Elisabeth she so desired.

The midwife carefully wrapped the baby in a shawl and held him out to her.

'A boy,' she enthused. 'With eyes as blue as his father's.'

But Katharine turned away burying her face in the deep pillow as silent tears dribbled into the exquisite embroidery.

Frowning the midwife looked up at the doctor. He motioned her to follow him as he crossed over to the window.

'Leave it for the time being,' he murmured. 'You've surely seen such a reaction before after a string of children of the same sex. The mother has so set her heart upon a change that the shock, after the shock of giving birth, temporarily unbalances her. Madame Montredon had obviously convinced herself she was carrying a daughter. But she'll come round.'

Maxime standing outside the door with Zag, as he had done for the birth of the twins, knocked timidly.

'Come in,' the doctor called cheerfully.

He took the baby from the nurse's arms and handed him to his father.

'Another fine boy,' he announced. 'Mother and baby both doing well.'

He glanced across to where Katharine's back remained resolutely turned towards them. Maxime looked at the doctor enquiringly.

'A momentary disappointment,' he murmured.

Maxime took the baby in his arms and tiptoed across to the bedside.

'Katharine,' he said tentatively.

But she didn't stir.

'Darling,' he pleaded, 'we've got a beautiful fourth son.'

Xavier who had entered with Maxime came and stood behind him. He smiled down at the bundle in Maxime's arms and with one finger gently eased the shawl away from the baby's face.

'And this one looks exactly like his father,' he added.

Katharine half-turned and her eyes looked straight into Maxime's.

'Why Maxime?' she pleaded. 'Why? I *so* wanted to

give you a daughter. A little Elisabeth in memory of your mother.'

Maxime handed the baby to his father-in-law and sat down on the edge of the bed.

'We don't arrange these things,' he smiled, taking hold of her hand, his thumb caressing her soft damp palm.

'But you *wanted* a daughter so much,' Katharine cried.

'*You* wanted a daughter,' Maxime laughed. 'I'm perfectly happy with another son. Don't get paranoid on my account.'

Katharine's eyes wandered to the bevelled ceiling.

'I wanted to give you one,' she said miserably.

And she felt a failure.

'I'd leave your wife to rest,' the doctor advised. 'Then when she is feeling stronger the other boys can come and visit their little brother.'

'Let's have breakfast in the nursery,' Xavier suggested, taking Maxime's arm and leading him from the room. 'Then we can all go and hunt for Easter eggs in the garden. Jehan was shrieking with excitement when he went to bed yesterday evening wondering what the Easter bunny would bring them.'

Maxime cheered up visibly. But when at ten o'clock he ushered his sons into the bedroom to kiss their mother and greet their new baby brother his spirits sank. Katharine was lying against the pillows, pale and listless.

Three-year-old Jehan rushed to his mother's bedside holding out a large marzipan fish.

'For my new bruvver', he announced, his blue eyes sparkling.

Katharine turned, stretching out her hand to ruffle his chestnut curls. The twins were both dark-haired, like Maxime, but Jehan had inherited his mother's colouring. In spite of herself Katharine smiled realising that his offering was not entirely altruistic. Jehan disliked marzipan. He'd certainly kept for himself the collection of chocolate rabbits and hens, which Maxime had hidden in the bushes and flower beds for the boys to find.

'What's he called?' Jehan bubbled on.

He was the chatterbox of the trio. The twins were quieter, communicating with each other in an invented language which no one else could understand. Jehan, in self-defence, talked non-stop to a twin he had invented for himself named Hercule after the ginger cat in a tattered book which Katharine was required to read daily to him.

'Maman,' he insisted when Katharine didn't immediately reply, 'What's his *name*?'

He turned towards the bundle in his father's arms which his elder brothers were admiring.

Katharine looked helplessly at Maxime.

'I – I don't know,' she hesitated.

The only name she had considered was Elisabeth.

She smiled tenderly at her ebullient youngest son.

'What would *you* like us to call him?'

'Hercule,' Jehan promptly replied, standing on tiptoe to admire the bundle.

'He's not very *big*,' he grumbled, poking the marzipan fish into his face.

Maxime retrieved it just in time.

'He'll soon grow', his father laughed. 'Then you'll be able to play together.'

Jehan turned away, his interest span exhausted.

'Xavier's taking the boys to morning service,' Maxime remarked as his father-in-law entered the room.

A spark of hope lit Katharine's eyes.

'And you?'

'I'll stay here with you.'

'Come along boys,' Xavier smiled. 'Time for church. No

Jehan, you'd better leave the eggs behind. Don't worry, the baby won't eat them.'

He smiled across at Katharine.

'Bon Papa's taking us for *ice-cream* on the Barques,* afterwards,' Jehan squealed excitedly, grabbing his grandfather's hand and catapulting from the room.

The nurse discreetly left the room as Maxime sat down beside the bed.

'Feeling better?' he enquired tenderly.

But Katharine didn't answer.

'Jehan raised a point,' he went on. 'What *shall* we call him?'

Katharine's bleak eyes met her husband's.

'You choose,' she answered disinterestedly.

'How about Hugues?' he suggested, 'after his great-great-grandfather.'

'If you wish.'

'Or . . . Léon?'

At that, the floodgates of pent up emotion burst as memories of Léonie came flooding back. Katharine hadn't realised how much she had missed her great-grandmother's wise counsel, her love. She remembered Léonie arriving unannounced the day after the twins' birth, demanding to see her first great-great-grandsons. That afternoon the strong bond which had always existed between them had been soldered. But when, the following year, Jehan had arrived on Léonie's one hundredth birthday, it had become indissoluble.

As Maxime held her close waiting for the storm of emotion to pass he realised that Katharine had not let Léonie go. She had clung to her memory, almost as if she believed that by doing so her great-grandmother would return.

He sighed.

When they married he had imagined that *he* had

become the rock, that strong fortress Katharine's fragile nature, which had been so buffeted and wounded, needed in order to find peace. Then she had had this conversion when the twins were born and become a committed Christian. Maxime didn't understand very much about it, but he had been delighted that she had at last found stability and serenity. But now the birth of their fourth son seemed to have upset the balance and put all her emotions into the melting-pot.

Maxime was tenderly wiping his wife's still-streaming eyes when the doctor walked into the room.

He smiled, believing that the crisis was over. Her emotions had been unlocked and the momentary depression which had descended like a bolt of lightning and held her in its grip for the past few hours would now lift. And as he predicted, once she got used to the idea, she would joyfully hold out her arms to her baby son.

Maxime rose stealthily from the bed. He could see that Katharine's lids were drooping, her eyes half-closed. As he reached the door he looked back. Katharine gave a last shuddering sigh then her breathing became low and regular and he knew that for the moment at least her problems were forgotten. She had fallen asleep.

But it was not a refreshing sleep. And Katharine awoke tired and listless.

By the end of the week, when her black mood did not lighten, the doctor took Maxime aside. 'With your permission I'd like to call in a specialist who may be able to help Madame Montredon,' he began hesitantly.

Maxime frowned.

'I hardly think this is the time to introduce someone new. You've looked after my wife for each of her pregnancies. You've delivered all the babies. Surely medically you know her better than anyone else. How can another gynaecologist help?'

The doctor pursed his lips and looked at the floor.

'I wasn't thinking of another gynaecologist,' he began.

'Then who?' Maxime interrupted.

'A psychiatrist.'

'A *psychiatrist*?' Maxime exploded. 'My wife doesn't need a pyschiatrist.'

He shrugged.

'I agree she is behaving strangely. Not at all the way she did after the others were born. But she's older, a third pregnancy must take its toll. Surely rest . . . possibly a change of air . . .'

'That's what I thought for the first few days,' Dr Massenon went on. 'That's what I *hoped* it was. But now, after a week, I'm afraid it's more serious.'

Maxime got up and walked across to the window and stood looking out over the park, his hands clenched tightly behind his back, a muscle in his cheek working furiously.

'I don't like the idea,' he said tightly, watching the endlessly shifting clouds sending darting shadows across the lawn.

He turned and his violet eyes were cold.

'You'll be suggesting next that my wife should be consigned to a home for the bewildered to spend the rest of her life weaving Moses baskets.'

He sat down abruptly, his hands gripping the sides of the chair as if fighting to regain his composure.

The doctor made no reply.

'I do apologise,' Maxime murmured at last. 'That remark was in very poor taste.'

'Understandable in the circumstances,' Dr Massenon answered kindly. 'But the doctor I'm suggesting I know personally. He has worked with me before on cases such as this.'

'Does it often happen?' Maxime asked in surprise.

20

'It's not infrequent. And no one can account for it, though with a post-natal depression such as Madame Montredon has I'm convinced there always *is* a reason. The problem is to discover it.'

'Surely it was the disappointment at not having the daughter she longed for.'

'Initially yes. But that usually only lasts a day, two at the most. It's eight days now and she's still showing no interest in the baby. Something is seriously wrong. And the longer we leave it the more difficult it will be to treat.'

He paused as if uncertain how to phrase his next question.

'Your father-in-law', he remarked. 'I believe there is a very strong bond between him and your wife?'

'There always has been,' Maxime replied.

'And he now lives in North Africa?'

Maxime nodded.

'Could be an explanation,' the doctor said thoughtfully. 'This depression might hide an unconscious blackmail on Madame Montredon's part. A means of keeping her father here. She knows he would not return to Africa leaving her in her present condition.'

'But that's ridiculous,' Maxime spluttered.

'After giving birth mothers often act out of character. It's a great shock to a woman's system creating another human being. People seem to forget that.'

He looked intently Maxime.

'Perhaps it would help us to understand if you told me a little of your wife's background.'

Maxime hesitated. Katharine was a very private person.

He got up and once again stood tensely looking out of the window, trying to come to a decision. Then, taking a deep breath, sat down again.

'Since her early teens my wife has experienced a series of tragedies,' he said hesitantly, 'beginning with her father's unexplained disappearance when she was twelve which resulted in her and her mother leaving Marrakesh and settling in England with her maternal grandparents, whom she scarcely knew.'

Maxime's hands, clasped between his knees, clenched and unclenched as he relived in his mind Katharine's pain.

'She never fully adapted to England. The life and culture were so different from the ones she had known from her birth in Morocco. In 1940 her mother was killed in an air raid and Katharine's world really collapsed. But, during the war she met and married a young British officer.'

He looked up and his eyes mirrored the pain Dr Massenon had seen in Katharine's.

'He was executed by a German firing squad just before D-Day. And my wife lost the baby she was carrying.'

He shook his head sadly.

'When we met she was afraid to love. She had this irrational fear that anyone she loved or even become close to would die a violent death. Or be snatched away from her. I thought that with our marriage everything had been sorted out.'

Maxime stopped as if finding it difficult to continue.

'Katharine is a loving mother. It can't just be disappointment at not having a daughter. She hoped for a daughter when she was expecting Jehan. But the disappointment didn't last more than a couple of minutes. I can't imagine what has gone wrong this time.'

He combed his fingers absently through his thick dark hair, a familiar gesture when he was worried or puzzled.

'Could it have anything to do with our great-grandmother's recent death? There was also a very strong bond between them. And in spite of her great age my wife was shattered when she died. I'd tried to prepare her for the inevitable happening. But she seemed to think that Bonne Maman was immortal.'

He shook his head sadly.

'It could be a clue,' the doctor mused. 'But what about your father-in-law. Why did he disappear?'

'Oh, it's a long story. A frightful misunderstanding.'

'At twelve years old, a young girl is very impressionable.'

'My wife is very sensitive. And rather reserved,' Maxime cut in. 'She tends to keep her feelings to herself.'

'I see.'

Dr Massenon thoughtfully stroked his chin.

'Thank you for telling me this. It certainly throws light on what has now happened. I think her great-grandmother's death may have released her fears again which have now been compounded by the birth. She feels guilty . . . and a failure.'

'But that's ridiculous,' Maxime protested.

'Most guilt feelings in a depression are,' the doctor said drily. 'But try telling the patient that.'

He rose to his feet.

'I need to think about this,' Maxime frowned, his face drawn as he accompanied Dr Massenon to the door. 'Your suggestion has given me a shock.'

'Do think about it,' the doctor interjected. 'Hopefully by tomorrow or the next day you will have reached a decision. The longer we leave this, the worse it is likely to become.'

Maxime walked back to his desk and sat down heavily. Glancing through the window he saw Xavier strolling across the lawn, a football under his arm, his three grandsons jumping around him. Going across he threw the window open.

'Xavier,' he called as they approached the house, 'can you spare a minute?'

Xavier dropped the ball, then gave it a kick.

'Play by yourselves for a while boys,' he shouted, as three pairs of legs dashed off to retrieve it.

Crossing the terrace he walked into the room.

'The doctor thinks Katharine should see a pyschiatrist,' Maxime said curtly, as Xavier sat down in one of the deep leather armchairs.

His father-in-law raised his eyebrows enquiringly.

'What do you think?' Maxime went on.

Xavier thoughtfully crossed his legs and reaching into his pocket for his pipe slowly began patting tobacco into the bowl. Striking a match he inhaled deeply. Then leant back in his chair watching the smoke spirals rise to the ceiling and disappear in a hazy cloud.

'What do *you* think?' he countered.

'I don't know,' Maxime hesitated. 'My first reaction was one of anger. I was totally against it. But . . .'

He shrugged.

'I don't know what to think. I trust Dr Massenon. He knows Katharine well and I'm sure he wouldn't suggest such a thing lightly.'

Maxime once again ran his hand distractedly through his hair. 'But a *psychiatrist* . . .'

Xavier sat puffing thoughtfully. Then, removing his pipe from his mouth he pointed it at Maxime.

'Why do you say that?'

'Say what?'

'You gave the impression that pyschiatrists were beyond the pale.'

'Well, aren't they?'

'I'm not sure,' Xavier mused.

And they lapsed into silence.

'Xavier,' Maxime pleaded at last when his father-in-law

showed no sign of continuing the conversation. 'I don't know what to do.'

Xavier looked at him then leaning forward tapped his pipe out against the fender.

'Will you let *me* talk to Katharine?'

'Of course. But . . .'

'I don't say it will do any good but I can always try.'

He got up and crossed the room.

'Is the doctor with her now?'

'No, he left about half an hour ago.'

'Then I'll go and see what we can work out between us.'

He turned in the doorway and looked back at his son-in-law.

'Jesus is the best psychiatrist,' he said softly.

Maxime's head shot up, an astonished expression on his face.

'But he *does* work through human doctors.'

Chapter 3

When Zag entered the room Katharine was sitting by the window staring listlessly out at the far distant peaks of the Pyrenees.

He drew up a chair and sat down beside her. But she did not react.

'Katharine,' he said gently.

She turned her head and looked straight at him. And in the depths of those topaz eyes he read despair.

'Shall we pray about this?'

'About what?' she asked disinterestedly.

'About whatever is worrying you.'

Katharine turned her eyes back to the window.

'You believe Jesus heals, don't you? You've seen it happen with little Xavier.'

'I'm not ill,' Katharine replied.

And her voice was lifeless.

'Not physically perhaps, but you're not yourself.'

She didn't reply.

Xavier's eyes followed his daughter's.

'I will lift up mine eyes unto the hills from whence cometh my help,' he quoted.

Katharine turned her head and met his gaze.

'My help cometh from the Lord,' he continued. 'Cast whatever burden you are carrying on him Katharine. It's too heavy for you to bear alone . . . and he doesn't *want* you to bear it alone.'

Katharine's eyes dropped to her hands lying aimlessly in her lap. The shadow of her thick curling lashes met the violet smudges beneath her eyes and seemed to accentuate them.

'I don't know what's the matter Zag,' she whispered. 'I wish I did. It's this terrible darkness. As if a heavy black curtain had been drawn in front of my eyes cutting me off from the world . . . from everyone. I don't seem to be able to get through it, or pierce the gloom.'

'It's not the baby?'

Katharine shrugged.

'I was disappointed because I really believed that this time I was going to give Maxime the daughter he so wanted.'

Xavier shook his head sadly.

'There's still so much insecurity in you,' he said sadly. 'If only you could realise that you don't have to prove anything in order to keep your husband's love. Maxime is *delighted* with his fourth son.'

Xavier leant back in his chair, the tips of his fingers touching beneath his chin.

'You two remind me of your mother and me,' he murmured thoughtfully. 'Ours was a beautiful love story. And yours can be the same.'

But he could see that Katharine was not convinced.

'Dr Massenon came to see Maxime this morning,' her father went on. 'He's worried about you. He feels that this depression you're in is more than just a passing phase. In fact, he wants to call in another doctor . . . a psychiatrist.'

Katharine suddenly sat bolt upright.

'A psychiatrist?' she choked. 'Whatever for? I don't need a psychiatrist.'

'Dr Massenon thinks you do. He no longer knows how

to treat you. In fact Maxime has promised to give him an answer by tomorrow.'

Katharine's eyes blazed with anger.

'How *dare* he,' she grated through clenched teeth. 'How dare Maxime even consider such a thing.'

Then as quickly as it had flared up the anger subsided. Burying her head in her hands she broke into heart-rending sobs.

'I'm suddenly so afraid Zag,' she whispered at last as he wordlessly passed her a crisp linen handkerchief.

'What of darling?'

There was a pause. Katharine was obviously struggling to find the right words.

'You'll think it foolish,' she hesitated. 'But . . . of Marie-Céleste.'

'Maxime's first wife?'

Katharine nodded.

Leaning towards her, Xavier gathered her trembling body into his arms.

'Does Maxime know about this?'

Katharine shook her head.

'I wish you'd tell him. He'd put your mind at rest immediately.'

Her father held her at arm's length and gazed lovingly down at her.

'Marie-Céleste has *gone* Katharine,' he enunciated. 'She's in Germany with her new husband. She and Maxime haven't seen each other for over ten years.'

'She could come back,' Katharine whispered haltingly.

'Why on earth *should* she come back?' Xavier exclaimed. 'And even if she did, what difference would it make to your marriage? Maxime loves *you* darling. Can't you believe that?'

'I want to believe it. And most of the time I do. But since Bonne Maman died I've realised that we can lose everything in the twinkling of an eye. I think when I saw her in her coffin it affected me more than when I saw Mother.'

'Bonne Maman *was* 103,' Xavier said gently.

'I know. But I'd refused to even consider the possibility of her one day dying and leaving us.'

She turned her tear-streaked face towards her father.

'Am I going mad Zag?' she pleaded.

He gently drew her head onto his shoulder and stroked her dishevelled curls.

'No darling', he soothed. 'You're just a very sensitive young woman who has suffered greatly. And, sadly, still can't believe she is now secure.'

'I did believe it,' Katharine whispered. 'When I married Maxime I really felt I had come home.'

'And now?'

'Since Léon's birth the world has become a grey sea with nothing but black clouds on the horizon. And me all alone in a small boat tossing helplessly on the churning waves.'

'I think,' her father said thoughtfully, 'the shock of your great-grandmother's death, followed by the birth and the disappointment at not having a daughter . . .'

'She was to have been Elisabeth Léonie . . .' Katharine put in wistfully.

'You have a beautiful little Léon Hugues instead,' he encouraged. 'And everyone is delighted with him. Unfortunately, he has revived these fears about Marie-Céleste.'

He held her at arm's length.

'I don't think you need a pyschiatrist my darling. You need Jesus. A psychiatrist can only see the outside. And in your present emotional state, he could easily turn you inwards raking up fears until you become totally self-absorbed. Jesus will look deep into your heart, unearth the hurts and pain, bring them to the surface for you to confront . . . and then dismiss them. Once you face your dread of Marie-Céleste's improbable return, you will see the futility of agonising over something which is unlikely ever to happen.'

He grasped her hands.

'Let's give this burden to the Lord,' he smiled. 'You asked him to come into your life and be your personal Saviour at a moment of terrible crisis and he came. You've been following him faithfully ever since.'

Her father paused and his eyes questioningly sought Katharine's.

'Until this blackness came,' Katharine faltered. 'Now . . . I can't pray. The words won't come.'

'This is an attack of the devil,' Xavier said ominously. 'He's trying to destroy your faith.'

He took a deep breath.

'The Bible says "Resist the devil and he will flee from you." Let's resist him in Jesus' name.'

Xavier knelt on the carpet in front of her and Katharine slipped to her knees beside him. He grasped her hands in his then with his face lifted upwards, he called on Jesus to put his healing hands on his daughter and give her his peace.

Katharine remained silent, her head bowed as her father prayed.

After a while words of praise began to flow from Xavier's lips and her body seemed to become lighter, almost weightless as strong arms cradled her. She leant back feeling safe and loved floating effortlessly on a warm sea of peace which gently washed over her till it reached the farthermost part of her being.

Katharine sighed.

Looking up Zag saw that she had relaxed, the tense lines had gone from her face. And her father knew that there would be no need to call a pyschiatrist. As he had done with Jairus' daughter Jesus, the great healer, had touched his daughter and brought her back to life.

She opened her eyes, and returned his gaze.

'Could you ring for the nurse?' she asked him, rising from her knees.

Xavier's brow rutted.

'Yes of course. But why? Is something wrong?'

Katharine glanced at the delicate porcelain clock on the mantelpiece where the gilded cherubs were preparing to strike the hour.

'It's time for the baby's feed,' she smiled. 'I want her to bring him to me.'

*   *   *

When Dr Massenon visited Katharine the next morning he was surprised to find the empty cot by her bed. Looking round the room he saw her sitting in her usual place by the window. But her eyes were not roaming listlessly over the park. They were gazing tenderly down at the little bundle she held in her arms as she rocked gently backwards and forwards crooning a Hebridean lullaby.

Turning to where Maxime was standing in the doorway he raised his eyebrows enquiringly. Maxime shrugged. But his face was relaxed. The lines of strain around his eyes had gone.

'Whatever happened?' Dr Massenon questioned, closing the door behind him. 'When I saw your wife yesterday morning she was in deep depression, refusing to have anything to do with the baby.'

'I don't know,' Maxime replied as they walked back along the gallery together. 'When I told my father-in-law what you proposed to do he asked if he could talk to her. Whatever he said seems to have worked. My wife slept

31

for fourteen hours last night and has been as right as rain ever since.'

'Probably what was needed,' the doctor conceded. 'She was not only emotionally, but physically exhausted.'

Maxime looked at him strangely recalling that sleep was not what he had suggested the previous day.

'So we won't need to call in your pyschiatrist?'

'Not for the moment,' the doctor hedged. 'Let's wait and see. This may be a temporary remission.'

'Somehow I don't think so,' Maxime went on. 'My father-in-law and my wife both have this incredible belief in divine healing.'

The older man looked at him curiously. Had the strain of the past few days affected the husband too? It was not impossible He'd heard before of mentally ill patients who had these strange delusions. Though they had usually been safely stowed away in an institution. But for a man like Montredon de la Livière . . .

The doctor shrugged.

'I have to admit I'm intrigued . . . and also a little envious,' Maxime said thoughtfully, as they reached the doctor's car. 'It must be wonderful to have a strong faith such as my father-in-law has. And which he seems to have passed on to my wife. Faith which he says can move mountains.'

'I'll call again in the morning,' Dr Massenon cut in hastily, clamping his foot on the accelerator.

'Never did understand the aristocracy,' he muttered to himself as the car sped along the drive. 'They behave very strangely at times.'

He pursed his lips, slowing down as he approached the wide open gates.

'Too much inbreeding!'

*　　*　　*

32

'He's a splendid little fellow,' the paediatrician enthused, turning the baby over and running his fingers down his spine.

He beamed across at Katharine over the top of his half-moon glasses as he examined her plump, naked son. Léon at six weeks old was a joy to them all.

The doctor rolled the baby onto his back and grasped his feet in both his hands.

Raising the baby's left leg, still firmly holding the foot he began making rotating movements turning and palpating it as he did so. Léon's blue eyes watched him intently as he repeated the movement with the right leg. Placing it carefully back in position, he frowned.

'Is something the matter doctor?' Katharine asked, getting up from her chair and walking across the room towards him.

Dr Lasserre felt gingerly around Léon's right foot. Then made a sharp upward movement.

The baby let out a piercing yelp.

Katharine bent to pick up her small son, but the doctor put out a restraining hand.

'Just a minute Madame,' he murmured, once again attempting to manipulate the foot.

But Léon's little face, which had turned red with the first effort, creased like an old beetroot as his howls became more penetrating.

Dr Lasserre straightened up.

'I'm afraid the treatment hasn't been effective on his right foot.'

Katharine's eyes widened.

'What treatment?' she cried. 'What is the matter with him?'

The doctor wrapped Léon in a shawl and handed him to his mother.

'Did you not notice that both his feet turned inwards?'

'Well yes I did. But . . . I thought it was something which would straighten as he grew. In the same way that his legs are still bent in the foetal position.'

'It is more than that, madame. Your son was born with two club feet.'

'Club *feet*,' Katharine stammered, her eyes widening with fear. 'But why didn't Dr Massenon notice when he was born?'

'Dr Massenon *did* notice. He informed your husband but I believe you were not very well at the time. They both thought it unwise to tell you then. Dr Massenon called in Nurse Saurin, who is specialised in these cases, to do the daily exercises on the baby's feet which he hoped would effect a cure. The left foot has responded. Unfortunately the right one hasn't.'

'But what will happen?' Katharine asked desperately. 'There must be *something* which can be done.'

'There is. I shall have a series of X-rays of both feet taken.'

'But you said it was only the right foot', Katharine protested. 'That the left one had responded to treatment.'

'It has,' the doctor went on patiently. 'But it may not be permanent. That is why we must continue the treatment on *both* feet. The X-rays will ascertain the damage and according to the result we shall do all we can to rectify the foot medically.'

'What does that imply?'

'The baby will have to wear an apparatus which will help correction as he makes his ordinary natural movements with his feet. Possibly even a plaster which will be changed each month. But if that fails we shall be obliged to resort to surgery. And I fear that as far as his right foot is concerned we will not have the choice.'

'An *operation*,' Katharine said weakly.

She sat down abruptly, and protectively gathered her baby son close to her.

'Oh *no*,' she agonised. 'He's so *small*.'

'I understand how you feel Madame,' the doctor said kindly. 'Surgery will be a last resort. But if it comes to that, I know a very fine orthopaedic surgeon in Toulouse in whom I have every confidence. But he could not operate before Léon is at least two years old. Between two and five is the best time.'

'And until then?' Katharine cried.

'I'm afraid once he begins to walk he will have to wear either calipers or an orthopaedic boot, possibly on both feet in order to be sure. The sooner treatment is started the better if we are to prevent him from being a cripple . . .'

'A *cripple*,' Katharine queried weakly. 'You can't mean . . .'

'If his feet are not treated then I can assure you Madame your son will be a cripple for the rest of his life.'

Katharine's thoughts strayed to Theo. His love had helped her on the path to wholeness, following her beloved first husband, Ashley's death. She remembered Theo's handicap and the sense of inferiority he felt and would always feel, since the war had robbed him of his right leg. But Theo had known twenty-five years of healthy manhood before disaster struck. Léon would be deprived of a normal life right from birth. An unbearable pain shot through her body at the thought. And she hugged the now sleeping infant closer in her arms fiercely kissing his soft blond hair. Léon, the dark-haired baby Zag had pronounced the image of his father on the day he was born, had changed dramatically and now resembled a Botticelli angel. As she gazed protectively down at him, Katharine's expression softened. Blue eyes, blond hair. He could have been Rowena's son.

And at that moment, she longed for her mother.

Chapter
4

When Maxime arrived home he was surprised not to find Katharine waiting for him as usual in the petit salon.* Peeping into the nursery he saw her sitting by the window in the old rocking chair, Léon dozing peacefully in her arms.

Tiptoeing across the room he bent and kissed her chestnut curls.

Katharine looked up. But she didn't smile.

'The paediatrician came this morning,' she said coldly. 'Why didn't you tell me?'

Maxime drew up a chair and sat down beside her.

'We thought it best not to say anything until you felt stronger. And I'd hoped that the treatment would have worked, and there'd be no need.'

He tilted her face towards him.

'I'm sorry darling. Was it an awful shock?'

'The shock was wondering what else you are hiding from me,' she replied tightly, turning away.

As the words left her lips they surprised her. And she realised that the old fears had resurged. Unconsciously she hugged the baby closer.

'Darling,' Maxime pleaded, taking her hand in spite of her resistance. 'You know I'm not hiding anything from you.'

'How can I be sure?'

'Because you're my wife and I love you,' he answered simply.

Katharine raised her head. Seeing the love for her shining in his eyes, her resentment faded.

'Oh *Maxime*,' she appealed.

He took the baby from her arms and crossing the room laid him in his cot. Léon grunted but did not wake.

'Let's work through this together,' Maxime said, returning to her side. 'I think the best thing would be to ask for a second opinion.'

'But the evidence is *there*,' Katharine cried. 'You've seen his feet. I can't believe I thought they were normal.'

'All the same, since the exercises Nurse Saurin was brought in to perform haven't had the desired result, I'd prefer to ask a specialist from the Hospital for Sick Children in Paris to come and examine Léon. Maybe there's some new treatment which Dr Lasserre hasn't heard of. After all, he's a paediatrician, not an orthopaedic surgeon.'

But Katharine didn't appear to have heard. She was sitting opposite him her face white and tense, a haunted expression in her eyes.

That same terrible blank emptiness which had crept over her on the evening after her mother's funeral had returned. Maxime's comforting words had momentarily anaesthetised her after the initial shock. Now the soothing effects were wearing off and she was once again faced with the reality of a handicapped son, perhaps condemned to live his life as a cripple. And as on that late September evening almost fourteen years before, she felt she couldn't bear the pain. But this time it was not for herself, but for Léon. And it was doubly agonising because she knew she was unable to shield him. She was unable to take away his deformity. She could only stand by and suffer with him.

'Katharine?' Maxime queried anxiously.

But as she lifted her anguished face to his he felt helpless.

Staring numbly in front of her, Katharine remembered the evening her father had led her to the Lord. That terrible night when Xavier, her firstborn son's life had been ebbing away, Jesus had stretched out his hands and healed him.

As the memory surfaced she smiled to herself, and her face relaxed. She would call again upon Jesus in her pain. Give Léon to him and ask him to heal her baby as he had healed his eldest brother.

'It's going to be all right darling,' she whispered. 'Jesus will heal Léon as he healed Xavier.'

Maxime frowned but said nothing. He didn't share his wife's faith. Didn't always understand what she said. But he was so relieved that the tension had left her taut features that he preferred to ignore the remark rather than question her further.

* * *

But the well-known Paris consultant merely confirmed Dr Lasserre's diagnosis. And after X-rays had revealed the extent of the damage to Léon's feet, the treatment the paediatrician had suggested was immediately begun.

At first Katharine remained serene, convinced that this was only a temporary measure and that sooner or later Jesus would surprise them all with a miracle.

After all, she reasoned, had her Saviour intervened immediately the doctors could have claimed the victory. Jesus would come to the rescue when all hope of an immediate cure was gone.

So she remained buoyant, daily thanking God in her prayers for the blessings with which he had surrounded her, confident of a happy solution to Léon's affliction.

Maybe, she mused one morning as she knelt in front of her open bedroom window gazing out over the park, maybe Lord this is your way of bringing Maxime to you. When he sees you working so powerfully in Léon's life, healing where the doctors failed, he cannot help but be convinced and turn to you.

'Oh Father,' she entreated. 'Bring Maxime to the foot of your cross.'

As these words left her lips, Katharine rejoiced, never realising the price she would have to pay for her husband's surrender.

Watching her sailing through this crisis in their lives Maxime relaxed. He knew Katharine's sensitive nature, knew her fears. And he had been afraid for her. But she appeared to have accepted the situation and found peace.

When the following spring, calipers were put on her baby and he attempted his first stumbling steps, Katharine faltered.

'Help him Madame, by all means,' Dr Lasserre said. 'But don't *carry* him through. He *must* learn to come to terms with what is happening. If you persist in watching his every step and preventing him from grappling with the difficulties you're only doing him a disservice.'

Katharine bit her lip and instinctively stretched out her arms as Léon stumbled and fell.

But the doctor restrained her.

Her youngest son let out a yell, his lip quivered and his eyes filled with tears. He looked appealingly at his mother.

Katharine's heart almost broke when Dr Lasserre stopped her going to his aid.

'He will learn,' he said placidly. 'I suggest you leave him to Nurse Saurin.'

A knowing look passed between him and the nurse.

Katharine bristled. But, still holding her arm, Dr Lasserre led her towards the door.

Léon, on the floor struggling to get to his feet, wailed pitifully.

'I know it's hard,' the doctor sympathised as he closed the door behind him. 'But I'm afraid it's the only way. After all, we *have* made progress. His left foot has responded well and will not need surgery.'

'Then why does he have to wear those awful things on *both* feet?' Katharine accused.

The doctor smiled sympathetically.

'It is done as a precautionary measure. There could be a relapse. But by this time next year if all goes well we should have the operation behind us.'

'And Léon will be able to walk normally and play with his brothers?' Katharine queried, her spirits rising.

'Not immediately. It's a long slow process which could continue almost into his teens.'

'His *teens*,' she gasped.

'I'm afraid so.'

Katharine sat down abruptly on a small tapestried chair in the corridor. Suddenly the bubble of joy and hope which had been keeping her buoyant burst. And she felt herself sinking back into a deep dark pit.

The doctor sat down beside her.

'Come now Madame,' he chided. 'Many a mother has borne a child like Léon and survived. It's not unusual, though more frequent in boys than girls. It is not a life and death situation. Just a question of time and patience.'

He looked down the long gallery papered with gold framed portraits of Montredon ancestors in every kind of dress and uniform, and felt irritated by this young woman who appeared to have everything.

'Be thankful you are in a position to give your son the best treatment available,' he said curtly.

Before the Dawn

Katharine looked up bleakly as he rose to his feet. She had scarcely heard a word he said.

'I will call in again next week,' Dr Lasserre ended coldly. 'No please don't get up, I know my way downstairs. If you need me, don't hesitate to telephone.'

And with a brief nod he left.

Suddenly Katharine came face to face with what was happening to her baby.

She got up and hurried back to the nursery.

Seeing her, Léon let out another pitiful wail. But Nurse Saurin made it obvious that his mother was not welcome.

'Léon will be having his lunch in a few minutes,' she said firmly, 'and then he must have his rest. When his brothers come back from their walk they will be playing together in the nursery. Perhaps you could come in and see him for a short while after tea?'

Katharine opened her mouth to protest. Then remembering the look she had seen exchanged between the doctor and nurse turned towards the door.

She felt like an unwanted intruder in her own child's life.

Walking in a daze down the long corridor her lips suddenly set in a determined line. Picking up the telephone she asked the operator for a number in Algiers.

It seemed ages before the operator announced that she was through.

'Zag,' she cried, relief flooding through her when her father took the call. 'I was *so* afraid you wouldn't be there.'

'If you'd tried tomorrow I wouldn't have been,' he laughed. 'I'm off before dawn.'

There was a pause and his voice became grave.

'Katharine,' he said gently. 'Is something the matter?'

'Yes . . . no,' she began. 'Oh I don't know. I suppose not really.'

'Is it Léon?' he prodded.

'In a way. Nothing's changed but . . .'

'But what?'

Then it all poured out. The anguish which had cut through her at seeing her little son's distress. Her helplessness at being unable to take away his pain.

'And you're angry with God,' her father added.

She nodded, forgetting that her father was not standing beside her.

'I understand,' he went on quietly as if he had sensed her gesture. 'And *he* understands too.'

'Then why doesn't he *do* something? his daughter burst out.

'I don't know Katharine. As I've said before, if I did know the answer I'd be God.'

'I've prayed so hard,' she pleaded, 'ever since I found out about Léon's foot. I was sure God would heal him. Why hasn't he answered my prayers?'

'God always answers prayers', her father replied calmly. 'But not always immediately or in the way we expect.'

'But I thought he loved children,' Katharine cut in belligerently. 'Didn't Jesus say "suffer the little children to come unto me"?'

'He did Katharine.'

'Then why should my baby suffer?'

'Are you sure he *is* suffering as much as you think? Or is it *you* who are suffering?'

'Zag, you haven't seen him struggling to walk with those awful things on his legs, falling over and crying.'

Zag smiled to himself.

'I remember you falling over and crying when you took your first steps,' he countered.

'Yes but I didn't have my legs in *irons*.'

'No,' her father replied thoughtfully, 'but you suffered

42

in other ways later on. None of us escapes suffering Katharine. It comes to everyone sooner or later in life. Being a Christian isn't an insurance policy against pain.'

'I never thought it was,' she said angrily, 'you told me that ages ago. But I did think God would answer my prayers and heal Léon as he did Xavier.'

'God is not a dispensing machine for blessings. You don't put your money in the slot and instantly receive the goods.'

'But *think*,' Katharine cut in, 'how his name would have been glorified if Léon *had* been cured instantly, when the doctors said it would be a long slow process.'

'God doesn't need man's glory,' her father answered evenly. 'He lets us believe he does because it pleases our puny little finite minds. We think he needs *us* to glorify his name. But he doesn't. God is omnipotent and his will is sovereign. I know he *will* answer our prayers for Léon. But in his time and in his way.'

'I wish you were here,' Katharine groaned brokenly.

'I couldn't say any more than I've already done. You have Jesus, Katharine, cling to him. Offer *him* this burden for your baby and you will be at peace.'

Katharine sniffed back the tears which were rising in her throat.

'Treat Léon as a normal little boy,' her father ended. 'And he will become one.'

When Katharine replaced the receiver she was still not convinced.

*   *   *

'We've been meaning to go to London for ages,' Maxime said after lunch that day. 'And now that Lawrence has been posted to Teheran if we don't go very soon it may be some time before we see him and Tatiana again. What do you say to leaving early next week?'

But Katharine didn't say anything. The mere idea of leaving Léon sent waves of terror streaking through her.

'We haven't seen them since Nicholas' christening almost two years ago. I'd like to check up how my godson is progressing,' Maxime continued.

He grinned across at her.

'And your goddaughter as well. How about it?'

'Perhaps Tatiana could come here for a visit with the children before she leaves,' Katharine demurred.

'But not Lawrence,' Maxime cut in. 'He'll be off before the end of the month. This is really our last chance.'

Since Katharine and Maxime's marriage the two couples, though separated by almost seven hundred miles, had become very close.

'What is it darling?' Maxime said softly. 'There's something worrying you.'

'It's . . . Léon,' she hesitated.

'I thought as much.'

Maxime leant back in his chair and filled his pipe.

'Léon will be all right. Nurse Saurin is very capable.'

A startled expression darted into Katharine's eyes.

'I know she's strict,' he went on quickly. 'But it won't do him any harm. Dr Lasserre is right darling, he's *got* to learn to cope. This could be a long business.'

Remembering her son's woebegone face when she left him before lunch, Katharine's eyes filled with tears.

'But Maxime, he's so tiny . . .'

'Then he'll learn more quickly. And Nanny's there to cuddle him and dry his tears.'

Maxime had insisted on having an English nanny for the boys so that they would grow up bilingual. Nurse Moffatt, a sensible down-to-earth Scotswoman highly recommended by Flora, had proved to be exactly right.

44

Young enough to be on their wavelength, yet old enough to have had experience. She was firm but kind. And the boys adored her.

'But *I'm* his mother,' Katharine protested, her hackles rising. 'He needs *me*.'

'Granted. But he needs you fit and well. At the moment you're neither. You need to get away and see this whole situation in perspective.'

But Katharine didn't reply.

* * *

'Have you thought any more about our trip to London?' Maxime enquired a few days later.

'Maxime I . . .'

'Katharine I really *have* to go to meet the wine merchants and plan the sale for next season. If you don't come with me I shall have to go alone. But I'd *so* much rather you came with me.'

Once again Katharine did not reply. She was torn between the husband she loved and the child she felt needed her.

In the end Léon won.

And Maxime left for London alone.

'If you change your mind you can always come and join me,' Maxime coaxed, raising his hat to kiss her as the night express from Barcelona to Paris snaked around the corner and sighed to a stop in Narbonne station. 'Promise?'

'Yes,' Katharine replied, clinging tightly to him as the guard blew his whistle. 'Yes darling, I promise.'

But Katharine did not join her husband.

Before they reached the station platform her choice had been made. And without her even realising it, that night a yawning gap began to open up between her and the husband she loved so much.

Chapter 5

The surgeon entered the room where Katharine and Maxime were waiting. Seeing him, Katharine's throat constricted. But he was smiling.

'I think we can say that it was a very successful operation,' he announced. 'Your son is now in the recovery room.'

'So everything went well?' Maxime enquired.

'*Very* well. Better than we had expected. One can never be quite sure what one will find. But it was smooth going and you should be able to take Léon home in a few days.'

Katharine clasped her hands together in delight, her eyes shining.

'So he's *cured*?' she cried delightedly. 'Finished with those awful appliances!'

'Not too quickly Madame.'

'We cannot be too cautious. Léon will have to wear an orthopaedic boot for the time being until we are sure that everything is back in order. And, of course, no sport.'

Katharine slumped back on the hard hospital chair.

'Leon's operation has been *successful* darling,' Maxime said gently, sitting down beside her. 'Let's take things one at a time.'

'Thank you doctor,' he went on. 'We are most grateful.'

The surgeon smiled again.

'It will be at least half an hour, maybe longer, before your son is returned to his room . . . and then some time before he regains consciousness.'

He looked across at Maxime.

'I suggest you take your wife out for a breath of fresh air.'

Katharine stubbornly shook her head. But Maxime placed his hand under her elbow and forced her to her feet.

'The doctor's right,' he said firmly, glancing out of the window shaded by blinds from the late spring sunshine. 'It's a beautiful afternoon. A stroll will do you good.'

As they walked together down the bright corridor towards the lift, Katharine suddenly stopped in her tracks.

'I want to be there when they bring Léon back,' she exclaimed.

'You will be,' Maxime reassured her. 'I promise.'

He felt her body relax and she gave him a brief smile.

But as they sauntered through the gate into the shimmering afternoon Maxime could feel that his wife was not with him, her thoughts were back in that small room overlooking the hospital garden. And he sighed.

In the fifteen months since the calipers had first been fitted on to Léon's legs, he had sensed Katharine quietly slipping away from him. There was nothing tangible. Nothing he could reproach her with. Alone at night in their canopied bed, their moments of intimacy were still as passionate, the afterglow still as sweet. And as he held her close and she responded willingly to his touch he convinced himself that his imagination had been playing him tricks.

But when the night sky faded it was as if Katharine also faded, becoming distant and remote. And the only person who counted in her life was Léon.

It had been a difficult fifteen months for them both he reflected, his thoughts travelling back to that night on the station when he and Katharine had said goodbye before he left for London.

'What do you think,' he had announced triumphantly upon his return. 'I've persuaded Tatiana to bring Alexandra and Nicholas for a visit before she leaves to join Lawrence in Teheran. They'll be arriving next week.'

Katharine had seemed delighted. She and Tatiana had always been close and Maxime was hopeful that whatever it was that was worrying his wife she would be able to open up and confide to her friend. Even though it hurt to think that Katharine couldn't at the moment share her fears with him.

But the visit had not been a success.

After the initial excitement of their arrival and meeting up again with Alexandra, her eight-year-old goddaughter whom she hadn't seen since her little brother's christening over two years before, Katharine seemed preoccupied.

'Why don't you and the boys come to Nice with me to visit Mamenka?' Tatiana suggested. 'Alexandra and the twins get along so well together and, in spite of the age gap, Jehan and Nickie seem to enjoy each other's company.'

'I couldn't,' Katharine murmured.

'Why ever not?' Tatiana frowned. 'Mamenka would be delighted to have us all. And goodness knows when we shall see each other again now that we're off to Teheran.'

'It's . . . Léon. I couldn't leave him.'

'Then *bring* him,' Tatiana laughed. 'I meant all four.'

'Oh no,' Katharine had protested. 'He's not well enough . . .'

'Katharine there is *nothing* wrong with Léon,' Tatiana said firmly. 'He's perfectly healthy and well. *Everyone* keeps telling you that, but you won't listen.'

Katharine bristled. It was the first time she and Tatiana had ever come to verbal blows.

'*Calipers* are not a disease,' Tatiana went on. 'Many children wear them and live perfectly normal lives. It

48

will do Léon good to get away. You're turning him into a chronic invalid. Don't you agree Maxime?'

Maxime smiled at his wife. He agreed privately with every word Tatiana had said but didn't think it the moment to voice his feelings.

'*Do* go darling,' he cajoled. 'Tatiana's right, it will do you all good to get away. And Tamara would be so pleased to see you and the boys again. I'm only sorry I can't come with you.'

Katharine did not reply. She had been stung by Tatiana's frank remark. Something inside her told her it was true, but she closed her mind to the warning.

'Come on Katharine,' Tatiana said warmly. 'I'm sorry, perhaps I should have kept my mouth shut but . . .'

'But what?' Katharine enquired frostily.

Seeing the steely glint in Katharine's eyes, Tatiana did not continue. But her heart went out to Maxime and, knowing her friend's fragility, she felt afraid. Afraid that this time the suffering she could see hovering on the horizon would be inevitable if someone didn't manage to pierce Katharine's blind obsession with Léon and show her just what she was doing not only to her own life but to her marriage as well.

Maxime threw down his napkin and rose from the table.

'I'm afraid I have to leave,' he said hurriedly, sensing the tension and deeming it wise to leave the two friends to work through their problem.

He bent to kiss his wife.

'You two make your plans and I'll see you for dinner.'

But Katharine did not accompany Tatiana.

In fact, a certain coldness sprang up between them after Tatiana's frank outburst. She longed to tell Katharine what she could see was happening. What she was afraid would surely happen to her marriage, and her family life if she persisted in this obsession with Léon. But they

49

parted without a word having been said. And for the first time, Katharine was pleased to see Tatiana go.

As Maxime reflected on these past events his natural good sense took the upper hand and his spirits suddenly brightened.

It will be different now, he convinced himself. Léon is on the road to recovery. Life will soon return to normal. And Katharine and I will recapture that wonderful happiness we shared during the first six years of our marriage.

He squeezed his wife's arm affectionately against his side as they re-entered the hospital, confident that they were about to walk together into a glorious future.

But he couldn't have been more wrong.

* * *

'Maman, why don't you ever have time to read my Brer Rabbit book to me any more?' Jehan grumbled one evening as Katharine hurriedly kissed him goodnight.

At that moment Maxime walked into the room.

'Here's Papa,' Katharine comforted. 'He'll read the story to you.'

'But he read it last night *and* the night before,' Jehan pouted. 'I want *you* to do it.'

'That's not very kind to Papa', Katharine smiled, getting up from the chair by his bed.

'You do better rabbit noises than Papa,' Jehan sulked. He turned to her pleadingly.

'Maman . . . *please*.'

'Darling, I have to go to see Léon now.'

Jehan's deep blue eyes filled with tears and his lower lip trembled.

'Léon, Léon,' he gulped. 'It's *always* Léon. I don't know why we had to have him. It was much better before he came. You had time to read to me then.'

'Jehan that's enough,' Katharine said sharply.

Throwing himself on his face Jehan buried his head in his pillow, his little body shaking with silent sobs.

Katharine looked appealingly at Maxime.

'Leave him to me,' her husband smiled reassuringly.

And sitting down by the bed, he gently turned his son towards him.

But Jehan covered his face with his hands and shrugged himself away from his father's grasp, refusing to be comforted.

*　　*　　*

'I really don't know what's the matter with Jehan,' Katharine frowned later that evening as they sat on the terrace listening to the click of crickets in the soft summer dusk. 'He's becoming more and more difficult.'

'I should have thought it was obvious what was the matter with him,' Maxime replied, clasping his hands behind his head and leaning back in the wicker chair, his eyes on the darkening horizon.

'What do you mean?'

'Simply that he wants a little of your attention from time to time.'

'But that's *ridiculous*,' Katharine flared.

'It's not,' Maxime said smoothly. 'The twins are feeling neglected too. But with them it's different, they have each other and have always been pretty self-contained. But poor Jehan is one on his own. And for the past two years he's scarcely had a mother.'

'Maxime,' Katharine exploded. 'What on earth do you mean?'

'Exactly what I say.'

He turned and smiled sadly at her.

'We're *all* feeling neglected darling. All us boys.'

'Maxime, you're being unfair!'

'I'm not Katharine. The only person you seem to have any time for these days is Léon.'

Katharine's eyes widened in amazement. She opened her mouth as if to speak then abruptly rose to her feet, her lips set in a hard line, a tinge of angry colour burning on her high cheekbones.

'I've never heard anything so absurd in all my life,' she snapped.

And turning, she walked through the terrace door across the drawing-room and up the stairs.

Watching her, Maxime sighed.

His hope that, once Léon's operation was safely behind them, life could return to normal finally dashed. Katharine's obsession with her youngest son had increased not lessened.

Picking up a newspaper he squinted at it in the fading light then, giving up the unequal struggle, rose in his turn and wearily crossing the hall went into his study.

When he finally entered their room, Katharine was lying in the semi-darkness of the warm summer night, her eyes staring aimlessly out of the window just as she had done in those dreadful days of black depression after Léon's birth.

And Maxime was suddenly afraid.

Had the last two years proved too much for her? And, not for the first time, he blamed himself for the birth of their fourth son.

Following her gaze he realised that at each crisis since their marriage her father had been there to shepherd Katharine through. And a feeling of anger and jealousy against his father-in-law whose place in his wife's life he longed, yet seemed unable, to fill overcame him.

The feeling passed as swiftly as it had come and he realised that Xavier was the last person to wish to intrude. He had given Katharine to Maxime on their wedding day and from then on tried to be only a shadow in their life.

Maxime wondered whether, had Xavier been with them he could have unravelled the tangle of emotions which were now binding and confusing Katharine.

On an impulse he left the room and telephoned Algiers. 'I'm afraid Brother Xavier has gone back into the desert,' said the voice which answered his call.

'When do you expect him back?' Maxime asked.

'We do not expect him back,' the voice went on. 'Not on any fixed date. He said he may be away for a long time. But if it is urgent . . .'

'It is not urgent,' Maxime replied. 'No, there is no message.'

Not sure whether he was relieved or disappointed to find his father-in-law unavailable, Maxime thoughtfully returned to the bedroom.

Katharine did not appear to have moved.

He climbed in beside her.

'Katharine,' he whispered, tentatively putting out a hand to her in the dark.

For a split second there was no response. Then throwing herself into his arms, she burst into tears sobbing as if her heart would break.

He gathered her to him, the rapid beat of her heart boring though his chest echoing his own. His pulses throbbed as the scent of rose petals which always clung to her soft skin hovered around them. And his body ached with longing for her. As his legs twined sensuously with hers a shudder of passion trembled through her. She whispered his name, the sobs died away and she willingly gave herself into his warm embrace.

'Better now?' he asked tenderly, as later she lay warm and yielding in his arms.

She snuggled closer to him.

'Don't let's quarrel Maxime,' she pleaded. 'I can't bear it.'

'We haven't quarrelled,' he smiled.

'But you said . . .'

'Forget what I said. I understand darling. Maybe it will just take time for you to realise that Léon is a normal little boy now.'

Maxime leant on one elbow and looked lovingly down at her.

At that moment a full moon slid effortlessly across the sky, gliding in and out of the spangle of stars. It seemed to stop as it passed their window. In the sudden light which momentarily flooded the room, Maxime saw his wife's flushed face, her full lips turned upwards in a slight smile, the glow in her tawny eyes. And, as always he was enslaved by her ethereal yet strangely earthy beauty. Groaning with love, he took her in his arms once again.

'Let's go away,' he whispered sleepily as the short summer night began to fade and rainbow shadows of purple wavered to pink before melting into the pale gold of early morning. 'We'll go to Léonie's house in Biarritz which she offered us for our honeymoon. Do you remember? The sea and the Atlantic breezes will do us all good. We won't even take Nanny. It will be just you and me and the boys.'

Maxime grinned.

'We'll take them to tea at the Hôtel du Palais and begin their education in the social graces.'

He lay back against the pillows, his hands clasped behind his head.

'The family always gathered at Gure Etchea for Easter in the old days,' he reminisced. 'I can't think why you and I never met there.'

'Because we only came over to France in the summer,' Katharine yawned.

'I remember Léonie taking me to tea at the Hôtel du Palais for the first time when I was about seven,' Maxime reflected.

'Me too,' Katharine smiled. 'That last summer we came to France as a family, Bonne Maman took Anne-Marie and me to lunch there. It was a favourite haunt of hers.

She remembered it being built in the 1850s as a Summer Palace for the Empress Eugénie.'

'Bonne Maman still called it the Villa Eugénie,' Maxime put in. 'It only became the Hôtel du Palais around the turn of the century.'

He turned on his pillows and smiled down at Katharine in the moonlight.

'Isn't it wonderful darling that we can relive all these happy childhood memories with our children?'

'Mmm,' Katharine murmured sleepily, convinced at that moment that the rift had been mended. That from now on life with Maxime was going to be as it always had been.

But Katharine had not realised the depth of her guilt which, without even realising it, she still harboured because of her early rejection of Léon. And although, as Maxime had predicted, the holiday at Gure Etchea did them all good, it did not provide a final solution to their problem.

When the following October Jehan, now six years old, joined the twins at Le Petit Séminaire* in Narbonne and only Léon remained at home during the day, panic gripped Katharine. The nursery which for over seven years had overflowed with exuberant boys was now strangely empty. Her old fear of rejection, the fruit of her youthful suffering which she had buried when she married Maxime, resurfaced. She convinced herself that her role in life was slipping away from her. And her strong maternal instincts focused even more fiercely on her youngest son.

Léon, now the butt for his elder brothers' natural jealousy, became fretful and petulant, refusing to let his doting mother out of his sight.

Maxime, standing on the sidelines, gradually withdrew into himself as Katharine in a vain attempt to stop the passage of time, that moment when Léon would join his brothers at school, became more and more obsessed with her youngest son.

Chapter
6

'I'm bringing Cristobel and her sweet little friend Laura to Paris for Easter.'

Flora's characteristic scrawl, spreading over several thick linen pages, arrived a few months later.

'It's hopeless trying to get away in the summer because of the shoot. But I decided it would be lovely for the girls to have this Easter break and Robert thinks it's a splendid idea. He and the boys are going to do something outrageously dangerous up mountains while we're away.

'I know it's no use asking you to join us, you *never* seem to be able to get away these days. What *do* you get up to? Anyway, since the mountain won't come to Mohamet, (that's us!) we'll just have to come to the mountain (that's you darling!). Could you *bear* to have us to stay for a few days? Cristobel is longing to see her godmother again and you'll *love* Laura, such a sweet child.

Katharine looked up as Maxime came into the room.

'A letter from Flora,' she remarked. 'She's thinking of visiting us for a few days at Easter.'

'I hope for more than a few days,' Maxime said warmly.

He knew of the strong bond which existed between Katharine and Flora and the calming influence the older woman had had on Katharine during earlier traumas in her life. Maxime had been hopeful that Tatiana's visit two years earlier would have helped Katharine to see things in perspective. Now, in desperation, seeing his wife slowly slipping away from him he clung stubbornly to the hope that Lady Flora might be able to break through this obsession which was eating into Katharine. And of which she herself seemed strangely unaware.

'Why don't you telephone Ardnakil now and ask Flora to stay longer?' Maxime suggested, afraid Katharine might find some excuse not to be reunited with her old friend. She seemed to resent every moment away from Léon. 'It's so much easier than writing.'

Katharine smiled.

'I might just do that,' she mused, gathering up her letters and rising from the table.

*   *   *

Flora arrived with a flurry of hat boxes and expensive leather suitcases.

When Maxime met her and the two bleary-eyed girls off the night train from Paris on a bright March morning Flora, as always, looked as if she had just stepped out of a beauty parlour.

'Maxime,' she exclaimed delightedly, a whiff of perfume enveloping him as she threw her arms round his neck.

She stepped back and gazed fondly at him.

'You look *splendid*,' she exulted. 'But then who wouldn't, living in this *marvellous* sunshine.'

Even at seven a.m. the station platform was bathed in a warm golden light.

Fora flashed her dazzling smile on the pale young girl with long golden plaits standing awkwardly to one side.

'This is Laura, Maxime. Cristobel's little friend.'

'And of course Cristobel you know. Or you *did* know. *How* long is it since you last saw her?'

'Far too long,' Maxime grinned, bending to kiss Cristobel on both cheeks.

'And how is my darling Katharine?' she went on, as Maxime pointed out to Emile the numerous pieces of luggage which were somehow to be stacked into the boot of the car.

Maxime looked at her strangely and for a moment his heart sank. So Katharine hadn't even confided in Flora. He decided to let their guest discover for herself.

'I can't *wait* to see the boys,' Flora prattled on, climbing into the back of the roomy car beside the girls. 'I've never met Léon you know. Tell me, does he look like the others? They're all so *handsome*. *Such* a pity they're too young for Cristobel and Laura. Just *think* what splendid marriages we could have arranged.'

Maxime turned round in the front seat and grinned at her.

'Young people don't allow their elders to arrange their marriages any more.'

'No. Well, perhaps it's a good thing. *Everyone* was against my marrying Robert, a man twenty-seven years my senior. But they were all *quite* wrong. We've had over twenty years of absolute bliss. And five wonderful children.'

She leant back against the leather upholstery and closed her eyes.

'You must have another child Maxime and catch us up,' she murmured sleepily. 'A little girl would make all the difference to Katharine.'

Maxime gave her a quick penetrating glance. Had Flora's Highland intuition guessed at the strange situation he and his wife now found themselves in? He smiled at Flora and the sleepy girls. But Flora's eyes were closed.

Turning round, as Emile drove the car through the open gates and gently purred to a standstill in front of his home, his spirits rose.

Flora was just what Katharine needed. Beneath that butterfly exterior was hidden a store of wisdom which he was sure would pierce through the veil of his wife's incomprehension.

* * *

'Cristobel and the boys are riding along the canal to Castérat,' Maxime announced, walking onto the terrace one morning, where Katharine and Flora were sunning themselves. 'I'm going to take Laura out on a leading rein and give her her first riding lesson. It might be a good time to start Léon.'

Léon, as usual, was sitting on his mother's knee.

At Maxime's suggestion he snuggled up to her, his eyes startled.

'Perhaps . . . another time,' Katharine said diffidently.

She looked appealingly at her husband. This was not the first time his father had suggested Léon should begin to learn to handle a pony.

Maxime clicked his tongue in annoyance.

'But darling, it's the *perfect* time,' he pleaded. 'Laura has never ridden before, they can have their first lesson together.'

Katharine hugged Léon closer.

'Maybe it's better to concentrate on Laura,' she ventured.

'I can perfectly well cope with the two of them.' Maxime's face relaxed and he smiled down into his wife's anxious eyes.

'If you're worried, darling, I'll take them one at a time.'

At this Léon set up a terrified wail.

'Stop it Léon,' Maxime burst out exasperatedly.

But Léon's wail only became more piercing.

'Shush baby,' Katharine soothed. 'It's all right.'

Maxime shot his wife a penetrating look.

'He's *not* a baby Katharine,' he said tightly. 'He's a perfectly healthy little boy of four. And it's time he started behaving like one. At his age his brothers were already adept at handling their ponies.'

'Yes but . . .' Katharine began.

Seeing the pain in his wife's eyes, Maxime relented.

'But *what* darling?' he asked gently.

Katharine didn't answer. She didn't know what to say. In her heart she knew that what her husband was saying was true. Yet something inside her would not let Léon go. Would not let him take the slightest risk.

'I see,' he sighed, after a few minutes. 'All right, we'll leave it for the time being.'

The pain faded from Katharine's eyes and she gave him a grateful smile.

Maxime knew that he had lost once again. And he hated himself for his weakness. But he also knew that he had no choice. Katharine meant more to him than anything in the world. More than the four sons he adored. He was even prepared to sacrifice Léon on the altar of her happiness.

Smiling diffidently at Flora who had remained apart during this conversation, he turned and walked away.

'Why don't we go for a walk,' Flora suggested as Katharine relaxed.

Now that his father was safely out of the way, Léon released his grip on his mother and slipped from her knee.

'Léon can't walk very far.'

'Then let him go back to the nursery to Nanny,' Flora said blithely.

And getting up, she took her hostess's arm.

'Come Katharine,' she said firmly. 'Léon, I think Nanny wants you in the nursery.'

Léon opened his mouth to protest. But seeing the glint in Flora's eyes he scrambled up from the floor, where he had been playing at his mother's feet, and limped hurriedly across the terrace.

'He seems to walk very well to me,' Flora remarked as they went down the steps and across the lawn.

'Oh yes,' Katharine said hurriedly. 'But not far.'

'Why not?' Flora enquired.

'Flora you don't know what Léon's been through,' Katharine burst out. 'You don't understand!'

They had arrived at the lake.

'I understand very well Katharine,' Flora calmly replied, sitting down on an old iron bench and patting the place beside her. 'And I know what Léon has been through. One of my brothers had the same problem and medicine was far less advanced in those days. It didn't stop him from being awarded the MC for an act of outstanding bravery a year before he was killed at Verdun during the First World War. He led a perfectly normal life. And Léon should now begin to do the same.'

She smiled at Katharine sitting on the bench beside her, her lips set in a stubborn line.

'That's sometimes the hardest part,' she said gently. 'Realising that he is not an invalid. No different from other children. And allowing him to have his wings and fly. Duncan, my brother, went to prep school when he was eight. And I'm sure they made no concessions to him there.'

But Katharine stared silently at the ground, her toe making small concentric circles in the earth beneath her feet.

'You're denying Léon the right to be a normal little

boy,' Flora went on. 'He'll be going to school with his brothers very soon. What's going to happen then?'

'I – I was thinking of engaging a governess and having him taught at home.'

'Katharine, do you realise what you are doing,' Flora admonished. 'You're setting him apart, making him different. You're denying him the immense joy of being one of a large family. You've told me so many times how much you missed not having brothers and sisters. How happy you were to come back to France after the war and rediscover this wonderful extended family. Do you want Léon to be an only child as well?'

Flora shook her head in dismay.

'Léon could be the twin Jehan misses. They could be great friends in spite of the age gap. But you won't let them. You're preventing him playing . . . and fighting with his brothers. And if I'm not mistaken you're alienating your other three sons. You're so obsessed with Léon and his supposed fragility that nothing else seems to matter.'

Flora took a deep breath.

'Not even Maxime!'

'Flora that's ridiculous,' Katharine spluttered, rising angrily from the bench.

But Flora restrained her.

'Darling,' she pleaded, 'don't let's quarrel. We've been friends for a very long time. We've shared so much and lived through many traumas together. Don't let this come between us.'

Reluctantly Katharine sat down.

'Perhaps I should not have said what I did,' Flora apologised. 'But I love you dearly Katharine. I know how much you have suffered and now that you have found happiness with Maxime I can't bear to see this rift between you.'

Katharine drew in her brows.

'Flora,' she said bewilderedly, 'there's no rift between Maxime and me, I promise you.'

A rising blush stained her ivory cheeks a delicate magnolia.

'We love each other very much.'

Flora smiled fondly at her friend.

'And that is very important,' she said. 'But it is not everything. In order for a marriage to work two people need to be together, . . . on a spiritual as well as a physical level. And I assure you Maxime is suffering. It's not only your *sons* who are feeling rejected. It's your *husband* as well.'

Flora took Katharine's hand in hers and held it tightly.

'Let Léon go Katharine. Let him have his wings. Not only for you and your marriage but also for Léon. He's a lovely little boy, but you're turning him into a whining invalid.'

As Flora spoke Katharine stiffened and withdrew her hand. And Flora knew that there was no point in continuing the conversation.

*   *   *

The rest of their time together passed uneventfully.

When they parted on the steps of Le Moulin the evening Flora and the girls returned to Scotland, Katharine kissed them all affectionately.

'We've had such fun with the twins and Jehan. *Do* bring them to Ardnakil very soon,' Cristobel begged.

Katharine smiled non-committally.

'This summer?' Cristobel called out of the window when the car slid away from the front door.

'Oh maman *please*,' the twins pleaded, jumping up and down on the steps beside her.

'Me too,' Jehan, called bombing down the drive after the car.

'Yes of course, you too,' Cristobel yelled back.

Flora wondered whether Katharine noticed that Cristobel had not included Léon in her invitation. As they swept through the open wrought-iron gates her heart was full of foreboding for what the future might hold for her friend. With dismay Flora realised that their conversation in the walled garden might never have taken place. Nothing had changed. Katharine and Léon remained in a world apart. And Maxime, though attentive and loving as ever to his wife, was slowly retreating into a shell of his own and taking his other three sons with him.

She sighed deeply and sank back in her seat.

Maxime, in the front beside Emile, turned round and their eyes met.

He raised his eyebrows. And Flora shrugged resignedly.

Nodding, he turned away, his eyes on the road ahead.

He knew that the hope he had clung to at Flora's arrival had been extinguished. If Flora had been unable to pierce this veil of incomprehension which enveloped Katharine he wondered whether anyone ever could.

'Perhaps a holiday?' Flora said tentatively. 'Just the two of you.'

'And Léon,' Maxime added.

Flora thought she detected a tinge of bitterness in his voice.

'Then a *family* holiday,' she continued. 'Away from everything, just you and Katharine and the children.'

Maxime sighed.

He had tried that once. Just after Léon's operation when they had all gone to Gure Etchea, Léonie's house in Biarritz. It had been pleasant, refreshing, a change. They had relived with their children the pleasures of their own childhood, and Maxime had believed that the breakthrough had come. That the chapter, opened on the day of Léon's birth, had been finally closed. But when they returned, everything had been as before.

'It's worth considering,' Flora remarked as the car drew up in front of the station.

'*Anything's* worth considering,' Maxime said desperately.

Then, as always, his natural good humour surfaced. He had weathered many storms in his life, he told himself. He would weather this one. Jumping from the car he went to help Flora and the girls alight.

Glancing up at him Flora noted that his face looked less strained, his smile seemed more spontaneous.

'There's always Ardnakil,' she murmured.

'Thank you Flora,' Maxime replied. 'But I think we'll try to work this one out by ourselves.'

Waving them goodbye when the train chunted away from the platform Maxime gritted his teeth.

He would try again.

*　　*　　*

Katharine opened the little white velvet box which Maxime had placed beside her plate. Lying on a blue silk lining was a slim gold bracelet, dotted with tiny pearls.

'Like it?' he enquired anxiously.

'It's beautiful', she murmured, removing the bracelet and twining it twice around her slim wrist.

Holding out her arm, she admired the filigree gold pattern which separated the pearls.

'I've never seen one like it,' she purred delightedly. 'Wherever did you find it?'

'I didn't,' he grinned. 'I had it specially designed for you.'

Getting up, Maxime walked round the table and,

twining his arms round his wife's neck gently rubbed his cheek against hers.

Katharine leant against him, her eyes closed.

'Maxime', she whispered, 'you're so good to me.'

'I love you', he answered simply.

'I love you too,' she whispered back.

And she held up her face for his kiss.

It was their tenth wedding anniversary.

Maxime had toyed with the idea of suggesting that they go away together on a second honeymoon. But he had been afraid of the answer. Katharine had not left Léon since the day he was born, and he didn't want to risk even suggesting it.

There was a discreet cough in the doorway.

Lost in their embrace, it took seconds before they realised that they were not alone.

'There is a call for Monsieur,' Alphonse announced.

He seemed embarrassed.

'Take a message will you Alphonse,' Maxime said testily.

The butler self-consciously cleared his throat.

'I'm afraid Monsieur, the caller is very insistent.'

Maxime frowned irritably.

'But who is it?'

Alphonse didn't reply. He gazed at his feet, his embarassment seeming to grow.

'Perhaps Monsieur would like to take it in his study?'

'I'll take it in the hall,' Maxime snapped.

The butler looked furtively at Katharine, then stood aside as Maxime stormed out of the room. With another glance in her direction, Alphonse carefully closed the door behind him.

Katharine poured herself a cup of coffee, then held out her arm, once again admiring the bracelet. And her thoughts went back to her wedding day.

Leaning back in her chair such an upsurge of love for her husband swept over her that Katharine caught her breath. Then abruptly it was as if a veil were torn away. And she saw herself as others had seen her during the four years since Léon's birth: completely wrapped up in her guilt and obsession. Shocked by the sudden revelation, every nerve in her body seemed to jangle, like the brass rings on a curtain which has been roughly drawn back, yet continues to send rippling echoes even after daylight has flooded the former obscurity.

'Father', she cried. 'What *happened* to me? *How* could I have been so blind?'

She crumpled and fell to her knees.

'What have I done?' she pleaded. 'Where did I go wrong?'

Into her now sharpened awareness it was as if a gentle voice replied.

'You kept forgetting, my child, which one of us is God.'

Katharine covered her face with her hands.

'Forgive me Lord', she whispered over and over again. 'Please forgive me. Help me to make up to Maxime and the boys for these past four years.'

As her trembling body gradually quietened Katharine rose from her knees, at peace with herself for the first time in many months. She had known that something was wrong, but had been unable to pinpoint what. And her prayers had seemed hollow. She now realised that Jesus had left her to find the reason, and the solution, for herself.

'Praise you Lord,' she exulted. 'You do indeed work in mysterious ways.'

As she spoke Maxime entered the dining-room. But he was no longer smiling. His face was tense and angry. He seemed preoccupied, even distant.

'Is something the matter darling?' she enquired, handing him his coffee.

Her husband looked up, almost as if he didn't see her.

'What is it darling?' she probed.

Maxime absently put down the cup. But he didn't reply.

Katharine frowned remembering Alphonse's embarrassment, his suggestion that Maxime take the telephone call in his study. The way he had avoided her eyes and furtively closed the dining-room door behind him.

And her mind leapt to her father.

'Maxime,' she said sharply 'Has something happened to Zag?'

Her anxious voice roused Maxime from his stupour. Getting up he walked quickly to her side.

'No darling', he soothed, drawing up a chair and sitting down beside her. 'It's nothing to be alarmed about.'

'But what was that telephone call about?' Katharine insisted. 'Who *was* it?'

Maxime avoided her eyes and his expression hardened.

'Maxime', she pleaded. 'I *must* know.'

He turned slowly round and looked into her puzzled eyes. And he knew that there was no escape. He had to tell her the truth.

'It was Marie-Céleste', he said blankly.

Katharine's eyes widened, her pupils almost black.

'Your first wife?'

Maxime nodded.

'Yes', he said, his voice expressionless. 'She's come back.'

Chapter
7

Katharine slumped in her chair.

For a few seconds there was silence in the room, broken only by the steady tick of the grandfather clock standing in the far corner. As the pendulum swung soporifically backwards and forwards there was a gentle whirr followed by eight deep chimes.

The sound brought Maxime back to earth. Kneeling beside his wife he gathered her into his arms. But she seemed limp, as if all life had been extinguished.

'Darling', he pleaded. 'Look at me. Say something.'

But Katharine remained staring blankly in front of her.

She remembered questioning Maxime on the day he asked her to marry him about what would happen if ever his first wife reappeared. He had been amused at the idea and replied that whatever she did Marie-Céleste was no longer any concern of his. On that golden spring afternoon Katharine had believed that the past, both their pasts, had been finally buried. But now she realised that her worst fears had been confirmed. The beautiful Marie-Céleste, her husband's first love, had returned.

And the peace and happiness which had surged through her only a few minutes before slowly drained away.

'What are you going to do?' she whispered.

'I honestly don't know,' Maxime answered, rising to his feet.

'You said she was no longer any concern of yours . . .'

'She's *not*', he cut in. 'But . . . oh Katharine I feel sorry for her. She's back in Paris, homeless and penniless.'

Katharine's brow furrowed.

'How can she be penniless?' she queried. 'What about her husband?'

'She doesn't *have* a husband', Maxime said tightly. 'Kurt never married her.'

'But I thought . . .'

'We *all* thought. Or we assumed. No one's had any contact with her for years. As I told you her family cut her off when she left. We believed Kurt had divorced and married her. But he didn't.'

Maxime shrugged.

'He's gone back to his wife and children . . . and left Marie-Céleste to fend for herself. She returned to Paris thinking that after all this time her family would have forgiven her. But her father refuses even to meet her. His wife died about five years ago and he remarried, a much younger woman who obviously doesn't want to be lumbered with Marie-Céleste.'

He looked at her hopelessly.

'She's desperate Katharine.'

'But what can *you* do?' Katharine said harshly, fear adding an unpleasant edge to her voice.

'I don't know', he answered miserably. 'Unfortunately she hadn't heard about my mother's death . . . or about our marriage.'

He paused, as if searching for words.

'She wants to come back', he ended dully.

'That's impossible,' Katharine gasped.

'Of *course* it's impossible', he soothed.

70

Then suddenly, all her terrifying nightmares fused in a thundering wave which bore screaming down upon her.

'You're not going to bring her here?' Katharine's voice rose hysterically.

'No, no of *course* not,' he cut in quickly.

'Then what?'

'As I said darling, I honestly don't know.'

He got to his feet and, walking over to the window, stood looking bleakly across the sun-dappled lawns. Katharine remained at the littered breakfast-table, staring blankly at the opposite wall, her eyes focused on nothing.

Maxime turned round, and suddenly his mood seemed lighter.

'Don't worry darling,' he smiled. 'It's a storm in a tea-cup which will soon blow over. Don't let's give it hurricane proportions. As you said, she's no longer any concern of mine. I'll try to get in touch with her brother, perhaps *he* can persuade their father to help her.'

Maxime came quickly across the room and lifting her in his arms held her close.

'Don't give Marie-Céleste another thought,' he said softly. 'Just think about tomorrow. We'll all be on our way to Gure Etchea with nothing to do for a whole month but go shrimping and build sand-castles with the boys. Aren't you looking forward to it?'

Katharine nodded absently.

'What are you going to do?' she enquired hesitantly.

'Sort something out before we leave. I'll try to get hold of Antoine, my ex-brother-in-law straight away.'

Maxime paused, a slight frown creasing his brow.

'Are you sure you're all right?' he enquired anxiously.

'Yes darling,' she murmured distantly, giving him a weak smile. 'You go and do what you have to do.'

He pressed her briefly to him then swiftly left the room.

*   *   *

Katharine went mechanically about the house all morning.

The boys were over-excited and teased Léon unmercifully until even Nanny Moffatt's equable temper was roused. When Katharine looked in on them after tea Nanny announced firmly that an early night was what they all needed and, ignoring Léon's wails for his mother, swept him off to his bath before six o'clock.

Katharine realised that her presence was superfluous and, after promising to read a story to Jehan once he was in bed, she wandered down to the drawing-room to wait for Maxime.

The steady, unchanging routine of the nursery and the prospect of a complete change had restored her spirits. She felt at peace again, confident that she could trust her husband, and prepared to leave this unpleasant interlude in their lives in his capable hands.

As she was glancing idly through a magazine she heard Alphonse's dignified step cross the hall to open the front door. Wondering who could be calling unannounced at this hour she put down the magazine and waited. Perhaps it was Armand popping in on his way back to Narbonne from Castérat to say goodbye. A warm glow suffused her at the thought of her great-uncle.

But the imperious voice coming from the hall was not Armand's. She heard the usually imperturbable Alphonse stammering a reply. Then the voice was raised again.

Getting up and crossing the room Katharine walked into the hall. A tall, curvaceous woman, fashionably dressed, with a mass of flaming red hair escaping from

her tight-fitting cloche hat, was organising a pile of
suitcases which the taxi driver was carrying into the
hall.

Seeing Katharine, Alphonse looked desperately around
him. He appeared not only embarrassed but hopelessly
confused.

'I don't think I have had the pleasure of meeting you,'
Katharine said coolly, advancing towards the intruder.

She neither understood why nor cared for the way
this unknown woman was ushering all this luggage into
the hall.

The stranger turned round and looked Katharine up
and down.

'Who are you?' she enquired frigidly.

Alphonse quickly stepped between them.

'Madame Montredon de la Livière,' he interjected
hurriedly, bowing towards Katharine.

'There must be some mistake,' the woman said icily.
'*I* am Madame Montredon de la Livière.'

In that instant Katharine knew who the intruder was.

She felt her legs go weak and begin to crumple
beneath her. But with a superhuman effort she regained
control.

'Perhaps,' Katharine breathed formally, 'you had better
come into the drawing-room.'

She nodded towards the agitated butler.

'That will be all Alphonse.'

'*No*, Alphonse,' the woman contradicted. 'Have these
suitcases taken up to *our* room.'

She heavily stressed the 'our'.

Alphonse looked helplessly from one to the other.

'That will be *all*, Alphonse,' Katharine ground out
through clenched teeth.

As the two women stood locked in a silent battle
Maxime rushed in through the open front door. He had

seen the taxi bowling back along the drive and a terrible premonition had struck him.

Alphonse gratefully hurried away before any further counter orders could be issued. For the first time in his career as a butler he was at a loss for words.

'Marie-Céleste,' Maxime burst out angrily. 'What is the meaning of this?'

'Meaning of what darling?' she enquired archly, giving him the full benefit of her dazzling smile.

'Coming here.'

'Why shouldn't I come here?' she enquired in syrupy tones.

And walking languidly across the hall she slipped her arm in his.

'I've returned home to the husband I love.'

Katharine gasped.

Maxime angrily shook himself free of Marie-Céleste's grasp and put his arm protectively around Katharine.

'This is *not* your home,' he said curtly. 'You left it some thirteen years ago.'

Marie-Céleste sighed deeply.

'I made a *terrible* mistake darling,' she purred.

'And stop calling me darling,' Maxime menaced, his voice rising dangerously.

He had felt Katharine's slight body stiffen at his side, and drew her protectively against him.

'I won't have a slanging-match in the hall,' he said tersely, and walking across to the drawing-room flung open the door.

'I've no intention of having a slanging-match anywhere,' Marie-Céleste announced coolly.

'I told you on the telephone this morning that I would try to arrange something for you.'

'But you don't *need* to arrange anything Maxime.'

'Then why are you here?'

'Because this is where I belong. We're married sweetie.'
She looked at him provocatively.

'Or had you forgotten?'

'We *were* married,' he replied, his voice like flint. 'But
we've been divorced for over eleven years.'

'Ah,' she smiled, sitting on the arm of a chair and
crossing her long, slim legs. You seem to forget that we
were married in the Catholic Church. And the Catholic
Church does not recognise divorce. According to *them* we
are married till death us do part. This lady . . .'

She pronounced the words with heavy sarcasm, snapping
her fingers in Katharine's direction before fitting a turkish
cigarette into a long ebony holder, 'is your mistress.'

Flicking a slim gold lighter, she bent her head to
the flame.

'I *quite* understand that you consoled yourself in my
absence Maxie darling,' she went on, blowing smoke
rings in Katharine's direction. 'But now the party's over.
I'm back. And your concubine must go.'

Katharine covered her face with her hands.

Maxime stood up and faced his ex-wife menacingly,
hands clenched tightly at his side.

'What is it you want Marie-Céleste?' he hissed.

'*Want* darling?' she queried innocently turning her
sparkling emerald eyes full on him. What *could* I want . . .
but *you*.'

'State your price,' Maxime said icily. 'Katharine is my
wife . . . and we have four children.'

Marie-Céleste languidly stubbed out her half-smoked
cigarette.

'You have four *bastards*,' she corrected.

Katharine put out her hand to restrain Maxime. A livid
spot of colour had appeared on each cheekbone and the
glint in his eyes frightened her. She feared he was about
to strike his ex-wife.

'I've told Alphonse to have my things taken up to our room,' Marie-Céleste drawled languidly. 'I was *so* sorry to hear about your mother, Max darling.'

She raised her eyebrows enquiringly. 'But does that mean *we* now have the master bedroom?'

Sliding gracefully off the chair, she blew him a kiss and left the room.

As the door closed behind her, Katharine collapsed.

For a few seconds Maxime remained motionless, his burning eyes fixed on the door. Then turning, he saw his wife and suddenly the anger drained from him. In one swift stride he was beside her.

'Katharine, *darling*,' he groaned. 'Don't look at me like that, I beg you.'

Katharine's eyes, black with fear were fixed on her husband.

'Everything's going to be all right, I promise you,' he went on urgently.

'What are you going to do?' she whispered, her voice barely audible.

'I haven't got a plan of action yet, but Marie-Céleste hasn't got a leg to stand on. All that talk about the Catholic Church is poppycock and she knows it. She doesn't care two hoots for the Catholic Church. Our wedding was just an excuse for a glittering social event with Marie-Céleste in the star role.'

He paused.

'The only thing which *does* slightly perturb me is that, although I was the innocent party, I did what I thought was the "right thing" and allowed her to divorce me. Legally I suppose she could play on that.'

He felt Katharine stiffen in his arms.

'But only to get money out of me darling, nothing else.'

He kissed the tip of her nose affectionately.

'*Don't worry.*'

Katharine gave a weak smile. Then her brow creased in a puzzled frown.

'Maxime,' she ventured hesitantly, 'her clothes, they're so beautiful. And all those expensive suitcases . . . she doesn't *look* penniless.'

Maxime smiled wryly.

'It's all relative. Penniless to Marie-Céleste means she hasn't got an endless supply of cash to spend on herself.'

He shook his head in bewilderment.

'How *could* I have been taken in by her?'

'She's very beautiful,' Katharine said raggedly.

'So are panthers,' Maxime remarked drily. 'But I've no desire to live with one.'

And the tension eased, they both laughed.

'I don't think I've got time to change,' Maxime announced, glancing at his watch 'Can you bear to dine with a farm labourer?'

As she snuggled against him they heard Alphonse's discreet cough.

'Dinner is served Madame,' he announced.

'Oh *no*, Alphonse, not *yet*,' a voice called silkily from the stairwell. 'I simply *must* have a drink.'

And drifting in a cloud of expensive perfume Marie-Céleste, resplendent in a shimmering green silk dress undulating sinuously around her hips, sailed into the room.

'My, *my*,' she mocked, 'we not only dine with the chickens but we no longer even dress for dinner.'

She sighed exaggeratedly.

'My poor sweet, how ghastly for you having to live like a peasant. But we'll soon change all that.'

Completely ignoring Katharine, she flashed her brilliant green eyes on Maxime.

'*Do* be an angel and mix me a cocktail Maxie darling. Or I'll *die* . . .'

77

Maxime ignored her request.

'My wife and I are going in to dinner,' he stated frigidly. 'If you do not wish to join us, Alphonse will have a tray sent up to your room.'

Katharine saw Alphonse still standing in the doorway, uncertain what to do.

'I think *I'll* have a tray in my room Maxime,' Katharine stammered. 'I promised I'd read Jehan his bedtime story . . . and I haven't kissed the twins goodnight.'

Marie-Céleste slowly removed a cigarette from a jew-elled case and as she bent her head to the flame the cleav-age of her dress clearly revealed her full creamy breasts.

Katharine gasped. Her beauty was overpowering.

'Run along to your nursery duties,' Marie-Céleste said off-handedly and added with a mocking smile, '*Such* a touching picture of domestic bliss.'

She laughed and lay back on the sofa, a deep slit at the side of her dress exposing her perfectly shaped thighs.

Maxime linked his arm in Katharine's and walked with her into the hall.

'Try to have an early night,' he smiled, 'I'll come up as soon as I can.'

As she mounted the stairs she saw him standing point-edly at the drawing-room door waiting for Marie-Céleste to cross into the dining room. But his ex-wife made no move.

'*Do* come and sit down, sweetie,' she heard her husky voice coax suggestively. 'Now that we're *alone* we can have that little cocktail.'

Walking blindly along the gallery to the night nursery Katharine imagined Marie-Céleste turning her sultry eyes on Maxime as she provocatively patted the empty place beside her on the sofa. And she suddenly felt defeated. Convinced that in spite of his protestations Maxime would not be able to help once again becoming enslaved by Marie-Céleste. How could any man resist such dazzling beauty?

*   *   *

Lying sleepless in bed gazing into the summer darkness, watching the moon, hanging in the dark sky like a great baroque pearl, glide in and out of her window, Katharine's vivid imagination reached fever pitch. Her emotional weather vane fluctuated between storms of anxiety and a feeling of numbed shock, in the agony of love and fear which the remembrance of the day's extraordinary events filled her. She was aware of a constant threat of danger which so overpowered her that she felt, in order to remain sane, she had to blanket her mind with oblivion.

As the clock in the turrett boomed eleven she agonised over why Maxime still hadn't come to join her, convinced that Marie-Céleste had entwined him in her coils once again. From the dark corners of the room it seemed that ugly, formless shapes were creeping out, leering at her, mocking her, savouring the moment when they would rise like a massed army, swoop down and destroy her.

'You've lost him', they taunted. 'You've lost him. And it's all your own fault.'

And Marie-Céleste's mocking laugh mingled with theirs. Only now her laughter held a note of triumph

'Jesus', Katharine cried. 'Help me.'

Tearing back the bedclothes she fell sobbing to her knees.

'Give me back my peace of mind,' she pleaded. 'Don't let them destroy me.'

The door opened softly. Maxime tiptoed into the room and gently lifting her in his arms laid her on the bed.

'She's gone,' he said, gently kissing her quivering lips.

Katharine's eyes searched his face.

'*Gone,*' she whispered incredulously. 'Gone where?'

Maxime sat down on the side of the bed and took her hands in his.

'I've just put her on the night train to Paris.'

'But . . . I don't understand.'

'There's not much to understand. I knew there was something behind this charade. Marie-Céleste isn't interested in me any more than I am in her. And the last thing she wants is to be buried down here.'

'But what did you do?'

'Booked her a room at the Crillon for the time being and promised I'd rent her a flat in Paris as soon as it can be arranged. *And* pay her expenses, which knowing Marie-Céleste could be considerable, on condition that she immediately reverts to her maiden name and never shows her face down here again. If she breaks either of those conditions, she fends for herself.'

He grinned down at Katharine.

'Knowing Marie-Céleste, that's the last thing she wants.' Maxime paused, as if uncertain how to continue. 'I'm afraid this means I have to go to Paris darling. I don't intend to be her benefactor indefinitely, so I need to see my lawyers and get this business tightly sewn up. If there's a loophole, Marie-Céleste will find it. Unfortunately I didn't manage to get hold of her brother. He's on business in the United States. But I'll do so as soon as he returns. He's a good chap and I know he'll help if he can.'

He smiled at Katharine, gently smoothing the hair away from her forehead.

'And that my darling, is the latest state of affairs.'

Just then the moon flooded the room with a pale eerie light, briefly outlining Katharine's taut white features. And Maxime realised the terrible strain Marie-Céleste's sudden appearance had inflicted on her. He groaned and taking her in his arms pressed her head against his broad chest.

'My darling,' he said hoarsely, 'what *have* I done to you.'

His faint masculine scent flooded her nostrils as Katharine reached up a hand and tenderly stroked his face.

'And that isn't all,' he went on gloomily. 'This upheaval means that I won't be able to stay very long in Biarritz. I'll come with you tomorrow, see you settled in at Gure Etchea . . . and then I'll have to leave.'

His lips tightened.

'Blast Marie-Céleste', he grated.

His hold tightened round her as his lips roved over her hair.

'I'm *so* sorry darling.'

'It's all right Maxime,' she whispered, biting back the tears which once again threatened to overflow.

It seemed so unfair that just when Jesus had lifted the veil on her past life and she had vowed to make up to Maxime for the years they had lost, he should be snatched from her. Then an immense outpouring of love swamped her feelings of self-pity. Lying back on the pillows she held out her arms to him.

'I thought I had lost you,' she said huskily. 'Now that you're here, nothing else matters.'

Chapter
8

'I'll be back as soon as I possibly can darling,' Maxime said, stooping to kiss her as the car's engine hummed softly.

They had been in Biarritz just a week. And the boys had made endless plans as to how they would occupy their father during the time he would be with them.

'*Why* do you have to go?' Jehan stamped. 'You promised to take me shrimping.'

'And I will,' Maxime smiled, tweaking his son's nose as he climbed into the car. 'Just as soon as I get back.'

'But I want you to take me *today*', Jehan pouted.

'Come back soon Papa,' the twins chorused in unison.

That was one of the offputting things about the twins. They always did everything in unison. And it usually meant double trouble.

Maxime wound down the window.

'A pity Léonie refused to have the telephone installed here. I could have rung you every evening.'

He caught hold of Katharine's hand and squeezed it.

'But you know how to get hold of me. And I'll send you little notes telling you how much I love you as often as I can. Don't worry if you don't have time to reply. Just concentrate on having a wonderful holiday with the boys.'

'Bye bye Papa,' the twins chorused, tap-dancing on the step, anxious for their father to be off so that they could begin the day's activities.

'Bye bye,' Jehan called morosely.

Léon held tightly to Katharine's hand, looking from one brother to the other.

'Bye bye Papa,' he mimicked, waving his other hand in salute.

Maxime looked at Katharine and raised his eyebrows as Emile manoeuvred the car away from the house. It was the first time he could remember Léon ever openly acknowledging his existence.

Katharine smiled to herself. Jesus could indeed work miracles. Her youngest son's attitude to everyone was already beginning to change.

'Léon,' Xavier called, 'we're going to play pétanque.* Want to come?'

Léon looked up at his mother, his eyes shining. In an involuntary gesture Katharine put out her hand to stop him then, remembering, checked herself. But Léon had already released himself from her grasp afraid, yet exulting in his new found freedom.

Watching him limp hurriedly across the lawn to join his brothers Katharine's heart rejoiced. She turned and entered the house. The morning's mail had just arrived, forwarded from Le Moulin. On top of the pile was a letter with an Algerian postmark and she ran delightedly across the chequered tile floor to pick it up. Mail from North Africa was erratic and it was some weeks since she had heard from her father.

As she slid her finger beneath the flap she noticed that it was addressed to her husband. For a fraction of a second she hesitated, frowning, then her brow cleared. Maxime wouldn't mind. It was bound to be for the two of them. And she tore open the envelope.

'Thank you for your telephone call,' her father had written.

Again Katharine frowned. What telephone call? Maxime hadn't mentioned that he'd spoken to her father. Then she shrugged. He must have forgotten.

'Luckily, you caught me just before I left,' she read, her eyes turning back to the pages in her hand. 'And of course I will do my very best to comply with your wishes. As you well know my dear Maxime, my daughter's happiness means more to me than anything else and she must come first. You can rely on me to fit in with your plans. I hesitate to telephone you in case Katharine takes the call since I realise that you do not want her to know anything about this. So I'm afraid this will be a very hurried note penned minutes before I set off.'

The letter dropped from Katharine's hand as, frowning once again, she sat down on a carved wooden chair.

What on earth did her father mean? What plans were being made between him and Maxime of which she was unaware?

A tiny stone of suspicion plopped insidiously into the now still waters of her mind, its swirling ripples eddying noiselessly outwards in ever-increasing circles. And suddenly, that old icy feeling gripped her heart.

Looking out of the open door through which she and Maxime had walked arm in arm such a very short time before, doubts and fears once again caught her in their web. Her husband was on his way to Paris to meet his ex-wife. Katharine's reason told her it was purely business. But her imagination reminded her of Marie-Céleste's sultry voice coaxing Maxime to the sofa that evening she had left the room. She also remembered that he had once loved her. It was not *he* who had left. Maxime's ex-wife was still unbelievably beautiful . . . and ruthless when it came to getting her own way.

And Katharine was suddenly very afraid.

'Maman,' Jehan wailed, ambling into the hall. 'You promised to take us to St Jean de Luz to see the fishing boats and have a picnic. When are we going?'

Her son's voice brought Katharine back from her encroaching nightmare.

'I thought you were playing pétanque?' she queried.

'We are,' Jehan continued, scuffing the toes of his sandals against the tiled floor. 'But I want to go on a picnic.'

Katharine smiled down at her small son. And the dark shadows fled. How could she have been so stupid? She and Maxime had so much.

'Run and fetch the others. I'll ask Nanny for your bathing things and then we'll be off.'

Jehan stopped sulking and dive-bombed through the door in search of his brothers. Tucking the letter into the belt of her dress Katharine ran up the stairs, telling herself that she had been ridiculous. She could trust Maxime utterly. There was no need to worry.

But after she had kissed the boys goodnight, alone in the cool tiled dining room, Katharine toyed with her dinner. And, remembering the letter, her anxiety returned.

At ten o'clock, inwardly cursing Léonie for not having the telephone installed at Gure Etchea she walked down into the town. It was a beautiful evening, warm and scented, the stars veiled in a haze which made them look like tiny powder puffs dotted around the sky.

The elegant old-world Hôtel du Palais, formerly the favourite summer residence of the Empress Eugénie during the Second Empire, was glittering with lights, chandeliers playing harsh tricks on ageing faces, when Katharine entered the foyer. As she waited for the call she

had requested, the distant throb of an orchestra drifted
through from one of the many reception rooms.

'Oh Berthe, I'm so sorry,' she apologised when the
old woman finally answered 'Did I get you out of
bed?'

Berthe gave a sleepy denial.

'I wanted to know whether Monsieur had arrived.'

'No, Mademoiselle Katharine.'

Katharine, the little girl she had known as a baby,
would always be Mademoiselle to Berthe, no matter
how old she was, or how long she had been married.

Katharine hesitated. Maxime's train had arrived in
Paris almost two hours ago.

'Monsieur telephoned from the station,' Berthe went
on. 'Manon took the call. He told us not to wait up for
him as he would be back very late.'

'I see,' Katharine replied slowly.

'Shall I tell Monsieur you rang?' Berthe enquired.

Suddenly Katharine felt an intruder: like a private
detective spying on her husband.

'No . . . no Berthe, don't bother. He might worry.'

As she put the telephone down and walked slowly
across the foyer peppered with elegant furniture and
priceless ornaments, the haunting strains of a tenor
saxophone playing 'All the things you are' drifted after
her. The music brought back memories of Ashley. That
faraway evening when they had met again. And all
those long-buried fears of losing the person she loved
most returned. There could only be one explanation for
her husband's late arrival, the gloating demons taunted.
He was with Marie-Céleste!

Lying sleepless in the moonlit room which only twenty-
four hours ago had witnessed their love, Katharine
tossed and turned, puzzling over her father's cryptic
letter. Maxime had been in Paris for three days the

week before they left for Biarritz, meeting with wine merchants interested in Le Moulin's vintage. He must have telephoned Zag then.

She suddenly sat up in bed.

Perhaps Maxime's business trip had been a foil. And he had really gone to Paris to see his ex-wife!

As she allowed her vivid imagination free rein, she convinced herself that Marie-Céleste's sudden appearance had not been the surprise it had appeared to be. Maxime had known that she was back in Paris. Perhaps she had been there when he went on that business trip. And he had now returned to join her.

Katharine's lips set in a hard line.

Angrily thumping the fluffy lace-edged pillow, she settled her head firmly into its depths and shut her eyes, trying to shut Maxime out of her mind.

But lying dry-eyed and sleepless, watching the sea shimmering silver and jet in the moonlight, she remembered their love.

'Maxime,' she cried brokenly as sleep finally overcame her.

The night had been traumatic but also decisive. Katharine decided that the only thing to do was to discover the truth for herself. She would telephone Maxime and tell him of her fears.

The boys were still having breakfast when Katharine called for Emile to fetch the car, and drove immediately to Biarritz. Giving the rue de la Faisanderie number to the clerk behind the Post Office counter she waited impatiently to hear her husband's voice.

'Engaged,' the clerk intoned laconically.

And returned to his counting.

Katharine pursed her lips in irritation.

'Could you try again?' she asked tersely.

The clerk sighed and put down his pen.

'Still engaged,' he replied, without looking up.

Katharine frowned and glanced at her watch.

Who could Maxime be telephoning at this early hour?

Then her heart missed a beat. Or who could be telephoning him? No one knew he was in Paris . . . except Marie-Céleste!

Her face hardened and she tapped at the grill separating them to get the clerk's attention.

'Would you please keep trying the number I gave you until you get through,' she instructed.

Pushing aside his sheaf of papers he dialled again. Then without a word replaced the receiver.

Katharine stood nervously drumming her fingers on the counter until a fat woman with three children in tow pushed her aside.

When her call was announced and the quartet had been directed to a cabin Katharine returned, her eyebrows raised enquiringly. Seeing her, the clerk squinted down at the number she had handed to him twenty minutes earlier and dialled again.

'Cabin three,' he announced disinterestedly, when the long persistent ring indicated that the line was now free.

Stumbling in her haste, Katharine pulled open the door of the cabin and grabbed the receiver.

But it was again Berthe who answered.

'I'm sorry Mademoiselle Katharine,' she apologised, 'the taxi has just left.'

Katharine gave a puzzled frown.

Maxine always complained when he was in Paris that he didn't get enough exercise and tended to walk everywhere. Why had he taken a taxi?

'Oh Berthe,' she groaned. 'I've been trying to get hold of you for over twenty minutes. But the number was always engaged.'

'Monsieur *did* make a lot of calls,' Berthe chatted on.

'Did he say when he would be back?' Katharine interrupted.

'Not for a week.'

'A *week*,' Katharine gasped.

'Yes Mademoiselle Katharine. Monsieur said he had to leave Paris and told Manon not to bother about meals for him once he returned because he'd be very busy.'

'I see,' Katharine answered weakly.

She suddenly felt faint, as if all her bones had been removed, leaving her in a jelly-like state.

'Thank you Berthe,' she managed to stammer, pulling herself together with a great effort. 'I didn't realise Monsieur was leaving Paris quite so soon.'

Putting down the receiver she pushed open the door of the cabin and, in a daze, walked back to the counter to pay for the call.

Maxime had gone to Paris to see his lawyers and arrange to rent a flat for Marie-Céleste. He hadn't said anything about leaving for a few days.

Mechanically picking up the change the bored clerk pushed through his little aperture, a vivid thought abruptly winded her. If, when he returned, Maxime did not intend to go back to the rue de la Faisanderie in the evening . . . then where *would* he be going?

And suddenly Katharine knew that Marie-Céleste had won.

She clung to the counter for support as the stuffy office began to spin crazily round and round.

You could be wrong, a little voice prodded. Surely Maxime wouldn't give up his family for a beautiful face?

Looking up, oblivious of the curious glances being cast in her direction, Katharine saw her reflection in

the Post Office window. The sleepless night had left
dark rings under her eyes, her usually creamy complexion was chalk-like. She compared herself with Marie-
Céleste.

And convinced herself that she had lost.

Blinded by fears and insecurity Katharine knew that
she could not wait a week to confront Maxime with
what she now believed to be the truth. She could not
remain tranquilly at Gure Etchea while her vivid imagination painted lurid pictures of her husband lost in
another woman's embrace. She had to do something
to fight the terrible feeling of jealousy. Get away from
the memories which were everywhere. And ward off by
any means this insanity which she felt was about to close
in on her.

On a sudden impulse she turned and walked swiftly
back to the counter.

'I want to place a call to Scotland,' she announced,
flipping through her address book to find the Ardnakil
number.

The clerk took it disinterestedly.

'Two hours wait,' he said, without looking up.

Katharine bit her lip in frustration.

'Never mind,' she replied tightly.

And walking swiftly back to the car told Emile to drive
her to the Hôtel du Palais. She would telephone from
there. Sitting in its opulent splendour which held so
many happy childhood memories, surrounded by time-
less beauty she might recover her peace and equilibrium
before speaking to Flora.

The car cruised along the Avenue de l'Impératrice
and, passing through the hotel's imposing wide-open
gates which reminded Katharine of those at Castérat,
skirted round the beautifully laid out formal gardens.
Katharine's breathing was becoming more regular, the

former erratic beating of her heart had almost returned to normal as the car stopped at the entrance. She even managed to smile at the uniformed doorman who sprang from under the glass marquise* to open the door.

Ardnakil had always been her refuge in times of pain and stress. As they had done in the past those mellow stone walls would give her shelter from this present storm.

* * *

'Are we going to see Papa?' the twins asked excitedly.

'No', Katharine replied, her mind elsewhere as she supervised the packing.

'But *why* do we have to go?' Jehan wailed. 'We've only just come.'

Katharine clicked her tongue in annoyance. Jehan seemed to wail perpetually these days. Having started school the previous September he had been obliged to discard Hercule, his imaginary twin. And, once Hercule disappeared from his life, Jehan had promptly replaced him with a passion for his father.

'Papa promised to take me shrimping as soon as he got back,' he moaned on and on. 'I want to wait here for him. I don't want to go to silly old Scotland.'

Katharine looked exasperatedly at Nanny, placidly emptying drawers and filling suitcases.

'Come with me Jehan', Nanny smiled. 'I have a little job for you.'

He opened his mouth to protest. But Nanny took him firmly by the hand and led him into the adjoining room. Katharine sighed with relief.

'But if we're going to Paris we *will* see Papa,' Léon beamed.

In his little mind Paris was merely an extension of Le

Moulin. They wouldn't be able to help bumping into Maxime.

For a moment Katharine wavered, recalling the trauma in her own young life when her father had inexplicably disappeared. Was history repeating itself, she agonised? Was *she* about to inflict the same bewildering pain on her own children? After all, Zag's sudden departure had been based on a misunderstanding which could so easily have been explained had he only told his wife of his fears. And those painful years for all three of them would never have been.

She leant back on her heels, remembering. Then the sultry mocking image of Marie-Céleste patting the empty place at her side on the sofa, her eyes turned provocatively on Maxime, rose again and blocked her vision. Katharine's expression hardened. No man could resist such bewitchment. By leaving she wasn't making a mistake. She was merely preventing a greater hurt.

'No darling,' she answered tightly. 'Papa is busy. And we won't be staying in Paris. Just going from one train to the other.'

Léon's ice-blue eyes opened wide. He had never been in a train.

'*Why* can't we stay . . .?' the twins began.

But Katharine silenced them with an usually sharp glare. And they subsided. They had never seen their mother in such a mood. Looking at each other, they backed away, then turning raced into the corridor.

'Nanny', Katharine called after them. 'Can you cope?'

Nanny popped her head round the door.

'Everything will be ready to be loaded into the car before the boys have their supper', she answered placidly.

Katharine looked at her gratefully, then fled.

* * *

'Perhaps we will see Papa after all,' Jehan squealed excitedly, peering through the window, his eyes darting round like little spinning wheels absorbing everything in microscopic detail as the taxi drew away from the Gare d'Austerlitz the following morning.

Katharine, following her son's gaze, suddenly panicked. What if by some unbelievable chance they *should* see Maxime? What would she do?

She glanced at the embankment along which they were crawling. The rush-hour traffic was doing anything but rush, rather limping along like a rheumaticky tortoise. Then she remembered. Maxime had gone away. And, for the first time since their marriage, she did not know where.

Her eyes rose to the bridges spanning the Seine and memories of that false spring in Paris with Theo came crowding back. And she wondered what she would do if their positions had been reversed. If Ashley had suddenly returned to disrupt their happiness. Would she have rushed back into the arms of her first love? Marie-Céleste was Maxime's first love.

And in her tortured mind she saw Maxime standing on the approaching bridge gazing down into the slowly moving waters his arm lightly thrown across Marie-Céleste's shoulders.

'Maman', Louis squealed, 'look . . . there's the Eiffel Tower!'

'I saw it first, I saw it first,' Jehan shrieked.

'No you didn't,' the twins yelped in unison.

Katharine turned appealingly to Nanny. But Nanny had already given the boys the kind of look which silenced them immediately. And the argument fizzled out.

The very ordinariness of the boys' bickering brought Katharine back to earth. Shaking her head in disbelief at her wild imaginings she smiled ironically. Marie-Céleste would certainly not be up and about at eight-thirty in the morning!

'What's the Eiffel Tower?' Léon asked, plucking at her sleeve.

Relieved, Katharine turned to answer his question.

*　　*　　*

When the Golden Arrow train arrived in London that evening they were all beginning to wilt.

Katharine was torn between her desire to blot out everything which reminded her of Maxime and escape to Ardnakil, and to stay the night in London. It would be so easy to go to their flat in Sloane Street. Aching with fatigue she thought longingly of that peaceful haven, bearing Elisabeth's inimitable stamp. The long avenue of rooms panelled in faded apple-green silk with a shining lake of parquet floor linking them together, the scattered carpets, the priceless trinkets. Then she remembered the last time she had been there. It had been with Maxime. They had gone to London to celebrate their fifth wedding anniversary. And her mind resolutely shut out those halcyon June days, afraid that the memories London would evoke would make her waver in her resolve.

By the time the night train chugged into Perth the following morning they were all so exhausted that Flora took one look at them as the car pulled up in front of the great doors of Ardnakil and promptly despatched Nanny and the children to the nursery.

'And I don't want to see you before lunch,' she admonished, affectionately taking Katharine's arm as they mounted the wide oak staircase. 'You look washed out. Mairi will run you a bath and your breakfast will be sent up. She opened the door of the beautiful

94

rose room where, in the past, Katharine had so often found peace.

'Don't worry about the boys,' Flora added. 'Morag is there.'

'*Morag*?' Katharine exclaimed. 'She's not *still* around?'

'Yes,' Flora smiled. 'No one dares ask her age but she must be nearly ninety. And *still* considers herself in charge in the nursery, even though there haven't been any children in it for the past few years. She knows Nanny Moffatt and I've asked Janet to come in and give a hand. Janet's delighted at the idea of having children to look after again.'

Katharine turned towards her old friend.

'Flora', she murmured. 'You think of everything.'

Flora gave her a long hard look.

She knew that this sudden arrival must have a reason behind it. But she also knew that this wasn't the time to ask questions. When Katharine was ready to confide in her, she would. In the meantime Flora was determined that Ardnakil would be, as it had always been, Katharine's haven.

'Lavinia's coming sometime soon,' she remarked casually, walking towards the door.

Katharine shot her friend a terrified look. She had thought that by coming here she would be safe from all prying eyes. What was she going to say to Lavinia, the great-aunt who had given her a home after her mother's tragic death. And who had a habit of seeing straight through her.

'Possibly not until August,' Flora soothed. 'She and William will be staying with the Farquharsons.'

And quietly drawing the door to behind her, she left the room.

Katharine stood by the window gazing out over the early morning mist creeping in soft curls across the distant mountains now purple and pink with heather. And her mind wandered back to the house in Biarritz which she had so precipitately left two days before.

She sighed and turned away, all the confusing thoughts once again jostling for supremacy in her mind.

When she had walked through the door of Le Moulin as Maxime's bride she had believed that after all those years of wandering she had at last come home. Until that fateful day when Marie-Céleste turned up like a ghost from the past and Katharine's worst fears were realised. Those fears which Maxime had laughingly tossed aside on the day he asked her to marry him. But his first wife's unexpected arrival had projected Maxime back into the past.

Katharine wearily sat down on one of the spindly Louis XV armchairs, and long-forgotten scenes began crawling out from the dark recesses of her mind as ghosts from the past paraded themselves before her. Rowena, her delicate complexion shaded by a large sun hat, watching from a deckchair on the beach at Biarritz as Zag, holding tightly to Katharine's hand, raced with her into the frothing Atlantic breakers. Léonie, presiding at the breakfast table at Castérat surrounded by her great-grandchildren. Ashley at their last meeting, holding her in his arms and promising to return. Yet he hadn't returned. In spite of their promises, they had all abandoned her. And now Maxime, the rock in whom she had placed her trust had done the same. Could she ever believe anyone again?

'Jesus,' she cried, dropping to her knees and burying her face in the worn pink silk of the delicate seat. 'I'm so alone. Show me what to do.'

For a moment there was a penetrating silence. Then it seemed as if a voice within her was saying:

'I led you to Maxime. He is your husband.'

The voice was so clear that Katharine raised her

head and looked around. But she was alone in the room.

'For the Catholic Church he is Marie-Céleste's husband,' she muttered bitterly, as if in reply.

Again that intense silence filled the room. Then from the very depths of her that same voice clearly spoke.

'I do not abide in buildings built by men.'

'Jesus,' Katharine whispered brokenly. 'I don't understand anything any more. Please help me.'

As she knelt in mute anguish, tormented by doubts, by pain, by the hollow feeling of having once again been abandoned, at the house in Biarritz Juanita removed from the box one letter, addressed to Katharine, which had come in the morning's mail.

It was from Maxime.

The first of many which were to arrive almost daily.

But Katharine, cowering in her Scottish hideout, tortured by doubts, never received them.

Chapter 9

The taxi drew up in front of Gure Etchea and Maxime leapt out. He had been surprised not to find Emile waiting for him at the station with the car.

As he paid the driver, the front door opened. Juanita, standing aside as he ran across the threshold, did not appear to be expecting him either. Maxime stopped abruptly. There was no sign of life. The house seemed dead and deserted. And yet at this time of the morning the boys should have finished breakfast and the whole place be jumping with activity.

'Has Madame already left for the beach?' he enquired, Juanita's mouth dropped open in surprise.

'Madame left Gure Etchea over three weeks ago,' she exclaimed.

'*Left*,' Maxime frowned.

He paled then pulled himself together.

'Of course,' he lied. 'How stupid of me. I've been so busy it slipped my mind. I imagine Emile left with her?'

'Yes Monsieur. Emile went back to Le Moulin.'

'I see,' Maxime answered tightly. 'Don't bother to have my bags taken up, Juanita I'll be leaving immediately for Le Moulin. Ask Peyo to go into town and bring me back a taxi.'

Maxime slowly mounted the stairs, bewilderment and fear mingling together. What could have happened?

Katharine had appeared delighted at the idea of spending the summer here with the boys. Whatever had prompted her to return to Le Moulin? And why hadn't she contacted him? It would have been so easy to telephone from there. And why, when she received his letter announcing his arrival hadn't she let him know that she was no longer in Biarritz?

'Juanita,' he called over the bannister.

The door leading to the kitchen corridor swung open and the maid reappeared.

'All the mail has been forwarded to Le Moulin I imagine?'

'Except the letters which arrived this morning Monsieur.'

He walked down a few steps and held out his hand.

Juanita, who had come into the hall to collect the mail when she heard the taxi arrive, removed them from her apron pocket.

Maxime quickly shuffled through the envelopes as he walked back up the stairs. But there was nothing from Katharine. Why should there be, he reasoned? There was no point in her writing to him here if she were already at Le Moulin. Then a chilling fear broke over him. Perhaps she was not at Le Moulin. Then what had happened? Where *could* she be?

Entering their silent shuttered bedroom he sat down heavily on the bed. And for the fist time in his life he felt angry with his beloved great-grandmother. Why on earth had Léonie refused to have the telephone installed? It would have been so easy to ring Le Moulin and find out.

It was almost a month since he had left.

An exhausting time trying to deal with his ex-wife's unreasonable demands. But he had finally installed Marie-Céleste in a flat on the Ile St Louis, an area of Paris which, since Elisabeth's death, he and Katharine had avoided. And where he reasoned they would be unlikely to bump into her on their rare visits to the capital. He now hoped that she could be put firmly back into the past where she belonged. And he and Katharine be allowed to get on with their lives without her shadow hanging over them. Wearily lifting his head, Maxime tried to puzzle out this inexplicable disappearance.

After the initial shock of Marie-Céleste's sudden arrival, Katharine had seemed to come to terms with what had happened. And to understand.

But had she?

Maxime's tired brain rummaged in the recent past desperately seeking an explanation. And he wondered whether the post-natal depression coming so soon after Léonie's death, followed by the trauma of Léon's handicap had not, in the end, proved too much for her highly-sensitive nature. And, after all these years of dramas she had finally cracked.

He cursed himself for having left her at such a vulnerable time. But what else could he have done? What option did he have?

Getting up, he walked over to the long window and throwing open the shutters stood gazing out at the starch-blue sea curling its way up the beach, deceptively calm, creeping sneakily along the sand only to suddenly burst against the walls of the house in a wild spray of foam just when it was least expected.

And in those waters he thought he saw the answer to Katharine's dilemma. The tensions inside her had never really been resolved since Léonie's death. On the surface everything had seemed peaceful. But Marie-Céleste's reappearance had revealed the hidden breakers lurking beneath the calm exterior. And suddenly those breakers had surfaced with a mighty roar, hurled themselves at Katharine and sucked her into their swirling currents.

Sighing he turned, at a loss to know where to go from here. The only thing he could do was return to Le Moulin and, if she wasn't there, try to discover her whereabouts.

But where was he to start?

* * *

By the time he had showered and changed Peyo had returned with the taxi. As it deposited him at Biarritz station Maxime looked up at the indicator board. But there wasn't a train for Bordeaux for another two hours and there he would have to wait an hour for the connection to Narbonne. It would be late that evening before he could hope to be back at Le Moulin and begin his search for Katharine.

Frowning impatiently Maxime momentarily considered hiring a car and driving himself home. Then reason came to his rescue. He realised that in his present state of fatigue, and with the détour he would have to make by road the time he would gain would be insignificant. At least in the train he could sleep, attempt to collect his thoughts and make plans. Sighing, he crossed to the ticket office.

Walking briskly along the Boulevard de l'Impératrice, named after Eugénie, Napoleon III's wife, whose love for Biarritz had turned it from a small fishing port on the Basque coast into 'the Queen of Resorts and the Resort of Kings', he entered the Hôtel du Palais, from where Katharine had tried in vain to contact him. And placed a call to Le Moulin. Almost immediately the butler's precise voice came down the line.

'Alphonse,' Maxime said. 'I'm leaving Biarritz by train this morning, arriving at Narbonne at 9.17. Have Emile meet me with the car, will you.'

'Very well, Monsieur. I trust you had a good holiday
And Madame and the young gentlemen are well.'

Maxime's heart tripped, missed a beat then caught in
his throat, momentarily preventing him from speaking.

So Katharine and the boys had not returned to Le Moulin.

'Thank you Alphonse,' he managed to stammer at last.
'Everyone is very well.'

Slowly replacing the receiver, he sat down thoughtfully
in one of the elegant period armchairs near the long
windows looking out on to the gardens, where memories
of the hotel's Imperial past still lingered in the entwined
initials of the Emperor and his wife planted in the
manicured lawns. Although impatience was bubbling
up inside him like a mounting volcano Maxime knew that
all he could do was wait. He suddenly realised that, in the
turmoil, he had not had breakfast and was very hungry.

Smiling grimly to himself he entered the now almost
deserted dining room. As the white-coated waiter glided
away after taking his order Maxime stared vacantly
through the window across the stretch of sand dotted
with gaily striped tents and sunshades and out towards
the sea, now reflecting the blue of the cloudless sky. His
lips twisted in a parody of a smile.

A perfect day for shrimping, he remarked to himself.

And his mind went to his sons.

*　　*　　*

'Watch me Maman, watch!'

Jehan dug his heels into the pony's flanks and clinging
to its mane, cantered towards the jump which Angus had
set up in the paddock for him. In one lithe movement he
and the pony soared together, paused for a fraction of a
second as they landed in the grass on the far side before
making a wide circle and returning to base.

'Hail the champion,' Sandy called as he and Cristobel and the twins cantered past on the other side of the paddock fence.

They all four waved their crops in Jehan's direction.

'Absolutely fearless,' Flora remarked. 'He rides as effortlessly as he switches backwards and forwards between English and French.'

Katharine nodded absently, her eyes on her panting child as once again Jehan raced towards the target.

'How about the young lad?' Angus called, nodding towards Léon who was standing at Katharine's side watching in awe.

Involuntarily, Katharine's hand tightened on her youngest son's. But Léon looked at her appealingly.

'Please Maman,' he begged.

'Let him go,' Flora smiled. 'You've no need to worry, Angus taught all our children.'

Katharine watched anxiously as Léon ran limping towards the old groom.

'Come on now lad,' Angus said kindly taking his hand. 'We'll saddle Thistle for you.'

His eyes twinkled down at the boy.

'She's not as prickly as her name.'

'He's . . . he's never been on a horse,' Katharine demurred.

'That's all right Madame,' Angus replied. 'I'll take him on a leading rein. He'll be riding as well as Miss Laura before long. Won't you young fella?'

Léon beamed up at him.

'I've saddled Georgina,' Angus called, as Laura opened the paddock gate and walked towards them. 'She'll give you a good safe ride.'

Laura had first mounted a horse with Maxime. Now, under Angus' careful guidance, she was a competent if not brilliant rider.

Angus grinned at her and his eyes, black like a panda's, crinkled up again, the lines around them jumping and mingling to converge in little rivulets which ran across his leathery walnut face. He removed his hat and thoughtfully scratched his head. His hair looked like tweed.

'You and Master Jehan can go off on your own,' he said over his shoulder to Laura. 'The others have ridden over to the Fort to cadge some scones from Jeannie.'

He winked at her as he replaced his worn cap.

The Fort, a jumble of old grey stones on another part of the estate was where Hamish, Flora's eccentric bachelor brother-in-law lived with Jeannie his equally dotty housekeeper. They shared a mutual passion. The Hamilton children. Who in Hamish and Jeanne's eyes could do no wrong.

As Laura and Jehan set off across the paddock Angus looked intently at Katharine, his wise old eyes missing nothing. He saw that she was apprehensive about her son's first riding lesson.

'There's a strong breeze starting up milady,' he remarked innocently. 'Could be cold for you and Mrs Montredon standing waiting. I'll bring the lad back to the house when he's had enough.'

Flora looked at the old man and their eyes met. Taking Katharine's arm she turned towards the gate.

'Let's leave them to it,' she urged.

Reluctantly Katharine allowed herself to be led from the paddock.

As they sat together in the beautiful, faded drawing-room sipping coffee, Flora smiled at her friend.

'Almost August,' she sighed. 'The peace won't last much longer. In little more than a week the house will be bulging with visitors up for the shoot.'

She shuddered.

'How I hate it. It's so cosy just being on our own. Don't you agree?'

Katharine nodded absently, her mind on Léon.

'It's amazing the way your boys ride,' Flora chatted on. 'They all seat their horses beautifully. Comes from learning bare-back without stirrups I suppose.'

'Yes, Maxime insisted. He taught them himself almost as soon as they could walk.'

Katharine sighed, a sudden longing for her husband overwhelming her.

'Maxime is a wonderful father,' Flora added.

Then just as suddenly the bewilderment and anger which had invaded Katharine almost a month before stamped out the longing and took the upper hand.

'And husband?' she asked tightly.

'And husband,' Flora quietly replied.

Katharine shot her friend an enquiring look. How much had Flora guessed? Perfect hostess that she was, she had asked no questions. But Katharine knew that she hadn't been fooled by their precipitate arrival, and the absence of letters or telephone calls from Maxime.

'Why don't you ask him to join us for the shoot?' Flora enquired innocently.

Katharine put down her cup and picking up a worn silk cushion began idly straightening out the tassles.

'You know, don't you?' she said.

'I guessed something was amiss. But . . . I was waiting for you to tell me when you were ready.'

Katharine didn't answer.

'Katharine you don't have to tell me anything. You and the boys are more than welcome to stay here as long as you wish. But . . . you're not happy without Maxime are you? And the boys are certainly missing their father.'

'They never say so,' Katharine cut in.

'Not in so many words. But haven't you noticed the

way they climb all over Robert? Even Alasdair and Ninian come in for their attention and they are barely out of their teens.'

Katharine shrugged.

Then abruptly tossing the cushion aside she burst into tears.

'Flora,' she cried pitifully. 'I don't know what to do. *Please* help me.'

*   *   *

Maxime picked up the pile of letters he had written almost daily to his wife during his stay in Paris, which had been redirected from Gure Etchea and were now lying unopened on her desk. And it was obvious to him that Katharine had not been back to Le Moulin. Wherever she had left for, she had gone directly from Biarritz.

As he had done earlier in the day he sat down on their bed, his head in his hands. It had been difficult to question the servants without arousing suspicion or leading them to believe that he was unaware of his family's whereabouts.

The clock in the turret solemnly struck midnight.

Lying wearily back against the pillows, his hands clasped behind his head, Maxime frowned.

He had telephoned his father-in-law from Paris in June asking him to join them in Biarritz. It had all been done in great secrecy as Maxime had wanted to prepare a surprise for his wife. Her father arriving unannounced at Gure Etchea to spend the month of August with Katharine and the boys, when he had to return to Le Moulin.

But he hadn't heard from Xavier. That must mean that he could be on his way.

Maxime leapt off the bed and switched on the light. He must telephone Algiers immediately and make some excuse. The last thing he wanted was his father-in-law to arrive and find Katharine and the boys gone.

Hastily getting through to the operator he asked for the number.

'One to two hours' wait,' she announced.

Maxime clicked his teeth in annoyance. It was already 2nd August. Xavier might even have left or be about to leave. But he could hardly call at two o'clock in the morning!

'I'd like to place a call for six a.m.,' he said.

The operator put down the details and hung up.

Without thinking he loosened his tie and flopped back on the bed. The next thing he remembered was the booming of the clock in the turret mingling with the insistent ring of the telephone at his side.

It was just six a.m.

When he heard his father-in-law's calm tones, Maxime suddenly floundered. And he didn't know what to say.

'Hallo, hallo,' Xavier said patiently. 'Hallo . . .'

'Xavier,' Maxime finally managed to stammer, afraid that he would hang up.

'*Maxime*,' Xavier replied. 'How nice to hear you.'

His voice betrayed no trace of anxiety. Though Maxime knew that his father-in-law must be concerned at receiving a call from him at such an early hour.

'I'm so glad I got you. I was afraid you might have left.'

'I'm just about to. Didn't you receive my letter?'

Maxime frowned.

'No.'

'Oh dear,' Xavier apologised. 'I'm so sorry. I wrote over a month ago saying that I would do everything in my power to be with you in August. And I've managed it. I shall be leaving for Biarritz . . .'

'Xavier,' Maxime cut in desperately. 'I'm afraid there has been a change of plan. Katharine and the boys are no longer at Gure Etchea. As she didn't know about our little secret, she has made other arrangements. I'm awfully sorry. So if it's more convenient for you to come for the family reunion in September . . .'

His voice trailed away, at a loss to know how to continue.

If his father-in-law sensed that something was wrong, he made no comment.

'I see,' Xavier said thoughtfully. 'In that case perhaps it *would* be easier if I came in September as originally planned.'

Maxime breathed a sigh of relief. How like Xavier to accept everything and change all his plans without recriminations or questioning.

As he replaced the receiver he almost felt his father-in-law's warm smile trickle over the line towards him.

Staring down at his crumpled clothes, he rose wearily from the bed and walked towards the bathroom, stripping as he went.

'Where do we go from here?' he sighed, turning the taps on full force.

Chapter
10

The house was silent when Maxime left.

Crossing the courtyard he entered the stable yard and walked over to Diamond's box. The great black hunter whinnied with delight when he saw him approaching. Quickly saddling him, Maxime clattered away and was soon cantering out of the park and through the vineyards. Once in open country he let the horse have his head and they galloped hard.

But Diamond, at sixteen, no longer had the stamina of a young stallion and after a while he slowed to a canter. Maxime leant forward to pat his withers. He and Diamond had been inseparable since he returned from the war and broke the horse in. But the time was fast approaching when his mount would need a more peaceful life.

Perhaps one of the twins could try him out, he reflected. It was time they were weaned from their ponies. And he could take over Hannibal, Diamond's grandson now a frisky four-year-old rearing to have his head.

'We're neither of us getting any younger old friend,' he murmured, settling comfortably back in the saddle.

And his thoughts meandered down the years to the day when he had brought Katharine to Le Moulin as his bride. That summer they had ridden together in the early morning, sharing their hopes and their dreams for the future . . . But that was before they began drifting apart.

Maxime reined Diamond to a jog as the gates of Le Moulin loomed into view.

Or had Katharine begun drifting apart from him, he mused, now devoting all her time and energy to their handicapped child? His love for his wife had never wavered, was still as strong as on the first day. And although on the surface she appeared to reciprocate, he realised that deep down a cloud had been forming. Something had come between them.

'Mornin' sir. Good to have you back.'

Maxime slithered to a halt.

'Thank you Achille,' he greeted his bailiff's assistant warmly. 'Everything going as planned for the grape harvest? No problems?'

'Not so far as I know,' Achille replied.

'Ask Lucien to come up to the house as soon as he has a moment will you?' Maxime asked, and raising his crop in salute he rode off.

The brisk ride in the fresh morning air had cleared his tired mind. The memories it had evoked had also made him realise that wherever Katharine had hidden herself he had to find her and persuade her to come back. Looking up at the imposing edifice as he approached his home he knew that without her it would once again become the empty shell it had been in the years he had lived in it alone.

'Have my breakfast sent up to the study Emmeline,' he smiled at the surprised cook, as he entered by the kitchen door. 'And when Lucien arrives tell him where he can find me.

He glanced at the heavy grandfather clock as he crossed the vast echoing hall.

Eight o'clock was about to strike.

110

Going into his study he closed the door and sitting down at his desk picked up the telephone and asked for the house in Narbonne.

Armand answered immediately.

'Maxime, my dear boy,' he exclaimed. 'What a pleasant surprise. You've just caught me. I arrived back from Castérat yesterday and shall be leaving in a few days for Biarritz. I'm so pleased Katharine and the boys are there, Gure Etchea is a tomb when one has it to oneself.'

'I'm afraid Katharine and the boys are no longer there Uncle,' Maxime cut in.

'Oh,' Armand queried, disappointment clearly showing in his voice. 'Have they come home with you?'

'No.'

There was a slight pause. And then Maxime took the plunge and quickly outlined the events of the past month beginning with Marie-Céleste's telephone call.

'That's why I'm ringing you,' he ended lamely. 'Would you have any idea where Katharine is? I'm at a loss to know where to start looking.'

'Have you tried contacting Katharine's Aunt Lavinia?' Armand enquired.

'I haven't contacted anyone,' Maxime went on miserably. 'After all, what can I say? Do you know where my wife is?'

'I admit it's not easy,' his great-uncle replied. 'But what else can you do?'

'I don't know.'

'Do you think she got lonely and went to stay with her friend in Nice? The Russian one.'

'Tamara?' Maxime queried.

Then he shrugged helplessly.

'She could be *anywhere*. But the problem remains the same. How can I make enquiries without giving the game away.'

'Start with Lavinia,' Armand said reasonably. 'And carry on from there. I'll come over later in the morning to see how you've got on.'

There was a knock at the door and the bailiff entered.

'Sit down Lucien,' Maxime smiled, waving towards a chair.

'If you can spare the time Uncle, that would be wonderful,' he ended.

But when after Lucien's progress report Maxime tentatively dialled Lavinia's number it was to be told by the faithful Elsie the Madame had gone with Canon Paget to visit Mrs Wellesley in Nice.

As Juliette entered with his breakfast-tray Maxime was considerably brighter. That might be an explanation. Katharine had taken advantage of Lavinia and William Paget's visit to Tamara to take the boys and meet up with them all. But, he reflected as he hungrily buttered a length of crisp fresh baguette, that didn't explain why she had left him in the dark as to her whereabouts.

Thumbing quickly through his address book he dialled Tamara's number and asked to speak to Lavinia.

'Are you thinking of paying us a visit while you're over here?' he enquired, not knowing what to say to justify his call, after they had exchanged the usual banalities about each other's health and the weather.

'Oh Maxime, you're too kind,' Lavinia replied. 'Katharine is always inviting us and it would have been lovely. But William and I are leaving on the lunch-time train for Paris, and then back to England tomorrow. Perhaps next time?'

So Katharine had not gone to Nice.

But where *had* she gone?

'Have you tried her friend in Scotland?' Armand enquired later that morning as they sat together in Maxime's study.

'Do you really think she'd have taken the boys all that way?' Maxime asked incredulously. 'Katharine does not like the idea of flying and Ardnakil's a couple of days' train journey from Biarritz.'

'Anything's possible,' Armand went on. 'Lady Flora and Katharine are very close friends. And now that Tatiana is in Teheran.'

His brow suddenly rutted.

'You don't suppose she could have gone to Teheran do you?'

Maxime's head shot up, a startled look in his eyes.

'No,' Armand soothed, regretting his question. 'I think Scotland is probably your best bet.'

He smiled affectionately across at his worried great-nephew.

'Why don't you try?'

Maxime's pursed his lips. He was obviously hesitant about contacting Lady Flora.

'The wonderful thing about the telephone,' the old man went on blandly, 'is that it's anonymous. Unless one announces oneself, no one knows who is at the other end. And it's possible to fade away without anyone being any the wiser.'

'What do you mean?'

'It's doubtful that a member of the family would answer. Why don't you simply ask to speak to Katharine? If she's not there, whoever picks up the receiver will be puzzled. You can then apologise and say you must have mistaken the number. But if she *is* there . . .'

Maxime looked up and for the first time since his arrival a smile slowly broke across his tense features.

'Uncle,' he grinned. 'You're a genius.'

The operator announced that there was only a quarter of an hour's wait so, replacing the receiver, Maxime sat down willing it to ring.

'Ardnakil House,' a voice with a soft Highland accent announced.

'May I speak to Mrs Montredon de la Livière,' Maxime asked, unable to control the tremor in his voice.

'Mrs Montredon has gone across to the paddock with Lady Flora,' the voice answered. 'May I take a message?'

Maxime's larynx suddenly constricted, leaving him gasping.

'May I take a message?' the voice repeated.

'No,' Maxime managed to croak. No, it's quite all right. It's not urgent. I will telephone later.'

'May I say who called?'

But Maxime's larynx had begun to constrict again, and without further ado, he put down the receiver.

'So,' Armand smiled. 'The mystery is solved.'

Maxime looked across at him with relief.

'For the moment,' he replied.

Then his blue eyes darkened and a look of fear shot across his face.

'But Uncle,' he cried wretchedly, 'what will be the final outcome! How will the story end?'

*　　*　　*

Flora gently released Katharine and crossing over to her wing chair picked up the coffee pot and filled both their cups. As Katharine dabbed at her eyes, Flora offered no advice, no comment, no comfort. She just waited for the flow to stop and Katharine to regain her composure.

Picking up her cup, Katharine thoughtfully sipped the cooling brew.

'So, where do I go from here?' she asked tightly.

'Where do you want to go?' Flora replied evenly.

Katharine looked bewilderedly across at her friend.

'Flora, don't you see,' she cried. 'I really don't know.

I had thought of taking the boys and going to live at Abbotts Priory. Since my mother's death it has belonged to me. At the time it was occupied by the Army and after the war all sorts of repairs had to be done.'

She shrugged.

'You know what a time it takes for any Ministry to get things moving. And of course, in 1945, there were so many requisitioned houses needing repairs. Maxime and I went down to see it the last time we were in London and agreed then that some decision had to be taken.'

'When was that?'

'Just before Léonie died.'

'Before *Léon* was born,' Flora put in pointedly.

A faint magnolia stain crept up Katharine's cheeks. She knew just what her friend was hinting at.

'You haven't been to England with Maxime since?'

Katharine shook her head, avoiding Flora's eyes.

'Yet he has had to come over on business from time to time?'

'Of course.'

Flora put down her cup and looked straight at Katharine. But she refused to meet her eyes.

'Do you realise what you are contemplating Katharine?' Flora asked steadily. 'Leaving your husband and uprooting the boys to Abbotts Priory to be brought up as English?'

Katharine began to protest. But Flora silenced her.

'Your sons are *not* English Katharine. They are *French*. You would be doing to them what your mother did to you. Uprooting them at a vulnerable age and trying to force them into a mould into which they wouldn't fit.'

Flora held up her hand as Katharine once again opened her mouth to protest.

'I know your father had left and Rowena thought she had no choice but to do what she did. But you *do* have a choice Katharine. You can learn from your mother's tragic mistake which was caused by a misunderstanding as I'm sure your dilemma is. Yet even if there *is* some other explanation, do you honestly think any of you would be happy living at Abbotts Priory?'

Katharine's lips set in a stubborn line and she didn't reply. She knew in her heart that what she was contemplating would be disastrous. But at the moment her sense of reason seemed to have deserted her.

'Maxime loves you darling,' Flora said gently. 'And he loves his sons. Can't you *see* that? Why don't you get hold of him and sort this whole thing out? He's probably frantic with worry, not knowing where any of you are.'

'He's more probably with his ex-wife,' Katharine snapped.

'Oh Katharine,' Flora put in sharply. 'You're being ridiculous and you know it.'

'But how can I be sure?' Katharine challenged. 'Maxime often goes to Paris on business. If I go back, every time he leaves I'll wonder whether he's not seeing *her*.'

'You can be sure by going with him,' Flora replied. 'You used to, didn't you?'

Katharine nodded.

'Then what stopped you?'

She knew very well that it was Katharine's preoccupation with her youngest son which had stopped her. But she wanted to hear it from her. She knew that the only way for Katharine to face reality was for her to admit that things had not been right since Léon's birth.

'I know what you mean Flora,' Katharine put in quietly. 'Jesus showed me myself as others must have seen me a few hours before Marie-Céleste came back.'

She raised her head and her eyes seemed luminous, too large for her face. Her gaze was far away as she relived those precious moments which, in the ensuing weeks she had pushed to the back of her mind.

'It was as if a heavy curtain was drawn aside,' Katharine said earnestly, and I was able to go through it and see my life from another angle. Almost an out-of-body experience, though I remained very firmly on the ground. Jesus showed me the havoc I had been creating in the years since Léon's birth, how I had hurt and neglected Maxime and the other boys. I confessed and repented and asked for help and forgiveness. I believed that from that moment onwards everything would be as before between Maxime and me. I wanted so much to make up to him for those years the locusts had eaten.'

Suddenly the light in her eyes dimmed and the joy left her face.

'Then when Maxime left for Paris I received that strange letter my father had written him. Knowing Marie-Céleste was there my imagination ran riot and all I could see was the two of them together. And I realised that, in the future, every time Maxime goes to Paris on business, he could be meeting her.'

'Why should he?' Flora interrupted. 'From what I've gathered she's not his favourite person.'

'But *Flora*,' Katharine cried. 'You don't *know* Maxime's ex-wife. She's the kind of woman who gets her own way. She's very determined and . . . she's so beautiful. I don't know how any man could resist her.'

'Have you ever looked in the mirror?' Flora smiled.

Katharine raised her eyes enquiringly.

'You're very beautiful too.'

'I'm no match for *her*,' Katharine replied miserably.

Flora leant back in her chair.

'Christians are not meant to find their own solutions to their problems,' she said softly. 'We're spared that. We just have to lay our burden before Jesus. And *he* will give us the answer. Have you done that?'

Once again Katharine shrugged in that typically gallic

fashion. Seeing it, Flora suppressed a smile. There was so little of the Englishwoman in her friend. How could she ever even contemplate life in the Cotswolds countryside.

'I thought I had. But I keep taking it back.'

'Then how do you expect him to solve your problem?' Flora smiled. 'Come darling. Let's ask him.'

But at that moment there was a knock on the drawing-room door and Sheana walked in.

'There is a telephone call for you milady,' she announced. 'The gentleman wouldn't give his name.'

Flora frowned and tutted in annoyance.

'I won't be a minute,' she said fishing in an embroidered bag hanging on the arm of her chair.

'Read Ephesians 4 while I'm gone,' she smiled, handing Katharine a small leather bound New Testament. 'It's all about happiness in marriage.'

Crossing the hall she picked up the receiver.

'Flora,' an anxious voice breathed down the telephone. There was a slight pause, then he announced.

'It's Maxime.'

Chapter
11

Katharine was sitting in the rose garden her face uplifted to the warm rays of the early August sunshine drinking in the sweet heady perfume as pollen drunk bees buzzed lazily overhead when she heard his step on the path. Then his shadow fell across the grass and she saw him standing at the entrance to the bower.

Raising her eyes she met his gaze.

His face looked thinner and his mouth was tense. But his amazingly blue eyes were still as brilliant. Gazing down at her as if wanting to memorise her every feature they darkened, then softened and his body seemed to relax.

'Katharine,' he murmured brokenly.

Dropping to his knees he tentatively took both her hands in his own. And at his touch, her pulses quickened. She noticed that, in spite of the warmth of the day, his fingers were cold.

She held his gaze. But he remained immobile, his hands tightly grasping hers. He seemed diffident, unsure what to do.

As they waited, each uncertain of the other's reaction there was a sudden eruption.

'Cristobel said Papa's arrived,' the twins shrieked, catapulting into the bower.

They stopped abruptly.

But Jehan, skidding after them, was less disconcerted.

'Oh hallo,' he panted, planting himself firmly in front of his father. 'Can we go shrimping now like you promised?'

His down-to-earth remark broke the tension.

Rising to his feet, Maxime gathered his sons to him. As they all three began making requests he felt a slight tug at his jacket and looking down saw Léon, who had limped after his brothers and arrived unnoticed in the midst of the turmoil.

'Papa,' he said shyly. 'I can ride a pony.'

Maxime disengaged himself and bent to pick up his youngest son.

'Can you *really*,' he smiled. 'Well, as soon as we're back home, we'll go riding together.'

Léon nestled happily against his father's shoulder.

'Let's go home now,' he whispered.

Maxime looked at his wife.

But Katharine avoided his eyes. All the doubts and confusion once again coming to the fore and fuddling her brain.

Jehan grasped his father's free hand and with the twins bouncing excitedly in front they walked out of the bower and across the lawn.

'Janet's making a chocolate cake for tea, with *icing* on it,' Léon announced, raising his head from his father's shoulders his eyes shining. 'She said I could have the first slice.'

'Not fair, not fair,' Jehan yelped. 'It's *always* you.'

Katharine sighed. The twins, sufficient in themselves, tended to ignore Léon. But Jehan's furious jealousy seemed to increase.

Maxime smiled down at her and squeezed Jehan's hand.

'Bet I get to the nursery first,' he screeched, thrusting

off his father's hand and shooting through the side door as they approached the house. The twins took up the challenge as Léon wriggled down and ran limping after them.

'They seem to be in fine form,' Maxime remarked.

'Yes,' Katharine agreed laconically.

Then fell silent.

She didn't know what to say.

As they crossed the hall Flora came out of the drawing-room.

'So you found her,' she beamed at Maxime. 'I'm sure you're both ready for tea. I'll tell Mairi to bring it up to your room, Maxime must be exhausted after his long journey.'

Katharine stiffened, suddenly afraid of being alone with her husband. But with a dazzling smile Flora glided away and, as they stood there, each waiting for the other to make a move, the green baize door leading to the kitchen swung open and Mairi, carrying a tray walked through it and headed for the stairs.

Maxime raised his eyebrows enquiringly at his wife.

'I'm afraid I don't know the way,' he apologised. 'Or shall I just follow the tray?'

Katharine turned and, in silence, they mounted the wide oak staircase together.

Entering the room where Mairi had set the tea-things on a small table in the window overlooking the rose garden, Katharine caught sight of Maxime's bag on the floor, and her heart contracted. Then seemed to expand until it filled her chest, cutting off her breath. And she felt trapped. Crossing to the table she lifted the heavy silver tea-pot and, careful to avoid her husband's eyes, began to pour.

'Katharine,' Maxime pleaded.

Putting the cup she handed him down on the table he tilted her averted face towards him.

Once again the strong emotion she had felt in the garden at the touch of his hands ricocheted through her. She looked up and saw his eyes, dark and strange gazing hungrily down at her. Then abruptly she recoiled. The emotions fizzled away and she withdrew into herself, as in their reflection she saw his ex-wife's mocking face.

Maxime watching her sighed.

'Why didn't you tell me where you were?' he pleaded.

But she didn't answer.

'Katharine,' he beseeched. 'You owe me *some* explanation.'

But again she remained silent.

Clicking his tongue exasperately Maxime sat down in the chair opposite her, forcing her to look at him.

'What's the matter?' he asked tightly. 'I simply don't understand. I arrive at Gure Etchea to find the house empty. No one knew where you'd gone.'

He threw up his arms in a hopeless gesture. 'I've been crazy with worry wondering what had happened to you all.'

Katharine raised her eyes, but they were dark and steely, the beautiful golden lights extinguished.

'If you'd stayed with us you'd have spared yourself the worry,' she answered coldly.

'*Katharine*,' he groaned. 'Be reasonable. You know I'd have much rather been on the beach with you and the boys than racing round Paris.'

'Then why weren't you?'

Maxime gave a deep sigh.

'This is impossible,' he said wearily. 'You know the answer to that question perfectly well.'

'I know that you left us to go to Paris to be with your ex-wife. I only hope you enjoyed yourself.'

He stared at her in stupefaction.

'According to Berthe you didn't require any meals,' she

122

ploughed on. 'In fact, you couldn't wait to leave the house in the morning and no one knows what time you returned at night – if you *did* return.'

Maxime put his head in his hands and groaned.

This was not the Katharine he knew. The wife he adored. Something had gone drastically wrong. But what? As far as he could see, everything was perfectly clear cut and straightforward. But Katharine had managed to twist what was already a difficult situation into something unravellable.

'I wasn't at the rue de la Faisanderie very much because I was doing what I went to Paris to do,' he insisted. 'Get Marie-Céleste off our back.'

'You told me before we were married that she was dead as far as you were concerned.'

He lifted his head and looked straight at her.

'And she is,' he said quietly.

'You also said she was no longer your responsibility.'

'She's not,' Maxime went on, his voice steady and poised.

'Then why . . .' Katharine exploded.

'Darling, don't you see . . .'

'No I don't see anything.'

'Then it's because you don't want to.'

Maxime's lips tightened.

'I spent the month of July, in a dreadful heatwave, not only in Paris but in London.'

'London?' Katharine queried.

'Yes, London. If you'd stayed at Gure Etchea you'd have known that. I sent the boys picture postcards of Big Ben and the Tower and the Beefeaters. And on your desk at Le Moulin is a pile of unopened letters from me explaining my every move.'

Maxime lips relaxed and his expression softened.

'I wanted everything to be absolutely watertight. So I

went to London to consult the brokers who manage the investments my mother left me over there. That took the best part of a week. Then what with lawyers and estate agents in Paris . . . it was all very time-consuming settling everything.'

'For someone who is not your responsibility?' Katharine cut in sarcastically.

'Yes.'

He leant across and tried to take her trembling hands. But she pushed him away.

'Darling,' he pleaded, 'can't you *try* to understand? Marie-Céleste means nothing to me but . . . I suppose I feel sorry for her.'

Katharine shot him a withering look. But he ignored it.

'I have so much,' he said gently. '*We* have so much. You've made me so happy Katharine. I know it's Marie-Céleste's own fault she's in this situation . . .'

Once again he shrugged.

For a moment Katharine wavered.

She recalled her telephone conversation with Berthe on the day she left Biarritz, and her shock at learning that Maxime was leaving Paris for a few days. The London trip was the explanation. She had totally misconstrued the remark immediately jumping to the conclusion that her husband was off on a jaunt with his ex-wife. Then she remembered her father's cryptic letter and the meaning she had placed on that. Perhaps there was also an equally plausible explanation for that.

She opened her mouth to ask Maxime what the letter meant. What it was he had been planning with Xavier behind her back.

But abruptly all the old fears and anxieties bubbled to the surface again and throttled her, cutting off communication. And she knew she was afraid of the truth.

She didn't want her suspicion that Marie-Céleste's arrival in Paris had not been a total surprise to Maxime to become reality.

And with that fear Katharine's heart hardened.

'It took you almost a month to get over your touching pity for her?' she threw out ironically, any vestige of a smile now wiped from her lips. 'What understanding lawyers you must have if they are willing to work with you until the early hours of the morning.'

Maxime raised his head and gave her a long, hard look.

'Just what are you implying?'

Katharine eyes shot venom towards him. She was suddenly beside herself, almost out of control. Fear, insecurity and the terrible feeling of rejection which had haunted her for so many years in a flash all suddenly fused together into a violent outburst of jealousy and rage.

'I may not be very worldly-wise Maxime,' she enunciated acidly, her breath coming in staccato gasps, 'but I'm not the fool you take me for. I don't believe a word of your fabricated story about Marie-Céleste's arrival in Paris being a surprise to you.'

She leant forward, her hands gripping the arms of the chair until the knuckles showed white, her eyes flashing with rage.

'You knew all the time she was there. In fact, if I hadn't been such a simpleton as to trust you, I'd have realised that that business trip you took to Paris only the week before *supposedly* to meet with wine dealers was just a trumped up excuse.'

She paused, white-faced, her chest heaving.

'There *were* no wine dealers. You were going to meet *her*. That telephone call and her sudden arrival at Le Moulin had been planned between you then. Sweet simple Katharine, you probably said. She'll swallow any story I choose to tell her.'

Katharine's voice was now rising to a point dangerously near hysteria.

'What a wonderful laugh you must have had at my expense during the last month, leaving me baby-sitting while you two lived it up in Paris. And as for working all hours with lawyers . . . It's perfectly obvious what you and she were up to once their offices closed.'

'Katharine be careful,' Maxime warned. 'Don't push me too far.'

She shot him a scornful look.

'Marie-Céleste,' she hissed. 'There's nothing *celestial* about *her*. Marie-Madeleine would be more appropriate. At least she had no option but to be a whore!'

Like a pricked balloon Katharine suddenly flopped back in the chair, her body shaking with emotion.

Maxime was so aghast at the terrible flow of words which Katharine had seemed unable to stop that he just sat and watched her, a look of utter disbelief on his face.

'Now you've gone too far,' he finally enunciated through tight lips. 'I never once met Marie-Céleste except in the presence of my lawyers or an estate agent. You know perfectly well that I have never been unfaithful to you.'

He passed a hand wearily through his thick dark hair, his features taut with barely-controlled rage.

'Though God knows in the past four years I've been tempted.'

He looked across at her, his eyes like flint.

'Perhaps you don't realise just what I've gone through since Léon's birth, having a wife who most of the time seemed to be merely going through the motions, hardly ever mentally there, so wrapped up in one child that she had no time or love or energy for any of the others.'

He clenched his teeth.

'And certainly not for her husband. I've felt like a piece of furniture. Yet never once did I look at another woman.'

Abruptly his anger evaporated and he looked at her appealingly.

'Even if you were dead, I'd never go back to Marie-Céleste.'

But Katharine turned her eyes away.

'I'm at my wit's end,' he pleaded. 'It's perfectly obvious you don't believe a word I say. You no longer trust me though I don't know what else I can do to convince you.'

Still Katharine remained ramrod stiff, refusing to meet his gaze.

'Tell me darling, please. What *can* I do? I love you so much and . . . until today I really thought you loved me.'

The atmosphere in the room was electric as they faced each other in a tense silence.

Once again Katharine's resolve wavered.

She longed to throw herself into his arms and blot out all the pain in the warmth of his embrace. But even as her hands loosened their grip on the chair a hazy cloud seemed to rise up behind Maxime's shoulder. And out of it Marie-Céleste's mocking face appeared, blowing smoke rings contemptuously at her as she had done that evening at Le Moulin.

Grasping the arm rests again Katharine clenched her teeth giving a short sarcastic laugh.

At the sound, the exhaustion, the anxiety and the anger which Maxime had been suppressing suddenly burst its bounds and overwhelmed him.

'Very well Katharine,' he said, his voice hard and chiselled. 'If that's the way you want it. You refuse to believe that what I did for my ex-wife I really did for us. You've convinced yourself that Marie-Céleste and I are lovers . . .'

Rising to his feet his tightly-clenched fists betraying his rage he looked down at her. And it seemed to Katharine that he towered above her as from a great height.

'You've asked for it . . .' he rasped through clenched teeth. 'You'll get it. At least my ex-wife wants me . . . which is more than my present one does.'

His outburst was so out of character that Katharine gasped. She did not know what reaction she had expected from him. But this was not the Maxime she knew. The husband who had always been so loving, so tender, so understanding. And, in her fear, she recoiled.

But Maxime mistook her reaction for revulsion.

Turning on his heel he picked up his bag and walked swiftly towards the door.

'But don't imagine you're going to have it all your own way,' he threatened, his hand on the knob. 'In French law you've done the worst thing you could possibly do, leave the conjugal home. You won't have a leg to stand on if it comes to the courts.'

His grip on the knob tightened.

'The boys are *my* sons as well as yours,' he went on stonily. 'And I do *not* intend to give them up. Stay here if you wish, or go to Abbotts Priory or wherever the fancy takes you . . . but you'll go alone. My sons will return to Le Moulin with me.'

And with that parting shot, he walked quickly from the room and down the stairs.

Katharine remained frozen in her seat, numb with shock and disbelief. She had no desire to weep. And when she did her tears seemed superficial, and brought no relief. She had no idea how long she remained there in a state of limbo. Her mind enveloped in a thick grey fog through which, try as she would, she could not grope her way. But out of the fog, mingling with the tinkling chimes of the clock on the chimney piece, she heard a car draw up at the front door. Getting up she walked to a side window and looked down.

Flora and Maxime were standing on the steps of the house in earnest conversation. As Katharine watched they walked slowly towards the car. Taking Flora's hand in his, Maxime raised it to his lips then, leaning forward, embraced her warmly. Climbing into the back seat he leant out of the window and waved as Malcolm let out the clutch and headed down the drive towards the tall wrought iron gates.

* * *

A light tap on her door dragged Katharine back from the stupor into which she had fallen when she saw her husband disappearing round the bend of the drive.

'Come in,' she called listlessly.

Janet put her head round the door. Nanny Moffatt had gone to Argyllshire to visit her family and, to her delight, Janet was once again in charge of a well-stocked nursery.

'The boys are ready for bed Madame,' she beamed. 'They're waiting for you to read them their story.'

Katharine dragged herself from the chair and followed the serene rosy-cheeked woman to the next floor.

The twins looked up from the jigsaw puzzle they were doing as she entered.

'Where's Papa?' they enquired.

'He's had to leave,' she answered, forcing herself to smile.

'But he's only just come,' they exclaimed, their eyes riveted on the numerous pieces scattered all over the table.

129

'Gone!' Jehan wailed, abandoning the cataloguing of his most treasured possessions – a collection of old toffee-papers and used bus tickets, several rusty nails, the remains of a squashed beetle, and some rather smelly fossilised snails. 'But he promised to take me shrimping.'

Katharine frowned. Jehan always seemed to be grumbling about something these days. But today his wails set her nerves on edge.

'He'll take you some other time,' she snapped.

Looking across the room she saw Léon, already tucked up in bed, his Christopher Robin book open on his lap, waiting for his story. When she walked towards him tears welled into his expressive china blue eyes, and slowly meandered down his cheeks. Turning his face to the wall, he pulled the covers over his head and, as the book slid to the floor, quietly sobbed.

Feeling totally out of her depth Katharine glanced appealingly at Janet.

'Léon will be all right,' Janet smiled reassuringly. 'He's overtired. They've all had a very busy day.'

She walked across to the child and tucking the sheets around him gently stroked his hair.

'You come with me Jehan,' she said, holding out her hand as Léon's hiccoughing sobs subsided. 'We'll play one game of ludo and then off to bed.'

Katharine looked helplessly around her. But the twins were absorbed in their puzzle and Jehan, the shrimping forgotten, was already busily setting out the counters for the game.

As she closed the nursery door behind her they none of them even noticed her leave. And she suddenly felt useless and totally superfluous.

Entering her room she saw a note in Flora's large flowing handwriting propped on the little inlaid writing desk.

'The "hearty hunters" have already begun to gather for

the glorious 12th, her friend had written. What's glorious about it! I'll have a tray sent up for you as the last thing you want this evening is to have to suffer a dinner of jaw-aching boredom with a crowd of tweedy women and their spouses all neighing in anticipation of the kill. Force yourself to eat something darling and then try to have a good night's sleep. If you need me, I'm here. You only have to ring.'

Katharine's eyes dropped to the PS 'Lavinia has just telephoned,' Flora had hurriedly scrawled. 'She and William arrived at the Farquharsons yesterday. I've invited them to lunch tomorrow. Just the four of us.'

'William,' Katharine murmured affectionately, as the letter dropped from her hand.

She sighed.

It was so long since she had last seen him. What would he think of the neurotic woman she had become?

Slumping into the spindly gold-legged chair by the window she thrust her head into her hands, aching for the relief of tears. But none came.

'What have I done?' she cried in anguish.

But there was no answering cry. No comfort in the still warm air, heady with the scent of late summer roses.

'Jesus,' she whispered brokenly. 'You are my Saviour. Have you sent William to bring me out of the pit and show me the way?'

She waited expectantly. But still there was no answering cry, no gentle call. Yet a strange peace slowly began to trickle through Katharine's tired body. And she knew that William had not arrived at that particular time by chance.

*   *   *

Maxime sat bolt upright, tense and sleepless, in the train snaking through the darkened countryside.

He had not been able to reserve a berth at Perth station

on the night express to London, so had taken a train to Edinburgh only to realise on arrival that the situation there was the same. It was the 12th of August, the height of the holiday season and all sleepers were fully booked in both directions.

Trying to settle himself into a more comfortable position as the train whistled through a station, the platform lights momentarily flashing into the darkened compartment casting eerie shadows on the sleeping figures on the seat opposite him, he felt in his pocket for his pipe. Viciously patting strands of tobacco into the bowl he jabbed the stem into his mouth and lit a match. And once again the lolling figures shot briefly into view. An elderly man hunched by the window, his short legs sticking out in front of him like twin pit props, gave a sudden shuddering snore.

Maxime looked enviously across at him as, puffing thoughtfully, he thought back over the day's events.

'Don't come immediately,' Flora had cautioned when he had first telephoned her from Le Moulin. 'Wait for a few days. Katharine's still very raw and bewildered and rather muddled in her mind. I must say when she arrived I thought she was heading for a breakdown. The one she didn't have when her mother and then Ashley were killed.'

She paused.

'You know that Katharine came here after parting from Theo, that German officer?' Flora asked diffidently.

'Yes,' Maxime reassured her. 'Katharine told me about it.'

He sighed.

'In fact she told me everything. We were both absolutely honest with each other before we married. That's why I'm bewildered also. I simply can't understand what has upset her so deeply.'

'I'm afraid all the hurts and insecurity . . . and especially the rejection she felt in the past has suddenly risen up and boiled over.'

'But Flora,' Maxime protested. '*No one* has rejected her.'

'I know that and so do you. But to some people, and Katharine is one of them, death is seen as a rejection. She's been repressing these feelings for years. And now with your first wife's unexpected return they have all come rushing back.'

'What can I do?' he asked desperately. 'Katharine seemed quite happy for me to go and sort out the Marie-Céleste problem. I only did it to get her off our back.'

'That's what I'm sure she'll end up believing,' Flora reassured him. 'But we're not there yet.'

Maxime had waited four more days, immersing himself in estate work which had been piling up in his absence. And when the tension became too great, saddling Diamond and galloping off into the surrounding countryside in an attempt to clear his mind and think rationally.

'Have you telephoned Lady Flora?' Armand enquired, at the end of the week.

Having watched Maxime become more and more drawn and anxious as the days passed, Armand was worried about his great-nephew.

'Not again,' Maxime replied.

'I think you should,' Armand replied serenely. 'Or preferably go to Scotland and see Katharine. There's nothing to be gained by both of you sitting on different sides of the fence. Better to face each other and get this unfortunate misunderstanding sorted out.'

So Maxime had left.

Rising heavily from his seat he pulled open the door of the compartment and walking into the corridor leant his arms on the window rail staring absently at the darkly-silhouetted countryside racing past.

The train gave a piercing whistle and roared through a station.

Maxime sighed deeply, resting his head against the cold pane as the flashing lights darted like a kaleidoscope across his face.

And he wondered whether Armand had been right.

He and Katharine had met face to face as his uncle had suggested. There had certainly been a confrontation. But with what result? Perhaps it would have been better to let things lie for the time being in the hope that they would simmer down.

His mind went back to the boys. And remembering Léon's whispered request to go home, Maxime's heart hardened. Nothing could excuse Katharine for what she was doing to their sons.

Raising his head his lips compressed into a hard line.

He'd done his best.

He had tried to reason with her, to convince her that she had no cause for worry, no need to fear. That he loved her and wanted only her. But she had refused to believe him. Recalling her mocking laugh, he found it easier to come to a decision.

'I warned her,' he muttered tightly. 'If that's the way she wants it . . . It's her choice .'

A woman walking along the corridor stopped abruptly. With an apologetic smile, he pressed himself against the window to let her pass. Giving him a strange look, she hurried by.

'But,' Maxime ended grimly, pulling back the compartment door before regaining his seat, 'my sons will remain with me.'

134

Chapter
12

William Paget took both her hands in his own, and looked fondly down at her, then bent to kiss her cheek.

'Katharine my dear,' he said warmly, 'how lovely to see you again.'

For a moment Katharine couldn't reply. Tears had welled into her throat at the sight of the silver-haired old man who had come to mean so much to her. Pulling herself together she rose on tiptoe and throwing her arms around his neck kissed him warmly in return.

Flora standing with Lavinia in front of the great empty fireplace, now banked with a profusion of multi-coloured flowers and ferns, which looked as if they had been gathered in brimming armfuls and tossed into the grate to arrange themselves, smiled happily as she motioned them to sit down.

'I want to hear all about your holiday in Nice,' she said, reaching across to pat Lavinia's hand. 'After lunch you and I can have a long cosy chat.'

Her expressive dark-grey eyes twinkled across at William.

'We'll leave these young people alone. I know they've got a lot of news to catch up on.'

Her eyes rested meaningfully on Katharine. But her friend didn't meet her gaze.

Seeing the way Flora was manoeuvring the conversation, Katharine realised that her supposition the previous evening when reading Flora's PS had been correct. It was not entirely by chance that her hostess had invited William and Lavinia to lunch today. Knowing of Katharine's deep affection for Ashley's father, Flora had done so deliberately.

Looking up, Katharine smiled across at her hostess, remembering words Flora had uttered many years before when Katharine had still been a churchgoer and not a committed Christian.

'There are no chances in our life with God,' she had murmured. 'What the world calls co-incidences, Christians call God-incidences.'

Katharine had not understood.

But now she did. And she realised that God had used Flora to bring about this meeting with Ashley's father, that wise godly man who had suffered so much and yet through it all still kept his eyes on Jesus.

Katharine blushed, at that moment doubting her own faith. Had her eyes been on Jesus during the past traumatic weeks, she wondered. Or had she been relying on herself and therefore open to the devil's insinuations?

She knew the answer, and sent up a quick prayer of repentance asking for forgiveness. She had wondered why Jesus hadn't answered her cries for help. But now she understood.

Turning to William she smiled.

'Flora's right,' she agreed warmly as lunch was announced. 'We have so much to talk about.'

Rising to her feet, her heart and her step lighter she walked across the hall and into the dining room.

*　　*　　*

Hailing a taxi Maxime gave the address of his flat in Sloane Street. Then sat wearily back against the pungent

136

leather and closed his eyes as the cab weaved its way out of the station yard and set off across London.

It was early morning, and the traffic was light. A soft drizzle was falling giving the city a grey washed-out look which exactly matched Maxime's mood.

Entering the flat he loosened his tie and flopping fully dressed on the bed immediately fell asleep. When he awoke it was almost eleven o'clock.

'Blast,' he hissed. 'I've missed the Golden Arrow.'

He sighed.

Now what?

Throwing his legs over the side of the bed, Maxime ran his hands through his hair, frowning in concentration.

'If I can get a plane to Paris,' he mused, 'I can still catch the night train to Narbonne.'

Picking up the telephone, he rang the airport. But the few flights were fully booked. All they could offer was one to Brussels in the early afternoon which, as long as it was not delayed, would enable him to catch a train to Paris in time for the Barcelona night express.

Exasperated, Maxime put down the receiver. The whole thing was just too complicated. He could leave after dinner by the night ferry and be in Narbonne by tomorrow evening. Then he suddenly remembered. Today was 13th August. The 15th was a public holiday in France. And this year it was also a Friday. That meant a long weekend. He would arrive back just as everything closed down for three days.

Maxime flopped back on the bed and a terrible lethargy, almost a paralysis, took possession of his tired limbs. An image of Katharine as he had last seen her, her hands clenched at her side, her face white and tense, her soft lips drawn into a hard unforgiving line, flashed before his eyes. And he was suddenly overwhelmed by a feeling of utter hopelessness.

'Home sweet home,' he reflected bitterly. 'Hardly any point in killing myself to go back now.'

He closed his eyes, his whole being aching with an unutterable weariness.

'If I'm going to be alone,' he slurred, as sleep once again overcame him. 'I may as well stay here.'

* * *

'Come Katharine,' William smiled, 'let us walk in the garden.'

He placed his empty coffee cup on the inlaid table at his side.

'These young people,' he teased, his eyes twinkling at Flora and Lavinia sitting together on the sofa, 'are longing to be alone so that they can gossip about us.'

Flora twinkled back at him as he offered Katharine his arm.

Walking down the steps from the terrace and across the lawn, they turned into the small walled garden hidden from the house. Guiding Katharine towards a worn stone bench, William released her arm

As they sat in a friendly silence Katharine's mind wandered down the years to that day at the Rectory when she had brought William news of his son's death. And the scene seemed to be repeating itself.

'I know what you are thinking Katharine,' William said softly, his gaze, as then, riveted on some distant view which she could not see. 'And I know that you are hurting now as you did on that far-off day.'

He turned and fixed her with his still-bright eyes.

'But it is not the same.'

'I know,' she whispered.

'*Do* you?' he queried.

Katharine didn't reply.

138

'If you remember, I told you then that God would make everything beautiful in his time. And he has. He has given you beauty for ashes. You have a husband and four sons.'

Katharine shrugged helplessly. All William was saying was true. But she couldn't wipe from her mind Maxime's visit. Her suspicions . . . and his harsh words.

'I wonder for how much longer,' she whispered brokenly.

And suddenly the sleepless night, the trauma of her meeting with Maxime and now William's kindness all fused into a gigantic bubble which hovered uncertainly. Then burst.

'Oh William,' she said painfully, 'you don't know it all.'

'Then perhaps it would help to tell me.'

His understanding and his love broke down Katharine's resistance. As he had done on that tragic May afternoon fourteen years before, William sat silently, waiting for the storm to pass.

'It's as I thought,' he commented at last, 'you are comparing a marriage which was perfect because it was so brief with a marriage which over the years is bound to have its ups and downs. Had Ashley lived you would have had your difficult times. Every couple has moments when they think they have made a dreadful mistake.'

Katharine creased her forehead thoughtfully.

'Maxime and I have never felt that way,' she reflected. 'Now I come to think of it this is the first serious disagreement we've ever had . . .'

'Then count your blessings,' William broke in. 'To be able to say that after ten years of marriage is *most* unusual.'

But Katharine, deep in thought, made no reply. She simply stared fixedly at her shoes.

'Let Ashley go,' William said quietly. 'Death is but a little thing compared with the fact that Ashley lived, and was the kind of person he was. Don't let that rope which seems to be holding you to the past keep yanking you back.'

In the distance a bell ringing on the terrace summoned them to tea.

'What a pity,' William said regretfully, rising to his feet and holding out his hand to Katharine. 'We must go back, otherwise Flora and Lavinia will send out a search party.'

His twinkling blue eyes shone down at Katharine.

'But let us continue this conversation tomorrow.'

*   *   *

During the next few days Katharine spent many hours in the garden with William Paget. His wisdom and his love for her had quietened her tormented spirit at their first meeting. And since then with his help she had been able to reflect on her life calmly and rationally. William had unravelled the strands which subconsciously tied her to her tragic past, helped her face that past and accept that it was behind her.

'Why don't you write to Maxime . . . or better still telephone him and say you are going home,' William suggested as they sat together in the walled garden after dinner on the Saturday evening.'

Twilight was creeping up on them and a light breeze trembled through the overhanging roses causing fragrant showers of petals to drift to the grass at their feet.

Katharine leant back and closed her eyes and a slow smile crept across her face.

Now seeing everything through William's clear eyes she finally felt able to pick up the threads of her life, tell Maxime that her fears had been unfounded . . . and start again.

'I will,' she agreed. 'I promise.'

Turning impulsively she kissed the old man's withered cheek.

'You must meet Maxime,' she burst out spontaneously. 'You'd like him. He's a wonderful man.'

William raised his eyebrows in amusement.

Understanding his thoughts, Katharine smiled.

'Thank you for helping me to rediscover that,' she whispered. 'Ashley and Maxime. So different and yet . . . in many ways so alike.'

She looked up at him her eyes warm and shining, her ivory complexion glowing.

'Oh William,' she cried, grasping the old man's hand and holding it tightly in her own. 'You've shown me what a very lucky woman I am . . . to have been loved by two such wonderful men.'

*   *   *

Armand's hand trembled as he picked up the receiver and asked the operator for the Ardnakil number. He was obliged to spell it out several times before she finally understood. The old man drummed his long dry fingers against the desk in an unusual bout of impatience as she rabbited on in an attempt to connect him.

'Two hours wait, Monsieur le Marquis,' the operator finally chirruped as triumphantly as if she were announcing that their team had won the Cup Final.

'And,' she added knowingly, 'that's what *they* say. To my way of thinking it will be *much* more.'

With this comforting piece of information ringing in his ears Armand replaced the receiver. Pulling a sheaf of papers towards him he tried to concentrate his thoughts. But his mind returned incessantly to the telephone call he had just received.

'My poor, poor child,' he groaned. 'How is she going to bear this on top of everything else?'

And he agonised over how he was going to break the news to Katharine.

Rising heavily to his feet he began to pace up and down the worn Persian carpet, his restless hands clasping and unclasping themselves behind his back.

When at last the shrill ring of the telephone broke in on his troubled thoughts Armand stumbled hastily back to his desk and picked up the receiver.

'Just putting you through, Monsieur le Marquis,' the girl chirped above the crackles.

Armand's mouth was dry and his pulse jumped erratically as he waited to be connected.

'Lord,' he breathed, as the explosions gradually subsided and a soft Highland voice announced that he was through. 'Give me the words!'

And taking a deep breath he struggled to steady his voice.

Chapter
13

'What is everybody doing this afternoon?' Flora enquired, glancing round the table when Janet came to claim Léon for his rest.

As a Sunday treat the four boys had been invited to lunch in the dining room.

'Sandy and I are challenging the twins to a tennis match,' Cristobel announced. 'And Jehan's going to be ball boy.'

'And you Laura?'

'I think I'll take a book and find a sunny spot in the garden,' Laura replied.

'Don't you want to play tennis?' Flora queried.

'Not today thank you Lady Flora,' she mumbled, abruptly excusing herself and walking hurriedly from the room.

As the young people clattered off to their various occupations Katharine fell in step beside Flora.

'Laura doesn't seem very happy,' she remarked.

'I don't think she is.'

Katharine raised her eyebrows enquiringly as they crossed the drawing-room and strolled out on to the terrace where coffee was awaiting them.

'Her sister Mary telephoned yesterday evening,' Flora explained. 'She's to be married in September and wants Laura to go back to London at the end of the week to have fittings for her bridesmaid's dress.'

'I should have thought she'd be pleased!'

'I suppose she is in a way. But unfortunately the end of the week is when Alasdair arrives back from mountaineering in Austria.'

Once again Katharine raised puzzled eyebrows.

'Laura's been in love with Alasdair since she was twelve,' Flora sighed, leaning forward to pour the coffee.

'You can't be serious,' Katharine laughed. 'How old is the child?'

'The same age as Cristobel, fifteen.'

'She'll get over it.'

'I'm not so sure,' Flora mused.

She looked across at Katharine.

'Laura's very like you.'

'Like *me*?' Katharine exclaimed.

'Yes,' Flora went on smoothly. 'Your backgrounds are very similar. She lost her mother at twelve and has been brought up by her father's sister Edwina. He's an Oxford don who hardly notices she's around. Now Mary's getting married I think she'll be even more alone.'

'How old is Mary?' Katharine frowned.

'Ten years older than Laura. And Philippa, the eldest of the three sisters who's been married some time, is twelve years her senior. So like you, Laura's practically an only child. Coming here is really the only family life she's ever had. And I have a feeling that, like you, when she falls in love it's for keeps.'

'But I wasn't *twelve* when I met Ashley.'

'No, but if you had been I don't think it would have made any difference. You'd have fallen deeply in love with him all the same.'

Katharine shrugged impatiently.

'Perhaps that's why Laura irritates you,' Flora concluded, 'because you are so alike.'

'Heavens Flora, why do you say that?'

'Because she does.'

'Perhaps you're right,' Katharine agreed. 'I'm afraid I find Laura rather wet. She's the exact opposite of Cristobel, who's so alive.'

Flora smiled to herself.

'I suppose now you're going to say that *I'm* wet,' Katharine challenged.

'No darling I'm not. Anything but. But I think in life, like you, Laura is going to feel things very deeply . . . and get hurt.'

'Does Alasdair know about her secret passion?'

'Nobody knows. And Laura would die with embarrassment if she knew I'd guessed. For Alasdair she's just his little sister's friend, the shy, skinny schoolgirl with the long blond plaits. He's not even noticed she's grown up. Still calls her "freckle-face"!'

Flora smiled across at Katharine.

'Poor little darling. Can you imagine the humiliation of it?'

Katharine didn't reply. She was trying to swallow the remark about she and Laura being alike. And finding it difficult to digest.

'It was a surprise when William preached at the service this morning,' Katharine remarked, changing the subject. 'Wasn't it a wonderful sermon?'

'John 4', Flora added. 'Jesus and the woman at the well.'

'What he said was so apt,' Katharine observed. 'It made me think. If we turn away from the source we dry up, the water of life ceases to flow in us and becomes sluggish and stagnant.'

Katharine sighed and leaning over tugged viciously at a weed peering hopefully through the fuschia overflowing from a stone vase at her side.

'It's been happening to me.'

She leant back and closed her eyes.

'I didn't realise it. It's so easy to move away from God when things are going well. One begins to imagine one doesn't need him and can manage one's own life. It takes a jolt to bring us back and make us understand that when Jesus said to his disciples "without me you can do nothing" he meant it. Talking to William these past few days has really brought me to my knees and forced me to see that I keep forgetting who is God.'

'We all do at times,' Flora murmured.

'To our sorrow,' Katharine remarked. 'But I do think if Maxime were a believer it would be easier.'

'Undoubtedly. But he doesn't stop *you*, does he?'

'No. And he doesn't mind my sharing my faith with the boys and bringing them up to know Jesus as their Saviour.'

'Like Robert,' Flora agreed.

She turned and gave Katharine one of her dazzling smiles.

'I don't want to pry darling. But does this conversation mean that you are seeing things in a different light? And have come to a decision?'

'Yes, with William's help. We'll be going home as soon as Nanny Moffatt returns from her holiday.'

Flora leant across and squeezed Katharine's hand.

'Why not go on ahead and leave the boys here to wait for Nanny,' she ventured.

'Thank you Flora,' Katharine replied thoughtfully. 'I might just do that.'

Stretching lazily she got to her feet.

'I think I'll take a stroll. Do you feel like coming with me?'

'Darling I'd love to,' Flora replied. 'But with the house bulging with all these hearty hunters I'm *so* behind with my correspondence. Why don't you walk over to the Fort? William and Lavinia are lunching with Hamish. I've invited them all to tea. You could walk back together.'

'Perhaps I will,' Katharine smiled and, turning as she tripped lightly down the terrace steps, kissed her finger-tips in Flora's direction.

Delighted that she had finally taken a decision and her life was about to return to its appointed groove, Katharine found herself retracing her steps to the walled garden where William had so patiently unravelled her fears.

As she approached she heard the unmistakeable sound of weeping. Tiptoeing inside she saw Laura, her book abandoned on the grass, her body hunched along the length of the bench across which her dishevelled golden hair was flowing.

'Laura,' she ventured, tentatively touching the slim shoulders heaving with uncontrollable sobs. 'Laura, what's the matter? Can I help?'

Slowly the girl raised a face blotched with tears, yet still etched with a delicate porcelain beauty.

Katharine sat down on the bench beside her and, in a sudden rush of compassion went to take the distressed girl in her arms. But Laura hunched her shoulders and drew away. Then abruptly slipping off the bench she picked up the book and, without a word, fled.

Looking after her Katharine recalled her conversation with Flora. And she understood what Flora had meant. Thinking back down the years, her heart ached for the unhappy child knowing that, at Laura's age, she would have reacted in exactly the same way. Sensing this, some of the irritation she had always felt towards Laura's shyness and diffidence melted.

'How true it is what the Bible says,' she murmured, 'that we always see our own faults in others. Perhaps in order to take the spotlight off ourselves.'

Katharine sighed.

But was it a fault to love so deeply that one was capable of being badly hurt? Looking back on her own life, she knew that it wasn't.

And her heart went out to Laura in her pain.

*   *   *

When she entered the dim hall an hour later the telephone was ringing.

'It is for you Madame,' Duncan announced, handing her the receiver. 'A call from France.'

Katharine's heart leapt.

She had waited for five days for Maxime to telephone. For some sign that their bitter parting words had been a terrible mistake and that, like her, all he wanted was to forget that angry meeting and be together again. And now the call had arrived. Just at the right time when she had at last come to terms with the past traumatic weeks and was ready to put them behind her and start again.

'Thank you Lord,' she breathed, her heart thumping excitedly as she hastened to take the receiver Duncan was holding out to her. 'Your timing is always perfect.'

As she grasped it, Duncan solicitously slid a chair beneath her and, revelling in the sweet moment of anticipation, Katharine sank gratefully down.

'Hallo,' she breathed, her voice throbbing with emotion.

Hearing her, Armand was suddenly taken back. He floundered, at a loss for words.

'Hallo,' Katharine repeated, puzzled at the silence at the other end of the line. 'Hallo . . . hallo.'

A note of anxiety had crept into her voice. Hearing it, Armand made a tremendous effort to pull himself together.

'Katharine, my dear,' he finally managed to stammer.

But his voice was strained.

'Uncle *Armand*!' she exclaimed.

Then abruptly stopped.

Why was Armand telephoning her?

Her happiness slowly evaporated. Her anxiety crystallised and those paralysing fears gripped her once again.

Something must have happened to Maxime!

'Uncle,' she choked. 'What is it?'

'Katharine,' Armand hesitated, suddenly feeling alone and helpless. 'I asked for Maxime.'

He cleared his throat.

'Nothing serious,' he lied, feeling the tension at the other end of the line.

'But . . .' she said bewilderedly, 'Maxime's at Le Moulin.'

'Did he not join you in Scotland?'

Katharine wavered, unsure what to reply.

'Yes,' she admitted at last. 'But . . . he couldn't stay long. He . . . had to leave.'

Armand's heart sank. And he realised that something was very wrong. Maxime was *not* at Le Moulin. In fact, there had been no news of him since he left for Ardnakil almost a week ago.

'How stupid of me,' the old man stuttered. 'I quite thought . . .'

'But where are you Uncle?' Katharine asked anxiously.

Taking a deep breath Armand prepared to lie for the second time in a few minutes.

'Biarritz,' he blurted, silently asking God if not for forgiveness at least for understanding for this web of lies which in the present situation he felt compelled to weave in order to avoid causing Katharine more pain.

'Oh that explains it,' she exclaimed with relief, knowing how difficult telephone communication was with Gure Etchea. 'Is there anything *I* can do?'

'No, no nothing,' Armand said hurriedly, now thoroughly flustered. 'It is quite all right. Don't worry my dear. Just enjoy your holiday.'

And to prevent himself having to lie still further he quickly replaced the receiver. He felt crushed and totally out of his depth. The news he had received weighed heavily on him. He knew he could not keep it from Katharine indefinitely. But what was he to do? And where was Maxime?

Wearily putting his head in his hands he sought help from the God who had always been his strength.

That help was to come almost immediately. But in a way he least expected.

*   *   *

Puzzled by her great-uncle's strange behaviour, Katharine thoughtfully put down the receiver and rose from the chair. Armand had seemed confused and evasive. So unlike his serene self. And she couldn't understand it.

Frowning, she crossed the dim hall in the direction of the drawing-room then abruptly, as if catapulted from a faraway place into an unfamiliar scene, she fell on to a hard oak settle near the corner turret. The turret was the favourite hidey-hole of Lady Flora's special pet, a dubious-tempered West Highland terrier. Hearing the creak, Laird wandered out from among the collection of skis, tennis rackets and golf clubs stored in a higgledy-piggledy jumble inside the turret and glared belligerently at her. Mechanically Katharine bent to pat him, but he growled and retreated to the safety of his den.

Leaning her head wearily against the back of the high settle Katharine closed her eyes replaying in her mind the strange, disjointed conversation she had just had with her favourite uncle. And she didn't understand why Armand had telephoned Ardnakil. Everyone believed she was spending July and August at Gure Etchea. Then she remembered that Armand had said he was there and realised that her absence must have caused questions. But how much had Maxime told him? And how did he know that Maxime had left to join her here?

As Katharine pondered over these questions another one wormed its way into her mind. Crossing unsteadily back to the telephone she lifted the receiver and asked for her home number. By some miracle the operator told her to hold the line she would put her straight through.

'Has Monsieur arrived yet?' she enquired innocently when Alphonse answered the call.

'No Madame,' the butler replied. 'We do not know when to expect him.'

Katharine caught her breath and her hand trembled on the receiver. Gripping it tightly she took a deep breath.

'Oh, he must have stopped over in Paris to finish some business,' she managed to reply. 'No, don't bother to tell him I rang Alphonse, he'll no doubt telephone me from there.'

And she hastily terminated the call.

In a daze she heard the click as she replaced the receiver on its cradle. It seemed to echo a click which snapped in her brain at the same time, causing an icy numbness to creep insidiously up from the soles of her feet to finally envelop her whole body.

Maxime was not at Le Moulin. Then where was he?

And abruptly her life which, the previous evening had come together again in the old happy pattern crumbled about her ears.

She remembered their angry conversation and Maxime's bitter parting threat that if *she* didn't want him his ex-wife did. And the awful truth of his whereabouts suddenly struck her.

If Maxime was not at Le Moulin, there was only one place he could be.

He had carried out his threat and gone to Paris to Marie-Céleste!

Chapter
14

As Armand sat in a kind of drunken stupor, his head in his hands, his body slumped wearily against the old-fashioned mahogany desk which had belonged to his great-great-grandfather, a groan trickled through his parched lips. And he wondered, not for the first time since Maxime had informed him of Katharine's sudden disappearance and the reason for it, just where the future was leading them all.

Léonie had held the family firmly together right until the end. But he had been beside her. But now, for the first time in his life he felt desperately alone and incapable of taking the strain, bearing the terrible burden of the news which he had received a few hours earlier. And which he knew would devastate Katharine.

Lifting his head he glanced across the room and his eyes fell on the delicate miniature of his sister Aurélie which had always stood on Léonie's dressing-table. And he wondered if the curse which seemed to have hit the family, and especially those who through no fault of their own had been involved in Aurélie's fateful union, was as the Old Testament prophesied to be visited upon the children until the third and fourth generation. Aurélie had died a tragic death. Elisabeth's life had not been easy. Maxime he thought had finally found happiness with Katharine. But now . . .

The sudden ring of the telephone in the stillness of

his shuttered room startled him. Apprehensively, he stretched out his hand to pick up the receiver. In the past few hours the instrument had shattered his peaceful world and brought nothing but disaster.

'Hallo,' he said, breathing deeply in an attempt to compose his voice.

'I'm so pleased to find you in. Could you bear to have a guest for dinner?'

Armand gasped.

It was Maxime.

'My dear boy,' he said shakily. 'Where are you?'

'At Le Moulin,' Maxime replied. 'Where else?'

'But I telephoned you just after lunch and Alphonse told me you were still in Scotland.'

'I was,' Maxime replied.

'I don't understand. I rang Ardnakil and Katharine said you had left last Tuesday.'

There was a slight tense pause.

'Look Uncle,' Maxime blurted out at last. 'It's too complicated to explain over the telephone . . .'

'Then do come and dine with me,' Armand broke in.

He stopped abruptly, uncertain whether to tell Maxime now of the news he had received. But Maxime did not notice his hesitation.

'Splendid,' he said.

And, as he rang off, he sounded relieved.

Thoroughly confused, Armand once more rose from his chair. Maxime would be with him in a couple of hours. It would give him time to prepare what he had to say. Bad news could always wait!

* * *

'Mamam, we won,' the twins shrieked, bursting into the hall. 'We beat Sandy and Cristobel.'

'Wimbledon beware,' Sandy laughed. 'The terrible twins are about to land!'

Seeing Katharine sitting immobile on the settle, he winked in her direction. But she did not react. She hardly seemed to notice their presence.

'Do we *have* to change for tea?' Jehan wailed, trailing in behind them. 'We've already changed *once* since we got up.'

His irritating moan brought Katharine out of her stupor.

'Yes you do,' she answered sharply, suddenly remembering that Lavinia and William were coming to tea. 'You can't have tea in the drawing-room wearing those clothes.'

'Then I'd rather have it in the nursery.'

'Oh *do* stop grumbling Jehan,' Katharine said irritably. 'And go and change at once.'

Loudly voicing his complaints, Jehan trailed behind his brothers up the wide oak staircase.

As the hall cleared of young people, and the cloud of labradors which had raced down the stairs to greet them slowly regained their baskets beneath the long arched window on the half-landing, Katharine rose unsteadily to her feet.

She had been looking forward to seeing William again and telling him that she was on her way home, back to Maxime and their life together at Le Moulin. But now . . . what could she say? She knew that she need not say anything. William was not one to pry. But she also knew that his perceptive sensibility would pierce whatever protective armour she might attempt to hide behind. He would know, instinctively, that the wound which they had both believed healed had broken open again. And was now bleeding remorselessly.

'Good news?' Flora enquired, popping her head round the drawing-room door.

Seeing Katharine's chalk-like face, she stopped.

'Darling,' she cried running across the hall towards her friend. 'What is it?'

'I don't know,' Katharine whispered unsteadily. 'I really don't know.'

As she spoke, she saw Marie-Céleste in Maxime's arms, her red-tipped fingers running sensuously through his dishevelled hair, her generous lips voluptuously caressing his neck. Then slowly exploring the contours of his face till they rested seductively on his own as they entwined in a passionate embrace.

She looked blankly at Flora standing anxiously by her side.

'I think I'm going mad,' she said hoarsely.

The accumulated strain of the past few weeks, combined with the succession of tragedies which had punctuated her young life and on which she had firmly closed the door, all fused together. Darkness closed around her. She trembled, her knees buckled beneath her and with a low moan she crumpled and fell to the floor at Flora's feet.

Flora's cry coincided with Sheana's appearance through the green baize door with the tea-tray. As the astonished maid ran to her aid a dark shadow fell across the dim hall. Lavinia and William stood open-mouthed in the doorway gazing unbelievingly at Katharine's prostrate form on the cold flagged tiles.

* * *

'Maxime, I'm so pleased to see you!'

Armand rose with difficulty from his chair when his great-nephew was announced. He was unbelievably tired. The events of the past few hours had drained him of all energy. And for the first time he felt the weight of his ninety years.

Holding out his heavily-veined hands he took both Maxime's in his own and leant his cheek forward for the younger man's embrace.

'Come and sit down,' he said ushering Maxime towards a chair placed opposite his own in the wide window embrasure.

His still-bright nut brown eyes pierced through his nephew. And he was shocked by the dark shadows under his eyes, the strain etched on Maxime's face.

'You look worn out,' he exclaimed. 'Have you had a difficult time?'

Armand knew that he should break the news which was weighing heavily on him to Maxime. But his heart ached for the younger man who seemed so dejected that he pushed it to the back of his mind. During dinner would be a better time.

Maxime, gazing idly out of the window at the banks of wisteria creeping over the stone walls of the balcony, raised his eyes and gave a wan smile as Armand handed him a glass.

'It wasn't very easy,' he admitted.

Then he frowned.

'But why did you telephone me at Ardnakil? Did you tell Katharine I wasn't at Le Moulin?'

'Not in so many words,' his uncle hedged. 'But I'm awfully afraid she guessed. I was caught off my guard when she said you had left several days ago.'

He looked directly at Maxime, the same thoughts which had tortured Katharine passing through his mind.

'I stayed in London,' Maxime remarked briefly.

And he told his uncle the whole sorry story.

For a moment Armand sat watching the level rise and fall in his glass as it trembled in his hand. How could he do what he had to do? How could he inflict more bad news on these two stricken people whom he loved so much.

'My poor dear children,' he murmured at last, when Jeanne announced that dinner was served.

As she closed the door behind her after serving the gaspacho, Maxime picked up his spoon.

'You didn't tell me why you rang me in Scotland Uncle,' he enquired. 'Was it anything important?'

Armand opened his mouth. But no words came. Glancing away he lifted his napkin and carefully wiped his dry lips.

'Is something the matter?' Maxime frowned.

He drew in his breath as Armand reluctantly raised his eyes. They had a stricken, hunted look in them.

'There *is* something the matter,' Maxime insisted.

Armand trembled, clasping his hands tightly together in an effort to control his body.

'Do you remember last year when Xavier was here,' he began waveringly, 'we discussed the situation in Algeria?'

Maxime nodded impatiently.

'He said it was rather unhealthy. There were anti-French rumblings coming from many sides . . . and he didn't know how things were going to turn out.'

'Yes,' Maxime urged, his face tense, his eyes never leaving his uncle's face.

'He also said that, should a crisis occur . . . should he be in danger . . .'

Armand stopped and reaching for his glass, gulped some water.

'Yes, yes, I remember,' Maxime prompted curtly.

'That instead of informing you, in case Katharine should take the call, I was to be told so that any news could be broken to her gently.'

Maxime's expressive eyes darkened and, involuntarily he clutched the edge of the table.

'You don't mean . . .'

Armand nodded sadly.

'I had a telephone call from the Mission this morning . . .'

'And?'

'Xavier has been kidnapped.'

'*Kidnapped?*' Maxime exclaimed, his tone incredulous. 'But that's ridiculous. By whom?'

'No one knows,' Armand answered raggedly. 'The line was not very clear. I tried to call back, but it was always engaged. Then the Ministry of Interior rang and confirmed it.'

Maxime slammed his napkin down on the table.

'This is a ridiculous story,' he expostulated. 'Who on earth would want to kidnap Xavier? And for what?'

Armand twiddled with the stem of his wine glass as Jeanne came in to change the plates. He was grateful for the pause. It enabled him to pull himself together.

'To hold as a hostage,' Armand said shakily, as Jeanne left the room. 'I know it sounds preposterous. But it's true. These Algerian nationalists are serious . . . and it appears ruthless. There are several of them imprisoned over there and the FLN* have taken Xavier prisoner in an attempt to secure their comrades' release.'

His voice trembled as he dealt the final blow.

'They say that unless their demands are met . . . Xavier will be executed.'

The two men stared at each other in horror.

'You can understand now why I needed to contact you. And why I was so flustered when it was Katharine who answered the telephone.'

'She mustn't know,' Maxime cut in swiftly.

He rose abruptly from the table. Walking over to the window he thrust his hands in his pockets and gazed unseeingly out.

'I don't see how it can be avoided,' Armand replied.

'It *must* be avoided,' Maxime said sharply. 'Katharine is in a very fragile state at the moment. I prefer not to think what such news might do to her.'

He turned and faced the old man.

'This is a nonsense,' he went on scathingly. 'A twenty-four-hour wonder which will all be cleared up before the news breaks.'

'That's not what the Ministry of Interior official told me,' Armand replied miserably. 'They are taking it very seriously.'

'Then what are they *doing* about it,' Maxime exploded. 'Did they tell you that?'

Armand shook his head.

'The official promised to keep in touch and to let me know as soon as anything further happens.'

'That's not good enough.'

Maxime sat down abruptly.

'Did the man give you his name?'

Armand shook his head.

'I'll go to Paris tomorrow and see what I can find out.'

He smiled at Armand's woebegone face.

'The authorities won't stand for blackmail,' he soothed. 'These bandits will soon capitulate.'

'I wouldn't be too sure.'

'Every man has his price,' Maxime said drily 'If the Ministry of the Interior can't do anything, we'll see how much the terrorists need to be bought off.'

'I'd be very sure of what you're doing before you enter into *that* kind of negotiation,' his uncle remarked cautiously. 'These Algerian nationalists are serious. We're going to have to give them their independence sooner or later.'

Armand sighed.

'In the meantime the thing to do is decide on some plan of action.'

Maxime sat down wearily.

'My poor darling,' he whispered. 'How much more can she take?'

He looked across at his uncle and his eyes were hard.

'And where is your God is all this?' he asked stonily. 'Hasn't Katharine suffered enough in the past twenty-five years? Does he *have* to exact the last drop of blood from her?'

'I know what you're thinking Maxime,' Armand replied quietly. 'And you're quite wrong.'

'Time alone will give us the answer to that one,' his nephew replied brusquely, getting up from the table.

Armand pushed aside his untouched plate.

'I'm not very hungry either,' he smiled shakily, rising unsteadily to his feet. 'We may as well go back to my study and try to work out a plan of action.'

Suddenly a wave of tenderness for the old man who meant so much to them all, swept over Maxime.

'I didn't mean to bite your head off,' he apologised. 'It was unforgivable of me.'

'But very understandable in the circumstances,' Armand smiled, as his great-nephew took his arm and led him from the room.

'Don't worry,' Maxime urged. 'We'll see this through together. The important thing is that Katharine doesn't find out before we've got it all sewn up. It's just a storm in a teacup which will quickly pass. Those bandits will soon give up, you'll see.'

Armand looked up at his nephew and sadly shook his head.

He was not convinced.

*   *   *

As he was thrust, manacled, into the foul-smelling cellar to fall on the damp dirt floor, Xavier looked up at the iron grill high above his head. In the thin trickle of pale

161

light squeezing itself through he noticed a filthy straw mattress lying against the opposite wall.

Crawling towards it, he eased himself onto the torn surface and wearily leant his head against the earth wall. He vaguely wondered what time it was. His watch and all his personal effects had been removed by his masked jailer.

It must be late afternoon, he surmised, watching the weak light gradually fade from the small barred opening.

His head ached and his shackled feet, separated only by a small length of iron chain, were beginning to chafe his ankles. Bending down in an attempt to ease their position, the chain which bound his hands pulled sharply. Not for the first time that day he wondered at his situation. And the reason for it.

It had been totally unexpected and unbelievably brutal. The sudden pad of feet behind him. A hand clasped roughly across his mouth jerking his head backwards, and a sharp prod from a bony knee propelling him into the back of a waiting car. A gag had been tied tightly round his mouth and a blanket thrust over his head as the car shot away from the pavement.

He had no idea how long the journey had taken from the centre of Algiers, stunned as he had been by the sharp blow he had received on his head as he was unceremoniously grabbed from behind. It was not until he was inside the building that the headgear and the gag had been removed; to be replaced by the iron chains and an undignified search of his body before he was kicked into this putrid underground room.

As his eyes became accustomed to the semi-darkness he looked around him at the tiny space, noticing small puddles of stagnant water in the far corner in which floated the upturned bodies of an assortment of insects.

And he shivered, his eyes travelling apprehensively round seeking their live companions.

And he wondered where he was. This was not a prison. He had visited many North African prisons and they were luxury compared to the filthy hovel in which he was now crouched.

'I suppose I'm in a disused cellar somewhere in the Medina*,' he mused.

Remembering the warren of narrow alleyways teeming with people which criss-crossed the Kasbah*, into which Europeans seldom ventured, Xavier sighed.

'Unless there's a miracle,' he mused wryly, 'there'll be no hope of anyone ever finding me here.'

And he wondered again what had happened. And why he was here.

Automatically he felt in his pocket for his Bible. Then remembered that he no longer possessed anything.

Sitting puzzling over the weird events of what had begun as a normal morning, he heard the sound of a very rusty lock being turned. His eyes now accustomed to the darkness, he looked towards the door, expecting to see one of his masked captors. As he watched, it grated open a few inches and a tin mug and plate were thrust through.

Crawling painfully towards them he saw that the plate contained the local gruel, a couscous* without the meat or vegetables which made it such a succulent dish. There was no spoon, so plunging his hand into it, he swallowed a mouthful. He was hungry. His captors had caught him as he was walking in the cool of the morning before breakfast. But the gruel was covered in a thin greasy liquid which tasted like dishwater. Retching slightly he pushed the plate away and drank thirstily from the tin mug.

Wearily regaining the mattress he noticed that the

cell was infested with cockroaches which now scuttled from every crevice to swarm over the unappetising dish. Looking up, he saw a number of scorpions crawling lazily down the red earth walls. And he recoiled in fear drawing his cloak tightly around him. Peering closely he was relieved to discover that they were not the red sand scorpions with the lethal bite but the black variety, whose bite was painful but not deadly. Xavier noticed that one of his ankles was beginning to swell and realised that he must already have been bitten he dozed.

The room was now in complete darkness. Even the trickle of light from the grilled aperture had been replaced by a curtain of impenetrable anthracite as the swift African night descended.

Xavier sighed. Not even a moon to lighten his darkness. Rolling over onto his side he fell into an exhausted sleep.

When he awoke his glance went immediately to the aperture through which a thin grey streak was seeping.

Must be morning, he yawned.

The plate was still where he had left it, though now wiped clean by the various bugs which shared his cell. He looked down at his ankle which had swelled considerably in the night, making the chafing of the irons almost unbearable. Without thinking, he scratched his cheek and realised that, having finished his supper, his cell-mates had started to feed off him.

And, his eyes on the aperture where the grey was gradually paling, he began to recite Psalm 139. When he came to verse 11 he cried out in triumph.

'If I say "Surely the darkness will hide me and the light become night around me even the darkness will not be dark to you: the night will shine like the day, for the darkness is as light to you".'

At those words hope entered his heart.

It was as if the chains melted, the walls disappeared and he was free.

'Thank you Lord,' he kept repeating. 'I still have my memory. They haven't taken that away. I know that when I am weak, then I am strong because you will pour your strength into me. I need not fear what mortal men can do to me, nor worry about what to say when I am brought before my captors. You have promised that your Holy Spirit will speak for me.'

'Father,' he cried at last. 'I do not know when that day will come. I do not know what tomorrow or even today holds. But I do know that nothing can separate me from your love. When I walk through deep waters they will not overcome me for you have promised never to leave me nor forsake me.'

Lying back against the damp wall Xavier raised his hands in supplication.

'Lord, keep me from bitterness and self-pity. Show me my captors as you see them, your lost children . . . and give me the grace to forgive them.'

As he lay, quietened, on his mattress the door once again ground open a fraction and a slice of stale dark bread and another mug of tepid water were thrust inside.

Crawling across to pick them up Xavier was able to find it in his heart to thank his Father for his daily bread.

As the day wore on, the claustrophic cell seemed to steam up and become hot and damp. Xavier was not sure whether the temperature was rising or he was becoming feverish. Various parts of his body were swelling from the insistent bites of the black scorpions which swarmed all over the cell. And he was beginning to feel lethargic and ill.

Towards the end of the afternoon, drifting in and out of a fitful sleep, he heard the bolt creak in the lock.

A masked man came in and retrieved the filthy plate, replacing the two empty mugs with a full one. His throat now parched with fever Xavier rolled off the mattress and heaved himself towards it. But as he reached out his hand to put the mug to his dry lips, a heavy foot crashed down on it, causing him to gasp with pain. Looking up, to his utter astonishment he saw the man who had been his constant companion for the past few months. A man he had come to love as a brother. And who he believed had become his brother in Christ.

'Khaled,' he exclaimed hoarsely.

The man removed his foot and directed it at Xavier's head with such force that he topppled over backwards and lay for a few seconds like a crab, unable to right himself.

'Get up,' he hissed.

Struggling onto his side Xavier forced himself to his feet.

The man was tall, almost as tall as he and, as they looked each other in the eyes Xavier saw hatred in his captor's dark stare.

'Khaled', he pleaded, '. . . why?'

The man's lip curled contemptuously.

Fumbling in the wide pocket of his djellabah* he brandished a small bound book.

It was the Bible which Xavier had given him.

'Infidel . . . dog', he shrieked.

And taking the Bible in both his hands he savagely tore off the cover. Then in a frenzy of hate began to rip the volume apart shrieking obscenities as he did so.

Xavier stared unbelievingly as the pages fluttered about his captor. When the last one had drifted to the floor Khaled stamped viciously on the pitiful pile of torn crumpled paper. Then in a final act of hate spat upon them.

'See if your God can save you now', he cried triumphantly, pushing Xavier roughly to his knees. 'Tell him to come down from his cross.'

He laughed maniacally. Then his eyes narrowed into two dark slits.

'*Nothing* can save you from the fate which awaits you', he hissed triumphantly. 'Nothing . . . Allah will not be mocked. And neither will Algeria. We Arabs will free ourselves from the yoke of you mealy-faced French colonist pigs. *Vive l'Algérie libre*.'

And with a final kick which sent Xavier reeling he slammed the door and turned the key.

Chapter 15

William and Lavinia hurried across the hall to where Flora and Sheana were doing their best to revive Katharine. Asking no questions, William knelt beside her, gently lifting her head.

'Let us get her to a place where she can lie down,' he said.

'The library's nearest,' Flora answered.

As the four of them lifted Katharine's slender body Jehan cannon-balled down the stairs.

'Oh hallo,' he chirped. 'Is this a new game? Can *we* play?'

Startled, Flora looked up.

'I think after all Janet it would be better if the boys had tea in the nursery,' she apologised.

Janet following Jehan down the stairs holding Léon's hand, the twins chattering behind her, had already turned and started to usher the boys back up.

'Come along Jehan dear,' she urged, when he remained staring, fascinated by the little procession making its way across the hall.

'But I thought we were having tea in the drawing-room?' Jehan protested.

'Not today,' Janet soothed. 'Come back to the nursery with your brothers.'

'But I want to play this new game,' he protested as Flora quietly closed the library door.

'It's *not* a game Jehan,' Janet said patiently. 'Your mother is not feeling well. Now come along, do.'

'It's not fair,' he stamped.

Then seeing the look in Janet's eye he stuck out his lower lip and began kicking his way back up the stairs.

'I suppose you'll tell me I've got to change my clothes *again*', he grumbled. 'That makes *three* times since I got up. Well I'm not changing them tomorrow no matter *what* happens. In fact, I think I'll stay in my pyjamas all day, so there.'

Janet took him by the arm and dragged him protesting up the stairs.

Lavinia bent over Katharine's prostrate form trying to force some brandy between her lips.

Suddenly, as the stinging liquid burnt her throat a jumble of confused memories leapt into Katharine's mind, twirling crazily round and round until one surfaced, agonisingly clear. Coughing violently she shot up on the couch.

'No', she cried, 'no. Lawrence has got it all wrong. He's made a terrible mistake. Ashley's not dead.'

She stopped abruptly, looking around her with glazed eyes.

'It's all right darling,' Flora soothed, bewildered by Katharine's strange outburst.

Katharine stared from one to the other. Then focused on William standing beside her. Her past life jerked before her, as if projected by a magic lantern. And she was back in that little room at the cottage on the day Lawrence brought her news of Ashley's death, prostrate on the old sofa as Rickie attempted to force brandy down her throat.

'I'm sorry,' she gasped, slowly returning to the present. 'It was the brandy. It . . . it must have brought back memories.'

169

Flora looked across at Lavinia as William sat down on the long leather couch beside her.

'Has anything happened within the past few minutes to upset you?' he asked kindly.

Katharine slowly shook her head. Then she remembered Armand's strange telephone call. And the vision it had conjured up. With this recollection she felt herself drifting off into a formless grey limbo as the pain and the fear returned to haunt her like the dull persistent ache of an old wound. And suddenly she wanted to wipe out the years between and float back down that long tunnel which joined her to the past. That past which had once held such promise.

Sinking helplessly back on the sofa her body shook uncontrollably. But no tears came. Only hard dry sobs which seemed to tear her body apart and leave her mutilated and bleeding. As Ashley had bled on the stones of that grim prison yard. Yet he had been released from further pain, further anguish while she had been left alone to carry the scars of war with her forever. In the darkness which was slowly closing around her she wondered why she had to go on living when Ashley was dead.

Lifting her arms towards his father, she held him tightly against her, as she had once held his son.

'William,' she whispered plaintively. 'Oh William. Why did Ashley leave me? Why did he have to die?'

* * *

'There doesn't appear to be anything we can do tonight,' Maxime announced, putting down the receiver. 'They are all very pleasant and helpful at the Place Beauvau*. But they seem to be as much in the dark as we are. I'd better go to Paris.'

He glanced at the clock.

'I've missed the overnight express. If I take the first train in the morning perhaps they'll have some news for me when I arrive.'

'Perhaps', Armand remarked, though not very convincingly. 'But what we must decide is what we tell Katharine. She'll have to know sooner or later and I'd hate her to hear from the newspapers.'

'One unknown Frenchman being kidnapped by a crowd of bandits is hardly likely to be headlines in rural Scotland,' Maxime answered drily.

'One never knows. But in any case, I don't think it's a risk we should take.'

'Perhaps I should go to Ardnakil and tell her myself,' Maxime suggested. 'Though after what happened at our last meeting, I wonder whether she'll even agree to see me.'

'Maxime', Armand said gently. 'The two of you are under a terrible strain, and it's obvious that you're both very unhappy. Why don't you telephone Katharine and try to sort things out? Get her to come back to Le Moulin. She'll see everything differently when she's in her own home setting again.'

'Would she come?'

'You won't know until you try.'

*   *   *

Dr Anderson's expression was serious as he ushered Flora from Katharine's room and quietly closed the door behind him.

'Would you like me to go and sit with her?' Lavinia enquired, getting up from one of the spindly tapestry-covered sofas which lined the gallery walls.

'Perhaps, in a moment', the doctor demurred. 'I'd like to talk to you all first.'

Flora led the way back down the staircase and into the drawing-room where William was waiting.

'Mrs Montredon has obviously been under a great strain,' the doctor announced sitting down in the wing armchair which Flora offered him. 'I don't know what and she doesn't seem to want to tell me. Or perhaps she isn't capable of expressing it at the moment. But I think it's very deep-rooted. Possibly even goes back many years.'

He crossed his legs and leant back, his eyes on the ceiling.

'Whatever it is, if we don't somehow get to the bottom of it I'm afraid she is heading for a complete breakdown.'

Lavinia carefully examined her hands. And only their slow clenching and unclenching betrayed her emotion.

'What can we do doctor?' William enquired.

'For the moment there is not a great deal we *can* do. A little sedation to help her to relax. And then we must try to get her to verbalise what is causing her such anguish.'

He looked across at Lady Flora.

'I would suggest temporary hospitalisation.'

'That won't be necessary,' Flora cut in quickly. 'If Katharine is under such a terrible strain it is here where she will find healing and peace.'

'Of course Lady Flora,' he acquiesced. 'Just as long as you realise that it *is* an illness.'

'I think we all understand that doctor,' William put in. 'And, with your help I am sure we shall win through.'

As the doctor left the telephone rang.

'It is for Mrs Montredon, milady,' Sheana announced.

With a helpless glance in William's direction Flora picked up the receiver.

'Flora', Maxime's voice came down the line. 'How is Katharine?'

'How did you know?' Flora gasped, taken back.

'Know what?' he enquired.

Flora realised that in her disarray she had spoken without thinking. And she didn't know how to continue.

'Flora', Maxime said anxiously. 'Is something the matter with Katharine?'

'Katharine is not very well at the moment,' she answered guardedly. 'She's sleeping and I'd rather not disturb her.'

'But what *is* it?' Maxime demanded.

'Oh Maxime,' Flora cried. 'I don't know what to say. Dr Anderson has just left. He thinks Katharine is on the verge of a complete breakdown.'

Maxime abruptly sat down.

'I'll be there tomorrow,' he said tightly.

'Maxime I don't think that is a very good idea,' Flora started to protest.

But Maxime had hung up.

* * *

When the taxi drew up at the house the following evening Maxime jumped out and raced through the open door. From the lighted drawing-room he heard voices and a burst of laughter. And he stood helplessly in the middle of the great hall, uncertain what to do.

As he stood there Flora, alerted by Sheana, came quickly through the drawing-room door and, running across the hall in her long gown threw her arms around his neck.

'Oh Maxime,' she cried. 'I'm not sure that this is a good idea.'

'Whatever do you mean?' he asked roughly. 'Where *is* Katharine?'

'She's in bed But she's still very weak. And terribly confused.'

Maxime turned quickly towards the stairs. But Flora laid a restraining hand on his arm.

'William is with her,' she said diffidently.

'William?'

'Ashley's father.'

Maxime stared hard at her for a moment. Then turning on his heel he ran up the wide staircase two at a time.

Katharine, lying on her back in the vast bed, looked smaller than ever. The evening shadows had clothed the room in misty pastel shades, but Maxime was able to make out a silver-haired man sitting beside his wife, her hand held lightly in his. As he tiptoed across the room, Katharine opened her eyes. But there was no recognition, no welcome, no warmth in them. It seemed that the golden lights which so fascinated him had been extinguished for ever.

Hearing him approach, William gently released Katharine's hand, and standing up held out his own.

'You must be Maxime,' he said softly.

He indicated the chair which he had just vacated.

'Come and sit beside her. I'm sure that now you are here Katharine will be able to tell you what is worrying her.'

Tentatively Maxime sat down and reached for his wife's hand.

But a look of fear leapt into her eyes and she drew away.

'No,' she cried, 'no.'

Plunging her head into the pillow she clutched the bedclothes tightly round her.

'William,' she cried, her voice a terrified plea. 'Don't let him touch me. Send him away.'

Maxime, stunned, abruptly rose to his feet, the chair crashing to the floor as he did so.

'What have you done to her?' he accused, turning his blazing eyes on William.

William came towards him and put a hand on his shoulder. But Maxime shrugged him off.

'What have you *said*?'

His body was shaking with rage. And he clenched his fists tightly at his side to prevent him hitting the older man.

William looked at him calmly and beneath his gaze Maxime's anger slowly defused. Distractedly picking up the chair, he sat wearily down on it and thrust his head in his hands.

William stood beside him, saying nothing. But his lips moved wordlessly as he waited for the younger man to regain control. At last Maxime raised his head. And their eyes met.

'I'm sorry', he whispered hoarsely. 'I don't know what came over me.'

'It was a perfectly natural reaction.'

Taking Maxime's arm William gently urged him from the chair. As they walked slowly towards the door Maxime glanced back. But all he could see was the huddled shape of Katharine's body beneath the bedclothes.

'What has *happened*?' he asked despairingly, as William closed the door behind them.

'We don't know', the older man replied as they walked back along the gallery. 'Katharine received a telephone call from her uncle which seems to have upset her terribly.'

'When?' Maxime barked.

'It must have been yesterday afternoon.'

Maxime relaxed. So Armand had not contacted Katharine since he left. She didn't know about Xavier.

'Katharine collapsed and was very confused afterwards. The doctor wanted to hospitalise her. Said she was heading for a complete breakdown and he needed to find out what was worrying her.'

Maxime said nothing. His tired mind almost unable to take in this last episode in the series of crushing events.

'I'll take her home,' he said at last, entering the deserted library and collapsing on the sofa.

'Do you think that wise,' William queried. 'In view of her reaction?'

Maxime shrugged.

'Flora refused to have Katharine hospitalised. She is quite willing to have her nursed here. And Lavinia and I will stay as long as is necessary.'

'But she's my wife,' Maxime burst out angrily. 'You all seem to be forgetting that.'

'We're not forgetting,' William said gently. 'And you must do as you think best. But, if you could leave her here until she feels stronger . . .'

Maxime's lips tightened.

'Stay a few days,' William went on calmly. 'Perhaps seeing you was a shock. Tomorrow she may feel differently. Don't take any hasty decisions.'

Maxime got to his feet. A terrible feeling of hopelessness creeping over him. And he didn't know where to go from here.

Apart from a quick call to the Ministry of Interior on his way through Paris and messages left for people who might be able to intervene he had not been able to do anything about his father-in-law's kidnapping. He knew that if Katharine recovered sufficiently to return home it would not be within the next few days. And in the meantime Xavier's plight was in abeyance.

Deflated and empty he slid helplessly back onto the sofa.

'You are carrying a great burden Maxime,' William said. 'And it is not only Katharine.'

Maxime had the impression that the older man was looking straight into his soul. He slowly raised his head and as their eyes met Maxime saw the compassion mirrored in William's gaze. It was as if a rushing torrent of pain which had been building up inside him suddenly broke its banks and overflowed leaving behind an overwhelming sense of relief.

And he instinctively knew that he could trust William.

'My poor dear children', William murmured, using the same words Armand had used, when he heard Maxime's story. 'Katharine does not need this on top of everything else.'

He pursed his lips.

'Since you asked for my advice, Maxime, I will give it to you. For the moment Katharine must not know what has happened to her father. Leave her here to recover while you return to Paris and try to sort out this drama. If you take her home now she is bound to find out about the kidnapping. And in her present state such a shock might finally break her.'

Maxime sat staring blankly at the shining parquet floor, his hands hanging loosely between his knees.

'The decision is yours of course,' William ended. 'But I don't think Katharine would forgive you if you didn't do everything in your power to have her father released.'

Maxime rose to his feet, every bone in his body aching with fatigue.

'You're right,' he said flatly.

Then he turned and smiled grimly at the older man.

'Doesn't it seem strange to you that it should be my wife's ex-father-in-law who has stepped in to advise me?'

William's eyes met his.

'It's not strange at all. Think of me as your friend Maxime. I wrote to Katharine when she told me of your engagement that if she loved you, you must be a wonderful man. I trusted her judgement then. And I see now that I was right to do so. Let us fight this attack of the devil together.'

Startled, Maxime drew back.

'God wants only what is good for us,' William said softly. 'And with his help, we shall win.'

Maxime looked away, embarrassed.

Then his eyes turned back to the serene old man standing before him. He remembered Zag, Armand, Katharine as she had been in the years following the twins' birth. And he shook his head in bewilderment. They all shared this faith in God. This strange intimacy with Jesus. And he wondered. Perhaps there was something in religion after all which had so far eluded him. Then suddenly the sight of his wife's pathetic form beneath the bedclothes, the look of horror in her eyes as he approached her, her terrified plea all flashed before him. And his face hardened.

'God doesn't seem to be very near to Katharine at the moment,' he remarked, avoiding William's penetrating eyes.

For a few seconds William remained silent.

'If that's the case', he said at last. 'It is not God who has moved.'

And with a final affectionate pat on Maxime's shoulder he left the room.

Chapter
16

Hearing the heavy door creak open, Xavier rolled weakly onto his side. He had no idea how long he had been lying on the filthy mattress alternately sweating and shivering in the semi-darkness of that claustrophobic cellar.

On the first morning he had tried with an edge of the chain which manacled his hands to scratch a sign in the damp earth to give him some idea of the passing days. But as the fever increased he became disorientated and lost all sense of time or place. Opening his eyes with difficulty, the blood pounding in his head, he saw Khaled glaring down at him. But when he struggled to rise, the Arab raised his foot and kicked him back onto the mattress.

'So infidel,' he jeered. 'Your God didn't come down from his cross to save you.'

He spat contemptuously at his prisoner.

And once again his maniacal laugh echoed round the damp walls.

As Xavier attempted to wipe the spittle from his face, Khaled bent down and slapped him viciously across his dry cracked lips.

'Well my friend, what have you to say for yourself?'

Xavier tried to look him in the eye. But the hatred in the other's dark gaze made him turn away.

'I don't understand Khaled,' he said hoarsely. 'But do with me as you wish.'

Khaled's lips turned downwards in a sneer.

'We will my friend. We will. But not yet.'

Once again he bent down. His face close to his captive's.

'You will not escape', he goaded. 'And neither will your countrymen. We will hound you ugly French swine from our land . . . Those of you who are still left alive.'

He crossed his arms in the folds of his djellabah, his mouth a hard slit in his bony face.

'Death would be a relief now wouldn't it?'

Lifting his forefinger he drew it slowly across his throat.

'Why should we give you that relief? We want to see you suffer and grovel and beg for mercy. But you will not receive it.'

Turning to the man standing behind him, he roughly pushed him forward.

'Treat him', he ordered. 'I want him kept alive for as long as it suits me.'

The man knelt beside Xavier. But he avoided the prisoner's eyes. For a split second Xavier drew back as the Arab produced from the folds of his djellabah a powder which he mixed with the remains of the fetid water in the mug beside his mattress. Then he relaxed. Whatever it was he was being forced to drink was certainly not poison. Khaled in his hatred would not grant him a merciful release.

As the man rose Khaled clapped his hands imperiously and the door once again creaked open. Xavier saw his masked jailer standing outside, a machine gun at the ready. With a final vicious kick at Xavier's aching chest Khaled swept from the room. The Arab scuttling behind him half-turned as they reached the door. And Xavier saw pity in his liquid brown eyes.

*　　*　　*

'Good-morning boys,' Flora said brightly, walking unex-
pectedly into the nursery as they were finishing breakfast.
'What are the plans for today?'

'Papa *still* hasn't taken me shrimping,' Jehan groused.

'I'm sure he will very soon,' Flora soothed. 'But there
aren't any shrimps in the lake, you'll have to wait till you
go to the seaside.'

Jehan opened his mouth to complain but Janet silenced
him with a glance. She sensed that Flora had something
to say to Maxime who, since his arrival, had taken to
breakfasting with his sons.

'Come along now all of you,' she said firmly, 'and we'll
make plans.'

As the boys trooped from the room Maxime walked
over to his hostess.

'Dr Anderson is with Katharine,' Flora said softly.
'Perhaps you'd like to go and see him.'

Maxime sighed. It was now two days since his arrival
and Katharine's attitude towards him had not changed.
Each time he tried to talk to her she turned away as if
overcome by fear. And he didn't understand. The only
person she wanted near her was William who sat beside
her bed hour after hour, saying nothing merely being
there as she stared bleakly out of the window.

'Give her time,' William said kindly. 'Sometimes in
such a crisis the best thing is to do nothing.'

'But for how long?' Maxime asked desperately, thoughts
of Xavier perpetually in his mind. 'I really have to get
back and see what I can do about my father-in-law. Here
I feel helpless.'

He had shrugged hopelessly.

'In more ways than one.'

'Then why don't you go back?' William had suggested
the previous evening after another fruitless attempt on
Maxime's part to communicate with his wife.

'But will anyone *ever* find out what is troubling her?' Maxime agonised.

'Of course we will,' William replied calmly. 'But one can't unravel the problems of many years in a few days.'

Maxime compressed his lips. He was afraid that with time and no apparent action being taken Katharine's state would worsen and become chronic. And as it had done on the night the twins were born, his heart contracted with fear.

'I can't bear the thought of losing her,' he said brokenly.

'You won't lose her', William soothed. 'I promise you.'

Maxime looked up and met the old man's tranquil eyes. But he had not been convinced. Now it seemed that he had come to a crossroads. The point where a decision had to be taken.

Straightening his shoulders, bracing himself for whatever lay ahead, Maxime knocked and entered the bedroom.

The doctor looked up. But before Maxime could introduce himself Katharine drew away.

'Don't let him touch me,' she whispered pitifully. 'Tell him to go away.'

The doctor raised his eyes enquiringly as Maxime quickly took the two steps which divided him from his wife.

'Katharine,' he pleaded, kneeling at her bedside. '*Darling*, what is it? Can't you tell me?'

But she huddled into an even smaller ball, her back towards him as she attempted to shield herself.

'No, no,' she cried. 'Send him away.'

The doctor gently touched his shoulder.

'I think it would be best if you left your wife for the time being. I'll see you downstairs in a few minutes.'

Grimly Maxime rose to his feet and without a backward glance left the room.

* * *

'And you can give no explanation at all for Mrs Montredon's behaviour?' Dr Anderson enquired, as they sat together in the morning-room.

'None,' Maxime answered grimly. 'I've told you all I know. The difficulties my wife has had since our youngest son's birth. But this . . .'

Once again he gave a helpless shrug.

'The last time I saw her she was perfectly normal.'

'But something must have happened in between,' the doctor probed.

'Obviously. But what?'

The tense uneasy silence which followed was broken by Sheana coming to announce that there was a call from France for Mr Montredon.

Excusing himself, Maxime rushed to the telephone.

* * *

'Have you read the newspapers?' Armand enquired.

His voice was querulous.

'No. What's happened?'

'The terrorists have issued an ultimatum. If a number of dangerous criminals inprisoned in Algiers are not released within a week Xavier will be executed.'

Maxime quickly drew in his breath.

'I'm sorry Maxime,' Armand continued. 'But I don't know what to do.'

'There's nothing you *can* do,' Maxime replied kindly his heart going out to his great-uncle. At ninety years of age he deserved a little peace.

'Do you know when you will be back?'

'I'll come straight away.'

'My dear boy,' Armand apologised. 'I didn't even ask about Katharine. Do forgive me. How is she? And the boys?'

'Everyone's fine,' Maxime lied. 'Katharine doesn't know anything and up here she's protected. So I'll persuade her to stay on for a while until we get things straightened out.

He glanced at his watch.

'With a bit of luck I may be able to get a plane from Edinburgh to Paris. I'll telephone you as soon as I arrive.'

Armand gave a great sigh of relief. He felt helpless in the face of this latest disaster.

'Flora,' Maxime said walking into the drawing-room where his hostess was sitting at the piano playing her favourite Chopin. 'I have to leave I'm afraid. As you've so kindly offered to keep Katharine I'd rather she stayed here.'

He briefly outlined the reason for Armand's call.

'Poor Maxime,' Flora exclaimed. 'Of *course* Katharine can stay with us. And the boys as well. We'd be delighted to have them.'

'No,' he interrupted. 'Nanny Moffatt will be back in two days' time from her holiday. I'd like her to bring the boys home. They need to be in their own surroundings. Léon especially seems perturbed by all these comings and goings.'

Flora nodded and wisely didn't insist.

'It might be better if they don't visit Katharine before they leave,' Maxime hesitated. 'I don't want them to see her as she is at the moment.'

'As you wish Maxime,' Flora remarked.

Though she was not entirely sure that Maxime was right.

'And now', she said briskly, 'planes from Edinburgh.'

Maxime smiled to himself. In spite of her vague appearance, there was a very practical side to Flora.

* * *

'So my friend', Khaled jeered, '*my Christian brother.*'

He threw back his head, his pointed black beard giving him a Mephistophelian look as the diabolical bellow broke from his lips once again. But this time it was more menacing. There was little resembling laughter in the sinister throaty screech.

'The time has perhaps come . . . yes?'

Raising one heavy dark eyebrow cynically in Xavier's direction he thoughtfully stroked his beard. Then suddenly his mood changed. A nasty glint appeared in his eyes as he lunged forward with his foot.

'Answer me scum,' he roared. 'And stand up when I speak to you.'

Xavier raised his eyes still showing the ravages of fever in his haggard face and struggled to his feet.

'If you say so Khaled,' he sighed.

'I do say so,' the other screamed, stamping his feet in frustration, incensed at his prisoner's calm.

He waved his arms wildly at the two masked men who had entered the cell with him, and they scuttled terrified to his side.

'Away with him,' he roared. 'You'll soon be grovelling, Frenchman, begging for mercy.'

Xavier looked at him. But the Arab merely raised his hand and brought it crashing down across his lips. As the blood spurted forth Xavier tried to stem it. But he was roughly seized by his two armed escorts and pushed out of the cell into the narrow dark tunnel outside.

So, Khaled mocked triumphantly after the blindfold had been removed from Xavier's eyes.

The place to which he had been brought was equally infested, equally dark and damp but smaller and the earth ceiling was low. Xavier had the feeling that it might at any minute cave in on them. Through a long funnel set in a corner he caught a glimpse of an iron grill and in the distance heard the swish of robes and the pad of sandalled feet passing over it. And he knew that he had been brought to one of the many underground passages criss-crossing the old city. An impossible place to find. And an even more impossible place to escape from. The greasy funnel was small in diameter and at least two metres in length. Even a monkey wouldn't have been able to scramble through it.

He smiled sadly to himself. So this is where he was to meet his Maker.

He had no regrets for himself. But thoughts of Katharine and his grandsons went through his mind. And he prayed that they might be spared the sordid details of his end. In the fleeting moments when he realised that his execution and preceding torture were being prepared, memories of his past life floated through his mind.

'Thank you Lord', he breathed, 'for this short time for reflection. Forgive me for the hurt I caused Rowena and Katharine. Watch over Katharine now that I shall no longer be able to, and reveal yourself to Maxime so that they may have the joy of worshipping you together.'

He looked across at Khaled who was striding agitatedly up and down the small cell, giving occasional impatient shrieks as if the arrangements were not being carried out fast enough. And he found it difficult to forgive him.

'Father', he breathed. 'Help me. Pour into my heart the compassion your son showed to his executioners. Give

186

me *his* love for these men. And the courage and the grace to forgive . . . and to ask your forgiveness for them.'

Seeing Xavier's lips move Khaled suddenly stopped and his shaggy black brows drew together in a frown. Then that devilish smile twisted his lips.

'So infidel,' he sneered. 'You still believe in your God?'

He pulled a long curved knife out of his belt, and pointed it in Xavier's face.

'You *still* think he can save you?'

He thrust his head forward until it almost touched his prisoner's, the knife held menacingly in his hand. Xavier could feel his fetid breath on his face.

'Yes?' he jeered.

'Yes,' Xavier answered quietly. 'I still believe he can save me.'

He looked straight into his captor's eyes.

'And he can save you too Khaled.'

At that Khaled's face turned dark with rage.

'Dog', he spat. 'Infidel, scum.'

He whirled his knife round his head, the blade glinting terrifyingly in the dim light.

'Enough', he screeched. 'Take him.'

The two masked men seized Xavier and one put an arm around his throat jerking his head back.

Khaled advanced towards him, the knife in his hands. He came face to face with Xavier then slowly manoeuvred his way round him. Xavier could feel his throat constricting, his breath escaping with difficulty.

'On your knees Frenchman,' Khaled shrieked triumphantly. 'Beg for mercy. Beg for your life like the rest of your compatriots who have trampled over our country for 130 years and made us grovel will soon be doing. None will be spared.'

The two men thrust Xavier roughly to his knees on the hard earth floor.

'Beg', Khaled screeched. 'Beg infidel. Call on your God. The God who saves.'

Once again the ear-splitting shriek distorted his face as he continued his macabre dance round and round, the knife quivering in his hand.

Suddenly he stopped and backed away. Then with slow deliberate steps his eyes never leaving Xavier's haggard face, he walked towards him.

Jerking his head at the man holding Xavier's throat so that he slightly released his hold Khaled rushed at his prisoner.

'Allah will not be mocked,' he screamed. 'And neither will my people. We will no longer be the Frenchman's slave. The time has come for the FLN to take over power and the defeated French to scuttle home like rats.'

His face distorted with hatred and rage, twisted almost beyond human recognition into a terrifying grimace.

'Or return in their coffins!'

Khaled was now completely out of control, his body convoluting and shaking as he executed his macabre sword dance.

'Death to the French colonist pig!' he hollered maniacally. 'Vive l'Algérie libre.'

And with a blood-curdling yell he brought the sharp blade down against Xavier's throat.

Chapter
17

'I'm at my wit's end,' Maxime sighed wearily walking into Armand's study.

Armand rose and took his arm.

'I can see that my boy. Let's sit on the terrace and have a drink.'

'I've tried every avenue I can think of,' Maxime went on, collapsing into a wicker chair. 'But I've come to a dead end. Everyone is very polite and concerned. But . . . for political reasons they can't get too involved.'

'So your original idea of trying to buy Xavier's freedom hasn't worked?'

Maxime shook his head.

'The Ministry of Interior people have no idea where he is . . . or even if he's still alive. Though they say they're doing everything they can to find out.'

Armand thoughtfully stroked his chin.

'What we need', he reflected, 'is an influential Arab, preferably a businessman who has contacts everywhere. If we knew someone like that I think we might be able to get somewhere.'

'But we don't do we?' Maxime answered miserably.

At that moment the telephone rang in Armand's study. Excusing himself, he left to answer it.

Maxime picked up one of Toinette's glossy magazines lying on the table and idly flicked through the pages. Suddenly he stopped, letting out a low whistle.

'I think we've found what we're looking for,' he breathed, handing Armand the magazine as he walked back into the room.

Armand adjusted his reading glasses, then frowned at the full-length picture of a smiling young woman on the arm of a thick-set older man.

'My goodness gracious,' he exclaimed incredulously. 'Marie-Céleste!'

'Exactly,' Maxime cut in jubilantly. 'And the man proudly escorting her from the Casino at Deauville is a well-known Arab millionaire financier. You must have heard of him.'

'Indeed I have,' Armand replied slowly. 'Of rather dubious reputation I believe.'

'Just the person we want.'

'But isn't he something to do with the Mafia?'

'I wouldn't be at all surprised. But . . . set a thief to catch a thief.'

'I very much doubt whether we'd have the sort of money *he'd* be interested in,' Armand remarked.

'Perhaps not. But he's got Marie-Céleste. Or, knowing her, *she's* got him. *That's* what we've got to work on.'

Armand thoughtfully put the magazine back on the table and a smile broke across his aristocratic face sending small parallel lines rippling out in every direction.

'Do you think she *would* help?' he enquired doubtfully.

'As you said to me when I hesitated about going to Scotland to see Katharine,' Maxime grinned, 'I won't know until I try. And I intend to try this very minute.'

When Maxime finally tracked down his ex-wife she was staying in a sumptuous villa in Antibes.

'Max *darling*,' she trilled, 'how wonderful to hear from you. Does this mean that you have at last ditched your pathetic little concubine and are coming to join your lawful wedded wife?'

But Maxime ignored her taunt.

'Marie-Céleste,' he said urgently. 'I need your help.'

'Isn't that what wives are for sweetie,' she cooed.

'I saw a photo of you taken with . . .'

'Oh yes darling. Wasn't it too divine. Are you in financial difficulties? I'm *sure* Bachir would help.'

She paused then added archly.

'If *I* asked him of course.'

'It's not financial,' he said desperately. 'You've no doubt heard that Comte Xavier de Montval has been kidnapped by Arab fanatics?'

'I did hear something angel,' she replied vaguely. 'Too dreary for words.'

'*That's* where I need your help,' Maxime ploughed on. 'The Ministry of Interior don't seem to be able to do anything to obtain his release. I'm looking for an influential Arab businessman to act as go-between . . . And your friend would be the ideal person.'

'I'm sure he would,' Marie-Céleste drawled. 'But darling, *why* do you want to get entangled with all these tedious do-gooders who can't mind their own business?'

'Because', Maxime said tightly, 'Xavier de Montval happens to be my father-in-law.'

'Your *what?*' Marie-Céleste spluttered.

Her voice had changed and become hard and metallic. Gone were the soft sultry tones. There was a slight pause. Then suddenly Marie-Céleste laughed.

'Of course I'll help you Maxime darling,' she rippled on. 'But naturally I shall want something in return.'

'Just say what it is.'

There was another slight pause.

'You,' his ex-wife breathed softly.

Taken off his guard Maxime mentally reeled.

'Marie-Céleste,' he said sharply, 'this isn't a joke.'

'I'm not joking,' she cut in.

'What is it you *really* want?'

'I want to be Madame Montredon de la Livère again.'
She paused dramatically.

'The *only* Madame Montredon de la Livère. And hold my salon at your mother's house on the Ile St Louis.'

'The house has been sold,' he interrupted curtly.

'It can be bought back,' she replied, her voice like icy silver. 'Every man has his price . . . even *you* Maxime.'

'Marie-Céleste,' he pleaded. 'You know what you're asking is impossible.'

'Then so is your request.'

'I don't understand,' he said desperately. 'What is this pantomine all about . . .'

'It's not a pantomine Maxime.'

'Of course it is. You don't love me . . . I doubt whether you ever did.'

'Who's talking about love?' she put in coolly.

'But if you want me back . . .'

'My dear Maxime,' she said silkily. 'Love has nothing to do with it. I find you irresistible at the moment. *Unbelievably* sexy . . . And even more so since you rejected me.'

She took a deep breath and whispered sultrily.

'I want you in my bed darling. Officially.'

Marie-Céleste paused dramatically.

'*And I want that intruder out . . .*'

'What you ask is impossible.'

'Then what you ask is *also* impossible,' she replied in syrupy tones.

Maxime replaced the receiver and went back to join Armand just as Jeanne announced that dinner was served.

'It's no use,' he said wearily as they walked together towards the dining room.

Then suddenly another idea hit him.

'Antoine has always had some sort of influence on his sister,' he said thoughtfully. 'He was very helpful when Marie-Céleste returned and I was sorting out the flat business in Paris. Maybe he could help again? I could always ask him.'

'Ask by all means', Armand replied, sitting down at the head of the table and carefully smoothing his table napkin across his lap. 'But, knowing Marie-Céleste, I wouldn't hold out any great hopes if I were you.'

* * *

Katharine opened her eyes and looked slowly round the room. For a few seconds she felt confused, wondering where she was. All the familiar objects which surrounded her in her bedroom at Le Moulin were missing. Then, as her gaze gradually focused she remembered. And her eyes fell on the photograph of her sons on her bedside table. Picking it up, her face softened.

There was a knock on the door and William walked in.

'You haven't met my sons, have you?' Katharine smiled, replacing the photograph.

'Indeed I have,' William replied warmly, drawing up a chair and sitting down beside her. 'They're a splendid bunch.'

Katharine's face glowed.

'Jehan and I are firm friends.'

William leant towards her, his blue eyes twinkling.

'I have a feeling he's adopted me as his missing twin. He's even invited me to live with you forever at Le Moulin.'

Katharine joined in his laughter, all her former irritation at Jehan's perpetual opposition to everything melting in a sudden rush of tenderness for them all.

William was encouraged. It was the first time he had heard her really laugh since he arrived.

'They'll be wondering what has happened to me,' she murmured. 'I must have been out of action for several days.'

William looked at her sharply.

It was over a month since Katharine had collapsed. And he realised that the prescribed sedation had been heavier than they had believed.

Katharine stretched luxuriously and glanced at the small carriage clock on her bedside table.

'I expect they're out riding now, but if I get up in about an hour I could go to the nursery and see them before lunch.'

Her wan face dimpled with pleasure at the thought.

'There's no need to worry about the boys,' William reassured her. 'Your husband came and took them back home.'

At his words something clicked in Katharine's brain. She remembered their last meeting . . . and Maxime's angry parting words.

'Go where you like . . . but my sons remain with me.'

'Maxime . . . took the boys . . . back to Le Moulin?' she gasped.

Not understanding, William nodded.

Katharine gaped at him in stupefaction, the laughter draining from her face, her eyes widening with fear as the events of that Sunday afternoon over a month before rushed back to her mind. Armand's evasive telephone call . . . and now William's revelation.

So Maxime had carried out both his parting threats.

He had joined Marie-Céleste in Paris . . . and had now claimed his sons.

'Oh . . . *No*.'

There was a light tap on the door and Dr Anderson arrived on his routine visit.

Seeing Katharine's ashen face, the terrified look in her eyes he raised his eyebrows enquiringly at William. But William could only shake his head in bewilderment. Katharine's abrupt change of mood was an enigma to him.

The doctor jerked his head towards the bedroom door.

'What happened?' he frowned, as he and William walked together down the long gallery. Mrs Montredon has been so much better lately. I was even able to drastically reduce her medication.'

William shrugged his shoulders in a helpless gesture.

'We don't seem to be getting anywhere,' the doctor sighed as they joined Flora and Lavinia in the drawing-room. It's one step forwards and three steps backwards. The month of heavy sedation has obviously benefited Mrs Montredon physically and I really thought she was on the road to recovery. But after what happened this morning, I realise that mentally she's still very fragile'

He scratched his balding head in bewilderment.

'And you can give absolutely no explanation for what triggered this latest set-back?'

'None at all,' William answered miserably.

Dr Anderson sighed.

'Well unless someone can get her to say what is worrying her, then I see no other solution but to have her hospitalised.'

'Give it another few days,' William pleaded. 'I'm sure we can get to the bottom of this with patience.'

'It's been over a *month* Canon,' the doctor protested.

He got up and walked slowly towards the door.

'I can't force hospitalisation but . . . frankly I don't

want to take the responsibility for what might happen
if something isn't done . . . and done soon.'

*   *   *

Contacting Marie-Céleste's brother was not as simple
as Maxime had imagined. He was on holiday cruising
round the Greek islands with his young family. When he
finally did manage to get hold of him Antoine was most
sympathetic. But, like Armand, not overly hopeful.

'I'll do my best Maxime,' he said warmly. 'However,
you know my sister isn't the easiest of people to deal
with. And when she's got an idea in her head . . .'

'But *why*,' Maxime agonised. 'Why this sudden interest in me?'

'I don't think she'd have given you a second thought if
you hadn't found happiness with someone else. She can't
bear to think that another woman has succeeded where
she failed.'

Antoine sighed.

'I'm afraid she's abysmally selfish. Always has been.
And now she's besotted with this money and power
game, that's why she's got herself entangled with that
awful man. He's as rich as Croesus but old enough to be
her father. Anyway, leave it to me. I'll get back to you as
soon as I have anything to report.'

It was the end of September before Antoine rang
again. In the meantime, everything seemed to stagnate
as far as Xavier was concerned. It was obvious that the
Ministry of Interior was working on the case, but no
concrete evidence could be produced that Xavier was
still alive. And Maxime fumed with impatience as the
days dragged by.

'I'm afraid I've reached a deadlock,' Antoine announced
glumly when he finally telephoned.

He paused.

'I suppose you couldn't play her game?'

'What do you mean?'

There was an awkward silence. Antoine seemed embarassed.

'Well, go along with her request.'

'You mean go to *bed* with her?'

'Perhaps not that far but . . . Well frankly Maxime if you want to get her to do anything at all, you'll have to meet her. And see where it goes from there.'

He paused again.

'If you explained the situation to your wife I'm sure she'd understand. After all, it's her father's life which is at stake.'

'I see, yes, well thank you Antoine.'

'I'm sorry that I haven't been able to pull off anything Max. But . . . you know your ex-wife.'

Maxime replaced the receiver and sank into the chair by the telephone. Where on earth did he go from here? Nothing appeared to be happening officially and Marie-Céleste's paramour was his only slight hope.

He gave a sardonic smile. Wasn't it in a *Tale of Two Cities* that a man had given up his life for his friend?

'Looks as if I'm being called upon to do the same,' Maxime remarked grimly. 'Only it won't be my life I'm giving up, it will be my *wife* . . . and my sons as well if Katharine finds out.'

* * *

Xavier felt the cold steel against his throat and braced himself for the quick slash which would end his life.

But Khaled did not move.

Looking up he saw his executioner towering motionless above him. Khaled smirked and slowly drew the knife across his taut throat. But no blood spurted out. And Xavier realised that this was all part of the torture. Khaled had no intention of killing him yet. He was going to play with him as a cat plays with a mouse, going through the motions of cutting his throat without actually slicing through his jugular vein. As he watched, the Arab drew the knife slowly back and forth so that his prisoner felt the hard steel but was denied the relief of death.

Xavier's knees were beginning to ache, but he dared not move.

'*Beg* infidel,' Khaled grated, removing the knife and raising it as if to make one quick final slash. 'Beg for mercy.'

But Xavier made no reply.

'Beg,' he screeched.

Xavier raised his eyes and looked at him.

'You know I never will Khaled,' he replied quietly.

The Arab's face darkened with rage. Howling like a dervish he swung the knife round his head then brought it down with a swift final blow. But just as the blade touched Xavier's throat he stopped. Beside himself with fury he snatched it away, then lunging forward aimed a vicious kick at his prisoner's chest. The blow sent not only Xavier but the masked men holding him reeling.

Khaled angrily thrust the knife back into his belt.

'Why should I kill you?' he screamed. 'A swift death is too good for a Frenchman.'

Turning on his heel he waved his arm imperiously at the two men hastily scrambling to their feet. And bellowing for the door to be opened swept through it without a backward glance.

Xavier picked himself up and looked around at his new surroundings. If possible, the room was grimmer than the one he had left. Smaller, more cramped, with no filthy mattress on which to lie. Sighing, he rubbed his bruised knees and wrapping his cloak round his now emaciated body he attempted to stretch his weary limbs. As he lay down on the hard earth a large black rat scuttled out from a corner, followed by another. They raced each other across his bare legs.

Speculating on how long it would be before Khaled returned to continue his torture, Xavier fell into a troubled sleep.

* * *

'Maxime darling, I'd *love* to meet you,' Marie-Céleste gushed. 'We're leaving with some too adorable friends of Bachir's on his yacht for a Carribean cruise next week but . . . if you'd like to join me in Nice beforehand. Why don't we meet at the Negresco* tomorrow evening?'

Maxime gritted his teeth as he replaced the receiver. The whole business was utterly distasteful to him. But he was desperate. News from Ardnakil was not as promising as he had hoped. It was now over a month since he had left, and he wondered whether it would not have been better to have brought Katharine home.

He sighed. Perhaps this was not the moment. And at least at Ardnakil she was shielded from the drama surrounding her father.

But in the end his journey to Nice proved fruitless. Marie-Céleste was adamant in her demands. And Maxime was unable to meet them.

'Bachir is the man you need', she said smoothly. 'And I'm the woman in his life at the moment.'

She smiled provocatively.

'I could get him to intervene if I wished.'

'Then why won't you?' he pleaded.

'So that you can live happily ever after? Come come

199

Maxie darling you surely don't *still* believe in the tooth fairy?'

'Then there is nothing more to be said.'

'That's where you're wrong,' she replied, her sultry voice tinged with steel. 'There is *one* more thing.'

Marie-Céleste paused and carefully inserted a black turkish cigarette into her ruby-studded holder.

'I can get Bachir to do anything I wish. To act for you . . . or *against* you. Had you thought of that?'

She glanced at him from beneath half-closed lids.

'What do you mean?'

'You want this man released . . .'

She raised her eyes and looked straight at him, casually blowing smoke rings into the scented air.

'I can make sure he is *not* released.'

'Marie-Céleste', Maxime broke in desperately, leaning forward and forcing her to look at him. 'You wouldn't do that.'

'Wouldn't I?' she smiled tantalisingly. 'Just watch me.'

Marie-Céleste made an almost imperceptible movement with her head and a man moved stealthily out of the shadows.

Turning her brilliant emerald eyes full upon Maxime, she placed her hand on his, smiling bewitchingly. Then playfully blew a cloud of smoke in his face.

It was at that moment, unnoticed by Maxime, that a camera silently clicked.

* * *

William walked into Katharine's bedroom determined to get to the bottom of her problem.

'How are you feeling?' he asked.

She smiled wanly at him.

'A fraud.'

'You're not a fraud', he answered quietly. 'You're just a very unhappy woman.'

William took her hand and idly turned it over.

'It is now more than a month since you collapsed, and you still refuse to say what upset you. You may not remember but when you came round you relived the day Lawrence brought you news of Ashley's death. You were crying out that he had made a mistake and Ashley was not dead.'

Katharine's eyes widened with surprise. And he saw that she had no recollection at all.

'We thought all that was behind you. That you had come to terms with what happened during the war. But . . . perhaps we've been mistaken.'

His blue eyes rested on her.

'I've met your husband,' William went on. 'Maxime's a fine man, who loves you dearly. He left everything and rushed here as soon as he heard you'd collapsed. But you refused even to speak to him.'

Katharine's brows drew together in a puzzled frown. And William realised that because of the heavy sedation the past month was nothing more than a hazy blur in her mind.

'Maxime's as bewildered as we all are by your present illness,' he said gently. 'Katharine, my dear, we've been through a great deal together in the past. Can't you tell me what's troubling you?'

For a moment Katharine's eyes left William's face and she hesitated. Then suddenly the emotions bottled inside her exploded, and she burst into tears.

'William,' she pleaded, 'what has happened to me? What has become of that woman who was able to weather every storm? When I lost my mother so tragically I survived. Then when Ashley was killed I picked up the pieces and carried on. Everyone thought I was so strong.'

She accepted the crisp white handkerchief William was holding out to her.

'I convinced myself that I was. But now I don't seem to be able to take anything any more. I'm like a game of skittles, collapsing at the first blow.'

She paused and her lips trembled.

'Can you recognise the woman you first met in '43? On the eve of her marriage to your son?'

William smiled.

'You're still that woman underneath, Katharine,' he said softly. 'The woman who took it on the chin. But it was wartime. Like many others who survived you haven't yet recovered from its terrible consequences. You thought the wounds were healed when you married Maxime. But the past can survive in the sub-conscious in many different disguises, and continue to cause pain. The series of shocks you have received since Léon's birth have compounded and revived your initial grief. Now at a time when you are most vulnerable, that pain has risen to the surface and crushed you.'

'I've made a complete mess of my life,' Katharine said flatly, as spears of rain began to beat against the window panes. 'And it's too late to start again now.'

There was no bitterness or anger in her voice. Just a terrible emptiness.

'It's never too late,' William replied. 'It's always possible to rise up from the pit of misery and despair.'

'Even when you feel you have been hit by a slab of concrete?' Katharine asked listlessly.

'Even then', he replied equably. 'But you have to want to.'

His light blue eyes seemed to bore right through her.

'I'm so bewildered William,' she pleaded. 'I need to know the truth.'

'About what?'

'About Maxime. His recent behaviour is a mystery.'

'I don't think we can ever know the whole truth about anyone. We just have to trust them and accept them as they are. As Jesus accepts us.'

'But how can I *ever* trust Maxime again . . . after what has happened?'

William smiled his slow sweet smile.

'What *has* happened Katharine?' he asked gently.

And he sat patiently waiting as, in fragmented portions the story came tumbling out.

'My dear child,' William said at last, wiping the tears streaming down her pale cheeks. 'My dear, dear child, what a chapter of misunderstandings.'

Katharine raised her eyes and looked at him.

'I'm sure there is some very simple explanation as to why Maxime did not go directly back home after he left here in August. But if you don't ask him you'll never find out.'

He thoughtfully stroked his chin.

'Doesn't he have a flat or a house in London?'

'Yes, in Sloane Street.'

'Perhaps he decided to break the journey and stay there. He must have been very tired after two nights in the train.'

'We *had* been meaning to go to London for some time', Katharine sniffed, giving her nose a final blow.

'That may well be the explanation. Why jump to the conclusion that he rushed off to Paris to be with his ex-wife?'

'But he said . . .'

'People say many things in anger,' William cut in.

Katharine sat for a few moments in thought. Then, a frown creased her brow.

'But the boys,' she pleaded. 'He threatened to take the boys from me . . . and he has.'

And once again the tears flowed.

'Maxime didn't take the boys from you,' William assured her. 'He took the boys home because that is where they belong. They *wanted* to go back to Le Moulin. And Maxime felt that all this coming and going was upsetting them. He was anxious to take *you* home as well, but the doctor persuaded him that it would be better for you to stay here until you felt stronger.'

He leant forward.

'If you telephone him Katharine I'm sure he will drop everything and come. Your husband loves you very much.'

Katharine took the sodden ball to which she had reduced William's handkerchief and rubbed it across her eyes.

'Thank you,' she whispered.

'If you really want to thank me, you'll telephone Maxime.'

She nodded.

'I will, I promise.'

William stood up and stretched his weary limbs. It had been a long struggle. But he felt that they had finally broken through.

'Why don't you have a rest and then come down to the drawing-room for tea?' he suggested. 'You can telephone Maxime at the same time.'

Katharine smiled and snuggled down on her pillows.

'Lavinia went back to Goudhurst to attend to some things which needed to be done,' he remarked, his hand on the door knob. 'At the bookstall on Euston station she bought a French magazine for you. It's on the bedside table.'

Reaching out a hand Katharine picked it up and began flicking idly through the pages.

Before the Dawn

As William walked down the long gallery towards the stairs a sharp cry rang out from Katharine's room.

'What is it?' he exclaimed, hurrying back. 'Katharine, what has happened?'

She turned to face him. Picking up the magazine lying open on the bed beside her Katharine pointed wordlessly to a large glossy photograph of a beautiful woman playfully blowing smoke into the face of the man sitting beside her, her hand clasped in his as he gazed into her eyes.

William groaned.

It was Maxime and Marie-Céleste!

Chapter
18

Maxime returned from Nice more discouraged than ever. His meeting with Marie-Céleste had not only proved fruitless but it had revealed a danger which he did not even dare to consider.

Entering the house an avalanche rocketed down the stairs as his sons and his dogs hurtled to meet him.

'Papa, *when* are we going shrimping?' Jehan demanded, his hands on his hips, defiance blazing in his blue eyes.

'Jehan I'm sorry,' Maxime apologised. 'I've let you down badly. But I promise you that very soon we *will* go. We'll all go back to Biarritz and shrimp till we drop.'

Satisfied, Jehan bumbled off.

'Did you bring Maman back with you?' Léon asked from behind a huge ginger cat purring in his arms as he sidled up to his father.

Maxime crouched down on his haunches in front of his small son.

'Not this time,' he said gently.

Léon's face fell and he turned away, quickly wiping his sleeve across his face as tears crept into his china-blue eyes.

'But it won't be long before I do,' Maxime went on hurriedly, in an attempt to reassure his woebe-gone son.

He rose to his feet and put his arm round Léon's drooping shoulders.

'Shall we go riding together?' he suggested.

But Léon shook his head and, escaping, limped back up the stairs.

Watching him go Maxime sighed. When was this nightmare going to end, he wondered. And when it did . . . He did not dare voice the fear uppermost in his mind, that terrifying 'if', what irreparable damage would it leave in its wake? His face hardened and he silently cursed Marie-Céleste, little realising that the trail of misery which she had begun was at that very moment creating even more havoc in his wife's bedroom at Ardnakil.

Crossing the hall and entering his study he dialled his ex-brother-in-law's number.

'I didn't say so at the time,' Antoine replied when Maxime told him of his meeting with Marie-Céleste. 'But knowing my sister, the possibility that it could work against you did occur to me.'

He paused.

'What a pity you told her that Montval was your father-in-law. Now I don't see what can be done. You know the saying, hell has no fury like a woman scorned.'

Maxime silently agreed with him. Marie-Céleste was certainly determined to extract her pound of flesh.

'I had thought when I saw that picture of you both that things were working out,' Antoine went on.

'What picture?' Maxime interrupted.

'Oh, didn't you see it? Génevieve noticed it in a magazine when she was at the hairdresser's and bought a copy. You and Marie-Céleste dining at the Negresco.'

Maxime groaned.

'But who on earth would want to photograph us?' he expostulated.

'Not *you*,' Antoine laughed. 'Marie-Céleste. Since she's had that Arab in tow she's perpetually being photographed. That's part of his attraction. She's always loved the limelight.'

'Thank goodness my wife's tucked away in Scotland,' Maxime said, his voice brittle. 'If she saw that . . . it would be playing right into Marie-Céleste's hands.'

'I never thought of that,' Antoine mused. 'I wouldn't mind betting my dear little sister organised the whole thing. She'll stop at nothing when she's thwarted.'

He paused, pursing his lips in thought.

'Hang on a minute', he went on reflectively. 'If we can deflect the limelight elsewhere for Marie-Céleste, she may take her claws out of you. Otherwise I fear she could carry out her threat to work against Montval's release.'

'I'm open to any suggestion,' Maxime answered wearily. 'Personally, I don't have any.'

'But I *have*,' Antoine cut in. 'You probably don't know this but when Marie-Céleste returned from Germany she had no intention of coming back to you . . . or even contacting you. She tried father first but he wouldn't have anything to do with her. He remarried after our mother's death, a much younger woman, and Gabrielle certainly didn't want a beautiful step-daughter almost her own age quering the pitch.

'Then she got hold of our Spanish grandmother, hoping no doubt to live in the lap of luxury in her ducal palace. But Abuela* told Marie-Céleste very bluntly what she thought of her. You were her last resort. She had been floating around Paris for some time before she contacted you and, contrary to what she may have told you, by no means penniless. Living it up at the Ritz as it happens.'

'Thanks,' Maxime put in drily, 'but I don't see the connection.'

'Our maternal grandmother always liked you Maxime.

She was furious when she heard that Marie-Céleste had left. If I can get her to take Marie-Céleste in, it might solve the problem.'

'But she's in Madrid.'

'Exactly. And Marie-Céleste loves Madrid . . . and all the pomp.'

Antoine paused, his brow rutted in thought.

'Look, I'll try to persuade Abuela to forgive Marie-Céleste's past and offer a home with her. Then she'd be off your hands for good.'

'But you say your grandmother doesn't want to have anything to do with her.'

'I think I can talk her into it. For your sake she might agree,' Antoine replied.

He paused.

'It wouldn't give you an introduction to her Arab boyfriend. But it *would* mean that the threat she'll delight in dangling over your head would be removed.'

'But what about the boyfriend?'

'Marie-Céleste would drop him like a hot cake if something better turned up,' Antoine replied confidently. 'I know my little sister. And in the meantime if I think of any strings I might be able to pull to help your father-in-law I'll get in touch immediately. But for the present, all I can do is try to remove the threat your ex-wife poses. And I think she's a threat which shouldn't be taken lightly.

Maxime replaced the receiver, his heart heavy. All his efforts had produced was a compromising photograph in a glossy magazine!

* * *

William frowned as he stared at the picture. He recognised Maxime and, in view of Katharine's reaction, he didn't need to be told who the woman was. Closing the magazine he placed it thoughtfully on the bedside table, then sat down and took Katharine's hand.

'Katharine my dear,' he soothed, shocked by her appearance. She seemed to have aged ten years in the past five minutes. 'I'm *sure* there's some innocent explanation.'

Katharine slowly turned to face him.

'How could there possibly be,' she said numbly. 'The evidence is there.'

Suddenly her face hardened.

'No William,' she rasped, abruptly sitting up in bed and pulling her hand from his grasp. 'I believed you because I wanted to believe you when you tried to whitewash Maxime, even though the evidence was there before my eyes. But I was too blind to see it.'

'I cannot give you an explanation for this picture Katharine,' William said slowly. 'But I am sure that there is one. I am also absolutely convinced that Maxime loves you.'

'You are too saint-like William,' she exploded. 'You never see any wrong in anyone.'

Katharine took a deep breath, her body tense and her eyes hard.

'Our marriage could have been a success if Marie-Céleste hadn't come back. But all that has happened since has shown me that I *have* no option. I must face the fact that it's a sham.'

* * *

'Things have reached such an impasse,' William said as he joined Flora and Lavinia in the drawing-room for tea, 'that unless something is done quickly I fear that Katharine may take matters into her own hands, with disastrous results.'

He produced the incriminating magazine and briefly outlined their conversation.

'Oh, *why* did I buy the wretched thing,' Lavinia groaned. 'I thought it might spark some interest in her.'

'It certainly did that,' William smiled.

'Perhaps we should telephone Maxime and ask him about it?' Flora suggested. 'As you say there's probably some very logical explanation which we can then pass on to Katharine.'

She rose from her chair and walked across the hall to the telephone.

'There's at least two hours wait,' she declared coming back into the room.

When the telephone rang, and Sheana announced that it was the call for France, they all looked at each other.

'It might be better if William spoke to him,' Flora suggested hesitantly. 'He was with Katharine when this all happened.'

William rose and went to pick up the receiver.

Maxime on the other end of the line was clearly on edge.

'Is everything all right,' he blurted out as soon as he heard William's voice.

'Katharine is much better,' the old man reassured him. 'But we have met with a slight problem.'

And he explained what had happened.

Maxime groaned.

'I was hoping she wouldn't see it. What bad luck that Lavinia should choose to buy *that* issue.'

'I told Katharine there must be some very simple explanation.'

'There is', Maxime interrupted.

'My poor boy,' William commiserated when Maxime told him.

'What on earth can I do?' Maxime agonised. 'Obviously

211

I can't tell her *why* I was with Marie-Céleste without telling her about Xavier. And I don't think she'd be able to stand that at the moment.'

William was silent for a few seconds.

'How are things going as far as your father-in-law is concerned?' he enquired.

'Absolute stalemate. No one seems to be able to tell us anything.'

'I wonder Maxime,' William murmured thoughtfully, 'whether in the circumstances it might not be better to tell Katharine why you were in Nice with your ex-wife.'

'But it would mean . . .'

'Telling her about her father. But she is now more alert than she was during that month on sedatives. She knows the boys have gone and she's upset thinking that you intend to take them from her. Then she sees this photograph . . . And she's bound to start wondering why she has no news from her father.'

'I see your point,' Maxime reflected.

He sighed deeply.

'I honestly don't know what to do for the best.'

'Leave it with me,' William said quietly. 'Will you agree to my breaking the news to her if there appears to be no other way?'

'Whatever you think best,' Maxime ended miserably. 'Honestly William I'm at the end of my tether.'

'I can well imagine.'

He paused.

'But Maxime do you realise that the end of man's tether is the beginning of God's power?'

'I don't understand.'

'As far as he is concerned,' William continued, 'it is when we are weakest that we are strongest. God can't work through strong people, they resist him. But when we are weak and at the end of our tether he takes us in his arms and carries us through.'

There was a pause. Then Maxime said self-consciously.

'I'm afraid I'm not very religious.'

'Neither am I,' William replied warmly. 'I'm just a simple Christian who believes in the promises of God and the power of prayer. Ask him to help you Maxime and he will give you strength and peace.'

'I'll try,' Maxime answered evasively.

'And I will pray for you,' William promised. 'With God's help we'll win through.'

'You're a wonderful man,' Maxime breathed. 'If your son was like you I feel unworthy to take his place in Katharine's life.'

'My son was like *you* Maxime,' William answered softly.

* * *

It was one of those rare October days when autumn distils a final whiff of sweetness to mingle with the pungent smell of burning wood.

Katharine was sitting in an armchair drawn up to the window. A lone tear stole down her ashen cheek.

William, sitting opposite, his head bowed, said nothing.

'I must go home,' she whispered at last.

William looked up and his eyes followed her gaze.

'It might be the best thing,' he replied.

Katharine shook her head in disbelief.

'How long has this news been kept from me?' she choked at last.

'I believe it was in August that your father was taken prisoner.'

'And no one had the courage to tell me.'

'It wasn't a question of courage Katharine. You were

ill. Nothing was to be gained by adding more anguish to your already tormented brain.'

'And had it not been for that photograph I wouldn't know even now?'

'Probably not.'

Suddenly her features hardened.

'How dare you,' she flamed. 'How dare you all treat me as if I were certified and locked up in a home.'

'Katharine, my dear . . .'

But she angrily brushed his hand away.

'Maxime had no right to behave as he did.'

'But what could you have done? Your husband is moving heaven and earth to have your father released.'

'If he's still there to *be* released,' she cut in icily.

William didn't reply. He realised that it was best to let the anger out rather than lock the pain inside her as she had been doing for so many years.

'Katharine,' William put in evenly, 'go home by all means. But what do you intend to do when you get there?'

Katharine looked at him enquiringly.

'Have all these misunderstandings with Maxime now been resolved?' he went on.

'Not all,' Katharine hesitated, suddenly remembering the letter from her father to her husband which she had mistakenly opened in Biarritz. She still did not know why Maxime had written to Xavier in secret, nor why her father's reply had been so cryptic. And once again Marie-Céleste's mocking face rose to taunt her.

'Then resolve them,' William said bluntly. 'With all the other problems he has on his mind at the moment Maxime needs a loving supportive wife, not someone who's holding a grudge.'

Katharine glanced quickly across at William. He had never spoken to her in that tone before.

Before the Dawn

'If you will allow me,' he went on, 'I will accompany you. You've been ill and it's a long journey to take on your own.'

'Oh William it's not necessary.'

'If you intend to go soon it *is* necessary.'

Although she started to protest, deep down Katharine was grateful. She still felt weak and had been shattered by the news William had just given her.

But it was not the journey which she was afraid to face alone.

It was her husband.

Chapter
19

'I'm afraid I do *not* share your opinion that taking Mrs Montredon back to France in her present condition is a wise move,' Dr Anderson remarked when told of Katharine's decision to leave Ardnakil.

'I understand your concern Doctor,' William sympathised. 'But we had to tell her about her father's kidnapping.'

The doctor looked up sharply.

'I thought we'd decided . . .'

'It was the lesser of two evils,' William explained.

'But in her fragile mental state it could have easily tipped the balance very unfavourably,' the doctor protested.

He shook his head, his sand-coloured eyes angry.

'I simply don't understand your absolute refusal to have her treated professionally. This illness has been dragging on for, how long, over two months. If you take her back to France without at least attempting to clear up the cause, then I cannot be responsible for what might happen.'

'No one will hold you responsible doctor,' William said quietly, as Flora and Lavinia sat in silence, at a loss as to what to say. 'And we are all very grateful for what you have done for Katharine. You said on the first day that if only she could talk and say what was troubling her we

216

could get to the bottom of this illness. Well, she has at last begun to talk. And you were quite right, the roots went back a very long way.'

He paused.

'It was as if there were a mental blind which she had firmly closed on all the pain she suffered during the war. All the hurtful memories. Her daily agony after my son, Katharine's husband, was killed.'

He looked up and saw that he had caught the doctor's attention.

'In the years after the war when she, like so many others, faced the reality of peace and the fact that the sacrifices of loved ones hadn't resulted in a perfect world, it seems that the shutter cutting off her memories became stuck and she was forced to face the pain. But now, having at last brought all the hurts to light I am convinced that, with God's help, she will be able to work her way through them.'

'I only hope you're right,' the doctor replied slowly.

He pursed his lips. Then suddenly smiled.

'Perhaps after all you were right to keep her here where she felt safe. You seem to have done the psychiatrists' work for them.'

William smiled to himself.

'The God I serve is the great psychiatrist,' he replied quietly.

Dr Anderson gave him a strange look as he rose to his feet. But he didn't comment.

*   *   *

In the dim grey light of the November dawn Maxime paced agitatedly up and down the deserted station platform. The Vent du Nord* had risen during the night and was screeching through the exit sending swirls of dust and the odd newspaper racing round his ankles. A lone cleaner disinterestedly pushing a broom in an attempt to capture escaped litter was the only other sign of life.

In his anxiety he had arrived at Narbonne station a good half an hour before the Barcelona night express from Paris was due. And a hurried cup of strong black coffee taken standing at the deserted buffet, one eye on the clock above the metal counter, had done nothing to soothe his agitation.

For the tenth time he walked to the edge of the platform and peered down the line.

When William had telephoned to tell him that he had explained the circumstances of the compromising photograph to Katharine but had been obliged to tell her about her father's kidnapping, Maxime had held his breath.

'It's all right,' William assured him. 'But she insists on returning home.'

'I'll come immediately', Maxime had cut in.

'There's no need for that,' William had continued. 'It would only worry her more knowing that you had left the scene of operations as it were. Lavinia and I will bring her back.'

'But I can't . . .'

'We had planned to visit Tamara this winter,' William put in equably. 'We'll go on to Nice from you.'

But Katharine had not returned immediately.

When she finally came downstairs they had all been shocked by her frailty and insisted she regain her strength before tackling the long journey.

'I'd rather not go by plane,' she said hesitantly, when Flora had tentatively suggested that it might be less tiring.

So the three of them had made the journey in two

stages, stopping at Goudhurst to rest and allow William and Lavinia to prepare for their winter in Nice before taking the Golden Arrow to Paris and the night train to Narbonne.

'She will no doubt be exhausted,' William had warned Maxime. 'Don't expect too much.'

'All I want is to have her back,' Maxime had replied.

Now as he strode impatiently backwards and forwards the announcement he had been waiting for suddenly blared from the loudspeaker. And in the distance he saw the long black line of the train. His heart beat faster as the engine clacked towards him, reducing speed with agonising slowness until it finally belched to a stop.

Immediately porters with barrows appeared from nowhere. And the station which a few minutes before had been deserted hummed with activity.

Running along the platform, his eyes darting frantically up and down the train, panic seized him. What if something had happened? What if at the last minute Katharine had changed her mind?

'Maxime!'

He stopped. Then he saw William's outstretched arm. And relief flooded through him.

He was just beside their compartment but in his anxiety he had not noticed.

William turned and held out his hand. Katharine, helped by Lavinia stepped down onto the platform. As she stood facing him, Maxime felt as if rough bony hands had seized him by the throat and were slowly strangling him. And he couldn't move. Then as if all the nerves in his body had risen to his rescue he grasped her hands, looking into her eyes.

But the eyes which gazed back into his were cavernous, so large that they seemed to fill her white face. Her clothes hung on her small body in loose folds and her high cheekbones stood out as if they were trying to pierce through the taut skin which covered them. He was shocked by her appearance. Overwhelmed by the change in his wife, with a cry, he put his arms around her and drew her to him.

She reached up and held him tightly. And they clung to each other on the windy platform in that chilly opal dawn.

But even as he held her, lovingly caressing her back, the nape of her neck, gently kissing her cold cheek pressing into his jacket he knew that their embrace was not the embrace of lovers. She was not clinging to him in the way she had done when he had kissed her goodbye all those months ago on the steps of Gure Etchea.

Then, in their embrace, had been the memory of the previous night when they had lain in each other's arms and listened to the breakers swishing up the beach towards the house. Now there was nothing sensuous in Katharine's embrace. It was asexual. She clung to him as a drowning child in its desperation would cling to a rescuer.

Seeing, above his wife's head William and Lavinia standing beside them as Emile coped with the luggage, Maxime kissed her cheek once again and gently released her.

* * *

'She is still taking a little medication,' William said as the three of them sat in the morning-room after breakfast. 'The doctor insisted.'

Katharine, exhausted, had been despatched to bed.

'I'm not sure it is entirely necessary.'

'Chasselin will be coming to see her later in the day,' Maxime put in. 'And then I'll get the best pyschiatrist . . .'

'Maxime', William said gently, leaning forward and looking straight into Maxime's face.

'Do you really think that a psychiatrist is the solution?'

Maxime looked at him blankly.

'Dr Anderson was consulting a psychiatrist about Katharine, although we preferred not to have her see him. It didn't produce any result.'

'But she looks terrible,' Maxime burst out.

'And do you think that by taking more drugs she will look any better?'

Maxime shrugged helplessly.

'What do you suggest?'

'She has at last begun to talk.'

Maxime sat in silence as William outlined all that had happened.

'If you are prepared to stay . . .' he ventured hesitantly.

'We are here to help you both Maxime. And we will stay as long as is necessary.'

At that moment the door crashed open and Jehan bombed into the room.

'Elise says Maman's back,' he shouted. 'Where is she?'

Maxime got to his feet.

'She's resting, Jehan.'

The twins sauntered in after him and through the open doorway he saw Léon limping hurriedly down the stairs, his face aglow.

'But I want to see her,' Jehan insisted.

'You will. Come and say good morning to your Aunt Lavinia and Canon Paget.'

The three boys stared in astonishment then made a bee-line for William.

'He's not *Canon Paget*,' Jehan scoffed. 'He's our *Grandpapa . . .*'

William looked across at Maxime.

'I hope you don't mind,' he apologised. 'I'm afraid they adopted me.'

'I'm delighted,' Maxime smiled.

A shadow flitted across his face and his lips tightened.

'At least they'll have *one* grandfather,' he remarked grimly as Léon limped into the room and climbed onto his knee.

They were all so busy listening to the boys' chatter that none of them noticed Katharine appear in the doorway. Suddenly Jehan looked up, and his eyes widened.

'*Maman*,' he whooped, racing across the room towards her.

'Katharine . . . darling,' Maxime chided. 'You should be resting.'

'It's all right Maxime', she smiled. 'I went to the nursery to see the boys but they had all escaped.'

She smiled at the twins who had each grabbed hold of one of her hands.

'I had to come down and see them.'

She walked slowly into the room. Léon, on his father's knee did not move. He sat staring, his limpid blue eyes wide with fright, as if he couldn't believe that they were focusing correctly.

'Papa *still* hasn't taken me shrimping,' Jehan trumpeted pompously, glancing accusingly at his father.

Katharine laughed. Her son's obsession with shrimping no longer irritating her.

Her eyes roved around the room. It was all as she remembered. Nothing had changed. Sitting down on a deep sofa she glanced across at her youngest son.

'Hallo Léon,' she smiled.

For a split second there was no reaction. Léon just stared unbelievingly at his mother. Then slowly slipping off his father's knee as if afraid that by any awkward movement he might break the spell he walked towards her, never taking his eyes off her face.

Katharine held out her arms. And suddenly he rushed into them, blotting himself against her.

'Maman, Maman,' he cried.

Gently lifting him onto her knee she encircled him with her arms. Pathetically calling her name, he burst into tears.

Katharine hugged him to her, rocking him backwards and forwards as she had so often done when he was a baby.

Jehan looked up from his machine-gun conversation with William.

'What's the matter with him?' he asked bluntly.

'He's pleased to see his mother again', William replied.

'Then why's he crying?'

Jehan sniffed disgustedly.

'Oh, that's *Léon*,' he remarked dismissing his brother out of hand before anyone could reply. 'He's stupid.'

He pulled at William's hand.

'Come on, I want to show you my collection. I've got two *London* bus tickets now *and* a rabbit's foot from Ardnakil. Donald gave it to me. Smells a bit, but I don't mind. As well as a crisp packet and an empty beer bottle I found in a dustbin on Perth station.'

He leant towards William.

'You won't tell Nanny will you?' he confided. 'I had to pick them up when she wasn't looking.'

'Your secret is safe with me,' William replied gravely.

And he winked at Katharine as Jehan hauled him from the room.

As Léon's sobs slowly hiccoughed and died away he looked up at his mother, then across at Maxime sitting opposite.

Slipping off her knee, he walked over and took Maxime's hand.

Bewildered, Maxime allowed Léon to lead him over to

the sofa and gently urge him to sit down beside his wife. Climbing back onto his mother's lap he held out his arms to his father.

Maxime looked above his son's head at his wife. But Katharine's face was buried in Léon's hair. Yet, as he looked, a tear stole down her wan cheeks and mingled with the golden curls.

Lavinia rose to her feet.

'I think I'll go upstairs and rest,' she remarked tactfully. And without a backward glance walked swiftly from the morning-room.

'Katharine', Maxime murmured. 'Oh Katharine.'

She raised her eyes to meet his. But all he could see in their depths was an immense sadness.

* * *

As they prepared for bed that evening Katharine stopped brushing her hair and turned round on her dressing-table stool.

'Maxime,' she said diffidently.

Her husband had been wavering uncertainly in the doorway of his dressing-room not knowing whether Katharine wanted him with her. Quickly tying the cord of his dressing-gown he walked across the room to her side.

'What is it darling?' he returned, standing behind her, still not daring to touch her.

But whatever it was she had wanted to say she seemed to have changed her mind. Avoiding his eyes, she slowly replaced her hairbrush on the tray.

Maxime slipped on to the long stool beside her. He had wondered as he nervously paced up and down that deserted station platform earlier in the day what his reaction would be at seeing her again. Would the tumult of the past few months, the angry, bitter words they had exchanged, and her terror of him which she had shown at their last meeting have changed things between them?

But as soon as he had seen her slowly descending the high steps from the train to the platform, even in her weak emaciated state, he had known that for him nothing had changed. She was still the most beautiful woman he had ever known. And his longing for her, for her physical closeness and her love had mounted within him as the day wore on. Now sitting beside her breathing in that faint scent of fallen rose petals which lingered on her skin, it was almost unbearable.

He could hear the blood pounding in his ears, his heart beating erratically, his body tense with suppressed desire. And he almost cried out in agony as the longing to be one with her, to soar together to those delirious heights they had attained so many times in the past rushed over him. And threatened to sweep away his iron self-control.

'What is it darling?' he whispered again, breathing deeply in an attempt to control his passion.

And daring to touch her, he slowly turned her face towards him.

'Is there *still* something worrying you?' he asked diffidently, when she didn't reply. 'Something which has happened to upset you which hasn't yet been explained?'

For a few seconds she did not move, just kept staring at her hands lying idly in her lap. Then lifting her eyes to meet his she nodded.

Maxime dropped her hands and put his arms round her.

'Can't you tell me?' he pleaded.

'I opened one of your letters,' she whispered almost inaudibly, '. . . at Gure Etchea . . . on the day you left.'

Maxime hugged her close.

'I would have done the same in the circumstances,' he smiled.

'But this was a very personal one. It was from Zag.'

And she explained the contents and her unfortunate reaction.

'Zag often told me that I jumped to conclusions without knowing the facts,' she ended hesitantly.

Maxime laughed.

'You certainly did in this case. It was a surprise I'd planned for you. Knowing I couldn't be at Gure Etchea in August I asked your father to join you there. That must have been his reply.'

He put his finger under Katharine's chin, and tentatively kissed the tip of her nose.

'Silly little darling,' he said tenderly. 'And that's been worrying you all this time . . .'

He broke off. Katharine was staring at him from wide-open horrified eyes, her face deathly white.

'Darling,' he said, drawing back, afraid that even his light touch had been too much. 'What's the matter?'

But his wife seemed incapable of speech. She just continued to stare at him fear turning her eyes almost black.

'It can't be true,' she whispered, her voice a croak.

'What can't be true darling?' he pleaded. 'Tell me.'

The light from the apricot-shaded lamp on her dressing-table slanted across her face turning the taut skin almost luminous. Maxime groaned and gathered her in his arms longing to comfort her in the only way he knew. Immediately all his senses leapt on fire but his closeness sounded no answering chord in her. There was no response to his touch.

She just lay cradled against his chest like a lifeless rag doll

'Zag,' she whispered pathetically, her voice so low it was like a wisp of mist. 'It's all my fault!'

Maxime's face puckered in a worried frown.

He wondered, not for the first time, whether the turmoil of the past months had not unhinged her mind.

'How can you say that?' he chided.

'But it's *true*,' she protested. 'I've just realised that I am responsible for what has happened to him.'

Katharine grasped her husband's hands and held them in a vice-like grip.

'If I hadn't opened that letter and jumped to the wrong conclusions, the boys and I would have stayed at Gure Etchea . . . and Zag would have joined us. He wouldn't have *been* in Algiers in August.'

Her haunted eyes bored into his.

'Through my stupidity I may have signed my own father's death warrant!'

*   *   *

'We seem to be going from one crisis to another,' Maxime said despairingly the following morning after recounting the previous night's drama to William.

'I must admit this is an eventuality we hadn't even considered,' William replied. 'I thought Katharine and I had thrashed everything out. But she didn't tell me about the letter.'

'It wouldn't have had any significance for her then,' Maxime remarked. 'It was only when I explained it that the truth struck home. I understand her anguish but . . .'

He shrugged helplessly.

'Oh William whatever will happen to Katharine if Xavier doesn't survive?'

'We don't know the end of the story,' William placated 'Perhaps your father-in-law will come out of this alive.'

Maxime sighed and passed his hand distractedly through his hair.

'Perhaps,' he conceded.

But he didn't sound very hopeful.

'Shall we pray about it together?' William asked.

Maxime looked startled but the old man had already dropped to his knees. Feeling as awkward as he had done on the night of the twins' birth when Xavier had suggested the same thing, Maxime followed suit.

'Heavenly Father,' William breathed. 'You know the beginning from the end. Xavier is your servant and if he is now in chains it is because he loves you. But you have promised never to leave us nor forsake us, so we ask you to give him your peace and let him know that he is not abandoned by those who love him. Give Katharine your peace also Father at this time of great distress. Take away her terrible feelings of guilt and show us what we can do to help her.'

He paused.

But Maxime remained silent.

'And please show yourself to Maxime, the man you chose to be Katharine's helpmate and companion,' William ended simply. 'So that they may worship you together. I ask it in the precious name of your son Jesus Christ.'

Maxime surreptitiously raised his eyes. But William was still kneeling, his face glowing with an inner radiance.

After a few minutes William opened his eyes and smiled across at Maxime.

'Jesus will show us the way,' he said confidently.

Maxime slowly rose from his knees and sat down

'I don't understand,' he faltered. 'But I'd like to. I'd like to have this strong faith which I've seen in you and my father-in-law. Which I saw in Katharine until all this happened.'

He looked up at William.

'It doesn't seem to be helping her now.'

'That's where you're wrong Maxime. Without her faith

I doubt Katharine would have survived this onslaught. She is like a tree bending in the face of the wind . . . but not breaking. Her faith is going through a very hard test, as happens to all of us at some time in our lives. But I'm confident she will come through . . . as long as she keeps her eyes on Jesus.'

Maxime carefully studied his shoes.

'Faith is not just about believing,' William explained. 'It is about living what we believe even when times are dark and it doesn't seem we are going to make it.'

The younger man longed to ask William more, but the morning-room door opened and Katharine walked in. She looked pale, but otherwise quite composed.

'Darling,' Maxime said anxiously, rising to his feet. 'How are you feeling?'

But at that moment a shriek which would have stopped Attila the Hun dead in his tracks echoed round the hall.

'*Maxime, Maxime, where are you?*'

And Toinette, wearing enough make-up to stock a beauty parlour, tottered into the room, her arsenal of jangling bracelets clinking and clanking like a member of a chain gang.

'Maxime,' she bleated, fighting a losing battle to retrieve an arm from inside the lining of her blue and orange hand-knitted coat which had been split in her struggle to remove it. Smiling to himself Maxime recovered his great-aunt's imprisoned limb and peeled off the coat to reveal a frock resembling an advertisement for Assorted Fruit Gums. The outfit was topped with a hat fit for the coronation of an African queen.

'*Maxime,*' Toinette wailed dramatically, looking like an over-dressed stick insect as she wobbled precariously on stiletto heels towards a chair 'Have you *heard*?'

'Heard what Toinette?'

'The *news* . . .' she gasped, fanning herself with a vast red handbag. '*This morning on the wireless . . .*'

Toinette's sentences were a rising crescendo of staccato italics.

'Those dreadful people say they've executed Xavier!'

There was a sudden silence.

No one dared move. The only sound came from Toinette's heavy breathing as she vigorously continued her fanning. Maxime looked quickly across at his wife. But Katharine remained motionless on her chair.

'You must *do* something Maxime,' Toinette whinnied on, oblivious to the disturbance her bombshell had caused. 'We can't have poor Xavier just *left* there. Telephone the President or someone and have his body sent home so that we can have a proper funeral.'

Her face brightened at the thought. And she stopped fanning to look around her delightedly.

'Xavier must be buried in the family vault, next to Maman after a full requiem mass in the cathedral,' Toinette rattled on, now that she knew she had everyone's undivided attention. 'I'll get Armand to telephone Father Anselme and arrange it. Of course there'll be a reception at home afterwards. And we *must* see about the *faire-parts**and announcements in the newspapers.'

She glanced around for approval.

'Perhaps Maxime you could invite the President or ask him to send a guard of honour and a few generals since Xavier died for his country. It would be *lovely* having soldiers blowing trumpets and things.'

Beaming with unadulterated joy at the prospect, Toinette unearthed a heavy gold compact from her handbag and began loading even more powder on to her already plastered face.

'I really *must* get a new set of mourning,' she twittered excitedly, grimacing at herself in the small mirror as she attempted to erase lipstick from her front teeth. 'I can't *possibly* wear the same one I wore for Honoré two years ago.'

She gave a final squint at her teeth and snapped the compact shut.

'Henriette dying so soon afterwards was *most* inconvenient. I had to wear the same hat for *both* funerals.'

Toinette leant back in her chair, relishing the prospect of such macabre festivities. She had always loved wallowing in blood and intestines and pointing out whose face was lop-sided because they'd just had a stroke.

'I *had* to come and tell you immediately', Toinette prattled gaily on. 'I tried to telephone but couldn't make the thing work. Kept getting a silly woman asking me for a number.'

But no one was listening. All eyes were on Katharine. Following their gaze Toinette suddenly noticed her great niece.

'*Katharine*,' she squealed. 'What *have* you been up to? You've not been to see me for *ages*.'

She peered short-sightedly over her improvised fan.

'You've lost a lot of weight', she remarked tartly. 'Are you on a diet or something? You look *dreadful*. Like someone from one of those concentration camps.'

She glared at Maxime who had risen and gone swiftly to his wife's side.

'You should be firmer with her Maxime. No man wants a wife who looks like a cheese straw.'

With a desperate glance in her great-aunt's direction Katharine ran from the room.

'What an extraordinary way to behave,' Toinette remarked raising her thinly-pencilled black eyebrows disapprovingly.

The effect was almost clownlike.

'She didn't even ask me how I was.'

Toinette shrugged and grappled her way to her feet, turning her ankle several times in the process.

'Give me my coat Maxime,' she said huffily 'And call me a taxi.'

'There's no need for that,' Maxime replied tersely, irritated beyond belief by his great-aunt's ill-timed appearance. 'Emile will drive you home.'

He turned to William.

'Would you mind,' he pleaded anxiously, jerking his eyes towards the door through which his wife had just vanished.

William immediately rose.

Shocked by the news, he feared for Katharine. But when he went up to her room, there was no sign of her. He glanced into the nursery, but Léon was alone, absorbed in a drawing. Desperate, realising the effect Toinette's announcement could have had on Katharine he quickly walked down to the drawing-room. But Katharine was nowhere to be found. Crossing the terrace he shaded his eyes and looked into the distance. And there he saw her, hair streaming out behind her running desperately towards the dark waters of the lake.

'Maxime,' he called sharply.

Hearing William's tone, Maxime rushed to his side.

Knowing that he could not catch up with her himself, William wordlessly pointed to the small speck in the far distance. With a quick intake of breath Maxime leapt down the terrace steps in one bound and raced off across the park.

'Oh Father,' William prayed, his voice ragged with fear. 'Let him arrive in time.'

Chapter
20

Xavier turned on his side as the door scraped open and the inevitable plate of dry flat bread and mug of water were thrust through. His eyes met those of his jailer and for a fleeting second their gaze locked. Then the man turned away. But his eyes had not been hard. There had been no hatred reflected in them. And Xavier felt a ray of warmth creep through his tired, emaciated body. They had been the eyes of the Arabs he had known and grown to love during his many years in North Africa, soft and dark and limpid. And he wondered why the man was here. Whether he too had been abducted and forced to do something he did not want to do. He decided to speak to him the next time he came.

Although Xavier had no watch, his body seemed to have developed a physical clock which told him when the meagre rations were due. So when the time came for his evening meal he crawled over to the door and waited. As their glance met once again, the look in his jailer's eyes had not changed. It lingered compassionately on the prisoner's dirty haggard face. But when Xavier opened his mouth to speak fear instantly leapt into the man's eyes. And the door was hastily slammed shut.

Sighing, Xavier picked up his plate and returned to his corner. He had not had a visit from Khaled for some time. And as he ate his stale bread, throwing a few crumbs to a small mouse who crept up beside him, he wondered why. He knew that Khaled would not have given up. That his torture was not at an end. But he couldn't understand this silence. Shrugging resignedly he thanked God for the remission even if it meant that when he returned, Khaled's onslaught would be even worse.

'Even though he slay me yet will I love him,' he said, stubbornly repeating words from the Book of Job.

And added the beautiful opening words of Psalm 56.

'Be merciful to me O God for men hotly pursue me; all day long they press their attack. When I am afraid I will trust in you.'

His mind went back to Khaled and again he wondered why. Why had this man whom he had rescued and come to love as a brother turned so viciously against him? Was it all a plot? Had Khaled planned the whole thing from the beginning? And his friendship and conversion been merely a mockery, a means to gain Xavier's confidence. Or had he perhaps been compelled by an Algerian nationalist organisation to infiltrate the mission?

Xavier's lips tightened and a wave of anger rose up in him. Then he remembered those days and nights he and Khaled had spent together in the desert. How little by little Khaled had opened up and told him his story. The story of an abandoned waif who had run barefoot and hungry through the winding alleys of the souk, begging and stealing. Until the day he had been hit by a piece of falling masonry and taken to the Mission Hospital. And Xavier had become his spiritual father. When he recovered Khaled had begged to be allowed to stay with him. Then Khaled had loved him . . . and he had loved Jesus. Or so Xavier thought.

He sighed deeply.

Khaled's betrayal had hurt him more than he cared to admit. He still hoped, though with each visit that hope was diminishing, that something of the teaching and love of Jesus which Xavier had nurtured in Khaled would pierce through the hatred which now corroded him. But now that hope seemed very remote.

What had happened? What devil had entered Khaled's heart and brought about such a dramatic change?

And he wondered whether he would ever know the answer. Lowering himself with difficulty to his bony knees he asked God to reveal himself to Khaled once again. To give him another chance.

'The Lord is my helper,' he ended. 'Why should I fear? Man can only kill my body, he cannot kill my soul. That is immortal.'

As the words left his lips he knew how his Saviour must have felt when he stumbled with his cross up the hill to Golgotha.

'Lord', he whispered brokenly. 'In the end there is only you. You are the only one who really understands.'

Comforted, he tossed the remnants of his crust to the mouse who had been joined by two companions.

'If God takes care of you, little vermin,' he smiled, 'how much more will he take care of me.'

And rolling himself in his cloak, he instantly fell asleep.

* * *

Breathless, Maxime raced to the lake just as Katharine tottered on the edge of the dark water shivering below.

Grabbing her round the waist he pulled her back. She collapsed against him, her face grey, her body almost lifeless.

'Darling,' he cried hoarsely, 'oh darling!'

Sweeping her into his arms, he carried her limp body back across the lawn and into the house.

'Get the doctor,' he called, seeing Lavinia and William hovering on the terrace.

Reaching their room he gently laid her on the bed and began to chafe her icy hands in his own.

Lavinia knocked on the door and came in.

'Dr Chasselin is on his way,' she whispered.

'Don't tell him,' Katharine begged, her voice diaphonous. *Please* don't tell him.'

She caught hold of Maxime's lapels attempting to sit up.

'I don't want anyone to know. I'm . . . so ashamed.'

'Lie back and rest darling,' he soothed. 'No one need know anything you don't want them to know.'

'It was Toinette,' she faltered weakly.

Maxime's face tightened.

'I've never thought her over-intelligent. But I didn't realise she was such a blithering idiot.'

'Is it true?' Katharine pleaded.

'I don't know darling. There are always all sorts of rumours going round in a situation like this. It may be just one more.'

'But if she heard it on the wireless . . .'

'Journalists can make mistakes,' he soothed.

He gently pressed her back on the pillows and covered her frail body with a blanket.

'Look darling, you've had about as much as you can take at the moment. As soon as you're settled I'm going to get on to the Ministry of Interior again and see what this is all about.'

'And you will tell me the truth?'

'Of *course* I'll tell you the truth. Have I ever lied to you?'

She turned her anguished eyes on him, then dropped

them to where her hands were idly plucking the blanket. And for the first time in many months she felt a faint stirring of love trickle back into her body.

'No Maxime,' she whispered shakily.

* * *

'Your wife is physically and mentally exhausted,' Dr Chasselin announced, as he and Maxime walked back down the long gallery together. 'She needs complete rest. Hardly surprising after the strain she's been under these past few months. Finally brought to a head by that broadcast this morning.'

The doctor's face hardened.

'Dreadful business.'

Maxime nodded.

'We'll keep her sedated for a few days and see what happens. It's important to build up her physical strength before tackling the mental problem. She's lost an awful lot of weight. But in the circumstances that's to be expected.'

He shook Maxime's hand warmly as they reached the front door.

'Don't hesitate to call me if you need me,' he ended and crunched across the gravel to his waiting car.

* * *

'Toinette's got it all wrong as usual,' Maxime exclaimed exasperatedly, walking into the dining room just as lunch was being served. 'If only Katharine hadn't been there when she barged in this morning all this upheaval could have been avoided.'

He sat down and spread his napkin on his lap.

237

'I got hold of the radio station. The journalist concerned played right into the terrorists' hands. It's apparently a well-known trick of theirs to spread false rumours in order to further torture the victim's relatives. It appears he had an anonymous telephone call announcing Xavier's execution just before going on the air. And he didn't have time to check. The radio people agreed that that was no excuse and apologised profusely. Since then the Ministry of Interior has come down on them like a ton of bricks and the poor journalist, who thought he'd got a scoop, has been severely reprimanded.'

He picked up his knife and dug into the pâté.

'I got on to my contact at the Ministry of Interior who says the rumour is without foundation. There have been no new developments.'

Maxime sighed.

'How tired I am of hearing that one. But he did say that they have reason to believe that Xavier is still alive.'

'That's good news,' Lavinia put in.

'Yes, but if they don't do something about rescuing him soon I wonder for how much longer. I doubt they are housing him at the Ritz!'

'When will you tell Katharine?' William enquired.

'As soon as she wakes.'

But Katharine received the news without any outward sign of emotion.

'For how long?' she asked bleakly. 'How long, Maxime, before the news is true?'

Sitting beside her, Maxime did not know what to reply.

'It will soon be Christmas,' he murmured on an impulse. 'I'm sure Xavier will be free by then.'

But Katharine didn't react to his enthusiasm.

'Why don't we ask William and Lavinia to stay on and make it an extra special Christmas for the boys. If you wish I can go to Paris and buy the presents . . . or perhaps in a week or two you'll be feeling strong enough to come with me.'

He squeezed her limp hand.

'Let's make plans darling . . . not only for Christmas but for our future.'

Katharine turned to look at him and as their eyes met a hesitant smile flitted across her pale lips.

'You're a wonderful husband Maxime,' she whispered. I'm sorry I misjudged you.'

She paused, her eyes pleading.

'This morning before I came downstairs I read the letters you sent to Gure Etchea which I never received. They explained everything.'

She reached across and took his hand.

'Can you ever forgive me?'

Stunned by her unexpected declaration, Maxime caught his breath. Gathering her into his arms they clung wordlessly to each other. With a deep sigh, Katharine nestled contentedly against him, then her heavy lids fluttered and closed, and Maxime heard her soft regular breathing. As he gently laid her back against the mound of pillows he looked down at his wife, his eyes warm and tender. He was grateful that their past misunderstandings were at last behind them. Katharine's words had confirmed that. But he wished she had been able to say that she still loved him.

Tenderly tucking her hand beneath the sheet he bent and kissed her forehead. She didn't stir. But as he tiptoed from the room his heart felt lighter than it had done for many months.

Xavier was still a prisoner and he and Katharine were not home and dry yet. But an inexplicable feeling of hope had risen in him. And he had a sudden urge to seek out William and ask him about this God of his who worked wonders in people's hearts. Although he wasn't entirely sure, he had a feeling that something was beginning to stir in his own. And he wanted to know more.

* * *

William was walking in the bare rose garden when Maxime finally found him. Falling into step beside him they strolled together in silence for a few minutes.

'Let us sit here on this bench,' William said as they came to a sheltered spot. 'Then I can explain it all to you.'

'Explain?' Maxime frowned.

'The love of Jesus,' William replied simply. 'That is why you were looking for me wasn't it? You've finally come to the point when you are ready to accept him as Lord of your life.'

Maxime sat down and stared at the older man in stupefaction.

'How did you *know*?' he stammered.

But William merely smiled.

'God is faithful. If we pray, believing, he grants our request as long as it is in line with his will. And what could be more in line with his will than that one of his children should come to him?'

He turned his warm blue eyes on Maxime.

And Maxime again had the feeling that William could see right through him, to the very depths of his soul. He was shattered by the revelation. The more so since he had never seriously considered that he had a soul.

'It obviously was not the right time for you,' William continued, 'because until now you were not willing to admit that you are a sinner, as we all are.'

Maxime was speechless. Like his wife before him he had never thought of himself as a sinner. He had imagined that only thieves and murderers and those who commited heinous crimes were sinners. He hadn't realised that even unkind thoughts were sins in God's sight.

But as William patiently explained to him the way of salvation and what he had to do to receive it, his whole concept of Christianity changed. And he understood that it was a personal God he was being called to serve. And that salvation could only come through repentance and accepting God's Son Jesus Christ as his Saviour.

Maxime sat slowly trying to digest these momentous, yet simple, truths which William was revealing to him.

'Katharine and I have been praying for you since her conversion,' William went on evenly. 'And so has her father. I'm sure that wherever he is he is still honouring his promise to his daughter to pray for you every day.'

Maxime raised his eyes, a looked of bewilderment on his face.

'Your wife loves you very much Maxime, but since she accepted Christ as her Saviour there has been this chasm between you. She longed for you to join her on her walk with Jesus. And I'm sure she has often felt very lonely spiritually.'

Maxime bit his lip. For the first time in many years he hovered on the brink of tears.

'My wife and I were able to pray through our problems and difficulties together,' William reflected. 'And it made all the difference to our marriage.'

'Do you think that is why Katharine is so attached to her father?' Maxime ventured huskily, deeply moved by what William was saying. 'Because of this spiritual bond?'

'I think Katharine has always been very attached to her father. But certainly when she became a committed Christian it must have drawn them even closer.'

For a few moments neither spoke. Maxime sat thoughtfully studying the grass beneath his feet, his hands hanging loosely between his knees. Then slowly raising his head he met William's eyes.

'Xavier once said there was a verse in the Bible claiming that God could bring good out of evil.'

'Romans chapter 8 verse 28,' William put in evenly. 'One of my favourites. All things work for good for those who love the Lord.'

'This morning I would never have believed that any good could come out of the dreadful mess we seem to have found ourselves in over the past six months,' Maxime mused.

Then he smiled.

'But it seems that God has kept his promise and worked his miracle. I'm ready to accept him William. And his Son as my personal Saviour. Please tell me what I have to do.'

Chapter
21

For over two weeks Katharine drifted in and out of sleep. But as the medication was gradually reduced and the periods of wakefulness lengthened she became aware of all the seemingly insurmountable problems which surrounded her. And her guilt at her father's captivity began increasingly to dominate her thoughts.

'No news?' she asked pathetically, one mid-December afternoon when Maxime crept into the room and sat at her bedside.

'Not yet darling', he soothed. 'But the Ministry of Interior has reason to believe that he is still alive.'

Katharine nodded. But it was obvious that the news gave her little hope. The guilt for what had happened was still there.

'Why don't we pray about it,' Maxime tentatively suggested.

His wife's hand suddenly tightened in his and her eyes opened even wider. Maxime caught his breath. Her hollow cheeks and her long lashes curling at the corners like a gull's wing emphasised their upward slant. He gazed at her adoringly, once again overwhelmed by her now fragile beauty.

'*Pray*, Maxime,' she whispered incredulously. '*You.*'

He smiled and lovingly smoothed the hair back from her forehead looking deep into her bewildered eyes.

'Yes darling, me. I finally capitulated, and William has led me to the Lord. But I need your help. I'm still only a baby Christian. William said you would take me the rest of the way.'

Katharine released his hand and gently stroked his face. And as he held her they whispered words of praise to the Lord they now both worshipped.

'The treatment seems to have worked splendidly,' Dr Chasselin announced the next day.

He had been hurriedly summoned by the nurse when Katharine had refused to take her morning medication and insisted on getting up.

When Dr Chasselin arrived Katharine was sitting in a chair drawn up to the window.

'I want to start living again,' she smiled wanly. 'My husband tells me that it is already the 15th of December.'

She shook her head sadly.

'What a lot of wasted time.'

'Don't start rushing things Madame,' the doctor warned.

But from that day on Katharine appeared to be almost herself again. No one knew whether she had been able to put her guilt for Xavier's kidnapping behind her or reason herself out of it. And for the time being they felt it best not to ask too many questions.

As Christmas approached the boys excitement mounted.

But there was still no news of Xavier.

On the 23rd, Maxime received a telephone call from Antoine.

'Mission accomplished,' he announced jubilantly. 'Happy Christmas!'

'What do you mean?' Maxime puzzled.

The tensions and dramas of the preceding weeks had put all thought of Marie-Céleste out of his mind.

'Marie-Céleste,' Antoine laughed. 'She left for Madrid this morning.'

'You mean your grandmother relented?'

'Took a bit of persuading but in the end she capitulated and invited my dear sister to spend the winter in the ducal palace with her. At least from there, and far from the Arab boyfriend, she can't harm your father-in-law. So that's *one* problem solved for you Max.'

On Christmas Eve Armand, Toinette and Marie-Louise came to Le Moulin for dinner. Henriette and Honoré, having practically ignored each other throughout their married life had been reunited by death within days of each other two years before. Honoré without having finished his book about Alfred the down-trodden horse which he had been working on since the turn of the century, or having patented his cure for hiccoughs!

No one knew exactly where Charles-Hubert was. Armand had thought he might return when he heard of Xavier's kidnapping. But all they had received was a choleric postcard from Istanbul, which he insisted on calling Constantinople, stating that if *he* were the governor-general those damned Arabs wouldn't be running around locking decent people up. He'd have 'em all horse-whipped!

The boys were allowed to stay up and join the family for dinner. They were beside themselves with excitement when they saw garlands of fairy-lights looped like jewels the length of the staircase and the enormous candle-lit tree standing in the hall, a heap of gaily-wrapped presents tumbling beneath it.

'It's been a splendid evening,' Armand said as, surrounded by discarded wrapping paper, the boys were escorted sleepily to bed. Léon had not managed to stay the course and was being carried upstairs in his father's arms.

Armand drew his heavy gold hunter watch from his waistcoat pocket and squinted down at it.

'But if we are not going to be late for midnight mass, I think we should be leaving.'

He glanced enquiringly at Katharine.

'William is going to give us communion here,' she said simply.

'But *darling*', Toinette squealed. 'Is that *proper*?'

'William is a clergyman.'

'Yes, but . . .'

She looked around her.

'Having mass *here*. It's not a *church* . . . I don't think that counts.'

'God doesn't live in churches made by man,' Maxime said, hearing the end of the conversation as he came back down the stairs. 'He's everywhere.'

Toinette's mouth dropped open.

'*You*, Maxime,' she whinnied, her voice mounting like a chromatic scale.

She shrugged herself huffily into the pink and magenta coloured coat Alphonse was holding out to her, and drew on gloves resembling a pair of dead rabbits.

'Come Armand,' she protested, her face suddenly bursting like an indignant hen through a tambourine festooned with brussels sprouts which passed for a hat. 'I don't know what Maman would have said. I'm pleased she didn't live to see it.'

Katharine looked helplessly from one to the other. It had been such a splendid evening. Why had Toinette to spoil it?

Armand took her arm as he bent to kiss her.

'Don't take any notice of Toinette,' he whispered. 'We all know she has a brain the size of a lentil. I only wish I could stay here and take part in the service with you.'

He winked conspiratorially at her as Alphonse handed him his hat.

'It would certainly be warmer than in the cathedral.'

'Armand,' Toinette called sulkily as she and Marie-Louise, looking like two early Christian martyrs teetered indignantly on the doorstep. 'We're going to be late.'

And with a final wink he was off.

*   *   *

Xavier was back at Castérat, in the bower with Katharine lazily watching the afternoon sun dapple her face as it filtered its way through the leaves. A feeling of immense happiness suddenly overwhelmed him and he leant over to take his daughter's hand in his. But as he did so there was a crash, the door flew open and Khaled strode defiantly in.

'So my friend,' he jeered, looking down at Xavier's huddled form crouched in the corner. 'We sleep our life away.'

Bewildered at being awakened from a deep sleep Xavier blinked open his eyes wondering what time it was. But the lack of light in the filthy cellar gave no hint as to the passing hours. Feeling groggy with sleep he gathered it must be the middle of the night. He knew what awaited him, and was loath to leave his dream and return to reality.

'Up man,' Khaled yelled.

Gathering together the remnants of his senses Xavier scrambled awkwardly to his feet, the shackles around his ankles acting as an efficient brake.

Khaled looked him up and down, his arms folded inside his djellabah.

'Well infidel. Do you know what day it is?'

'I don't even know whether it is day or night Khaled,' Xavier replied simply.

He glanced up at the barred aperture way above him.

'Insolence!' Khaled shrieked.

And an angry glint came into his eyes.

'Answer my question.'

'No Khaled,' Xavier sighed. 'I do not know what day it is. And does it really matter?'

Khaled threw back his head and laughed.

'Not for us. But for *Christians*.'

His eyes shot venom as he pronounced the word and to further emphasise his contempt he spat on the floor.

'It is Christmas Eve my friend . . . In less than an hour it will be Christmas Day. The day your Lord came to earth to *save* you.'

Khaled looked witheringly at Xavier's pitiful body.

'But he hasn't saved you, has he?' he jeered.

Xavier looked up but did not reply.

'Perhaps you would like to give your friends a little present?'

'What do you want of me Khaled?' Xavier asked wearily.

'Just a signature my friend. Just a signature. Then you will be free.'

With a flourish he produced a paper from the folds of his djellabah.

'There,' he said, thrusting it in Xavier's face. 'Sign that.'

Xavier peered at the closely-typed sheets. But in the almost complete darkness could not make out what it said.

'What is it?' he asked.

'A present,' Khaled wheedled. 'A Christmas present for the French authorities.'

He pronounced the word 'French' with loathing. As if Algeria were already divorced from the metropolis.

He thrust his face close to Xavier's.

'Your *confession*!'

'My confession?' Xavier queried. 'For what?'

Khaled snapped his fingers and the masked man accompanying him produced a torch and shone it in Xavier's eyes, blinding him.

'Read,' Khaled ordered.

Taking the paper in trembling hands Xavier's eyes carefully read it. Then without a word he handed it back.

'You know I can't sign that.'

Khaled's shaggy black brows drew together, and his eyes became slits in his swarthy face.

'I don't agree with everything about colonialism,' Xavier said evenly, 'and I think that perhaps it would be better if Algeria were free to run her own affairs. But, as you well know, I have never meddled in politics. What you also know is that I will never give in to the threats of a band of fanatics who are not interested in Algeria but only in achieving their own ends through bloodshed and violence. Asking me to sign a paper condemning my own country and stating that I agree with what Algerian terrorists are doing is a waste of time.'

Khaled drew his dagger and waved it menacingly in Xavier's face.

'Sign it,' he screeched. 'Sign it, or else . . .'

'Do what you will,' Xavier said resignedly. 'Kill me if you wish. But don't ask me to be a liar and a traitor.'

Khaled let out an unearthly yell and lunged forward with his sword. Then abruptly he stopped, the blade quivering in mid-air. Giving Xavier a vicious kick which sent him reeling he yelled for the door to be opened and, still screaming obscenities, crashed out.

Shattered, Xavier crawled back into his corner and sat shivering in a crumpled heap. His cloak was now almost threadbare and afforded little warmth. But Xavier hugged it around him as cold beads of sweat gathered on his forehead and trickled down his back.

He knew now that his days were numbered. Khaled would not forget. And looking down at his emaciated body, his muscles flaccid and limp from lack of exercise and the cramped position he was obliged to adopt for most of the day, he wondered whether his Lord would not take him before Khaled had the satisfaction of slicing off his head. And for the first time since his capture he sincerely hoped so. He no longer held out any hope of a reprieve. And the rescue he had at first thought would surely come now seemed just as illusion.

He thought back to Khaled's words.

So it was Christmas Eve. Nearly five months since his capture. Five months living alone in almost total darkness with only vermin for company.

'Jesus, this is the day when you came into the world to save us from our sins,' he said hoarsely.

He paused and smiled to himself, remembering other Christmases with Rowena and Katharine when she was a little girl. And he saw once again the golden lights dancing in her tawny eyes as she opened her presents and gazed rapturously at the candle-lit Christmas tree. He wondered what she was doing at this moment. Whether his captivity would prevent them rejoicing.

'Lord,' he said, 'give my child your peace. May her little family be able to rejoice today because of what you have done for them, because of your coming into the world as a baby almost two thousand years ago. Don't let my grandsons suffer through what has happened to me. And Jesus I give them to you, all those who are dear to me. Help them to accept whatever happens.'

He closed his tired eyes and the blackness was complete.

'Father,' he whispered, as weariness crept over his aching limbs. 'Into your hands I commit my Spirit.'

Before the Dawn

* * *

'On this evening when we remember the first Christmas and celebrate our Saviour's coming into the world to save us from our sins,' William said quietly as they gathered together in the drawing-room where he had set up an improvised altar, 'we must not forget that behind the beauty of the star shining over the manger lay the ugliness and the agony of the cross. So let us first thank our Lord for the terrible sacrifice he made for us. And because of that sacrifice meditate on how deeply he loves us.'

They remained silent for a few minutes, each one giving thanks in the quietness of their own hearts.

But William's heart was troubled. He had a strange feeling that Xavier was in mortal danger. That there was something evil surrounding him at this very minute. But he did not know what.

'Now let us praise God and thank him for all his blessings and his protection throughout this past year', William continued, trying to empty his mind of everything but his Saviour.

But the terrible feeling of evil persisted.

'His blessings may not always be apparent to us at the time,' he stumbled on, his mind still troubled. 'Often it is only later that we learn about the dangers from which he has snatched us. And the heartaches we have been spared.'

William paused, willing the evil to leave him. But it clung tenaciously, viciously tormenting his mind until it was almost a physical pain.

'As we remember Xavier wherever he is,' he said with a great effort, the feeling mounting now into his throat and choking him, 'let us also remember those who are holding him captive. And pray especially for them.'

'But William,' Katharine protested, raising her eyes. 'I find it so hard to pray for them.'

'God loves them as much as he loves us,' William replied gently. 'Jesus longs for them to turn from their wicked ways and acknowledge him. If we don't pray for them, then who will? But if they find our Saviour *he* will convict them of their sin.'

As he spoke those words the terrible constriction of his throat was released and the evil which had been tormenting him slithered away.

'Those who are evil today can become Christlike tomorrow,' he said softly. 'There is surely one who is their leader, one who is responsible for what has happened. Let us kneel before the throne of God and hold him up to the Lord especially. Ask Jesus to come into his black heart so that he will see what he has done . . . and repent.'

Slipping to his knees on the thick carpet, Maxime felt for his wife's hand and held her trembling fingers tightly in his own.

As she knelt before William and he placed the chalice in her hands murmuring 'the blood of our Lord Jesus Christ that was shed for you', she raised her head and saw that his eyes were upon her. For a long moment they looked at each other, suspended in time and space, as their thoughts went back down the years to William's little stone church in Buckinghamshire on the first Christmas morning after Ashley's death. As the memories flooded back Katharine's eyes clouded with tears. But there were no tears rolling down William's face as there had been on that cold Christmas morning. Just a radiance. He smiled at her and, as the tears slowly receded, she smiled back.

It was at that moment that Khaled's heavy sword was abruptly arrested in mid-air. And he crashed out of the cellar howling like a dervish.

Before the Dawn

*   *   *

The door ground open and the inevitable stale bread and water was thrust inside. Xavier wearily opened one eye. He had no desire to eat or even to drink. He had slept fitfully, badly shaken after Khaled's departure, and his intermittent dozing had been peopled with frightening macabre dreams. Attempting to sit up, his body felt as if a steam-roller had bulldozed over it, his head throbbed, every muscle and bone ached intolerably. And he flopped helplessly back into his corner.

As his mind cleared slightly he remembered Khaled's visit. And he realised that as his wasted body weakened he was becoming less and less able to withstand his tormentor's vicious onslaughts. Shivering, he pulled the remnants of his cloak around him and closed his eyes.

It was not until his evening meal was brought that Xavier awoke and realised he had slept the day away.

The terrible lassitude bordering on depression which had held him in his grip that morning had lifted and, feeling slightly refreshed, he realised that no matter what the cost, he had to do everything in his power to stay alive.

Absently chewing on the hard, dry, tasteless bread he suddenly brightened. If what Khaled said was true, and today was Christmas Day from now on he could at least keep a count of time. Next week would begin a new year. With a wry twisted smile he wondered what it would bring.

Then suddenly his natural good humour rose to the fore.

'I must be positive,' he stressed. 'I must trust the Lord's promise that he will deliver me from my enemies, and not let Satan goad me into believing otherwise. I must believe that next year I shall be back at Castérat with my family, with Katharine and my grandsons.'

He felt the tangled beard covering his face.

'I wonder what they will think of this?' he smiled.

And quickly swallowing the rest of the bread, he gathered up the meagre crumbs in his grimy hands and threw them to the mice.

'Sorry boys,' he smiled. 'Only reduced rations from now on. I've got to keep up my strength for my home-coming.'

The crisis had passed. That moment when Xavier, at the end of his tether, had threatened to succumb to despair and give up. Now he gathered together what little strength remained to him and determined that whatever happened he would fight on. Opening his mouth he began to sing the 23rd Psalm at the top of his voice. As his once-rich baritone feebly rang out, the door opened a crack and he saw his jailer's eyes watching him in bewilderment. Waving to him, Xavier smiled.

'There's a new year just around the corner my friend,' he croaked gaily.

But the jailer, terrified, slammed the door shut and scuttled away.

For the first time since his capture, Xavier laughed.

After all these months, something had changed and he did not know what. It wasn't only his attitude. It went deeper than that. He had never ceased to pray for those he knew were suffering because of his captivity. But now he suddenly felt liberated, tucked out of harm's way in the bosom of Jesus. And he no longer had any desire to pray for his own safety.

Throwing up his wasted arms in a gesture of adoration to the God who had brought him thus far, with what little voice he had left he began to praise.

Chapter
22

William and Lavinia stayed at Le Moulin until the beginning of January. Then they said they must be moving on to Nice to see Tamara who had returned from Teheran after being present, at the beginning of December, at the birth of Paul, Lawrence and Tatiana's third child and Tamara's second grandson.

'We shall miss you,' Katharine said wistfully as she stood on the steps of Le Moulin, Maxime's arm encircling her waist.

William bent to kiss her.

'If ever you need me . . .' he whispered as she clung to him, loath to let him go.

'It's true, we shall miss them,' Maxime said as they walked slowly back into the house. 'And so will the boys.'

He shook his head in bewilderment.

'Isn't it strange darling,' he remarked, 'that it was your first husband's father who led me to the Lord? If it were in a novel no one would believe it. They'd say it was too far-fetched.'

They stopped and their eyes met. But the brief moment of intimacy was interrupted by the shrill ring of the telephone.

'We have reason to believe that Comte de Montval's release is imminent,' an impersonal voice at the other end of the line announced.

Maxime stiffened.

'When shall we know for certain?'

'I'm afraid I can't say. But you will of course be informed as soon as it happens.'

Maxime walked thoughtfully back into the hall but Katharine had disappeared. In a way he was glad. He longed to tell her, but he did not want to hold out any false hopes. And as yet there was no proof.

'I thought you had things to do with Lucien,' Katharine remarked, seeing her husband hovering over the telephone in his study later that morning. 'You said you expected to be busy all day and might not be back for lunch.'

'Yes, well I'll be with you for lunch after all,' Maxime answered guardedly. 'I've got a lot of paperwork to clear up so Lucien is coming here to see me'

Although Maxime remained glued to the telephone all day, afraid that Katharine might receive a message in his absence, the Ministry of Interior did not call back. And when after three days of hanging around the house he finally telephoned them it was to be told that there was no further information.

'But you said three days ago that his release was *imminent*,' Maxime protested.

'I'm afraid for the time being negotiations have broken down. I cannot say any more. We will let you know as soon as there is any further development.'

Angry and disappointed Maxime replaced the receiver, sending up a quick prayer of thanks that he had not raised Katharine's hopes unnecessarily.

* * *

With his thumb Xavier carefully erased the figure four in the dirt behind the corner where he slept and faintly outlined a five against the one.

'The 15th of January', he said triumphantly. 'Perhaps today will bring my release.'

Each morning after his plate and mug had been removed he went through the ritual of marking off the days. And each time he did so he willed himself to be positive, clinging to Jesus' promise that he would never leave him nor forsake him.

'Jesus will either remove me from this hell-hole, or he will take me to be with him,' he whispered through his dry cracked lips which were now surrounded with weeping sores.

Then he smiled.

'Either way little mouse,' he remarked to his only companion who was busily licking his whiskers after picking up the few crumbs which remained, 'I win. Don't you agree?'

But the mouse merely flopped back to the ground and scuttled to its corner. The battalion of friends which had once invaded the cellar, faced with certain starvation, had deserted him. Even the rats, which had horrified Xavier when he first arrived, realising that there was nothing to be nibbled from his gaunt skeleton, had disappeared.

The day dragged by and, exhausted merely with the attempt to stay alive, Xavier was unable to summon enough energy to lift his feeble croaking voice in song. Each movement cost him. He had arrived at the point where even reminiscing was an effort and memories tended to become blurred and confused in his mind.

Rolling himself in his cloak, now almost useless against the damp cold which invaded the cellar, he tried to sleep. And was surprised when the door opened and his evening meal arrived. He listlessly chewed the unappetising bread and drank the greasy water, not because he had any appetite but because it gave him something to do. A purpose in life. A reason to stay alive. Even prayer had now become an intolerable effort and he tended to lose the thread of his sentences after a few words.

'I'll chalk up sixteen before I go to sleep,' he said as he crawled into his corner. 'In case my memory has left me completely by the morning.'

Then his bearded face, ingrained now with grime, softened and a wan smile touched his sore lips.

'The 16th of January,' he reminisced. 'Rowena's birthday. She would have been fifty-nine.'

His fevered mind wandered back through the veils of time. And he was with Rowena again. Her primrose-coloured hair shining in the sunlight, her sapphire-blue eyes laughing up at him as they ran, hand in hand down the beach at Medhiya to plunge into the warm surf. Revelling in the feeling of the water rushing over his body Xavier sighed, completely happy again.

The sudden jar of the door crashing open startled him as he and Rowena plunged in and out of the surf her hands tightly clasped in his. Xavier opened his eyes and for a few seconds was completely disorientated. Raising his eyes he saw Khaled leering down at him. And his mind reluctantly returned to the present.

'So my friend,' Khaled mocked. 'We still sleep'.

Xavier didn't answer.

'Up French pig when I speak to you,' he roared.

With an enormous effort Xavier managed to crawl to his feet.

Khaled watched him contemptuously.

'I have come to give you one last chance,' he threatened.

Producing the same paper from the folds of his djellabah he waved it in Xavier's face.

'You sign . . . or else.'

But Xavier remained motionless.

'Answer me when I speak to you, dog,' Khaled yelped.

'No Khaled,' Xavier answered, his voice almost inaudible.

'Speak up *Christian*,' Khaled jeered. 'Or has your fear of meeting your Heavenly Father paralysed you?'

Xavier took a deep breath. So this was to be it, he thought, Jesus has decided to take me to him.

'No Khaled,' he replied, enunciating each word with a great effort.

And his voice came out loud and clear.

In a terrible fury Khaled tossed the paper into the corner where the mouse immediately scuttled out and began nibbling at its edges. Then with a dramatic flourish he slowly drew his gleaming sword from his belt.

'On your knees scum,' he screeched, signalling with an imperious wave of his arm to the two masked men who had accompanied him. They immediately thrust Xavier's wasted body to the floor, pushing his head downwards, dragging back his long, matted hair so that his neck was bared.

'You still won't sign?' Khaled hissed menacingly.

'No,' Xavier croaked.

With an ear-splitting roar Khaled swung the sword upwards. Xavier heard the swish as it came towards his outstretched neck. But, just as the cold steel touched him Khaled held back. With a maniacal laugh he thrust the blade into his belt and grabbing Xavier by the hair forced him to look at him.

'Not here,' he gloated, his foul breath hot on his prisoner's face. 'No Christian, we will take you nearer your friends, the *Sunday* people.'"

He put all the loathing of which he was capable into the last three words.

'I want you to see for the last time the place where you are attempting to pollute the minds of the followers of Allah.'

He spat contemptuously and the spittle ran in a thick slime down Xavier's emaciated cheeks.

'We will give them your head on a platter . . . like John the Baptist.'

Once again his diabolical laugh rang out.

Letting go of Xavier's hair he pushed him aside.

In his weak state he toppled over.

'Get up,' Khaled screeched, dealing him a vicious kick.

Thwarted in his desire to humiliate his prisoner, Khaled's fury knew no bounds.

'Take him,' he roared as Xavier dragged himself to his feet.

The door crashed open and, his legs threatening to buckle beneath him, Xavier was dragged into the corridor.

As he passed his jailer, for a fleeting second their eyes met. And once again Xavier was sure he saw compassion and sadness mirrored in the other's gaze. He attempted to smile, but the man quickly turned away, trembling in every limb. Stumbling into a narrow alleyway where a van was waiting Xavier was thrust into the back wedged between his masked escorts.

'Now, my friend,' Khaled sneered, getting in beside the driver, 'let us see Algiers by night. You Frenchmen love Algiers by night don't you? And our beautiful Arab women. So different from your horse-faced wives. But soon when we take our glorious revenge, your countrymen will be running screaming in fear from the bloodbath Algiers by night is preparing for them.'

His nostrils quivered with scorn as his hooded eyes looked his prisoner up and down.

'But *you*, my friend, shall see our city one more time. *Then* you can go to meet your Maker.'

He gave his piercing screech of a laugh once again. And felt for his sword.

The van wound in and out of the steep narrow streets finally turning into a broad tree-lined highway. And Xavier knew where he was. The Mission was not more than twenty-minutes walk from where he had been kept prisoner for all those months.

He smiled grimly to himself at the irony of the situation. So near and yet so far.

'Look,' Khaled triumphed. 'Look infidel.'

He pointed a long bony finger.

'There is the house of the *Sunday* people. Look at it Christian dog for the last time.'

He leant over the back seat, his face close to his prisoner's. And once again Xavier smelt his fetid breath.

'You will never see it again,' he mocked. 'You will never see anything again. Only your lifeless eyes when we throw your head to your infidel brothers will gaze vacantly upon it.'

He smirked.

'Or perhaps we will wrap your severed head in a parcel . . . a little present for your friend the Chief of Police. He can share it with your illustrious generals who parade in pomp down our streets thinking they have the right to govern our people. It will be an hors d'oeuvre. A foretaste of what they can expect when the FLN and the Algerian people rise up against the French pigs and begin the slaughter.'

Xavier clenched his teeth tightly as he tried to control the revulsion which rose in his throat.

Without turning his head he glanced sideways out of the corner of his eye at the dark shuttered Mission House which for so many years had been his home. The car slid slowly past then suddenly accelerated and drove a short way out of the town to a dumping ground.

'Out,' Khaled ordered, removing his sword menacingly

from his belt. 'This is where *the rest* of your body will lie and rot.'

He waved his arm across an expanse of twisted, broken bicycles, worn-out tyres and decaying rubbish.

'Here where you belong.'

In a final gesture of loathing and contempt he spat in Xavier's face.

'Among the garbage!'

Chapter
23

William awoke with a start, bathed in sweat. Slowly raising himself on his pillows he frowned, not understanding what had roused him. Switching on the bedside light he peered at his travelling clock. The hands stood at ten minutes past three. Turning on his side he closed his eyes, but sleep evaded him.

'Lord,' he queried. 'Have you awakened me for a reason? Is there someone you want me to pray for?'

As the words left his lips that chilling sense of evil which had engulfed him on Christmas Eve during the midnight communion service in the drawing-room at Le Moulin, returned.

Gasping at the intensity of it, William cast his mind back trying to remember what had caused it. And suddenly it all came flooding back. Their prayers for Xavier . . . and Katharine's difficulty with his suggestion that they should pray for his captors. His brows drawn together in concentration, William tried to recall what had made the evil abruptly snake away and disappear. And then he remembered. It was when he had asked Jesus to reveal himself to the one who was causing Xavier so much pain, and turn him from his evil ways.

But with the remembrance came an overpowering conviction that Xavier was again in mortal danger.

Slipping to his knees William began to praise. But the

evil did not go away. It crushed down upon him, gripping him in a terrible stranglehold. Distraught and bewildered William called out to his Lord for help. And the answer came immediately 'this demon will only be cast out by prayer and fasting'.

'Father,' he cried. 'There is not time. You know I will fast, for as long as you put it on my heart to do so. But I beg you to hear my prayer and act now. Your Spirit has shown me that Xavier is at this very moment in mortal danger. His life hangs in the balance.'

The sweat with which William had been bathed when he awoke so abruptly was now pouring down his face as he lifted his hands in supplication.

'Lord speak to this man whoever he is,' he begged. 'Open his heart to receive your love. Show him what he is doing . . . and . . . I beseech you Jesus, save Xavier.'

He fell to the floor exhausted and remained motionless unable to move or to pray, silently pleading with his Heavenly Father, lying there in agony, his body writhing in pain because of the suffering which he knew was now tearing Xavier apart, he felt the touch of a hand on his shoulder. He looked around him. But there was no one there. Yet it was as though a gentle voice said: 'You have done what I asked you. Xavier is in my hands. Leave the rest to me'.

And the evil vanished.

Slowly rising to his feet William climbed back into bed. And he suddenly felt totally exhausted.

*   *   *

As Xavier was roughly pushed from the van, he blinked. His eyes, unaccustomed after so many months of almost complete darkness to even the charcoal grey of the fading night, were momentarily unable to focus. And he stumbled.

Khaled's lip curled contemptuously. He lunged at his prisoner with his foot and the little wind which remained in Xavier's thin chest wheezed out, leaving him gasping.

'We'll see whether your God will save you,' he sneered.

Once again he gave that hard metallic laugh.

'My God will save me Khaled,' Xavier replied, summoning all his strength in a last gasp. 'But perhaps not in the way you expect. You can kill my body, but you cannot kill my soul. That is immortal.'

He looked up at his tormentor from where he was lying, Khaled's foot resting heavily on his chest.

'Have *you* that assurance Khaled?'

At those words fear shot into Khaled's black eyes. Looking wildly round him he staggered backwards, an arm raised as if to shield his face.

Then emitting a satanic shriek which sent cascading echoes reverberating in the semi-darkness like the fury of an avalanche of rocks gathering speed to destroy all in their path, Khaled suddenly became volcanic with rage.

Kicking wildly with both feet, still maniacally screeching abuse, he backed drunkenly away zigzagging crazily across the debris, crashing blindly into everything in his path, as if fleeing from mortal danger.

Visibly shaken, the two masked men forced Xavier to his feet. And stumbling behind their screaming, half-crazed leader they dragged Xavier to the waiting van.

With an ear-splitting crash of gears it rocketed off, heading back to the town. As they drew near the Mission House Khaled, still writhing with diabolical rage, bellowed an order. There was a sudden screech of brakes and the van abruptly stopped. Thrown forward by the brutal impact Xavier felt a sharp arrow pain stab through his chest.

'Out,' Khaled screamed hysterically, waving his arms dementedly. 'Out, out, *out.*'

Xavier felt rough hands grab him. The van door flew open and his body shot through it to land heavily on the Mission doorstep. As it did so his head crashed against a stone pillar spurting blood across the pavement.

Opening his eyes he saw the van zigzagging wildly in the distance. Then, as the warm sticky blood now gushing down his face veiled his sight, his vision became blurred. Sinking back onto the hard pavement an immense weariness such as he had never experienced in all his months of captivity crept over his body. And past and present began to merge together in a hazy mist. Making one last superhuman effort he tried to stagger to his feet and ring the doorbell. It was so near, that freedom he craved. But every remaining ounce of strength seemed to have been drained from him. And the bell slipped from his grasp.

He sank wearily back on to the hard pavement, consciousness ebbing and flowing like a caressing summer tide. Suddenly all the terror and anguish of the preceding months vanished. Slowly raising his eyes Xavier stared unbelievingly. Rowena was standing beside him, smiling and beckoning him towards her. With a cry of joy, he held out his arms for her embrace.

* * *

The shrill ring of the telephone echoing through the deserted police station momentarily startled the Chief Inspector, sitting tensely drumming his fingers on his desk. The ultimatum ended at dawn. And he had been nervously watching long fingers of pearly grey begin to lighten the inky blackness of the night

Leaning quickly forward he grabbed the receiver before the second ring.

'Our part of the bargain has been completed,' a voice which did not identify itself announced. 'The goods have been delivered *alive* to the Mission House door. *Vive l'Algérie Libre.*'

There was a click as the unknown caller hung up.

Rising swiftly the Chief Inspector reached for his gun, vaguely wondering why the terrorist had stressed the word 'alive'.

He was soon to find out.

'Chartier, Dandieu, Archambaud,' he barked, striding quickly into the corridor and heading for the main door.

Immediately three uniformed policemen appeared.

'The doctor?' the Chief Inspector queried tersely.

'Just coming sir.'

As they leapt down the steps and into the waiting police van the doctor hurried after them.

'Mission House,' the Chief Inspector ordered.

The car shot away from the pavement and raced along the deserted street.

Dawn was just breaking as it lurched to a stop. Before it was fully stationary the doors flew open and the five men leapt out.

'My *God*,' the Chief Inspector exclaimed, seeing the filthy bundle of rags huddled lifeless on the Mission doorstep. 'They've tricked us, the bastards. That surely can't be him.'

He dropped to his knees then recoiled, overwhelmed by the stench of almost six months of unwashed humanity. Turning the body over he drew the tangled blood soaked hair away from the grimy face, and carefully studied the man's features.

'Without the beard, and stretching the imagination to its limits this *could* be the man we're looking for.'

He glanced up at the doctor hovering at his side.

'I understand now why the caller emphasised that they had delivered the goods *alive*,' he continued grimly. 'Doesn't look as if there's much life in him now.'

He stood up and the doctor pulled aside the reeking cloak and placed his stethoscope on Xavier's chest.

'There is still a beat,' he hestitated, 'but it's very faint. Unless we get him to hospital quickly he won't last the hour.'

Pulling a syringe from his bag he bared Xavier's arm, and felt around the empty skin hanging from the bone to find a vein into which he could inject.

'Ring the doorbell,' he ordered. 'Get to a telephone and contact Dr Legendre at the hospital. Make sure it's Dr Legendre and no one else. I told him to stand by for the call. Say we'll be at the hospital in a quarter of an hour and to be prepared. The *goods* have been delivered in very poor condition.'

As he spoke, soft footsteps padded across the Mission courtyard. A heavy bolt was drawn back and the old Arab doorman stood framed in the porch.

Seeing the police gathered in force he drew back, startled. Then he glanced at the bundle of rags which the doctor was instructing the policemen to carry very carefully. Running into the street he peered intently into the ashen dirt-ingrained face gasped and clutched at his throat, his eyes wide with a mixture of fear and surprise.

'Brother *Xavier*,' he cried, reaching out to stroke the sunken cheeks.

The Chief Inspector exchanged glances with the doctor.

'You know this man?' he asked curtly.

'It's Brother Xavier,' the old man moaned brokenly, tears meandering down his withered face.

Turning he scuttled back into the courtyard, calling hysterically for the rest of the community.

'Shut him up,' the Chief Inspector barked to the remaining policeman. 'Stay here and explain that until I give the order no one is to know *anything* . . . you understand.'

'Yes sir.'

The policeman saluted and ran across the courtyard. As he did so, shutters were rattling open and heads appearing at every window.

'Well, that's our confirmation, doctor,' the Chief Inspector remarked as he climbed into the van. 'I only hope Chartier puts the fear of God into them so that they *do* keep their mouths shut. Until the Ministry of Interior is informed the last thing we want is a leakage.'

The doctor nodded absently, his finger on Xavier's pulse.

'If we don't do something within a few minutes,' he said tersely as the van hurtled towards the hospital, 'it won't matter. Nobody's going to bargain over a *corpse*!'

Chapter
24

Katharine was still asleep when the telephone rang.

Maxime, in his study surrounded by an avalanche of neglected paperwork, frowned with annoyance as he stretched out his hand to pick up the receiver. He had expected at this early hour of the morning to be left in peace.

'Comte de Montval has been released,' the impersonal voice of the official from the Ministry of Interior announced. His neutral tones betrayed as little emotion as they had done with every previous announcement.

Maxime felt as if he had been winded.

'Can you repeat that,' he stammered. 'I'm not sure I heard correctly.'

The man, still with the same lack of emotion, repeated his previous phrase.

Maxime leant back in his leather chair staring vacantly into space. Now that the call had come, he couldn't believe it. There had been so many rumours and false alarms in the past five months.

'You're absolutely *sure*,' he probed.

There was a slight pause. The man was obviously irritated by Maxime's incredulity.

'Absolutely sure Monsieur,' he said coldly. 'The Chief Inspector of the central police station in Algiers accompanied your father-in-law to hospital just after dawn.'

'And it *was* my father-in-law?'

'He has been identified by a member of the Mission where he lived,' the man replied testily.

Suddenly Maxime realised that it was true. The long agony was over.

'Forgive me,' he apologised. 'The news is a shock. Can you tell me what happened?'

'I'm afraid I cannot say more. Only that the negotiations finally had a positive outcome.'

'And my father-in-law? How is he?'

'I regret to say that his life is hanging in the balance. According to the hospital he must have been thrown from a moving vehicle and knocked his head when he landed, fracturing his skull. Nothing serious, but he is still unconscious. There is also a deep gash on his forehead. And there appears to be some damage to his kidneys probably caused when he hit the pavement and landed heavily on his back.'

He paused.

'Had he been found half an hour later, we would be making arrangements for the return of his body. As it is, I can assure you that every effort is being made to save him.'

He gave a short laugh.

'Not only for the sake of his family', he remarked drily. 'We are hoping he will be able to provide us with some very useful information concerning his captors.'

'I'll leave for Algiers immediately,' Maxime cut in.

'I would not advise that. Comte de Montval will be brought back to Paris, to the Val de Grâce*, as soon as it is possible. You could arrive only to find that he had left.'

'Very well,' Maxime said tightly. 'I'll sit and wait for news.'

'We are hoping to withhold the announcement of

Comte de Montval's release until he is safely back in Paris.'

'But you surely don't have any objection to my telling my wife,' Maxime broke in.

'On the contrary, it would be advisable to do so. With the press one never knows. There could be a leakage which means she might hear of it from another source. But . . . prepare her for the worst.'

'What about the rest of the family?' Maxime interrupted. 'I can hardly keep the news from them.'

'Monsieur Montredon,' the unknown voice said patiently, but Maxime could sense the underlying exasperation. 'Until your father-in-law is out of Algeria his life is still in danger.'

'Why?' Maxime puzzled. 'I don't understand.'

'It's very simple. These terrorists are ruthless. Part of the bargain was to deliver Comte de Montval alive.'

He took a deep breath.

'Those conditions were met . . . but only just. Now, if they can eliminate him before he has a chance to talk . . .'

'I see,' Maxime ruminated. 'So he's not home and dry yet?'

'Not entirely. We will keep you informed.'

There was a click as the man replaced the receiver.

As always when he had a problem, Maxime turned to his great-uncle. Picking up the receiver he asked the operator for the house in Narbonne.

Armand listened intently without interrupting.

'So you see Uncle,' Maxime said desperately. 'In view of the danger Xavier is still in, I wonder whether I should tell Katharine. After all, I might be raising her hopes only to have them dashed again.'

Armand frowned in concentration.

'I think you should tell her Maxime,' he replied at last. 'Should Xavier not survive and Katharine discovers that you have withheld the news of his release . . . After all you've both gone through during these past few months I hate to think what her reaction might be.'

Maxime nodded grimly, wondering just how he was going to phrase it, to cushion the blow which he might later have to deliver.

'I don't want to interfere,' Armand went on hesitantly, 'but if you wish, I could come over to Le Moulin straight away . . . and be there if you need me.'

'Oh *Uncle*,' Maxime exclaimed, relieved now that the entire responsibility for what he had to do no longer rested with him. 'If you could . . .'

He replaced the receiver just as the clock in the tower boomed out the hour.

Eight o'clock. Katharine would be awake now.

Taking a deep breath, Maxime walked determinedly towards the stairs, bracing himself for what lay ahead.

* * *

'The Ministry of Interior has been informed,' the Chief Inspector said, 'and I've arranged to have a 24-hour security guard at the hospital. There will also be two armed policeman inside Comte de Montval's room and two outside the door . . . just in case.'

'By the looks of him,' Dr Legendre remarked, glancing back at the door of Xavier's room, 'I don't think it will be necessary for very long.'

'It's as bad as that?'

'I'm afraid so. His constitution has been wrecked by malnutrition and lack of light and air during his months in captivity. Then that blow to his head when he landed on the pavement hasn't helped. As things stand, I don't see how he can possibly pull through.'

The Chief Inspector creased his brow.

'Does his body shows signs of torture?' he enquired after a few minutes.

'No, oddly enough, nothing at all, apart from what looks like a few vicous kicks. But there's very little left of it. He's a skeleton. Nothing more than skin and bone.'

'I see. Then I imagine they employed their usual methods.'

The doctor raised his eyebrows enquiringly.

'They have other means of torture,' the Chief Inspector said curtly.

'Learned from us perhaps?' the doctor remarked drily.

The Chief Inspector shot him a hard look.

'I like to think not,' he replied as four armed police officers appeared in the corridor.

'Marcillac and Béranger you are to sit on each side of the bed,' he instructed. 'One watch the door and one the window. Scherer and Baulieu stand guard outside the door. *No one* is allowed to enter the room without Dr Legendre's permission. Is that quite clear?'

'Yes sir,' they answered smartly.

The police officer held open the door and Marcillac and Béranger entered the silent shaded room.

'What *are* those means of torture Chief Inspector?' Dr Legendre enquired, as he and the police officer walked away.

'Psychological,' the Chief Inspector replied laconically. 'Usually far worse than physical torture. They make threats and stage mock executions, usually in the middle of the night, drawing back just as the sword hits the neck or they are about to fire the gun. With these terrorists, it's usually the sword . . . infinitely more terrifying. And that way they can prolong the agony. Enough to make the toughest prisoner collapse and "confess" after a few enactments.'

The doctor shuddered.

'And of course solitary confinement for months on end on a starvation diet in a dark filthy cell with only a hole in the corner for all their bodily functions. I hardly need to tell you what *that* can be like after a few days, much less a few months. I imagine this poor devil has been through all that. Much worse than any beating. If he recovers he could have quite a story to tell.'

'*If* he recovers,' the doctor grimaced. 'But what state will he be in if he does? I should imagine his mind would be shattered. After all, he's not a young man.'

'We shall see,' the Chief Inspector replied tersely, with a final backward glance towards Xavier's closed door.

* * *

'Good morning darling,' Maxime said softly.

Katharine was just stirring as he entered the room. Opening her eyes she blinked up at him.

'What time is it?' she enquired sleepily.

He sat down on the bed and took her hands in his.

'Just eight o'clock. But don't hurry to get up,' he parried, playing for time, praying that God would give him the words which would prepare Katharine for whatever the days ahead might bring.

'I've just had a call from the Ministry of Interior,' he went on, lightly caressing her fingers.

Katharine shot up in bed. A flash of fear darting into her eyes.

'Zag?' she trembled.

'He's been rescued darling.'

With a low cry she flung her arms round his neck and held him tight, as if it were a dream from which she would awaken if she didn't cling desperately to it.

'Maxime,' she whispered, her voice muffled. 'Oh

Maxime, thank God. The nightmare's over. It's finally ended.'

She leant back on her pillows, her face radiant, the golden lights which he had not seen reflected in her topaz eyes for so long now leaping and dancing. Maxime's heart constricted and caught in his throat, like a caged bird battering its wings in an attempt to be free. And for a moment he couldn't bear to mar her happiness. He could not bear to tell her the truth.

'When did it happen?' Katharine gasped excitedly. 'Where is he? When can I see him?'

She leapt out of bed and, running to the window, flung back the heavy curtains. Lifting up her arms in sheer joy, she threw back her head and drunkenly breathed in great gulps of early morning air.

'Maxime,' she cried jubilantly. 'I'm so *happy*.'

And dancing towards him, she caught him in her arms and pirouetted round the room.

In spite of his anxiety Maxime could not help laughing. This was his Katharine, the Katharine he had married. The wife he had known for the first five years of their life together but who lately had been hidden from him behind a heavy dark cloud.

'Steady on', he chided, easing her into a chair. 'Calm down, there's something else I have to tell you.'

Immediately Katharine's expression changed.

'Your father is in hospital,' he said gently. 'It was to be expected. Almost six months imprisonment has left him suffering from malnutrition among other things.'

'What other things?' she faltered.

'I don't know exactly darling. Xavier was only released a few hours ago. The Ministry of Interior telephoned as soon as they received the news. But the man didn't have a lot of information to give.'

'So he's still in Algiers?'

276

'For the moment.'

'But when is he coming back?'

'Very soon,' Maxime soothed, seeing Katharine's euphoric mood rapidly evaporating.

'Then I must go to Algiers immediately.'

'I suggested that darling. But they advised against it. We could easily arrive in Algiers to find that Xavier had already left for Paris.'

He took her hands in his.

'I'm afraid we must just be patient . . . and pray.'

As their eyes met, Katharine slowly withdrew her fingers from his steady grasp.

'It's not as rosy as it at first appeared is it?' she said slowly. 'Zag's ill, isn't he?'

Maxime nodded.

Katharine said nothing, merely sat looking down at her clasped hands now twisting agitatedly in her lap.

Maxime's heart ached as he saw the sudden downward swing her happy mood had taken. Leaning forward he gently tilted her face towards him. She looked up and her eyes were dark again.

'You're right,' she said quietly. 'All we can do is pray.'

And, covering her face with her hands to hide the tears which had sprung to her eyes, she dropped to her knees.

At that moment there was a hurried tap on the door and the boys burst in sent by Nanny to say good morning to their mother before leaving for school. Seeing their parents on their knees they stopped abruptly, then stealthily crept towards them. They were used to praying with their mother at bedtime. But this was the first time they had seen their parents kneeling together.

'Can we talk to Jesus with you?' Léon asked simply, gently tapping his father's shoulder.

Although not yet of school age he always accompanied his brothers on their morning visit.

Maxime looked up and held out his hand to his youngest son.

'Maman and I were asking Jesus to take care of Bon Papa and bring him safely home,' he smiled.

The twins clasped hands and knelt reverently. Slipping his hand in his father's, Léon knelt between his parents and took Katharine's hand in his.

Katharine looked up, tears of joy and gratitude trickling down her pale cheeks, momentarily washing away her anxiety, as Jehan grasped her free hand.

How could Jesus who had said 'suffer the little children to come unto me' resist their trusting prayer she reasoned as her little sons, ignorant of the true facts, began one by one to pray. Their childlike faith never doubting, convinced that Jesus would honour their request.

And for the moment, Katharine felt at peace.

* * *

Lavinia was crossing the hall of Tamara's villa in Nice when William walked down the stairs. At eighty years of age, his disturbed night had taken its toll on him. He had overslept and was feeling drained and weary.

'I'm so sorry I'm late,' he apologised to Tamara, sitting at the cluttered breakfast-table reading her mail.

Tamara looked up and smiled, pushing the coffee pot across the table towards him as Lavinia rushed back into the dining room.

'You'll never believe the news,' she exclaimed excitedly. 'Xavier's been released!'

William and Tamara stared at her open-mouthed.

Then William remembered the fears which had awakened him. His anguished pleading with God for

Xavier's life. His desperate struggle with the powers of darkness which had kept him on his knees until dawn.

'Thank you Lord,' he breathed. 'Oh thank you Father.'

'How did you find out?' he enquired as Lavinia sat down and poured herself another cup of coffee.

'Félicie told me. She was listening to the wireless in the kitchen when they suddenly interrupted the programme to make the announcement. She was bursting with excitement.'

Lavinia put down her cup.

'I *must* telephone Katharine. She'll be ecstatic.'

As the dring-dring sounded at the other end of the line Lavinia's eyes shone with happiness. Maxime, alone in his study, all thoughts of his accumulation of work far from his mind, grabbed it.

'Maxime,' Lavinia exulted. 'What wonderful news. We are all *so* happy for you. Katharine must be out of her mind with relief.'

Maxime frowned. Did Lavinia mean what he thought she meant. And, if so, how on earth had she found out?

'*Maxime*,' Lavinia probed, not understanding his silence. 'Are you there?'

'I'm sorry Lavinia,' he apologised. 'I'm afraid you took me by surprise.'

'But you do *know* . . .'

She gave a startled gasp.

'Oh surely they've told you the wonderful news. Xavier's been freed!'

Maxime groaned inwardly.

At that moment Katharine, who had been idling over breakfast with Armand, having heard the telephone appeared in the doorway. Maxime put his hand over the receiver.

'It's Lavinia,' he mouthed. 'Do you want to talk to her.'

Katharine nodded and crossed to his side

'Yes Lavinia, I do know', Maxime went on. 'I'm sorry but we're all rather bewildered at the moment. I was informed earlier this morning but was told not to spread the news around. For some reason the authorities want it kept secret.'

'I can't think why,' Lavinia laughed. 'It's *wonderful* news. Anyway they haven't managed it. Tamara's maid heard it on the wireless about ten minutes ago.

Maxime's lips tightened in frustration.

'I'll pass you to Katharine,' he said crisply, She's here beside me and would love to talk to you.'

Getting up he handed his wife the receiver and left the room.

'*Now* what do we do?' he asked desperately, sitting down beside Armand.

'I don't see there's a great deal we can do,' his uncle replied calmly. 'The press has somehow got hold of it. And that's that. Just hope for the best my boy.'

'I think I'll ring that chap at the Ministry of Interior,' Maxime frowned.

'It's most unfortunate but it's happened,' the unknown man replied. 'We must just reinforce the security surrounding your father-in-law, and get him back to Paris as soon as possible. But don't, under any circumstances, mention where he is. We'll spread the word around that he's already left Algeria.'

Maxime replaced the receiver, his heart heavy.

How was he going to explain this one to Katharine?

From that moment onwards the telephone did not stop ringing. The flash news broadcast appeared to have been heard by everyone. And everyone wanted to know more. Maxime spent the day fending off questions and attempting to remain polite with, at times, almost complete strangers who had telephoned in order to be in on any gory details.

At the end of the afternoon he told Alphonse to say he was not available and to take a message from anyone other than close family members.

'If the Ministry of Interior chap has tried to get hold of us today,' he remarked to Armand, 'he won't have been able to. I think I'll telephone and see if there have been any further developments.'

But the news was the same. Xavier was still unconscious and growing weaker by the hour.

'In other words,' Maxime said grimly, 'the doctors don't hold out much hope.'

'I'm afraid that seems to be the general consensus,' was the laconic reply. 'But we may have more to tell you soon. I'll keep in touch.'

After a sleepless night Maxime finally got up.

He knew that Katharine's night had been equally disturbed and he had longed to hold her in his arms and comfort her. But she had not turned to him. Her body had remained rigid and taut whenever he had tentatively approached her. And he sensed that whatever her outward appearance might suggest, her mind was once again held in a tight grip of tormented emotions. Looking down at her as he carefully tucked the covers around her bare shoulders he saw that she had finally fallen asleep.

It was still dark and the house was as silent as a tomb when he walked down the stairs and entered his study. It was too early to telephone the Ministry of Interior. And, he reasoned, there was hardly likely to be any news since the previous evening . . . unless it was bad news. Maxime quickly dismissed the thought from his mind. Refusing even to consider that after all these months of anguish, now that victory was within their grasp, Xavier would finally not come out of this horrendous experience alive.

Sitting down at his desk he wearily passed his hand

across his face. Then, with a sigh, drew a sheaf of papers towards him and attempted to immerse himself in the estate accounts.

'Would Monsieur like breakfast served in his study?' Alphonse enquired, padding silently into the room with the morning's mail.

Maxime looked up, surprised to see that the night had gone and dawn was creeping through the stained glass windows.

'Thank you Alphonse,' he replied. 'But I'll wait and have it with Madame.'

He smiled as the elderly butler placed the salver with the letters on the desk in front of him.

Since Auguste, who had been the local postman for over sixty years, had finally retired the mail arrived promptly at seven and not, as had been the case in the old days, any time between ten and four in the afternoon, depending on how many kitchens Auguste stopped in to chat and down a glass of local red wine.

Sorting quickly through the pile Maxime saw that there was nothing of any great importance. Taking a paper-knife he slit open an oblong envelope with 'Association of Wine Growers' printed in one corner. Glancing quickly down the few lines written on the page he frowned. Then, peering closely, read them again.

'We hope to be able to inform you very shortly that the goods you are expecting will be arriving by air at Le Bourget. Time and date to be confirmed.'

It was signed: Jean Lelièvre.

Jean Lelièvre was the name of his contact at the Ministry of Interior!

Maxime's lips twisted in an amused smile.

'Obviously a false name,' he murmured. 'I wonder who he really is?'

Little did he realise how close he was to finding out.

Chapter
25

The Chief Inspector looked grave as he entered Dr Legendre's office.

'It is becoming increasingly difficult to guarantee Comte de Montval's safety,' he announced. 'I've doubled the number of men on guard but these terrorists are diabolical and will stop at nothing. The Arabs haven't forgotten what has happened since the insurrection. They've seen the crack in the French fabric and are rubbing their hands in glee, just biding their time. There's an undercurrent of rebellion brewing up all over the city and the FLN could openly erupt *en masse* at any moment. Once they do I hate to think of the bloodbath which could result . . . especially for us. And I'm not convinced the French Army would be able to crush it this time.'

The doctor pursed his lips then, picking up a paper knife lying on his desk idly transferred it from one hand to the other as if attempting to guess the weight.

The Chief Inspector frowned, irritated by the lack of response.

'The situation is becoming critical,' he stated curtly leaning forward in his chair to add emphasis to his words. 'If we don't get the patient out of the country within the next few days . . .'

He shrugged expressively.

'The next few *hours* would be better.'

'His heart is a little stronger,' Dr Legendre murmured thoughtfully. 'But he's still unconscious . . . and very weak. I'm not sure he would stand the journey by air.'

'Well he can't be sent by sea,' the Chief Inspector exploded.

'No, no I quite see that.'

He looked up and met the police officer's gaze.

'How long can you give me?'

'All I can say is the sooner the better. Otherwise I cannot take the responsibility for what might happen.'

His hands gripped the desk in front of him.

'Doctor,' he said earnestly. 'Montval is a very valuable prisoner. He comes from a well-known influential family. And he knows a great deal. The terrorists are terrified of what he might reveal.'

The doctor frowned.

'Are you suggesting that Comte de Montval was working for your services? I had understood he was some kind of missionary.'

'I'm not suggesting anything. I'm just saying that the terrorists are gunning for him. And they'll get him by any means if we don't act soon.'

The doctor stood up and walking from behind his desk took the police officer's arm.

'Well Chief Inspector,' he said evenly. 'It seems we have no option. *I* don't think he's fit to stand the journey. Frankly, I don't think he'd make it. And *you* don't think he stands a chance if he stays here. So it seems that my patient is between the devil and the deep blue sea. In other words, in a no-win situation.'

The Chief Inspector shrugged.

'The decision is yours Doctor. But don't say I didn't warn you.'

* * *

'May I come with you?' Armand asked diffidently when Maxime announced during lunch the following day that he had decided to take Katharine to Paris to await Xavier's arrival. Anything was better than remaining at Le Moulin feeling helpless.

Armand had scarcely left Katharine's side since the news of Xavier's release. And Maxime was grateful. Their uncle's calm presence seemed to soothe her and give her hope and courage where he himself had failed.

'I don't want to intrude . . .' Armand put in hurriedly when Maxime, surprised by his suggestion, did not immediately reply.

'*Intrude* Uncle,' Maxime exclaimed. 'You could never intrude. We'd be *delighted* to have you with us, wouldn't we darling?'

Katharine leant across the table and squeezed Armand's hand.

'Do come,' she added.

'But what about Toinette and Marie-Louise?' Maxime enquired.

'It would be good to give them a break from me,' Armand smiled. 'Then they could bicker day *and* night without my being there to act as referee. Anyway they probably wouldn't even notice my absence. Marie-Louise is up to her eyes interfering in everyone's private affairs and Toinette has developed this passion for antiques. I returned home on Tuesday evening to find she'd bought a ten-ton marble statue of an Austrian archduke, an absolute monstrosity, whom she insists was one of our ancestors.'

His lips twitched in amusement.

'He wasn't of course. Toinette intended giving it a place of honour in our already overcrowded drawing-room. But it apparently took six men to carry it into the house who then all got wedged trying to manoeuvre it round the bend in the stairs. In the end it was dumped in the hall next to the hat stand. And there I imagine it will stay. Toinette was furious. After running hysterically around like a headless chicken for several hours she's now lying prostrate in a pitch-black room, pretending she's dying.'

Armand looked sadly at them both.

'And today they're delivering a portrait of Napoleon which is so large they'll either have to cut it in two or knock down a wall to get it in. So that will cause *more* shrieking between Toinette and Marie-Louise who, as you know, is royalist to the core.'

Katharine and Maxime both burst out laughing. Seeing them, Armand relaxed and his nut-brown eyes twinkled.

'So you see my dears,' he assured them, 'you'd be doing me a great favour by allowing me to accompany you.'

His smile faded and he absently stroked the stem of his wine glass.

'Xavier has always had a very special place in my heart,' he said quietly. 'Perhaps the son I never had.'

*   *   *

They all three left for Paris that evening.

It was two days later at two o'clock in the morning that Maxime was awakened by the insistent ring of the telephone. Dragging on his dressing-gown he hurried down the stairs just as a bleary-eyed Berthe, her grey hair hanging in a plait down her back, stumbled into the hall.

'It's all right Berthe,' he smiled. 'Go back to bed. I'm sorry you've been disturbed.'

'The goods you are expecting will be arriving at Le Bourget at zero three thirty hours.'

There was a click and the line went dead.

As the car slowed down at the approach to Le Bourget Katharine was surprised to see no sign of life. The airport was in complete darkness. Puzzled, as soon as it slid to a standstill she was the first to jump out. It was just a quarter past three. A tall man in his mid-forties, hovering in the shadows, came forward, his hand outstretched.

'Madame Montredon de la Livière?' he enquired as Maxime came up beside her and took her arm.

Katharine nodded, unable to speak, the full impact of what was about to happen suddenly striking her.

'Jean Lelièvre,' he announced.

He smiled as Maxime raised his eyebrows in surprise.

'Perhaps I should introduce myself as Jean Lechat,' Maxime teased, immediately recognising the fictious Jean Lelièvre as Axel d'Aste, one of his old school friends from his days at Sorèze.* Isn't the world a small place?'

Katharine looked in bewilderment from one to the other as the two men, smiling broadly, grasped hands.

'But why the secrecy?' Maxime enquired.

'All part of the cloak and dagger set-up I work for,' d'Aste smiled.

He turned to Katharine.

'If you would like to come this way, Madame.'

And he led them, not into the deserted airport as she had expected, but round the side on to the tarmac where a car was waiting. Katharine looked apprehensively at her husband as d'Aste held open the door and motioned her to enter.

'It's all right darling,' Maxime reassured her, climbing in beside her. 'I can vouch for this rogue.'

Smiling broadly, d'Aste alias Lelièvre got in beside the driver.

'I said Le Bourget,' he explained leaning over the front seat as the car moved away. 'But in actual fact, for tighter security, Comte de Montval is being brought back in an Army Ambulance plane which will land at the military air base not far from here. Can't take too many precautions. We don't want the press on our heels just yet.'

It was now twenty past three and Katharine was becoming anxious. But a few minutes later the car halted beside a military patrol post then bumped across the turf towards a prefabricated hut. Standing in splendid isolation on the tarmac was an ambulance.

'There's no point in going on to the airstrip until the plane is announced,' d'Aste remarked as he handed Katharine down.

He pushed open a door. Five men were sitting smoking inside. They rose to their feet as the little party was ushered in.

'Colleagues from the DST* who've been working with me on this case,' d'Aste explained, introducing them one by one. Katharine was surprised at such a large reception committee, but thankful when the last man to be introduced turned out to be a doctor.

Sitting down in the stuffy room, she glanced surreptitiously at her watch. The hands stood at twenty-five minutes past three.

'Shouldn't we perhaps be going outside?' she ventured.

'The plane has not yet been announced,' d'Aste smiled.

'But I thought it was due at half-past three.'

He shrugged.

'There appears to be some delay. Don't worry Madame, we shall be informed of its arrival in good time.'

He leant forward and held up a flask.

'Coffee?'

She shook her head.

Sitting apart as the men chatted together Katharine counted the minutes. When her watch registered four o'clock she began to feel apprehensive. Maxime, deep in conversation with the mysterious Jean Lelièvre, seeing her face tighten with anxiety excused himself and crossed the room to her side.

'It's all right darling', he soothed 'Delays *can* occur. There's nothing to worry about.'

She smiled weakly. Far from reassured.

When another twenty-five minutes went by with still no sign of anything happening she felt she could bear it no longer.

'Has *no* one any news?' she pleaded. 'I suppose the plane did *leave* Algiers?'

'It left on time Madame,' one of the DST officials answered. 'I don't know why there's this delay.'

He turned and smiled at her.

'I'm sorry we dragged you out of bed so early for nothing.'

His words struck a chord in Katharine's heart and her faced turned ashen. What if they *had* come for nothing? What if there had been an accident . . . or Zag had died on the way?

She sat there, her body rigid with fear, remembering another arrival at Le Bourget from Algiers in 1946. Then the small private plane had crashed on landing. And Zag had been the only survivor. Could the same thing happen this time? Or could the plane have gone down in the sea? Zag had had so many brushes with death in the past twenty years. Surely his luck couldn't last for ever.

Maxime, guessing what was going through her mind felt for her hand. But it was cold and lifeless. And as he gently caressed it in his own he felt no answering response. He looked helplessly across at Armand thoughtfully sipping a cup of coffee. Seeing his nephew's anguished glance Armand put down the cup and walking over to where they were sitting eased himself into a chair beside Katharine.

'Shall we put the matter in God's hands,' her great-uncle said softly. 'Xavier is his child.'

Katharine turned a blank stare on him. Then suddenly her vision cleared.

'What a fool', she whispered. 'What a fool I've been. I had convinced myself that Zag's luck could not hold out indefinitely. As if God's will depended on *luck*.'

She shook her head bewilderedly.

'How *can* God put up with me?' she asked herself pathetically. 'I had completely left him out of this.'

She bowed her head and the three of them began to quietly pray.

The little group of men standing near the window looked curiously in their direction. But Katharine was oblivious of their puzzled stares. In her desperation and fear she cried out to the Jesus who had saved her so many times in the past, pleading with him to intervene once again for her father.

Raising her head, Katharine glanced for the umpteenth time at the clock on the opposite wall. It was now half-past five. She noticed that Axel d'Aste was doing the same thing.

The men huddled by the window were conferring anxiously together and scanning the night sky, straining their ears for the hum of a distant aircraft. But not a leaf stirred. Only the twinkling stars sailing serenely across the dark sky gave any sign of life.

Suddenly the shrill ring of a telephone broke the tense silence. Picking it up d'Aste listened intently.

'That was the Control Tower,' he said. 'The plane has been sighted. If all goes well it should be here within the next twenty minutes.'

Katharine's nails bit hard into the palm of Maxime's

hand. He looked anxiously down at her. Her face was deathly pale, but expressionless, as she sat rigidly on her chair, willing herself not to break down.

Armand got up and walked over to the group clustered by the tiny window. As he stood there, a small pinpoint of light appeared in the distance. It seemed to be flashing on and off as if giving a signal. And he breathed a sigh of relief. That small light in the darkness heralded the end of the long tunnel, or so he hoped. Then he thoughtfully stroked his chin. Or would it open a chapter of more pain, more heartache? No one could say.

'Only he who knows all, who holds the future in his hands,' he murmured softly.

The doctor turned round and smiled enquiringly at him.

'Just an old man talking to himself,' Armand reassured him.

And added under his breath.

'Oh God let this be the end of the tunnel for Katharine. May you now bring her into calm waters away from the depths which have threatened to submerge her . . . and grant her your peace.'

As he said it, the droning became louder, mingling now with the ringing of the telephone bell.

'Plane about to land,' a voice from the control tower announced.

Rising abruptly, the little group hastened towards the door.

As the plane broke through the clouds like a giant cigar, nine pairs of eyes swivelled anxiously towards the dark sky. It slowly circled the airport and then began to descend, dropping lower as the seconds ticked past.

Katharine, holding tightly to her husband's hand, felt her throat constrict. Her head began to spin and she wanted to be sick. Breathing deeply as the plane skimmed overhead, with a tremendous effort she pulled herself together. It dipped and touched the ground then slowly taxied along the runway finally stopping a few yards from where the ambulance was parked.

And suddenly the landing strip became a hive of frenzied activity. Men appeared from nowhere, running towards the stationary grey sheath. The plane door was yanked open, a ladder adjusted into position and a man in a white coat stood silhouetted at the top of the steps motioning to someone behind him.

'What caused the delay,' she heard a voice call up to the pilot.

'Dunno exactly', he replied, climbing down. 'Better ask the doctor. But it was panic stations back there.'

He cocked his head in the direction of the plane.

'I think they almost lost him. If we could have landed we would have done. But we were cruising over the Med miles from anywhere when the crisis occurred.'

He reached the ground and pushed up his flying helmet.

'There was some question of stopping off in Marseille to get the patient to a hospital there. But in the end they decided it was better to try to make Paris. There's apparently some topnotch specialist waiting for him at the Val de Grâce. But I can tell you it was touch and go. We had to slow down almost to full stop.'

His voice died away as he strode from the plane.

Shocked further by what she had just heard Katharine watched, trembling in every limb, as the white-coated man began to descend the steps, his head turned as he issued orders to those coming behind, signalling with his hands to go carefully. And suddenly, as arms were held up to steady it, she saw the stretcher appear. A male nurse was walking behind holding up a bottle of liquid with a tube dangling as, with great care, they slowly negotiated the steps.

The reception committee surged forward.

But Katharine's legs refused to move.

Her feet remained rooted to the spot. Armand and Maxime looked anxiously down at her but she didn't see them. She only had eyes for that stretcher which had now reached the ground and was being carried towards the waiting ambulance.

Suddenly it seemed as if every nerve in her body jangled and leapt to life. She began to walk mechanically forwards, hardly aware of what she was doing. Then without warning she broke away from Maxime's protecting arm and ran wildly to that still figure about to be lifted into the ambulance.

'Zag', she cried hoarsely, as she reached his side. 'Oh *Zag*.'

She stared in horror at his shaven head, his thin aristocratic nose protruding grotesquely between his hollow sunken cheeks. And the shrivelled dried-up skin on the fleshless arm lying lifeless at his side as the fluid dripped rythmically into the flattened vein.

'Zag,' she pleaded pitifully. '*Please* speak to me.'

But her father's eyes remained closed. His wasted body showed no sign of life. And he didn't respond.

Chapter
26

For three days Xavier's life hung in the balance. His emaciated body lay motionless on the bed, his eyes closed as Armand, Maxime and Katharine sat beside him hour after hour praying for his recovery.

'He *can* regain consciousness,' Katharine said desperately as the doctor quietly closed the sick room door behind him and followed her into the corridor. 'It happened before, nearly thirteen years ago when his skull was fractured in a plane crash. He was in a deep coma for over two weeks before he showed any sign of life.'

She looked up at him pleadingly.

'He's not in a coma,' the doctor replied. 'Dr Drancourt sent me the notes from his accident in 1946. This is not the same thing at all. Then he had a severe fracture of the skull, as well as multiple injuries, and they feared brain damage. Your father's present condition is not the result of an accident. The fracture he sustained this time was very slight, not serious at all. There's no brain damage. They had to shave his head because his hair was long and matted and infested with lice. It had nothing to do with the wound. That bled a lot but was very superficial.'

'Then why?' Katharine panicked.

'I don't know Madame,' he said kindly. 'This is a psychological illness . . . not physical at all. Comte de Montval regained consciousness before he left Algiers.

In fact the doctor who accompanied him on the plane said he was lucid for most of the way until his heart suddenly failed. They managed to revive him within seconds so the oxygen supply to his brain was not cut off. Though they were very afraid he would not make it to Paris.'

The doctor pursed his lips thoughtfully.

'He's been through an horrendous experience and is terribly debilitated, which *could* inhibit his speech. But I'm convinced it's not only that.'

He shrugged helplessly.

'He seems to have lost the will to live.'

Katharine clapped a hand to her mouth.

'*Why* doctor,' she stammered brokenly, now that he has been released and the ordeal is over?'

The doctor shook his head.

'It can happen. Your father has lived through hell and survived. But now that the danger is over . . .'

He shrugged.

'It's almost like a counter-shock, leaving him empty and deflated.'

Suddenly Katharine's mind went back to those days of emptiness she had experienced at Ardnakil. The feeling of nothingness and total despair, everything blunted and numb, wandering alone in an impenetrable grey fog. And she wondered whether the same hopelessness had enveloped her father's mind and taken away his will to live.

Recalling with gratitude the long hours William had spent sitting quietly at her bedside holding her hand, saying nothing, just letting his peace flow into her tormented mind, she knew that she could do the same for her father.

As they left the hospital that evening Katharine noticed for the first time the large dome dominating the old building and the steps leading up to the covered arch. Her thoughts went back thirteen years to that May afternoon at the Invalides when she had walked through a similar high stone arch and stood with her father beneath an almost identical dome to receive Ashley's posthumous Legion of Honour medal.

Ashley had died a brutal death.

And she began to wonder whether that threat of death and destruction which had seemed to strike those she dared to love had not, as she had believed, been exorcised in the security of Maxime's arms.

Turning into the Boulevard St Michel they drove along the embankment, passing in front of the 'Copper Kettle'. And her mind returned to the day she and Elisabeth had had tea there. She had loved Elisabeth. But she had died shortly afterwards in tragic circumstances.

As they crossed the Pont du Caroussel and skirted round the Louvre she remembered Theo and those halcyon weeks they had spent together in Paris before they realised that their love was doomed. Her days of waiting at the Val de Grâce had revived vivid memories of that other Paris hospital where she and Theo had sat beside Zag's bed day after day pleading with him to live. Had she also destroyed Theo's life she wondered? Almost five years after they parted he had still been clinging to their unfulfilled dream.

And now Zag.

Katharine shuddered, firmly clamping down her mind which was insidiously painting pictures of what his future might hold.

As she climbed wearily from the taxi and walked towards the house, William's face seemed to appear, smiling back at her from the shining door knocker. And a feeling of peace mingled with excited anticipation pushed its way into her tormented mind.

'Ask Manon to serve dinner in half an hour,' she called

over her shoulder to Maxime as she entered the house. 'I'm going upstairs to rest.'

But once the two men were safely settled behind the drawing-room door Katharine crept down to the hall and picking up the receiver dialled Tamara's number in Nice.

'William,' she said urgently when he was called to the telephone. 'I need your help.'

She quickly outlined her fears for her father.

'I don't know what else we can do,' she ended pathetically.

'Exactly what the Bible tells us to do,' William replied evenly. 'Jesus said that if we believe, in his name we will lay hands on the sick and they will be healed, we will cast out demons . . . and much more.'

'Can you come?' she whispered.

'There's no need my dear. I will intercede for your father in a 24-hour vigil, beginning now.'

'Oh William, I can't ask you to do that.'

'Why not Katharine?' he smiled. 'I'm an old man. I don't need much sleep. I am happy to spend time with the Lord, and to do this for your father.'

'William,' Katharine gasped. 'It's too much to ask you.'

'Don't worry my dear, I have done it before.'

He paused.

'And I hope if ever the occasion arises, the Lord will give me the opportunity to do it again.'

He paused but Katharine had the feeling that the conversation was not at an end.

'If, during tomorrow, you feel like joining me in prayer across the miles which separate us, then please do. After all, didn't Jesus say "whenever two or three are gathered together in my name I will be with them". He also promised that if we believe he would give us the desires of our heart.'

As they walked under the dome of the Val de Grâce the next morning Katharine's heart was beating rapidly, her eyes alight with expectation.

But when she tiptoed into her father's room he was still lying in the same lifeless position, only the monotonous drip from the bottle suspended above his left arm showing any movement at all. And she suddenly felt deflated. She had got up early to pray and been convinced that the miracle they longed for had happened.

Maxime and Armand walking in behind her, seeing her shoulders droop, exchanged concerned glances.

As they looked down at Zag's still form on the bed the doctor came into the room.

Katharine raised her eyebrows enquiringly. But he shook his head.

'No change I'm afraid. But he's still holding his own. If *only* we could get him to react in some way.'

He sat down beside Katharine. Then leaning forward gently shook Zag's bony shoulder.

'Comte de Montval,' he said urgently, 'your daughter's here *and* your son-in-law. Don't you want to open your eyes and talk to them?'

But Zag's face remained impassive.

'It's all over', the doctor stressed. 'The nightmare's finished. You're back in Paris. Your family's here, waiting to take you home.'

But only the steady drip of the fluid trickling through the rubber tube broke the silence.

The doctor shook his head in bewilderment.

'I can't understand it,' he said, his face perplexed. 'I'm convinced he can hear me.'

Katharine sat nervously twisting and untwisting her hands, clinging fervently to her belief that Jesus whom her father had so faithfully served would not abandon him now that the end was in sight.

She remembered William's calm confidence on the telephone the evening before and seeing him, in her mind's eye, in prayer for her father at that very minute, she slowly regained her confidence.

But the day dragged by as the ones before it had done.

'I've brought the Bible Zag gave me,' Katharine ventured diffidently when a distant church clock struck seven. 'I'd like to read a passage.'

Flipping through the pages to the eighth chapter of the Book of Romans, she began to read.

'For I am convinced that neither death nor life, neither angels nor demons, neither the present nor the future, nor any powers, neither height nor depth, nor anything else in creation, will be able to separate us from the love of God that is in Christ Jesus our Lord.'

'That was a favourite passage of Zag's,' she insisted, placing the Bible on the small bedside locker. 'Let us pray that hearing it will revive him and give him the will to live.'

Closing her eyes she slipped to her knees.

Maxime and Armand looked at each other, then at Xavier's pitiful body. Sighing, they followed suit.

The church clock chimed again then boomed out eight strokes. Katharine, exhausted, opened her eyes. Rising stiffly from her knees she glanced at the bed. Then suddenly staggered and almost fell. Her father's shaven head was turned towards her, his wide-open eyes looking straight into hers.

As she recovered her balance and stumbled towards him, a ghost of a smile flitted briefly across his cavernous face.

'Kate,' he whispered weakly.

Then, with a tremendous effort, he stretched out his bony almost transparent hand and feebly grasped her own.

Chapter 27

From that day onwards Xavier never looked back. And as his strength slowly returned he was finally able to talk about his experience.

At first the doctor refused to allow any official to question him. But in the end it was Xavier himself who persuaded him to let them come.

'It's what you doctors call therapy,' he grinned. 'You know, thrashing over the details. It's supposed to help me as well as them.'

But in spite of recounting his experience in the minutest detail he refused to identify his captors.

'Why Xavier?' Maxime puzzled when his friend Axel d'Aste complained to him that Xavier was not being very co-operative. 'Why don't you want to say who they were? They were a band of murderous thugs after all.'

But Xavier was not convinced. His betrayal by Khaled had wounded him deeply and he did not want to repay in the same coin.

'I still cannot believe that of Khaled. That all the time I knew him he was living a lie.'

'What other explanation can there be?' Maxime asked bluntly.

'He *could* have been forced by the FLN or the Islamic fundamentalists to carry out their orders . . . threatened,

300

even tortured. They are without mercy when a Muslim becomes a Christian.'

Xavier turned towards his son-in-law.

'If they wanted to suppress me what better tool for the job than someone I trusted? It's one of their ploys for breaking a prisoner.'

'It all sounds very far fetched to me,' Maxime protested.

'Not when you know the fanaticism of these people,' Xavier answered grimly. 'Their minds have become so twisted with hatred you realise that *anything* is possible.'

Looking up his eyes met Maxime's.

'Is it not narrow-minded to judge all men, all foreigners, all Muslims or Christians by the activities of a group of extremists? I've come to realise that fanaticism in any form is always a sign of suppressed doubt. And I'm convinced that Khaled had his doubts. I don't think he really intended to kill me. Except perhaps that last time. Then he had become so eaten up with indoctrinated hatred he *could* have done it. And left my *body* on the Mission steps. But, at the last minute, something stopped him.'

'Could it have been our prayers?' Maxime suggested.

'It could have been. But I like to think that, coupled with prayer, it was that last vestige of the Christian faith we had once shared which suddenly surged . . . and stayed his hand.'

Xavier leant back in his chair, his eyes far away.

'I'm sure if we could meet again on equal terms he would come back to Jesus,' he murmured.

'But surely you're not considering going back and trying to reconvert him,' Maxime exclaimed.

'I very much doubt whether I'd be allowed to go back,' Xavier replied sadly. 'And even if I did I'd be more of a liability than anything else. No Maxime, it's not easy to explain. But I *still* believe that Khaled could come to repentance, if only I keep praying for him. Imprisoning or executing him is not the answer.'

Maxime shook his head in bewilderment.

Until that January evening when Xavier had finally opened his eyes Maxime had never witnessed the full power of prayer, nor seen the promises of Jesus fulfilled in a person's life. He was not even convinced that such things could happen. But confronted with the reality of divine healing in his own family, and the doctors' evasiveness when pressed for an explanation, had caused him to think more deeply about his new-found faith.

And he remembered William Paget's words on the evening of Xavier's recovery when Katharine had been too overcome by emotion to announce the news herself, and Maxime had telephoned William on her behalf.

'There is nothing miraculous about the things one can explain,' the old man had quietly remarked, when told of the doctors' reaction. 'It's a question of faith and absolute trust in the promises of God.'

Now, hearing Xavier's words completing William's by adding love and forgiveness, Maxime's faith and his admiration for these two men of God had been strengthened and consolidated.

And he longed to be more like them.

*   *   *

'I wonder darling,' Maxime said tentatively at the beginning of February, 'whether you would mind if I returned home. We left in such a hurry that I hardly had time to give any instructions to Lucien. And there are certain matters which I need to attend to.'

He paused and looked anxiously at his wife.

'The doctor assures me that your father is well on the way to recovery. He just needs to rest and build up his strength. It's only a question of time before he's released.'

'I'll stay with Katharine if she wishes,' Armand put in, walking into the drawing-room where Katharine and Maxime were waiting for dinner to be anounced.

'Do go Maxime,' Katharine assured him. 'Uncle Armand and I will keep each other company. Maybe it won't be for very much longer.'

She turned to her husband with a smile.

'Have you noticed Zag's hair's already beginning to grow again?' she dimpled. 'And it's *white*. I'm not sure he'll like that.'

When a month later the doctor said that Xavier could now leave the hospital, he already had a sprouting crop of snowy white locks.

'*Very* distinguished', he chuckled, looking at himself in the mirror. 'Very distinguished indeed! Different from my clothes.'

He glanced down at his suit.

'I look like a coat hanger!'

Katharine insisted that Zag return with her to Le Moulin and not to the house in Narbonne, where the combined nursing efforts of Toinette and Marie-Louise would doubtless have put him straight back into hospital.

And Armand agreed.

When the car drew up in front of the house the boys, warned that their grandfather was arriving, were racing up and down the steps bursting with excitement.

Almost before Emile had opened the door they were clamouring round him.

'What have you done to your hair?' Jehan frowned, jumping like a kangaroo out of a red laurel bush. 'You look funny!'

Léon, his black and white puppy lolling over his arm, sidled up and slipped his hand in Zag's.

'I like you like that,' he said shyly. 'You look like my other Grandpa.'

Zag raised his eyebrows enquiringly at Katharine as, with the boys dive bombing around them, they walked into the hall.

'William Paget', she smiled. 'Ashley's father. The boys adopted him as a surrogate grandfather when they were in Scotland. Hope you don't mind.'

Zag's gaunt faced softened into a smile.

'I'm honoured,' he said quietly.

For Katharine, in the weeks following her father's return, the most difficult thing was to fend off all the people, interested, curious or just plain morbid, who wanted to see him and hear his story. But after a while the nine-day wonder of his release died down and life for them all settled into a pleasant routine. With the clement weather, the exuberance of his grandsons and Katharine's devotion, Xavier gradually began to build up to his former weight and regain his strength.

* * *

Spring was around the corner and Xavier was growing stronger every day. But to his annoyance, the doctors would not allow him to get up before lunch. So after breakfast Katharine often kept him company.

'It must have been a difficult time for you all,' he remarked one morning as Katharine sat beside him. 'All those months when you were without news.'

He smiled at her.

'I'm sorry darling,' he said remorsefully, 'for the pain and worry I caused you.'

Katharine's eyes widened and she caught her breath in a startled gasp.

'For *us* Zag,' she blurted out. 'Oh *no*. It was for *you*.'

Their eyes joined and before her father's steady gaze Katharine dropped her own.

'I knew there was something worrying you as soon as I was well enough to start taking notice,' Zag went on.

Katharine fiddled with the belt of his dressing-gown, lying across the bed.

'Do you want to talk about it?'

'The doctors said you weren't to have any worries.'

'If you remember, that's what you said last time I was convalescing,' her father answered drily. 'And I told you then that you'd worry me less if you told me what was bothering you.'

She got up and walked over to the window.

'I felt so *guilty*,' she said at last, her voice barely audible. 'If you had been killed I don't think I would ever have got over it.'

She paused.

'As it is,' she went on brokenly. 'Sometimes I can hardly bear to look at you, realising that if you suffered as you did . . . *it was all my fault.*'

Xavier drew his brows together in a puzzled frown.

'*Your* fault. What on earth are you talking about?'

He eased himself up on his pillows.

'Come here,' he said tenderly, holding out his arms. 'And explain to me what this nonsense is all about.'

Xavier listened until the storm of self-accusations had died away.

'So you see Zag,' she choked. 'If I hadn't left Biarritz you would have been with us at Gure Etchea . . . and none of this would have happened.'

'Why did you leave Biarritz?' he put in quietly.

But Katharine ignored the question.

'You've suffered so much,' she said hoarsely. 'I can't bear even to think about it.'

'Katharine,' Xavier said quietly. 'You are in no way responsible for what happened.'

'But . . .'

'Now listen to me,' he went on firmly. 'When I received Maxime's telephone call it was six o'clock in the morning. I was booked to leave on a plane from Algiers to Paris that afternoon. Ten minutes after putting down the receiver I was kidnapped as I left the Mission for my usual early morning stroll. The terrorists must have known my habits and planned it all in advance. It would have happened anyway. It had nothing whatever to do with you. The only difference it might have made had you been in Gure Etchea was that the news would have broken sooner, because Maxime or Armand would have telephoned the Mission to ask why I hadn't arrived.'

Katharine looked at her father, dumbfounded. Tears still shining like tiny crystal droplets on her curling dark lashes.

'But . . . we thought you had been kidnapped much later. Why wasn't Maxime informed immediately?'

'Because the authorities didn't know. It's part of the terrorists' tactics. They say nothing for four or five days which increases the family's anxiety about the person who has disappeared, making them more receptive to threats and extortions.'

Xavier smiled sardonically.

'Unfortunately, in my case it didn't work. There was no hue and cry because no one knew I was missing.'

'But what about the people at the Mission? Didn't *they* wonder where you were?'

'They all thought I'd left. We rarely met except in the evening. And I was notorious for missing meals. So when I didn't turn up for lunch no one gave it a second thought.'

'But they must have realised you *hadn't* left. All your things would still be in your room.'

'I had very few possessions there. It was only after the kidnapping became known that the police searched my room and found my unused plane ticket in a drawer.'

Xavier looked sadly across at his daughter.

'What a dreadful misunderstanding. And what a lot of unnecessary pain you've had to bear.'

He leant forward and took her heart-shaped face in his hands.

'Look at me Katharine, and tell me that this guilty feeling which never should have been there is now gone.'

Katharine raised her head. The tears were still glistening on her lashes. But the sadness had left her eyes, the shadow of pain been wiped from her face.

'Yes Zag,' she said, her voice a caress. 'It's gone . . . I'm finally whole again.'

* * *

It was towards the end of March that Maxime received the mysterious parcel.

He was alone in his study in the early morning when Alphonse entered with the mail.

'There is also this parcel for Monsieur,' Alphonse announced, laying a flat square box on the desk.

Maxime picked it up and turned it over. The handwriting was unfamiliar and there was no sender's address. He shrugged and put it down.

'Thank you Alphonse,' he said absently and, sifting through the pile of letters, took his paper knife and began methodically slitting them open.

When he had finished glancing through them he heard the breakfast gong and thankfully got to his feet. He had been sitting at his desk for two hours and was feeling cramped and stiff . . . and in need of a cup of coffee.

Maxime was busy going round the estate with Lucien

supervising the ploughing and draining of the vineyards for most of the day. And it was not until after dinner when he returned to his study that he remembered the parcel.

Picking it up he untied the string. The brown paper wrapping fell open to reveal a small cardboard box.

Intrigued he removed the lid. There, lying on some tissue paper was a set of keys.

More intrigued than ever Maxime picked them up and searched for a card or a note, something to indicate the name of the sender. But there was nothing. The box had no marking either. Reaching for the discarded brown paper he examined it in an attempt to unravel the mystery. It was postmarked Paris. But he could find no other clue.

Frowning with irritation he threw the keys onto his desk. As they landed a faint whiff of perfume rose from the tasselled key-ring, skimmed his nostrils and vanished. And he suddenly he knew. That perfume was unmistakeable. Marie-Céleste had worn it for years. Picking up the keys again he examined them closely. They must be the keys to the flat on the Ile St Louis which he had rented for her, and which she had obviously carried around with her in her handbag.

Maxime sat back in his chair, his brow rutted in a puzzled frown.

What did this anonymous parcel mean? What trick was Marie-Céleste about to play now?

His lips tightened as a sudden thought darted into his mind.

If she no longer needed the flat, then where *did* she intend to live?

There seemed to be only one possible explanation. His ex-wife must be on her way back to Le Moulin.

Leaning his elbows on the table and placing his head in his hands he groaned.

'Oh no Lord,' he said. 'Not that. Not now when everything has finally turned out right.'

*   *   *

Suddenly galvanised to action by the awful thought, Maxime picked up the telephone. Something had to be done and done quickly if disaster was to be averted.

Calling the operator he asked for Antoine's number.

'Monsieur is not at home', a prim voice answered.

'Is Madame there?'

'Monsieur and Madame are dining with friends.'

Maxime sucked in his breath in annoyance.

'Please ask Monsieur to telephone me as soon as he returns,' he said urgently. 'It doesn't matter how late it is. I shall wait for his call.'

It was gone midnight when Antoine finally rang.

'What's the panic Max?' he enquired cheerfully.

'I don't know whether panic is the right word,' Maxime replied. 'More a mystery. I received the keys of Marie-Céleste's Paris flat in the post today. And I don't know what it means. If she's no longer there I'm very afraid she might be considering returning here again.'

Antoine laughed heartily.

'My dear little sister,' he remarked drily, 'histrionic to the end.'

'Antoine please . . .' Maxime said testily.

'Marie-Céleste's still in Madrid. She won't be bothering you any more Max. If you read the social column in Le Figaro tomorrow morning you'll see the announcement of her marriage. That's why she no longer needs the flat.'

Antoine paused.

'Though she could have found another way of informing you.'

Maxime sat down abruptly, a mixture of relief and astonishment making his legs suddenly go weak.

'Geneviève and I are leaving in a few hours to attend the nuptials in two days time. I'm sorry, I should have told you.'

Maxime gave a dazed response.

'She's done what she set out to do,' Antoine went on dispassionately. 'Marrying the Duke del Alva, a very old family of impeccable lineage and almost as rich as her Arab boyfriend. Got estates and land all over the place. He's twenty years older than she is, with three married daughters almost her age but quite a catch. His wife died last year and he's been inconsolable ever since. But it appears that Marie-Céleste has found a way to dry his tears . . . according to what I've been told he's wild about her. Even managed to get a papal dispensation annulling her marriage to you. Can you believe it?'

Antoine gave a curt laugh.

'I wouldn't put it past my little sister to be married in white!'

Maxime sat in stunned silence, waves of relief and gratitude for this final deliverance from the ever-present threat of his first wife casting a shadow over his marriage washing through his mind.

'From what my grandmother tells me,' Antoine went on, 'the one dark spot on the duke's first marriage was the fact that his duchess produced only daughters. So, he has no son to succeed him. *Now* Don Alfonso is looking to his *new* Duquesa to deliver the goods.'

He laughed shortly.

'What a hope! Oh well, they say there's no fool like an old fool. I imagine the key incident is the last unpleasant surprise you'll receive from Marie-Céleste.'

Antoine paused.

'Has that put your mind at rest Maxime?'

'Yes Antoine,' Maxime floundered. 'Thank you so much. I'm sorry to have kept you up so late.'

As he replaced the receiver his eyes wandered slowly towards the stairs, at the top of which was the room where Katharine lay sleeping. And suddenly the relief which had begun to gush through him as Antoine spoke now changed to bubbling joy as an immense surge of love for his wife almost swept him off his feet.

Slowly rising, he mechanically switched off the lights and crossed the hall towards the stairs. Then, as if suddenly on fire he raced up them two at a time and slithered to an unsteady halt outside their bedroom. As he entered, a new sickle moon, a curved thread of silver veiled in mist sent a pale beam of light to where she lay asleep, her arms thrown above her head in childish abandon. Crossing the room he gazed at her sleeping profile, her chestnut curls framed in the snowy whiteness of the pillow, her light regular breathing gently lifting her still-youthful rounded breasts. Once again her ethereal yet strangely earthy beauty overwhelmed him. And he groaned.

Katharine stirred and opened her eyes.

'Maxime?' she murmured blinking sleepily up at him.

He sat down burying his face in her hair, not trusting himself to speak.

She lifted her hand and stroked his cheek.

'Maxime,' she queried gently. 'What is it?'

He raised his head and looked straight into her enquiring eyes hungrily drinking in every contour of her fragile beauty, as is if he could never have enough of it.

'It's all over darling', he choked hoarsely. 'It's finished. The pain, the anguish, the misunderstandings. They're all behind us.'

Katharine, now wide awake, shook her head in bewilderment.

Gathering her in his arms he recounted the day's extraordinary events.

'So you see my darling,' he whispered huskily, there's nothing more to fear. No ghost in the cupboard threatening to leap out and haunt you. The past is *really* dead this time. It's gone . . . our future lies ahead. And there isn't a cloud on the horizon.'

He smiled tenderly down at her, as she lay back in his arms and closed her eyes.

Then to his astonishment she suddenly laughed, and drawing him to her, folded him in her arms. He held his breath, an outpouring of love zigzagging through him as he felt her warmth, the tick of her heart fluttering in her bosom, the cascades of laughter vibrating in her breast. And the soft smooth curves of her body calling out to him.

But it was contagious.

In spite of himself, as the fire of passion roared through him he found his body also shaking with laughter. Together they rocked on the wide bed, neither really sure why they were so convulsed, until the ripples became a trickle then slowly died out altogether.

Maxime drew back and looked down at his wife.

'It's so long since I heard you laugh,' he smiled.

Katharine didn't reply but as their eyes met in a silent embrace the past pain melted and drifted away. And in a kaleidoscopic flash she recaptured the tender moments of their life together when they had been so happy, content just to be lost in each other's arms.

As her eyes held his he saw the golden lights come dancing back into their tawny depths. Slowly he leant his face towards hers.

She lifted up her hand and once again gently stroked his cheek, their eyes still locked in a mute embrace. Then suddenly it was as if a flash of lightning streaking like a meteor across the sky blotted out the moon and hurtled into the room. Maxime caught his breath as it shot between them. His grip on her tightened and they clung together as she reached up in an overpowering surge of passion to draw him to her. He groaned, drinking in the scent of rose petals clinging to her. Then shivered in anticipation and ecstasy as her soft body yielded to his embrace.

Katharine trembled, his kisses a drugging delight. In that first frenzied hungry embrace their love reflowered and burst into blossom with a greater depth and intensity as their moulded bodies seemed to rise effortlessly and whirl around the room with the force of their passion. And Katharine longed never again to feel solid ground beneath her feet. She wanted to stay forever in this suspended world with Maxime in her arms, caressing her, possessing her, totally hers and she completely his.

As the cascading waves of passion gradually diminished in gentle swirls like a beautiful woman in a shimmering gown gracefully gliding down a winding staircase, her satiated body floated effortlessly earthwards. And it seemed to Katharine, cradled in her husband's arms, that their return was serenaded by the mellow sound of softly playing violins, rocking them gently in their cadences as, like falling petals they drifted down.

'Maxime,' she breathed at last.

And with that one word all the pent-up emotion, the frustrations and the pain of the past few months were released.

'Oh *Maxime*', she whispered, her voice a gentle caress.

And all passion spent, safe in his arms Katharine fell asleep.

* * *

'You're looking very beautiful this morning,' Zag remarked.

Katharine blushed.

And he noticed that the tender magnolia bloom had returned to her previously pale, gaunt cheeks. The contours of her face seemed softer and more rounded. Her eyes had lost their haunted expression and were glowing with a new depth and lustre.

'I'm not worried about *you* any more,' she teased, drawing up a chair and sitting down beside the bed.

'Is that the real reason?' he probed.

Their eyes met.

'No', she breathed.

The clock in the turret solemnly striking ten broke the silence which had fallen between them.

'Zag', she ventured slowly. 'Do you remember on that morning when I told you I felt responsible for your kidnapping, you asked me why I left Gure Etchea?'

Xavier nodded.

'I didn't answer you then. But I can now because it's all been explained . . . If you can bear it I'd like to tell you the whole story.'

And with her father's eyes never leaving her face Katharine began at the beginning and recounted all that had happened since Marie-Céleste's arrival at Le Moulin the previous June.

When she had finished, Xavier wordlessly reached for the morning's edition of *Le Figaro* which he had been scanning when she arrived. Shuffling through the pages he folded it in half and handed it to her, pinpointing a paragraph.

'Here it is,' he smiled. 'Just in case you need any further proof.'

Picking it up Katharine looked down to where his finger was pointing. And there in the middle of the social column was the announcement of Marie-Céleste's marriage which was to be celebrated the following day.

She smiled as she read it.

Before the Dawn

In a final gesture of defiance Marie-Céleste had used Maxime's family name.

But the sight of it didn't hurt Katharine. Nothing that Marie-Céleste did could hurt her any more. She knew that, secure in her husband's love, *she* was the only Madame Montredon de la Livière.

'Doesn't give the poor duke much time to change his mind between the announcement and the nuptials,' Xavier remarked, breaking in on her reverie.

Handing back the paper, Katharine laughed with him. She hadn't needed proof that Marie-Céleste had really gone out of their lives. But now that she had seen it in black and white it was as if an immense burden had been lifted and she felt free to take Maxime's hand and joyfully face the future with him.

It was not long before she discovered the surprise which that future held in store.

Chapter
28

'I've heard so much about William Paget,' Xavier remarked to Katharine one morning. 'I'd love to meet him. Is there any chance he might come here?'

Katharine rutted her brow.

'I don't see why not,' she remarked. 'He and Lavinia should be leaving Nice and returning to England about now. They could easily drop off here for a visit on the way.'

And so it was that a week later the two men who had played such a crucial part in both Katharine and Maxime's conversions finally met. And an instant rapport sprang up between them. So much so that before William and Lavinia left Xavier announced that he and William had decided to visit Jerusalem together that winter.

'Zag you *can't*,' Katharine protested. 'Not after what you've been through.'

'But it's all over darling,' her father smiled. 'And we're not thinking of going before December.'

'What about Lavinia?' Katharine demanded, thoroughly upset and angry. 'Surely you're not going to drag her along with you.'

'Lavinia and Tamara are going to spend Christmas with Tatiana and Lawrence and the children,' William cut in. 'Now that Lawrence has been posted to Rome it's a wonderful opportunity for doting grannies and great-aunts to visit them.'

And Katharine knew she was defeated.

'I still think it's crazy,' she sulked. 'Jerusalem is a hot bed of intrigue at the moment. Haven't you suffered enough at the hands of the Arabs.'

'Israel is a long way from Algeria,' Zag consoled her. 'I doubt that the Arabs there will find me very interesting.'

'All the same I don't like it,' she grumbled. 'What are you trying to be, another Père de Foucauld?"

'Katharine,' Xavier said patiently. 'I'm not *yet* in my dotage. I still have many years of service to give my Lord. Please don't try to hold me back. William and I are going as tourists. We'll be staying at an Anglican Mission house in Jerusalem. I don't think you have any need to worry.'

But Katharine did worry.

'I don't like it Maxime,' she frowned when they were alone together that night. 'Why can't he settle down and just be a grandfather.'

Maxime smiled.

'You won't change him darling. You know the saying: if you love someone let them go. They'll return.'

Katharine smiled back at him in her dressing-table mirror. But she was not convinced.

'I may have reacted rather strongly to Zag's suggestion for a reason,' she mused later, as they lay contentedly side by side.

But Maxime didn't reply.

'Don't you want to know the reason?' she insisted. 'You're not very curious.'

'I'm just gloriously sleepy,' he slurred. 'But come on then let's have it. What *was* the reason?'

'Elisabeth,' Katharine replied enigmatically.

'Darling,' Maxime sighed, 'it's awfully late and I've got a very heavy day tomorrow, could we stop playing games.'

'It's not a game', Katharine insisted. 'My reason is *Elisabeth*.'

'My mother?' Maxime queried.

'No darling. Your *daughter!*'

As the realisation of what Katharine was saying dawned on him, Maxime sat up and looked down at her incredulously.

'You can't mean . . .'

'I do. I saw Dr Massenon this afternoon. She'll be arriving about the 20th December.'

'But Katharine darling, you're almost thirty-eight.'

'I thought you'd be pleased,' Katharine faltered, suddenly deflated.

'Of *course* I'm pleased. But I'm also terrified. I nearly lost you when the twins were born.'

'But there was no problem with the other two.'

'Yes, but you were younger then. Léon's nearly five years old. I dread to think . . . the danger you might be in.'

He took her in his arms and held her in a crushing embrace as if afraid she were at that very moment slipping away from him.

'There'll be no danger darling,' she soothed. 'I promise. And we'll have the little daughter we've both longed for.'

'I *really* don't mind what sex the baby is,' Maxime said anxiously, remembering the bleak weeks after Léon's birth. '*Don't* set your heart on a girl.'

Katharine held him tight.

'It *will* be a girl,' she whispered. 'This time I *know*.'

'If I remember rightly, you *knew* last time,' Maxime put in wryly. 'And Léon turned up.'

'Darling', he said tensely. 'I don't care if it's boy

triplets. It's *you* I'm worried about. Just when I've got you back again.'

'Don't worry,' Katharine purred happily, snuggling up against him. 'We'll get William and Zag to put off their trip to Jerusalem until after the baby is born. Then they can both be on hand to pray for us.'

When Katharine announced her news the next morning both William and Zag agreed to postpone their journey until after the birth.

'I'm wondering whether I should go to Rome,' Lavinia brooded. 'You're no longer young Katharine. I'm worried about you.'

'Oh please,' Katharine groaned. 'Don't *you* start. I've had enough of that from Maxime. *Do* go to Rome as planned. It's not the other end of the world. My little daughter and I will be will fine.'

Lavinia looked at her curiously.

But Katharine just smiled. She had that special feeling. This time she was sure.

As the summer months enfolded and then gracefully gave way to the vivid colours of autumn, Katharine bloomed. And, as before she waltzed through her pregnancy without a tremor or a problem.

Maxime, still unsure of the outcome watched her like a hawk, grateful for his father-in-law's calm presence to quieten his fears. And, as he had done with Katharine ten years before, Xavier guided Maxime on his new Christian walk as together they prayed for the safe delivery of the child to come.

William arrived on 18th December to wild whoops of joy from the boys.

'We're going to have *two* grandpas for Christmas,' Jehan cheered.

As if William were a trussed turkey about to be popped into the oven.

On the 20th all eyes turned towards Katharine. But she was still sailing serenely, if somewhat cumbersomely, around the house, putting the finishing touches to the arrangements for the Christmas festivities. On the 21st, Maxime began to show signs of tension. And on the 22nd when Katharine had still not gone into labour, although a midwife and a nurse had been installed at Le Moulin for the past four days, in his agitation he called the gynaecologist and suggested that Katharine should go to the hospital.

Dr Massenon arrived and said there was no sign of the baby's imminent arrival and perhaps it would be advisable. But Katharine refused to go. When on the evening of the 23rd there was still no change Maxime was beside himself with worry for his wife. Dr Chasselin, hurriedly summoned, conferred with the gynaecologist and they decided that it would be better to induce the baby.

'But I don't want my baby induced,' Katharine burst out.

'Darling,' Maxime pleaded. 'You're already four days overdue. I think you should do as Dr Massenon suggests.'

Katharine looked calmly at the anxious faces gathered around her.

'My baby will come when *God* decides it is time', she said firmly.

And flatly refused to allow them to do anything to hasten the birth.

On the 24th Katharine was sparkling.

'I'm going to be able to celebrate Christmas Eve with the family after all', she announced joyfully.

Maxime frowned. His wife's composure, her almost flippant attitude towards the approaching birth when he himself was distracted out of his mind, was incomprehensible to him.

'Let's put dinner forward to seven o'clock,' Katharine suggested, ignoring his anxiety. 'Then Toinette can't spoil everything by screaming when we're only half-way through that they'll be late for midnight mass.'

For the first time since anyone could remember Charles-Hubert was to be present. He was at last beginning to feel the weight of his advancing years and had not left for foreign parts after the reunion at Castérat that September. But returned with the other elderly members of the family to the house in Narbonne where, not believing in electricity, he frequently and triumphantly fused everything

He now spent his time exchanging insults with Toinette, flying into senile panics, avidly reading the obituaries in every newspaper he could lay his hands on and gleefully discussing who had just dropped dead. The rest of the day was amply filled pulling everyone to pieces before selecting a few favoured individuals to stick back together before noisily consigning the rest to the rubbish heap.

'Garbage,' yelped at the top of his voice had become his favourite expletive when discussing other members of the human race.

That evening as the family gathered around the vast table in the dining room at Le Moulin Katharine, radiant with happiness in a pale-green evening gown, was hoping that this special annual reunion in her home would not be spoilt by one of Charles-Hubert's epic outbursts. He had already brought shrieks from Marie-Louise and Toinette, for once forming a united front, by turning up with his own wine glass, the size of a goldfish bowl, wearing an outfit suggestive of an eccentric gondolier.

'Are you coming to midnight mass with us Charles-Hubert?' Toinette enquired, glaring at him through bristling eyelashes sooty with mascara as she wound herself like a mummy in the numerous multi-coloured wraps and scarves which Alphonse was holding out for her.

Toinette had excelled herself this year in a dress resembling a wilted leek. As her hair had now been dyed the colour of rancid margarine, the effect was striking to say the least.

'No', Charles-Hubert replied belligerently, giving her one of the stares he reserved for those he considered sub-human. 'Last time I went the priest promised it would only last an hour and it went on for nearly two. That was in 1910. Haven't been since. Those chaps never keep their promises.'

He pulled one of his amazing faces suggestive of someone suffering from a burst appendix and raging toothache at the same time.

'You didn't keep yours when you promised to love and cherish me,' Marie-Louise bleated plaintively.

Marie-Louise's face, like her voice, resembled a goat.

She had not so much changed as solidified over the years, so that no matter what she wore she always looked like a balloon. Strongly disapproving of Toinette's frivolous outfits Marie-Louise gave the impression that all her clothes had been bought at the Oxfam shop. And her choice of dress for the Christmas festivities bore out this theory. It was a museum piece in an interesting shade of mud.

Marie-Louise was the kind of woman who could be relied upon to clean the church brasses, a compulsive do-gooder from whose efficient interference many worthy causes had suffered over the years. Being a firm believer in the adage that the devil finds work for idle hands she had spent the entire evening knitting a purple bucket-shaped garment which defied identification.

Charles-Hubert glared at her through his mane of white hair which had fallen into his eyes making him look like a neglected sheepdog.

'That was in church,' he spluttered, firing a torpedo of saliva at anyone within range. 'It doesn't count.'

And harrumphing in indignation he frog-marched himself across the hall.

Lips twitching with suppressed laughter Armand ushered them through the door. Katharine managed to contain herself until it closed behind them before crumpling with giggles into Maxime's arms. It was as he held her shaking body that he felt her stiffen, gasp, then catch her breath as the first pain shot through her, leaving her feeling as if she had been sliced in two.

'Nurse,' he shouted, sweeping Katharine up in his arms and hurrying towards the stairs.

'Call Dr Massenon,' he threw over his shoulder to Zag as he reached the top.

Katharine moaned as another pain diced through her and the waters suddenly burst.

'Doesn't look as if there's time,' the midwife said tightly.

Running ahead of them she tore open the bed and hurriedly smoothed some towels across it.

'Quickly, put her down,' she ordered, as Maxime gently lowered his wife, now doubled with pain.

'The head's already there,' the midwife said tensely.

Maxime, standing behind her watched as a small black round head covered in hair appeared and then retracted. He gasped.

'It's gone!'

But the midwife ignored him.

'Push now Madame,' she urged.

'I – I can't,' Katharine panted.

'Go and stand at your wife's head, hold her up, it might make it easier.'

Tenderly Maxime lifted Katharine in his arms. She laid her damp curls against his jacket. As he looked down he could see beads of sweat forming above her lips and trickling down her brow. Pulling out his handkerchief, he started to wipe them away. But at that moment, Katharine convulsed and drew away from him, her face contorted with pain.

'Push Madame, push,' the midwife ordered. 'The baby's almost here.'

'Push darling,' Maxime urged.

He felt frightened and helpless. Merely repeating the midwife's instructions steadied his nerves and gave him the feeling that he was somehow helping Katharine through this ordeal.

'Again,' the midwife cried. 'And again. That's it, you're doing very well. Fine . . . *STOP.*'

The suddenness of the order took Maxime off his guard. He looked down at Katharine. She was panting, her face twisted with pain. He held her tight, longing to kiss her but afraid to do so. It was all so clinical. Suddenly she gave a sharp cry, then like a deflated balloon collapsed in his arms.

'Katharine,' he cried, terrified. '*Katharine!*'

With a great effort she opened her eyes and managed a weak smile.

'It's all right', she gasped. 'It's almost over.'

'Let her lie back,' the midwife said without looking up, her eyes on something which she was manoeuvring between her hands. Then suddenly as Katharine lay exhausted against the banked pillows there was a squelching sound and the midwife triumphantly held up an elongated body.

It was at that moment that Dr Massenon rushed into the room.

Chapter
29

The doctor looked surprised when he saw that he had arrived too late.

'Just in time to sign the birth certificate,' the midwife remarked laconically.

Dr Massenon walked to her side.

'Even for a fifth baby that was quick,' he remarked.

He beamed across at Katharine.

'Another fine specimen.'

Katharine looked mutely at Maxime. And he realised that no one had thought to announce the baby's sex.

The midwife had just cut the cord when Maxime put a hand on her arm. Picking up the baby he carefully wrapped a towel round it and, walking back to the bed, laid the child in Katharine's arms.

In the distance the cathedral bells rang out on the silent night air to announce the birth of the Saviour of the world, their deep sonorous tones joined by countless neighbouring churches as Katharine looked down at the tiny unwashed scrap. She turned her starry eyes towards Maxime and they gazed at each other, once again lost in a silent embrace.

'Elisabeth,' Katharine whispered incredulously, as the baby opened violet blue eyes and attempted to focus.

Maxime smiled tenderly down at her and gently stroked her cheek.

'Yes Elisabeth,' he whispered back. 'And born on the same day as her great-great-grandmother'.

Katharine looked at him in surprise.

'The Empress Elisabeth was born on Christmas Eve in 1837.'

'I can't believe it,' Katharine exclaimed huskily. 'It almost seems prophetic.'

She gently stroked the baby's damp hair.

'Don't you want to give her your own mother's name as well?' Maxime smiled. 'Or are you still adamant about the Elisabeth Léonie our youngest son was supposed to be?'

'Neither,' Katharine answered dreamily. 'I want to call her Elisabeth Aurélie after her great-grandmother and her great-great-grandmother.'

'Two very tragic women,' Maxime said uncertainly. 'Aren't you afraid to saddle her with such an unhappy legacy?'

'There will be no unhappy legacy for our little Empress,' Katharine glowed. 'Oh Maxime, I have such hopes and dreams for her. Such expectations for her future.'

Maxime looked lovingly down at his wife.

But there were misgivings in his eyes. And he held them both close.

'In that case why not go the whole way and add Eugénie as well.'

Katharine's brows drew together in a puzzled frown.

'That was the Empress' name. Elisabeth Aurélie Eugénie.'

'She was called Aurélie too?' Katharine queried.

'Yes. Perhaps it was one of the reasons why she was so fond of our baby's great-grandmother.'

Katharine gazed tenderly at the naked scrap in her arms.

'Then that will be her name also,' she whispered, cradling her little daughter close to her heart. 'Welcome

Elisabeth Aurélie Eugénie. We've been waiting for you for a very long time.'

Maxime, the ordeal safely over and their dream at last fulfilled, firmly banished from his mind his misgivings about the future consequences such a tragic name might have for their long-awaited daughter.

Overcome with emotion, he tenderly stroked his wife's pale cheek.

'Maxime,' Katharine murmured, 'didn't someone once say that the darkest hour is before the dawn?'

She stretched up a hand to draw his face close to hers.

'We've had our darkest hour,' she whispered. 'Now Elisabeth has brought the dawn . . . with all its promise.'

As their lips met, oblivious of the activity going on around them they clung together in a lingering kiss.

And Katharine felt her husband's tears of undiluted happiness mingle with her own.

Glossary of Terms Used

Abuela	Grandmother in Spanish.
Barques	A promenade in Narbonne along the Canal de la Robine.
Couscous	North African dish made of semolina, meat and vegetables.
Djellabah	Long robe with a hood worn in North Africa.
D.S.T.	Direction de la Surveillance du Territoire (French Counter-espionage Agency.)
Faire part	Death notice.
F.L.N.	National Liberation Front, Algerian independence organisation.
Invalides	A national monument in Paris housing Napoleon's tomb and a home for disabled soldiers.
Kasbah	Arab quarters.
Le Petit Séminaire	A preparatory school in Narbonne.
Marquise	A glass porch.

Medina	The old town in Arab countries.
Negresco	Famous top-class hotel in Nice.
Père de Foucauld	French viscount and Army officer who, after his conversion, became a missionary in Southern Algeria and the Sahara, where he was murdered by looters.
Pétanque	Popular game of bowls.
Petit salon	Smaller drawing-room where family receive visitors less formally.
Place Beauvau	Location of French Ministry of Interior, near Elysée Palace.
Sorèze	A renowned private school in Southern France dating back to the 17th century.
Souk	Arab market.
Val de Grâce	An 18th century convent in Paris transformed into a well-known military hospital.
Vive l'Algérie Libre	Long live free Algeria.